D0929775

Guernsey Memorial Library
3 Court Street, Norwich, NY 13815
(607) 334-4034
www.guernseylibrary.org

ANVIL OF GOD

ANVIL OF GOD

Book One

of the Carolingian Chronicles

J. Boyce Gleason

iUniverse LLC
Bloomington

ANVIL OF GOD
BOOK ONE OF THE CAROLINGIAN CHRONICLES

iUniverse books may be ordered through booksellers or by contacting:

iUniverse
1663 Liberty Drive
Bloomington, IN 47403
www.iuniverse.com
1-800-Authors (1-800-288-4677)

ISBN: 978-1-4759-9019-5 (sc)
ISBN: 978-1-4759-9020-1 (hc)
ISBN: 978-1-4759-9021-8 (e)

Library of Congress Control Number: 2013908278

Printed in the United States of America

iUniverse rev. date: 7/25/2013

To my wife, Mary Margaret Puglisi Gleason. A beautiful, generous, and caring woman, Mary Margaret has been the great love in my life and, in the best sense of the term, my better half. I could never have written this book if she had not supported willingly my illusions of literary grandeur.

We married young, two brave souls committing our hearts at life's door, and grew up together as most young couples do. She gave birth to our three sons and shaped our family, imbuing it with love and the strong values she inherited from her two wonderful parents, Joe and Josephine Puglisi. She also had the grace to welcome the love and values I inherited from my parents, Jan and Bud Gleason.

Although we faced the challenges that life threw our way—illness, financial hardship, the death of parents, the challenge of raising three boys—Mary Margaret was and remains the grounding force in the whirlwind of our lives. She is the tie that binds us. The walking definition of good, she is selfless, caring, and always committed to doing the right thing. She makes us a better family and has made me a better father, a better husband, and a better man. She is my love, my heart, and my life.

Thank you, sweetie. I'll stand at life's door with you anytime.

Acknowledgments

Many people helped make this book possible: author Barbara Dimmick, who refused to let me put down my pen; the late Upton Brady who, as my editor and agent, brought humor, wisdom, and a substantial knowledge of the Catholic Church to the process; author Merle Drown who, as my editor, "clears out the underbrush" of the stuff I put down on paper; and the dozens of readers who kept pace with my drafts and offered comments and criticism to help me make this a better story.

Source: H.G. Wells, History of the World

CAROLINGIAN DYNASTY

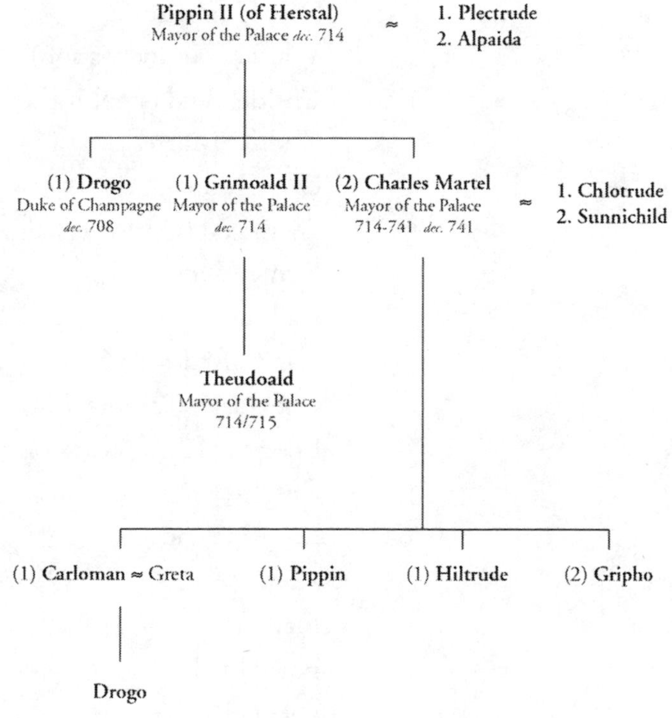

Nobles of the Realm

Region/Affiliation	**Name**
Alemannia	Liutfred
Aquitaine	Duc Hunoald
	Waifar (Hunoald's son)
Austrasia	Childebrand (stepbrother to Charles Martel)
Bavaria	Duc Odilo
	Grimoald (Odilo's cousin, the former duc)
Frisia	Radbod
Neustria	Ragomfred
	Charibert, Compte de Laon
	Bertrada (Compte de Laon's daughter)
	Lady Hélène
Provence	Ateni
Thuringia	Heden
	Bart (Heden's son)
	Petr (Heden's son)

Allies	
Lombardy	King Liutbrand
	Aistulf (King Liutbrand's son)

The Church

His Holiness the Pope	Gregory III
Bishop, Legate to the Holy See	Boniface
Bishop of Auxerre	Aidolf
Bishop of Paris	Gairhard
Bishop of St. Wandrille	Wido
Parish Priest, Paris	Father Daniel
Parish Priest, Laon	Father Martin

Rebels

Provence	Maurontus
Burgundy	Bradius

Austrasian Knights

(Loyal to Carloman)	Johann
	Ansel
	Brand
	Monty
(Loyal to Pippin)	Gunther
	Arnot

Bavarian Knights

(Loyal to Odilo)	Juergen
	Hans

Prologue

Maurontus

Outside Narbonne
AD 740

"God's will be done," Carloman whispered as the forward line closed on the enemy. One hundred and fifty men across, they moved in a syncopated march—left foot first to support their four-foot shields, the right behind for power and balance. With each forward step, the Frankish line shouted, "Hyuh!" while the rebels relied on drums to keep their men in formation.

"Stay close," one of his captains called. "Meet them as one. Meet them with force." Left foot forward, right foot behind, the shield walls slammed into each other, the men grunting as their shoulders strained under the impact. The second lines closed behind the first, pressing their shields against the backs of their comrades to add their weight to the wall. The third, in its turn, supported the second.

"Engage!" the captain shouted, and the second line stabbed their short swords above and below the forward shields, attempting to catch an eye or a foot to weaken the enemy wall. Shouts and curses echoed across both lines as the blades found flesh and the wounded were pinned between the shields. No one, not even the dead, could leave a shield wall.

Carloman's father, the great Charles the Hammer, had brought his army south to quell a disorganized pagan uprising and instead found a well-organized enemy. The rebel Maurontus had plundered a wide swath through the rich lands of the south, recruiting hundreds to his banner. Making matters worse, the rebel had enlisted the support of the Saracen holding Narbonne and augmented his troops with regulars. The Franks fought men well-seasoned by battle.

Initially, Maurontus attacked in skirmishes, targeting Charles's rear guard and supply lines to weaken them as they marched south. But after two months of sporadic fighting, Charles had lured Maurontus into a frontal assault by pretending to split his army for an attack on Narbonne. Maurontus took the bait, attacking with the full weight of his army. To Charles and Carloman's surprise, even with their army reunited, the two sides were closely matched. They were now in danger of falling victim to their own trap.

As the sun rose across the sky, Carloman began to worry that the heat would be a factor. Coming from the north, the Franks wore leathers and animal skin beneath their armor; they would tire more quickly than their southern counterparts. He looked to the far side of the field for his men of horse. Twice as large as the enemy's cavalry, it was the one significant advantage they had over Maurontus. To be a factor, however, the shields needed to force a break in the line.

"There!" Charles pointed to the near side of the enemy line where several shields had fallen. "Can't you see it, Carloman? Strike, God damn it. Strike!"

Carloman made the sign of the cross for his father's blasphemy and then waved for the signalman to order a cavalry charge. He couldn't help but smile at his father's exuberance. During the past twenty years, Charles had brought to heel every army from the Pyrenees to the Danube, and the man still thrilled at the turn of a battle.

Maurontus, however, reacted to the threat, storming across the field to push his reserves into line. The Frankish cavalry would be too late.

Then Pippin was there, crashing his warhorse into the gap. Carloman's younger brother trampled a spearman, wheeled his horse behind the enemy shield wall, and hacked down on the unprotected backs of the men on foot. More of the wall crumpled under his assault, and the Frankish shields pushed forward.

"He is a madman," Carloman said.

"He'll be surrounded. Cavalry's too far away." Charles spurred his warhorse, racing to the line. Carloman followed, veering toward their cavalry. It would take more than two knights to save his brother.

Maurontus called up his own cavalry, and Pippin was forced to turn his back to the shields to face the oncoming threat. The rebels closed on him from three sides. Carloman groaned. Pippin had no shield. He carried only a broadsword into the melee.

Pippin's warhorse reared at the rider in front of him while Pippin swung at the knight to his left. His blade caught the Saracen at the base of his shoulder and clipped off his left arm. Blood splashed over Pippin as he tried to turn to his right, but his warhorse came down heavily on its fore legs, throwing Pippin off balance.

The Saracen knight to Pippin's right lifted his blade for a double-handed blow. At the last second, Pippin raised his broadsword in an attempt to protect his right side. The move saved his life. He caught the knight's blow near the pommel, and their hands froze above his head. Had the Saracen held a heavier blade, Pippin wouldn't have had a chance.

Pippin struggled to turn his mount as the Saracen drew back his sword. *He won't make it,* thought Carloman. Although large enough to stop the blow from the lighter Saracen blade, Pippin's broadsword would be too long and heavy for him to recover in time for the next. The other knight's curved blade descended. Pippin's blade circled behind his head.

"No!" Charles's voice raged over the battlefield.

Pippin slammed the pommel of his sword into his opponent's faceplate. The metal crumpled inward, and the knight reeled in his saddle. The man's intended blow veered right, and Pippin's horse stepped left to restore its balance.

Charles crashed into the frenzy and took off the rebel's head. The man's torso momentarily sat erect in its saddle and then fell backward.

Sidling his horse next to Pippin's, Charles fell into a rhythm of attack with his son that held the enemy at bay.

Carloman led the cavalry through the gap in the line and struck the enemy's men of horse like a cudgel. Swords fell in every direction, but in the end, the size of the Frankish cavalry won out. The enemy broke into disarray, and Carloman's men fell on them like butchers. Those who lived fled early. Carloman ordered his men to give chase.

Charles and Pippin had run out of horsed knights to fight and were busy chopping away at what was left of the rebel shields. Aided by the break in the line, the Frankish infantry surged past them, and then there was no one left to fight. Maurontus's army was in rout.

Charles, Carloman, and Pippin screamed war cries at their retreating foes. And then they laughed—a great, rich laugh of men who knew they were safe for a moment on a field where death came easily. They clasped forearms, and Pippin raced off to rejoin the butchery.

Carloman stayed with Charles. "He's reckless."

Charles nodded. "But he has a talent for battle. He saw that opening before we did. He knew it could turn the day. And he trusted his men to follow."

"But, he—" Carloman froze. Charles was hunched over in his saddle, holding his left arm.

"Father?"

Charles's face was deathly pale. He groaned and struggled for breath. "A bolt."

Carloman moved his horse closer and used both hands to search his father's body. "There's no arrow, Father."

"A rock then. Something struck me. I can barely lift my arm."

Carloman looked to the back of their line. His son Drogo was there, as was his half brother Gripho. He waved for them to come.

"Accompany Father back to the tent. A rock-thrower must have clipped him."

"I'm fine." Charles straightened in his saddle, flexing his left hand. "Gripho, go with your brother. Make sure we find Maurontus's treasure. And Carloman, bring me that bastard's head."

Carloman nodded. Charles's word was law. He and Gripho turned away to give chase, circling the body-strewn battlefield to speed their pace. A sudden pang of doubt struck Carloman, and he reined in his horse to look back across the field. Charles had his hand on Drogo's shoulder as the two trotted their horses back to camp. Carloman could not tell if the gesture was out of affection or his father's need for support.

Chapter 1

Charles Arrives

Quierzy
AD 741

Stepping into the darkness of the stairwell, Sunni inhaled the musty scent of aging stone and stretched out her hand as a guide. Although the stairs were steep, she climbed with ease, having made this journey to watch for Charles every night since her husband left for Narbonne.

She did this more out of duty than necessity. When the army's banners were sighted, news of their arrival would be shouted from the rampart and echoed throughout the town. The fate of the entire court was tied up in Charles's success, and everyone from the lowest servant to Bishop Boniface would storm the staircase to see who had returned from campaign and who had not.

The banners would appear above the horizon along the eastern road, advancing in successive waves of color. The ranks of cavalry and foot soldiers would follow. In time, the sounds of their march would reach the walls, and the court would strain to see the knights' standards.

Because the absence of a standard from the ranks foretold a knight's death, those who could see would call out to those who could not, and a strange dichotomy would take over the assembled crowd. Cheers would greet the names announced while shouts for those unnamed were called forward. "Where is Stephen D'Anjou? Can you see Stephen?" and "What about Wilfred? Oh my God, not Wilfred!"

Sunni had seen families collapse in grief beside others who danced in celebration. Sobs and laughter would blend on the rampart in a discordant release until the hands of the celebrants stretched out to those who mourned, and the court would grieve its loss.

Arriving at the top of the stairs, Sunni discovered she would not be alone. A dozen steps away, Charles's daughter Trudi stared out at the horizon. They watched as the sun dipped low, casting a reddish glow to the underside of the cloud cover. A cold blast of wind made the girl shiver. Without thinking, Sunni kissed the locket she wore around her neck to ward off the night spirits.

"God help me," Trudi said. There was pain in her lament, but Sunni was reluctant to intrude. Stepmothers, she knew, are not always welcome. She found her own place on the rampart to watch the eastern road.

Trudi had her own reasons to await Charles's return. She was eighteen, old for a maiden. Charles had declared that, upon his return, he would decide whom the girl would marry. Although Trudi had never spoken to Sunni of this decision, her distaste was visible to any that knew her. Her body was coiled tight, her face a stew of emotions.

Sunni had argued for the girl, hoping to stop Charles from using his daughter as an instrument of his diplomacy, but he had insisted. Trudi would wed someone of noble blood. Charles would send her away to marry a noble on the Roman peninsula, or in Alemannia or Frisia, wherever there was an alliance to solidify, a political gain to be made. Her marriage would seal a bargain she knew nothing about.

She would be forced from the people she loved, away from the life she knew. She would be alone. Sunni's eyes welled. It was not so many years ago that she had shared a similar fate. It was, perhaps, the only thing they had in common.

Trudi had her father's face, which, although a man's face, was still handsome on her. Unfortunately, it was not the only trait she had inherited from him. She was tall for a woman, with broad shoulders and uncommon strength. *Thank God, the girl had breasts and hips,* Sunni thought, *or she might be mistaken for a man*. Trudi's hair was by far her best feature. It cascaded past her shoulders in waves of brown curls that Sunni envied for their thickness.

To Sunni's frustration, Trudi rarely did anything to enhance her beauty. Most girls her age were using the latest creams and powders. Trudi wore none. She refused to wear a dress, preferring pantaloons and vestments more suited to boys. Sunni had never seen her flirt. She had never seen her blush. The girl talked to boys her age the way they talked to each other.

Sunni had, over the years, tried to involve Trudi with the other girls at court. Such efforts, however, never kept Trudi's attention.

"They spend their time spinning thread and mooning over knights," Trudi would say, her eyes rolling. "They talk about each of the boys as if he was a prized horse. 'Look at his legs,' or 'I just love his shoulders.'" Trudi preferred to find her friends among the boys her age.

Making matters worse, Charles had indulged the girl's fantasy of becoming a warrior. Against Sunni's objections, he let Trudi train with the boys who would become his knights. Trudi strutted about court in armor and dismissed Sunni's advice. Sunni gently persisted, only to suffer the girl's continued rebuff. The one time Sunni's advice had been welcomed was when the girl's menses had set in. Even then, Trudi had declared it nothing more than "a nuisance."

"How do you stand it?" Trudi demanded, without turning to look at her. Sunni jumped in surprise. She hadn't thought the girl was aware of her.

"Your pardon?"

"How do you stand being married to someone you don't love?"

"I do love your father."

Trudi turned to confront her. "It wasn't even an arranged marriage. He just took you."

"That's not true."

"Of course, it's true." Trudi turned back again to the horizon, reciting the history. "When Charles stormed Bavaria, he deposed the crazed pagan duc—"

"Grimoald isn't crazed."

"Grimoald married his own brother's widow, flogged a priest, and performed pagan rituals over his own son."

"His son was dying. The doctors couldn't save him," Sunni said.

"So Charles got rid of Grimoald, put your uncle Odilo in his place, and married you, a Bavarian princess, to bear his third son. Am I missing anything?"

Sunni's face flushed. She looked down at her hands.

"So how do you stand it?" Trudi repeated.

How dare the girl? Of course, Sunni knew the stories. She had helped spread most of them. She was the "price" for making young Odilo duc de Bavaria in place of Grimoald. She had been "tamed" by Charles, who subdued her pagan upbringing through his iron will and firm hand.

The truth was that Sunni had seduced Charles from the start. She had seen the reality of their situation. The Bavarian royal family was in disarray, and Charles's army was too large to resist. Poor Grimoald would never be acceptable to Charles or his alter ego, Bishop Boniface. And an alliance between her family and the Franks offered not only a solution, but a tremendous advantage to both families.

The day she met Charles, Sunni knew she would have him. Tall, strong, fearless, Charles had been forty-two and a widower for a year when he came to Bavaria. He had a light in his eyes that made everyone else's seem dull. He was magnificent.

And he looked at her in that way that a man does when he needs to bury himself between the legs of a woman. In less than a week, she had bound him to her. He was bound to her still.

Now at thirty-two, she played the part of the "tamed" Sunnichild for Boniface and the court. She said all the Christian words, performed their rites so that she could have Charles. But she was no Christian. She still had her cache of herbs. She still prayed to the morning sun and the phasing moon. She still communed in secret with her brethren. She even shared some of their rites with Charles. Wedding Charles Martel had been her choice. She hadn't lied to Trudi. She did love the man.

"Hiltrude," she said, "mostly I find that men's stories tend to be about men. I do love your father. And if truth be told, I chose him. Women are not powerless, despite what you think. I wasn't powerless when I met your father any more than you are powerless now."

"What do you mean?" Trudi turned abruptly.

"Rarely do men tell you anything about the role that women play in their stories."

"No. Why do you say that I'm not powerless?"

"Because you are not."

"You of all people should know my plight," the girl said.

"Women are never powerless," Sunni said. "Perhaps when you are better prepared to listen and less prepared to judge, I will tell you about it."

Sunni started for the stairs. She could feel Trudi's stare follow her.

"If anyone is interested," Trudi called down after her, "the army has arrived."

Back on the rampart, Sunni saw Boniface raise a green and red signal flag to let Charles know there was urgent business to discuss. She groaned inwardly. To Charles, matters of state always took precedence over his family. She and Trudi would have to wait until Boniface had his say.

She turned her attention to the approaching army and saw Carloman's bold red banner with the white cross and the lion of St. Mark. Charles's eldest, at least, was safe. Although, she had never been close to Carloman, Sunni liked the serious, young man he had become. Her only reservation was Carloman's rabid devotion to the Church. Boniface had been named godfather to both Charles's older boys, and the bishop had taken the role to heart. He had taught them the catechism and imbued in them a strong foundation of faith. Of the two, he was closest to Carloman. The young man willingly accepted the bishop's counsel and shared the man's passion in Christ. At twenty-seven, Carloman had grown into a formidable warrior and a clever politician, but it was Boniface who pulled his strings. And that made Sunni nervous.

Charles's second son, Pippin, was another matter. In many ways, the young man was a mystery. He had spent six years being educated on the Roman peninsula in the court of King Liutbrand and become so close to the Lombards that Liutbrand had formally adopted him as a son.

Sunni took solace in the fact that Pippin was very much like his father. Pippin looked like him, swaggered like him, commanded troops like him. And much like Charles, there was a sullenness that clung to Pippin that oft times made him combative and cruel. Sunni enjoyed a closer relationship with Pippin, but she had to admit that the young man could exhaust her. One Charles in her life was more than enough.

Pippin's green banner with the white eagle flew alongside the blue hawk of Charles's stepbrother, Childebrand. Carloman's son, Drogo, flew his banner next to Charles, as did Gripho, her son by Charles. Sunni at last let herself smile. Gripho was safe. All the heirs were safe.

Sunni descended to the main hall, but, as she suspected, Charles chose to meet with Boniface to discuss the priest's urgent news. The two disappeared with Carloman into Charles's private chambers off the main hall. Never one to be left out, Sunni went up to her quarters and stole down the back stairs into the servants' quarters. She snuck through the kitchen, stopping to taste the evening's stew, and stepped into a closet that bordered the room where Charles and Boniface met. Years ago, she had bored a small spy hole into the wall.

Through it, she could see Boniface to her right with Charles and Carloman facing her. The bishop appeared to have just finished relating his news. Silently, Sunni cursed her tardiness.

She heard Charles reply, however. "Tell him, no."

"It is a tremendous opportunity, worthy of a great deal of consideration and debate," Boniface said.

Charles dismissed this with a wave of hand. "We're not going to Rome."

Sunni's mind raced. *Rome?*

"It's a perfect opportunity," Boniface pleaded. "By aligning your house with the pope, you elevate it above all other families. It grants you stature with churches in every region. The pope is in a desperate place. The Lombards threaten him from the south. The emperor in Constantinople won't help. His ancient ally Eudo of Aquitaine is dead. You are the only power who can come to his aid. He's offering you the protectorate of Rome."

"No."

"We may not get this opportunity again," Carloman said.

"We're not going, Carloman. We just returned from war in Provence, and there's trouble in Burgundy."

"We crushed Maurontus and the Saracen," Carloman said. "We plundered half of Provence. And it will only take a small force to handle Burgundy. We could do it with half our troops."

"If the Saracen are committed to campaigning on this side of the Pyrenees as they did with Maurontus," Charles said, "we will need the Lombards' help ourselves. Or are you so anxious to become a follower of Muhammad?"

Carloman looked insulted. "We could split our armies. Leave Pippin at home, and I'll ride with you to Rome."

"I think you underestimate the threat, Carloman. The Lombards are formidable."

Sunni couldn't agree more. Liutbrand was a strong and clever ally, but if Charles marched on Rome, the king would become a strong and clever enemy. Charles spent years cultivating relations with him.

"If we turn up in Rome," Charles continued, "Liutbrand will unite his cousins against us as a common foe. No, they won't be so easily mastered. It will take more than a title like 'protectorate of Rome' for me to turn on them."

"How about 'king'?" Boniface asked. Sunni held her breath.

Charles squinted. "Did Pope Gregory say that?"

"Without a Merovingian on the throne, and with you controlling all realms of the kingdom, it's the next logical step."

"Did he say that?" Charles insisted.

"The subject can be raised."

"Then there will be too many strings attached."

"Father, this isn't like you!"

"We're not going, Carloman."

Sunni turned to go. She had known Charles long enough to know this conversation was over.

Trudi ducked under the sword and spun right, away from her attacker. The thrust had been clumsy. She positioned herself to his right, where he could do the least damage. Ansel, she knew, was better with his right arm. She would have better luck defending against a backhanded blow.

He came again. This time she parried, feinted right, and spun left, going for the back of his right knee. He dropped his shield to take the blow and chopped downward with his sword toward her shoulder. Again, he was too slow.

Trudi had been training with the warriors since the age of eight. She had started a year later than most of the boys because it had taken her a year to convince her father to give his permission. Ultimately, Charles had relented and given her a sword made by the Saracen. It had a curved blade that was lighter and more flexible than the broadswords the boys used, though it had only one edge and tended to break against the larger blades.

Her armor too was different. She didn't wear the heavy chain mail the older boys draped over their torsos. She favored the Saracen leathers protected by small armor plates strapped to her chest, shoulders, legs, and arms. She could move more quickly than they could and had developed a number of spinning moves that gave her an advantage over them. The boys liked to challenge her because she presented a different kind of swordplay. It required more than brute strength to beat her.

She and Ansel often sparred at the end of the day on the practice grounds, choosing to compete again after the others had finished. Today, the air was so thick and hot that her armor felt like it weighed three stone, and her leathers stuck to her skin like tar. Waving for a rematch, Ansel stripped to his waist and grabbed a lighter practice sword. Trudi almost wept with relief and doffed her small plates of armor to fight in her leathers. At nineteen, Ansel was massive, his muscles shining with sweat in the heat of the day. Trudi noticed that he was smiling—not at her, but to himself. Clearly, he was doing more than staying cool; he was trying to limit her advantage.

Ansel picked up a small shield. Trudi picked up a second but shorter practice sword. A shield would help her little against Ansel. He was so strong that he'd break her arm if she tried to withstand one of his blows. Speed was her only ally.

They circled inside the practice ground wall, each looking for an opening. After several feints, Ansel rushed her, hoping that the force of his larger body would unbalance her. She spun to her left. As he lumbered past, she tried but failed to trip him. They circled once more.

Trudi feinted and kicked to make Ansel overreact. The slightest opening could be exploited when fighting with two swords. Ansel blocked each legitimate threat and refrained from reacting to her feints. Trudi swore under her breath. He knew too many of her moves. They circled again.

She looked to Ansel's eyes to anticipate his next move. But what she saw didn't make sense. She stepped back. She was certain that he had been looking at her breasts. He noticed her look and backed away, averting his eyes. And in the breadth of that moment, everything changed.

Her breasts, straining against her leathers, suddenly felt out of place. And she was terribly aware of his naked chest and shoulders. Again he looked at her, this time openly. Her heart raced, and she took another step back. Her stomach clenched. Blood rushed down her torso and coursed back up to her face. Ansel saw her reaction and smiled.

Furious, she took three steps forward, swung her short sword in a feint across his body, and used its momentum to throw her upper torso toward the ground. Pivoting on her left foot, Trudi swung her right leg in an arc high over her body so that her foot caught Ansel on the side of his head. The blow nearly toppled him. He stumbled. She hurled herself at him, spinning and hurling blow after blow with her two swords, pressing her advantage. Ansel backed and twisted to meet the attack, suffering the onslaught off balance. She went for a killing blow to end the contest, but he blocked it and slammed her square in the chest with his shield.

Stunned, Trudi backed up to regain her footing. Ansel, with an anger she had never seen before, drove at her with a series of blows that she barely checked. He advanced. She retreated. She tried to spin. He blocked her. She found herself backed up against the wall of the practice grounds. Ansel barely hesitated before he chopped his practice sword down in a finishing blow. She crossed both her swords over her head to catch his blade. Had it reached her, her head would have been crushed. They stood motionless against the wall, straining against each other.

Trudi looked up into Ansel's face and spat out the words, "I yield." When that produced no reaction, she shoved his arms away and let down her swords. He still didn't move. They stood against each other, breathing heavily. She saw his face change from rage to something else, something hungry. She looked away. Her face grew flushed. Short of breath, she dropped her sword and put her hand against him. He didn't move.

"Ansel," she said, looking back into his eyes. She had to get clear. She pushed against his chest until he gave way. Without a word, she left the training ground. She didn't look back at him. When he called after her, it took everything she had not to run.

In the following days, Trudi refrained from warrior training, which brought a serious rebuke from the warrior master. She avoided church, because Ansel was one of Carloman's "Knights in Christ," who attended mass every day. That brought a rebuke from Boniface. She ate in her room and went out only in the company of women—if she went out at all. When Ansel passed her on the villa grounds and called to her, Trudi ignored him. When he saw her on the street, she turned away.

She knew Ansel couldn't very well call on her in her rooms. He couldn't send her a note; neither of them could read or write. At best, he could send an intermediary. But there was little chance of that. The court was too small, and she was too central to it for any chance of secrecy.

Try as she might, however, Trudi could not stop thinking about him. How long had he been looking at her like that? Why had she reacted the way she did? She had never felt this way before. She had always thought of her breasts as something that got in her way.

Alone in her room, Trudi sat on her bed and thought of Ansel looking down at her breasts. A ripple of heat descended into her. She closed her eyes and imagined him pushing against her. Her stomach fluttered, and her skin flushed. Lying back, she pictured their last combat and imagined Ansel pressing her against the wall. She felt him pin her hands above her head while his mouth descended to her neck. His arm circled her waist to draw her to him, and he pressed into her with the length of his torso. Looking up into his eyes, she saw that raw look of hunger take over his face.

She imagined that her hands were Ansel's hands and that they followed the heat down the length of her body to the wetness she found there. "Oh, Ansel!" she gasped, her body convulsing as a flash of white blanketed her vision. Again it happened, this time stronger, and she collapsed into her pillows.

Shame filled her. Then anger. She covered herself with her sheets and lay still for a long time. She wanted Ansel. She wanted to feel his hands on her body. She finally understood the desire to be desired. She rolled onto her stomach and buried her head in her pillows. She had no idea what to do. She had no one to turn to. Most of her friends were the boys who trained with her. They would be of no help. The girls at court were not like her, and she was afraid that they would gossip. Her father, if he knew, would kill Ansel and marry her off to some faraway ancient noble, or worse, send her to a nunnery. She never felt more powerless.

Then she thought of Sunni. Sunni had said that women were never powerless. She would know what to do. She would help her have Ansel. For the first time since she had fought Ansel, Trudi smiled. In a moment, her fingers again were buried deep inside her.

"Good Lord, man. Have you lost your senses?" Boniface folded his hands in prayer and brought them to his lips, struggling to contain his outrage. If Charles or any of his sons had heard the confession he had just received, they would have killed the knight kneeling before him.

"She felt something too. I'm sure of—"

"Enough!" Boniface held up his hand and prayed to Michael the Archangel for strength. Boniface shuddered. This was dangerous ground. He rose to ensure that they were alone in the sacristy and closed the door to keep away any acolytes that might happen by. Charles would take Ansel's head if so much as a rumor of this reached his ears. And he would not respect the fact that Boniface was bound by the confessional to tell no one of the boy's sin. Thank the Blessed Mother that the boy had come to him before anything more serious had happened.

He had to think. Ansel had confessed to lusting openly for Charles's daughter and to pinning her body against the practice field wall with his own. The two had had no further contact, but the panic in the young knight's eyes suggested that this was still a very volatile situation. The pain on his face was palpable. Ansel did not trust himself. Lust had the better of him. Boniface sat back down and put his hand on Ansel's shoulder.

"You do recognize, my son, that you cannot marry Hiltrude."

"Yes, Father." The boy looked miserable. "But I have this ... this *need* for her. I can't stop it. I tried to pray it away. I tried exhausting myself on the training ground. I even touched myself to rid my body of this demon seed."

"All appropriate responses." Boniface nodded.

"But it only makes it worse. Thoughts of Trudi, of, of Hiltrude return. And she is always naked and—"

Boniface again raised his hand to stop him.

"You are not to speak of this again. Not to anyone. Not to Hiltrude. Not to me. Not even to yourself. And you will stay away from Hiltrude. You will no longer 'practice' your swords with her. You are forbidden to be in the same place as her. She arouses a demon in you that you can barely control.

"Now. As to your penance." Rising again, Boniface went to a closet in the back of the sacristy and brought out a leather flagellum. He held it by the handle so that the whip's tails hung before the young man's eyes.

"Do you know what this is?" Boniface let the fear grow in the young man's eyes. Ansel nodded. "This will be your path to salvation. And you must not spare yourself from its power. In the end, you will be stronger for it. And with God's help, you will tame your demon and restore your self-control."

"Thank you, Father."

Boniface put his left hand on Ansel's head and with his right made the sign of the cross, saying, "*Dominus noster Jesus Christus te absolvat; et ego auctoritate ipsius te absolvo ab omni vinculo excommunicationis et interdicti in quantum possum et tu indiges. Deinde, ego te absolvo a peccatis tuis in nomine Patris, et Filii, et Spiritus Sancti. Amen.*

Boniface found his godson inside the family chapel praying.

"*Sed libera nos a malo,*" Carloman said, one hand extended before him across the altar with its palm turned upward in supplication. The other hand clasped a holy icon that Boniface had given Carloman the day of his elevation to knighthood. It was a finger bone of the blessed St. Martin of Tours. Carloman wore it around his neck in a small wooden canister.

Though still young, Carloman's unusual height and lean body gave the impression that he was a man hardened by time. The right side of his face and his nose had been broken in battle and had never quite healed. From time to time, he had to sniffle the small amount of mucus that occasionally dripped from it. Though he reeked of intensity, Carloman's actions always were measured. Boniface took great pride in the religious conviction of his godson. Together, they had planned an alliance with the larger monasteries to rid the world of the pagan horde. Carloman's "Knights in Christ" were dedicated to this work. *Yes,* thought Boniface, *Carloman was the key.*

When his godson stood, Boniface led him back to his chambers.

"Charles has announced that he will raise Gripho to knighthood," Boniface said. "He named a day early in September to let it coincide with the fall assembly."

"How he dotes on that boy," Carloman said. "Gripho's barely been in battle. In Provence, my father kept him with the rear guard until Maurontus's line broke. He only sent him in for the kill."

"He is young, Carloman."

"My father is growing soft. He had me in the front lines at that age, Pippin as well. He's raising this one differently."

As the two walked down the hallway, Carloman glanced into a chamber off the hallway and stopped abruptly. Boniface followed his gaze and saw Ansel, kneeling on the floor, naked to the waist, flogging himself. A grunt escaped the knight's lips as each blow landed. Blood covered his back. Ansel's face was distorted. His eyes shined with fanaticism. Carloman looked questioningly at Boniface, who merely waved his hand at the chamber.

"Nothing to worry about. The young man came to me in the act of confession. Sometimes mortification of the flesh is the only solution to the carnal desires of young knights."

"He seems awfully intense about it," Carloman said.

"It is ... a special case," Boniface said.

Once in his chambers, Boniface unrolled the maps to show Carloman the monasteries whose allegiance they would need. "There are some, such as Saint Wandrille, we could approach now," Boniface said. "Others will have to wait until you and your brothers are named mayor."

"Brother," Carloman corrected. "Gripho is too young to be mayor. Father will never raise him up as an equal to Pippin and me."

"Nonetheless, you'll have to regard him as a successor. Bavaria and Neustria will help him assert his rights."

"Let them." Carloman pointed to the map. "Why will these monasteries have to wait?"

"Charles seized much of their land early in his career and left them with less than a third of the resources they had acquired."

"Are you saying we should give it all back?" Carloman asked.

"Only to those that are important for the relics they house or the influence they wield. If we combine your endowment with a papal decree to centralize the Church, we can align your family with the Church and mandate Christianity throughout the continent."

"What about the pagans?"

"Conquer them. Take their hostages. Baptize them."

"If they refuse?"

"Over time, the Church will win out. We supplant local rituals with our own, oftentimes using their words and rites. Birth, death, wedlock, knighthood—it is our rituals that tie us to God. It may take a generation or two to succeed."

"You're being optimistic," Carloman said.

"Then we will take stronger measures," Boniface said.

Carloman frowned.

"Have you seen their rites?" Boniface began to pace. "They are an affront to God. They drink blood. They sacrifice humans. Their 'communion,' a name that insults the Church, involves unspeakable debauchery.

"Yes, stronger measures may need to be taken," Boniface repeated, his face reddening. "Christians cannot coexist with such as them. If they do not submit to the Church, we must drive them from the land, imprison the leaders, and purge their followers. They are sin itself."

"Yet you suffered Charles's marriage to Sunnichild."

"Charles was adamant that he have her. She converted and married him within the Church. There was little I could do."

"I've heard rumors that she still practices the lore."

"If she does, she hides it well," Boniface said. "The real question, however, has always been Gripho. What if a son of Charles was pagan? Imagine the legitimacy that would give their lore."

"I asked him to join the Knights in Christ," Carloman said. "He refused."

"Perhaps that is merely a younger brother wanting to be seen as an equal."

"Let's hope so," Carloman said, "for his sake as well as ours."

Twice Trudi turned away from the door to her stepmother's chambers, and twice she turned back. Could Sunni be trusted? What could she do, if Charles made all the decisions? And what did she mean by "power"? Trudi had disdained Sunni's advice so often that she couldn't believe she was asking for the woman's help now.

She offered, Trudi reminded herself. Standing outside Sunni's chambers, however, she felt a new fear take hold. *How do I dare tell her about my thoughts of Ansel?* She flushed with embarrassment. *How can I tell Sunni about the hunger inside me, my need for him? Oh Jesus, how can I tell Sunni any of it?*

I can't. The clarity of this knowledge swept across her, quickly followed by enormous relief. *I can't tell her,* Trudi decided. *I won't.* She turned to go.

"I was beginning to think you had changed your mind," Sunni said, appearing in the doorway.

Trudi's stomach squeezed into a knot. "I can't."

Sunni took her hand and smiled. "Of course, you can. You have nothing to fear from me." Without waiting for Trudi's response, Sunni led her into her private quarters.

The rooms were small but thoughtfully adorned. Though too feminine for Trudi's tastes, the rooms were not overdone like those of some girls at court. Sunni used color as a subtle weapon to banish the coldness of the plaster walls. Red pillows lined the bed, and blue tapestries adorned the walls. And her furniture, though delicate, was purposeful and reserved—a desk and chair in the outer room, a small couch and chairs inside. In the bedroom, a gray mat lay in front of the hearth, which housed a small fire that took the chill from the air. Across the room, Sunni's bed was piled high with blue and gray pillows and white blankets. It was there that Sunni led her, and together they sat on the edge of her bed.

Oh my God, thought Trudi, *I'm going to tell her.* Trudi's face reddened, and her breath grew short.

"Tell me," Sunni said, her eyes reassuring.

To Trudi's horror, tears flooded from her. Before she could stop them, sobs wracked her frame, and she fell helplessly into Sunni's arms. The older woman cradled her, rocking her like a child until the tears were gone. When Trudi spoke, the words poured from her mouth in a torrent. Sunni said nothing. She just stroked Trudi's hair. When Trudi finished, Sunni sighed.

"That boy will never do," Sunni said.

"But I can't stop thinking about him."

"You need a man," Sunni said.

Trudi didn't understand.

"You have grown into a powerful young woman," Sunni said. "Why should you be surprised to find powerful forces inside your body?"

"You know I can't sleep with a man out of wedlock," Trudi said, reeling internally. "Father would—"

"No one condemns Pippin or the girl he lies with."

"That's different." Although she wasn't sure why it was different.

"Your father wants to barter with your body for an allegiance or a treaty. That is why he will not suffer you lying with a man out of wedlock. There are fewer questions about succession if the bride is a virgin. Boniface, of course, will condemn your sin. But you must remember that you are the daughter of Charles Martel. You will be his daughter even if you have lain with a man. In the end, your hand will still be sought by every noble family on the continent."

Sunni's calm in the face of Trudi's emotion was troubling. *She sees no shame in desire? Another man?* It was inconceivable. "But isn't lust one of the seven deadly sins?" she asked.

"There are no deadly sins," Sunni said. "Those are the teachings of people who seek to steal your passion for their own purposes."

There it was. Heresy. And Sunni had stated it as if it were obvious.

"So," Trudi whispered, "the rumors are true. You are pagan. This is what the Church warns about."

"A Church run by men," Sunni said. "It banishes all teaching that is not focused on serving the needs of men, particularly those men who run the Church. You were born of woman. Your body is a vessel that brings the power of the earth into focus. The passion for physical communion is only one of these focal points. You have many. Instead of subjugating those passions, you need to harness them."

"I don't think I could do that," Trudi said.

"Can you live without the passion you feel for Ansel?"

Trudi hesitated. "No," she said.

"Then you have already defied the Church. The question you must ask is: will you defy yourself?"

"But I want Ansel."

"You already know you cannot have Ansel. Your father would have him flayed, then drawn and quartered. Besides, Ansel is a brute, unworthy of a woman like you. He wouldn't come close to satisfying your needs. No, you need a man."

"I don't think I could do that," Trudi repeated.

"You have more power than you know," Sunni said. "When you are ready to harness that power, come to me. But you must promise me that you will speak of this to no one. Not your father. Not Boniface. Not Carloman or Pippin. They are men and do not understand our bodies or our needs. Helping you will put me in grave danger. But I can see that your need is great, so I am willing."

"I can't take your advice," Trudi said. "But I came to you in confidence, so I will leave you in confidence."

Sunni walked Trudi to the door, hugged her, and kissed both her cheeks. "Consider who has been teaching you and ask yourself whose interest they are trying to protect. If you decide you want my help, come see me."

Trudi left more disturbed than when she had arrived.

Two days later, Trudi rounded a corner to find herself directly in front of Ansel. Her heart leapt at the sight of him. Her face blushed deeply as she took a tentative step toward him. "Ansel." She reached out her hand to touch his chest.

"Stop!" Ansel said, his voice so strained it sounded like a gurgle.

"Ansel," she said again, surprised.

Ansel's face twisted into a grimace. "Temptress! Stay away from me!" His eyes seemed to push out of his head. "I must have nothing to do with you. Hear me, she-devil? Nothing!"

That night, she returned to Sunni's chambers, pausing again on the threshold. Sunni invited her in and closed the door behind her.

"How can I help you?" Sunni asked.

"Tell me about power."

CHAPTER 2

Jeu de Moulin

After Charles announced that he would raise Gripho to knighthood, Sunni whirled into action. She lorded over couriers, cooks, servants, and stable hands to make the villa at Quierzy suitable for her son to become a knight. She persuaded Carloman's wife, Greta, to host a celebration the evening after Gripho's elevation and summoned minstrels from Aachen and musicians from Paris.

Though the fête would strain the skills of the local seamstresses and the pocketbooks of his nobles, Charles did not complain about it to Sunni. So she decided to carry on until he did. She ordered hunts to gather venison and boar meat. She ordered bulls butchered, pigs slaughtered, and warehouses tapped for grain and grog. She even bullied Boniface when the bishop insisted that the knighting ceremony be followed by a high mass, saying that if there were going to be a mass, it should be a mass worthy of her only son.

Nothing escaped her eye. Tapestries were cleaned, rugs beaten, hallways mopped, stairwells scrubbed. She enlisted the local monastery to letter invitations on rare parchment intended for nobles across the continent. To ensure full attendance, she asked Charles to convene an autumn assembly of knights. It was the one time Sunni actually paid him attention. When he agreed, she grabbed both his cheeks in her hands and kissed him full on the mouth in front of Boniface, Carloman, and Greta.

Charles inquired after her on several evenings only to wait outside her chambers like a petitioner until she demurely came out to greet him and beg his indulgence as she and Trudi attended to matters "more appropriate for women."

After nearly a week of neglect, Charles sent for her. She blew into his chambers, bringing with her a seamstress, a cook, enormous bolts of cloth, and a minstrel. She showed him her two favorite gowns and asked his opinion. When he gave it, she frowned and said she'd have to "think about it." She made him taste the specialties the cook was preparing for the feast and showed him bolts of cloth to be used as decoration for the ball. He sat patiently until the minstrel started playing a ballad written specifically for Gripho's elevation.

"Everyone out of the room," he ordered. When Sunni stood to leave with the others, he roared, "Not you, Sunni!"

"As my lord wishes."

"Stop that!"

"Yes, milord."

"Sunnichild!"

Laughing, she threw herself into his arms and kissed him hungrily on the mouth.

"God, I've missed you," she said, pressing the length of her body against him.

He kissed her neck.

"Are you sure you don't want to hear the ballad I had written?" she asked. "I can have the minstrel back here in a second."

He laughed and started pulling off her clothes.

When they finished their lovemaking, Charles padded naked across the room and told the sentry outside his door to order bread, cheese, and wine from the kitchen. When it arrived, he sat at the opposite end of the bed.

"You don't look well, Charles."

"It is nice to see you too."

"Your color is bad, your skin is clammy, and you look exhausted. Was it a hard campaign?"

"Harder than we expected."

"Have you spoken to the doctors?"

"They had nothing to offer."

Sunni crossed the bed quickly and took his face in her hands. She looked at his eyes and then placed both hands at the base of his neck to feel his pulse. She grabbed his forearm and turned it over, inspecting it like a piece of meat. "They bled you," she stated. "What did the doctors say?"

"Nothing of value. 'Demons in my blood,' that sort of thing."

She leapt out of bed, took the bread and cheese from his hands, and upon finding her robe, turned on him.

"You are not getting out of this bed, and you will fast for at least two days."

"Sunni—"

"Why didn't you tell me? I'll have cold compresses sent up immediately. Of all times for this to happen! I've got to finish the menu and select the wine. Decide on the—"

"Sunnichild!"

"There's so much—"

"Stop. I am fine. I rested well after the battle. I've been bled. I've fasted and had my fill of compresses. Now it's time for me to be mayor." When she still didn't move, he said, "I will be fine, my love."

After a few moments, Sunni bent and kissed his forehead. "All right," she said. "But no sex."

"You would take away my reason to live?"

She hugged him, and he wrestled her back into bed.

"We have to talk about Trudi." Sunni pushed him away.

Charles groaned. "Let's get through this knighting. Then we will talk about wedding plans."

"It won't wait, Charles. She's been of age for years. The anticipation is killing her ... not to mention that she's an attractive and healthy young woman."

"What do you think of Liutbrand?"

"The Lombard? He's ancient, Charles. She'd be a widow inside three years."

"His son, Aistulf?"

"I'm not sure he can keep the other Lombards in line."

"Liutbrand is the only one who seems capable of keeping all of them from civil war. That's why I suggested him. Ateni of Provence?"

"If he is so powerful, why did you have to save him from Maurontus?"

"Look, Sunni, I can't have both Italy and Provence in rebellion. I need to align one of them more closely so that if the other becomes a problem, I won't get attacked from two sides."

"What about Odilo?" Sunni asked.

"I like Odilo, but with you and Gripho, we don't need further alignment with Bavaria."

"There just aren't many suitable choices for Trudi," Sunni said. "I would rather she wed someone she can love."

"Duty is a burden, Sunni. It always has been."

"We are a political marriage and yet love each other. Why can't she?"

"All of our potential choices should be here for Gripho's elevation. We can see how she is with them. But, Sunni," he paused, "no promises. If I need to make a political choice, I will."

"Yes, milord," she said, bowing.

Charles threw a pillow at her.

Sunni made her way down the hall to her chambers. Charles looked terrible. Others might not see it, but she did. Herbs or poultices would strengthen his blood. She would send for the lore master in town to see about potential remedies.

She ran across a young man who didn't seem to have enough to do, so she sent him to the stable master to help muck out stalls in preparation for the visiting dignitaries. She stopped to greet Pippin's mistress, Bertrada, who had come to offer Greta help with the fête. Sunni liked the girl; she was always pleasant and good-natured, if somewhat bawdy. As he had with Trudi, Charles kept Pippin's marital status open. But anyone could see Pippin was clearly in love with the girl. Sooner or later, they would have children, either in or out of wedlock. And as Charles himself had proven, bastards couldn't be counted out of the mayor's succession.

She found Gripho in her rooms pacing back and forth.

"I want you to tell that pious buffoon to stay out of my affairs!" Gripho said.

I don't have the heart for this, thought Sunni. *Not today.* "I suppose you are referring to Boniface," she answered.

"He is making the Church the center of my elevation. First they are having a prayer breakfast—"

"That's Carloman's doing. His knights are, after all, called Knights in Christ."

"Then there is to be a high mass following the ceremony—"

"I couldn't change that. You know I tried. There is too much precedent."

"Now they want me to fast for an entire day before I'm knighted. They want me to pray, lying prostrate before the altar all night. They even want me to name a sainted 'benefactor.' I could piss on their saints!"

He's still a boy, Sunni reminded herself. *Of course, he's frustrated.* "We walk a tight line, Gripho. You know your father gives a great deal of discretion to Boniface—"

"That sanctimonious old fart. I did all that you said. Learned the lessons, gave the right answers, let him believe I was devout. But I'll not fast. I'll not be 'reborn in Christ' as a Christian knight. I'll not join Carloman's zealots."

"I'll discuss it."

"I already told Boniface and Carloman what they could do with their ceremonies."

"Gripho—"

"No. Carloman and Pippin walk around as if they are already mayors and I'm one of their subjects. And Charles thinks they walk on water. Why do I have to put up with this? Once Charles makes me a knight, I am their equal, aren't I? It's time they started treating me that way."

Sunni fought to calm herself. "Gripho, you're fourteen. You are just becoming a knight. They are men. Your time will come. If you make them your enemies now, they will destroy you. Succession is no game. And believe me, this is all about succession."

"How would you know? Your idea of succession was to be taken hostage. And then you married the man who took you."

"Gripho—"

"Now you've gone over to their side." He imitated her voice. *"Don't move too quickly, Gripho. Walk a fine line, Gripho. Don't make them your enemies, Gripho."*

"Gripho!"

"I'm not doing it," he said and was gone.

Sunni blinked back the tears that lined her eyes. *There are times,* she thought, *when I could strangle that boy.*

"Your move," Charles said.

Boniface looked up from the *Jeu de Moulin* board and wondered if Charles would see the trap. Boniface had made his last three moves look careless, and they all seemed to leave key crossroads exposed. If Charles took the bait, Boniface would have him.

They had known each other for a long time, even before the bishop had taken his Christian name. In those days, he had been "Wynnfred," a lowly priest who spent his days spreading the faith to pagan strongholds like Frisia, Hesse, and Bavaria.

He had had more success than most. It helped that he was a big man and looked more like a blacksmith than a priest. His hands were huge, and he had a bulbous nose and a craggy face. If not for his habit, he might have passed for a pagan warlord. Still, he often returned from those sojourns needing to be patched up like a knight returning from battle. In recognition of his service, the pope had made him a bishop.

When Charles began to consolidate power throughout Francia, Boniface took it upon himself to minister the faith to Charles's family and became one of the mayor's closest advisors. Charles had never hidden his ambitions, and Boniface had never doubted the man's ability to succeed. The two became fast friends. And when it became obvious to all that Charles was the single power behind the throne, the pope made Boniface an archbishop and legate to the Holy See.

Although he had failed the pope's mission to return the powerful monasteries and lands Charles had seized from the Church in his younger days, Boniface had succeeded in strengthening the Church's authority and doctrine across the continent.

Many monasteries were powers in their own right, more moneylenders than houses of God. Some had knights of their own and fighting men. Many displayed holy relics and professed a special connection to one or more heavenly saints. So often did these churches celebrate unique rites that a Christian from one town attending mass in another might not recognize that he was in a church of the same faith. Using Charles's influence, Boniface had made great progress in bringing the practice of the faith into line and in reminding the clergy of their fealty to the Holy See.

"I need your help, Wynnfred." Charles moved a piece into Boniface's trap.

"It must be something important if you are using my given name." Boniface moved a second piece into line. The third would capture one of Charles's men.

"It is important." Charles placed a man across the board.

"How important?" Boniface licked his lips and completed the line. "*Tué!*" he called and plucked one of Charles's pieces off the board.

Charles placed a second piece in line across the board. Boniface blocked him, leaving Charles with a devil's choice. No matter where he placed his next piece, Charles would lose a man. "I want you to preside over my funeral."

The bishop looked up from the board, his surprise quickly replaced by doubt. He squinted, peering hard into Charles's eyes. After a moment, he nodded his head.

"Of course, I will. Although I will be sorry to do it, Charles."

"I haven't much time. After Gripho's elevation, I will hold an assembly of all the knights. I will name Carloman, Pippin, and Gripho as mayors and ask the entire assembly to submit their hands to them."

"Gripho's not old enough, Charles."

"Pippin and Carloman were given counties at that age."

"Those were counties. You are talking about making him a mayor of the palace. Your other two sons will be furious."

"I'll carve out a middle kingdom for him. Bavaria, Provence, the areas closest to the Lombard Peninsula. Sunni's relations will support him from Bavaria."

"He'll need them."

"Boniface, the boys will be tested on almost every front. They have Hunoald to worry about in Aquitaine, Liutfred in Alemannia, and the Saracen in Narbonne. If the boys fight amongst themselves, they will fail. You must support Gripho and Sunni and keep Carloman and Pippin from going after him."

"Pippin is not the problem, Charles."

"I know. Carloman can't stand the boy. But he'll do as I say."

"Are you sure the nobles will support them?"

"By appointing the boys as mayors at the assembly, no one will have an opportunity to debate my decision. And each of them will have to state their loyalty in front of the other nobles. If you make my funeral worthy of a king, the boys will look like princes. The nobles will be awed, and you will keep the peace between them."

"What if there are calls for naming a Merovingian as king?"

Charles spat. "I don't think there are any still alive. If they do find one, ignore all such demands. If they persist, shout them down. Under no circumstances allow my sons to name a Merovingian king. *They* will be kings."

After a long silence, Boniface returned his eyes to the *Jeu de Moulin* board. Charles moved a third piece into line to take one of Boniface's men.

Boniface looked surprised. "You must be distracted; you just sacrificed a corner of the board." He completed his own line of three and took the last of Charles's men from the crossroad. He clapped his hands and chuckled.

It took Charles only six more moves to beat him.

Many of the nobles returning from the Provence campaign decided to stay on at Quierzy to await Gripho's elevation and Charles's new assembly. To accommodate them, Sunni unleashed a small army of servants to ready rooms in the guest wings. She moved Childebrand of Austrasia and Theudoald of Neustria into temporary quarters inside the main house. Both men were related to Charles. Childebrand, a brooding giant of a man, shared Charles's mother and was fiercely devoted to his half brother. Theudoald was the grandson of Charles's father, Pippin of Herstal, and his wife, Plectrude. The man was a dilettante who distinguished himself only by harping on the claim that he was rightfully entitled to Charles's title as mayor. Sunni put the two in adjacent rooms, knowing that Childebrand would keep an eye on Charles's "rival."

As September drew near, nobles from across the continent began to arrive with their contingents. Patrice of Burgundy, Ateni of Provence, Liutfred of Alemannia, and King Liutbrand of the Lombards each made his way along the River Oise to the mayoral residence. Even the rebellious Hunoald of Aquitaine and the pagan Radbod of Frisia came for the elevation. Sunni had arranged for each of them to receive horn fanfares as they approached the villa and again when they entered the villa's grounds.

Knights on horse led each party up to the main house. For each knight on horse, there were at least six attendants and twenty fighting men afoot. Behind these came carts filled with supplies, gifts, and, on occasion, the nobles' wives. Another set of knights brought up the rear. For the most part, a dozen knights represented each region. Hunoald, the one-handed knight of Aquitaine, however, came with a contingent twice the size of his peers.

Upon arrival at the villa, the men afoot were dispatched to make camp on the grounds outside Quierzy while Sunni had the nobles and gentlewomen shown to their chambers. Knowing that Carloman would keep the Neustrian camp situated far from the Austrasian camp and the

Burgundians far from the Bavarians, Sunni made similar arrangements for her guests' chambers inside the mayoral residence.

As each party arrived, Sunni had their banners hung from the rampart and in the main feasting hall. The mix of colors and designs gave the grounds a festive character, and soon the people in town began to follow suit, decking their houses and shops in colors and marking up the cost of everything from a loaf of bread to a suit of armor. Booths were constructed on the outskirts of town for those merchants arriving from nearby counties who knew that there was money to be made.

When word came that the Bavarian contingent approached the villa, Sunni was in the kitchen checking on preparations for that night's meal. She shocked the kitchen staff by squealing for joy and performing the first steps to the Estampie with the head cook. Seeing the disapproval in the woman's eyes, Sunni stifled a laugh, curtsied gracefully, and rushed to the rampart to welcome her kinsmen.

Despite the distance the Bavarians had traveled, Sunni was surprised to find their retinue fresh and kempt. Men in polished armor rode beautiful white horses into the villa with a measured gait. Each knight sat erect in his saddle and sported a huge and waxed mustache after the Bavarian fashion.

Not Odilo. Sunni found her grandmother's youngest son riding casually among his men, his face clean-shaven and his armor well used. He looked as if he were taking a leisurely ride in the country. Sunni waved to him, jumping up and down to be noticed. Odilo laughed when he saw her and waved in return. He laughed again when, at Sunni's signal, trumpets blared into fanfare and the blue Bavarian banners unfurled over the wall.

He blew Sunni a kiss just as Trudi joined her on the rampart. Seeing the young woman take her arm, Odilo graced Trudi with a broad smile and bowed to her as formally as one can bow on horseback.

Both women laughed in response.

"He's the one?" Trudi asked.

"Yes."

"He seems young to be your uncle."

"He is thirty-six, four years older than I."

"He's quite amusing."

That isn't what she's thinking, Sunni thought. Trudi's cheeks already were flushed.

"Do you think he'll be willing?" Trudi asked.

Sunni smiled to herself. She had helped Trudi shed her plates of armor for attire more appropriate to a young noblewoman at court. She was dressed simply but elegantly in a soft, white robe held together at the waist with a rose colored sash. The sash accentuated the leanness of her body and the strength of her limbs. Trudi's hair was brushed until it shone and hung luxuriously over her shoulders. She wore a necklace with a golden amulet that Sunni had given her. It was a secret pagan symbol of fertility and a declaration of womanhood. There was no more powerful talisman.

"You are beautiful," Sunni said. "And it is a sacred right. He will be honored to share it with you."

Trudi's fingers played with the amulet. Her eyes never left Odilo.

They found him in the courtyard just inside the gate, giving his horse into the care of an attendant. Sunni swept into Odilo's arms, and together the two spun in circles like a child's top.

"How is it that you have been gone three years?" Sunni chided. "You abandoned me to these Neustrians and Austrasians without a second thought. What have I done to deserve such a fate?"

"You married Charles Martel," Odilo said, a smile on his face

Sunni took him by the arm and drew him toward Trudi.

"I have someone special for you to meet," she said. "May I present Charles's daughter, Trudi?"

Trudi smiled and curtsied with all the grace Sunni could have desired.

"How could I have overlooked someone so beautiful?" Odilo asked, bowing. "I don't remember Charles even having a daughter."

"You flatter me, sir," Trudi said, rising.

Sunni almost laughed aloud when Odilo's eyes caught the sparkle of the amulet around Trudi's neck. He leaned closer, and his eyes opened wide with shock. He looked to Sunni to confirm what he saw.

"Some gifts are eternal," she said.

Odilo looked to Trudi. She smiled as well, the blush creeping back to her cheeks.

Sunni could see Odilo's mind racing through the implications; Trudi was studying pagan lore and preparing for the rite of communion. And if that look on her face was any indication, he was meant to share in it.

"We have much to discuss, Uncle," Sunni said, laughing.

"I should visit more often," he replied.

Odilo would not miss the political ramifications; Trudi was of age to be married. With Gripho in line for succession and Charles's only daughter breaking with Christianity, a number of possibilities presented themselves, many leading to official sanction of the pagan lore. It could lead to an end of the purges and the pogroms.

Trudi winked at Sunni and turned her gaze to Odilo. She bent her head a little to the right and swept her hair back over her right shoulder. Odilo's eyes followed every movement.

Yes, things were moving along very nicely.

Boniface appeared out of the crowd near the main hall and bowed deeply to Odilo.

"May honor strengthen your sword," he said in the Bavarian dialect.

"And may truth guide its way," Odilo finished for him.

Boniface grasped him by the shoulders and hugged him to his chest. Odilo rolled his eyes at the display and wrinkled his nose at Sunni.

"Ah, I'm delighted to see you," Boniface said. "It's been too many years. How is that new bishopric I put into Regensburg? I trust that you've welcomed Gregor with open arms?"

"Of course," Odilo replied, "although, the bishop seems to spend most of his time preaching to prostitutes and beggars."

"As did our Lord," Boniface said. "Having a bit of a family reunion, are we?"

"Sunni was just introducing me to Trudi."

"And such a beauty!" the priest exclaimed. "Don't you agree?"

"She is delightful," Odilo said.

"But where is our guest of honor?" Boniface asked. "Where is Gripho? The Bavarian contingent won't be complete without him."

"He is probably in the main hall," Sunni said. She sensed that Boniface knew he was interrupting something important. His eyebrows had soared when Odilo mentioned Trudi. Sunni could almost hear him thinking. *What is she doing with them?* Sunni would have to be careful. Boniface knew that Trudi was of an age to be married. She was sure that he would inquire of Charles.

"Carloman is having a prayer breakfast on Friday to honor Gripho's pending knighthood," Boniface said to Odilo. "I would be delighted if you join us."

Sunni reached out to rearrange Trudi's hair and flashed Odilo a signal from their family's battle code, meaning *beware*. She did not look to see if he caught the warning.

"Ah, my apologies, good priest," Odilo said. "Had I only known in time. I am hosting a boar hunt on Friday. I thought it would be useful to engage the visiting knights in a pursuit where they can kill animals rather than each other."

"A noble gesture," Boniface said. "Carloman thought that prayer might accomplish much the same thing."

"I'm sure it will. Please give Carloman my respects and thank him for the invitation. My prayers will be with you."

Boniface bowed and made a hasty retreat.

"Prayer breakfast?" Odilo asked.

"Boniface is trying to ensure that the Church is the center of Gripho's elevation," Sunni said. "He sees Gripho as a symbol. A Christian knight of Bavarian blood is an enormous boon to Boniface. He believes that it will sway nobles and commoners alike to Christianity."

"Is Gripho willing to be used for such a purpose?"

"I'm not sure he can help it," Sunni said. "To break with the Church at this point would be suicide."

"But the boy doesn't support this, does he?"

"No. But even if Gripho doesn't participate in person, Boniface can still use his knighthood to sow the seeds of Christianity."

"Perhaps Gripho could join us on the hunt?"

"He already tried to refuse Carloman, and Charles nearly threw him from the rampart. There are, however, a number of visiting knights who are grumbling about the breakfast. They think of knighthood as separate from the Church and already feel they spend too much time in front of the altar. I think the idea of a hunt is wonderful. A brilliant stroke! Trudi and I would love to join you."

"Milady?" Odilo asked Trudi.

"Of course, I'll join you," she said. "A gold solidus on the first boar."

"You hunt?" Odilo asked.

"Would you have me watch you have all the fun?" Trudi retorted with a smile. "Sunni can handle the watching part."

Odilo laughed and shook his head. Trudi played with her pendant. Sunni smiled.

News of Odilo's hunt spread quickly. Many knights and visiting dignitaries seized the chance to avoid Carloman's breakfast. Hunoald of Aquitaine put up a wager for the largest boar killed. Ateni of Provence boasted that he would bring home three. Radbod of Frisia who, as a pagan, had been uncomfortable with Carloman's invitation from the beginning, jumped at Odilo's offer. And Liutfred of Alemannia gave his assent as well. Odilo had secured the lands of a nearby chateau and promised a roasting party after the kill. Those in attendance could stay the night as guests at the chateau.

To bolster his attendance, Carloman announced that Charles would attend the prayer breakfast with Gripho. All of the Knights in Christ accepted, as did the Neustrians and many of the Austrasians. Liutbrand, the Lombard king, and his son, Aistulf, assented, as had Patrice of Burgundy. No one had heard from Pippin.

To Carloman, it wouldn't suffice. With Boniface in tow, he sought out Charles.

"We can't let this stand. It's bad enough that the man is holding a hunt, but it is an insult that Sunni and Trudi go!"

"It is a sign of their pagan leanings," Boniface said. "Is it lost on anyone that the Bavarians, *from a former pagan country,* the Alemannians, *from a former pagan country,* and the Frisians, *from a still-pagan country,* have chosen the hunt over the breakfast?"

"And I don't like the idea that Hunoald is going with them," Carloman said. "He is as much a rebel as his father. We shouldn't let him out of our sight."

"This is a slap at the Church," Boniface said. "And with Sunnichild going, it gives the hunt your implied sanction."

"It has my sanction," Charles said. "Look at the two of you! All puffed up over court politics and some imaginary slight. The knights under our roof don't need any encouragement from you to point out our differences. They are more than happy to do that all by themselves. And while I am willing to support the religious agenda of the Church, this is not some catechism class. These are men of war. They live in their saddles and fight every day. Truth is, *I* would rather be going on the hunt with *them*."

Charles rose from his couch to face the two of them. "Boniface, you scheduled a high mass. Then you asked for twenty-four hours of fasting and prayer. And now, Carloman, you've decided to have a prayer breakfast. I'm raising Gripho to knighthood, not the priesthood. But the two of you have inserted the Church into every nook of this affair.

"And, so far, I've backed you. I insisted that Gripho be there, and I've insisted that he fast. I've told everyone that I will attend the breakfast with you. But I'd rather be throwing spears at boars than bowing my head yet again in church. And as for Sunni, I'm glad she is going. The implied sanction of the hunt makes me look as if I haven't lost touch with those who fight battles for a living. It also makes me look magnanimous to those who feel a little too uncomfortable with this much religion."

Charles focused on Carloman. "*I* defeated every one of those knights. They submitted to *me*. They continue to rule in their lands because I decided that they are the best equipped to rule. I have called them here, and they have come. They'll do my bidding, if I ask. At my word, they will wage war and besiege cities." Charles poked his right index finger in Carloman's sternum. "I won't waste that power on a prayer breakfast."

Carloman made sure that the prayer breakfast began precisely at seventh bells, Friday morning. A section of the main hall had been roped off to make the gathering as intimate as possible. Curtains had been raised on two sides to curtail the noise from others in the hall. He was pleased that Sunnichild had organized the hunt's departure from another entrance of the villa to cut down on the disruption of the event.

Even so, Hunoald of Aquitaine and his son, Waifar, came down into the hall on their way to the hunt. They were laughing and boisterous. Carloman raised his voice to continue his welcome, but many near the back turned their heads at the distraction.

Making matters worse, Hunoald came up short once he realized that he had disrupted the affair. Waifar bumped into him, and the two smiled comically at the glares from those attending the breakfast. Several of the Knights in Christ, marked by their red doublets with a white cross, put hands to swords. Hunoald raised his in a placating gesture. With a deep and ceremonious bow to Carloman, Hunoald waved with his good arm and strode out of the hall, his head held high in an overly dignified manner. Waifar followed him, with an equally affected posture. The moment they left the hall, Carloman heard them erupt into laughter.

Once the echoing revelry died down, Carloman resumed his welcome, trying to keep the anger from his voice. He recognized all the visiting dignitaries and local nobles in attendance by name and asked Boniface to bless the meal. Boniface, who on most occasions was not above wearing beautiful ecclesiastical garments, wore only a monk's brown robe tied at the waist with a rope, affecting a more humble demeanor.

Boniface asked those in attendance to bow their heads. Many of the Knights in Christ left their chairs to drop one knee to the ground.

"Thank you, Lord, for this moment of reflection by those of earthly power who consider the will of God in their defense of the realm." Boniface then blessed the repast, and the knights sat down to eat.

Carloman had arranged the seating with Gripho at the head table next to Charles. The boy looked uncomfortable, and Carloman couldn't tell if it was due to his distaste for so much ceremony or his distaste for so much religion. He still had doubts about the boy.

The visiting nobles were dispersed throughout the room as "hosts" at each table. Carloman then had graced their guests with the presence of his Knights in Christ, each wearing the order's white cross on his right shoulder and Carloman's lion on his left. "One arm a sword for God," as their motto read, "the other a shield for the realm." Carloman had instructed his knights to keep the conversation lively at each table by stating their opinions about barbaric pagan rites and the destructive influence that paganism had on peace and security. *Perhaps it was just as well,* thought Carloman, *that Odilo had lured some of Charles's pagan guests away from the breakfast.*

At the end of the meal, Carloman rose to introduce Boniface. The bishop left the head table and walked out among the nobles and knights. He greeted many by name, shook hands with a few, and clapped a number on the shoulder as he walked. Carloman did not have to turn his head to see Charles's disapproval. His father always bristled when someone else lorded over a room.

"We are here in God's name," began Boniface, "for we are men of God." He turned and swept his arms to encompass all of them. "We are His Knights in Christ. We are nobles of incredible power who have chosen to dedicate this morning to God rather than to the pursuit of wild animals, sport, and revelry." Boniface lifted his right hand and bowed his head. When he looked up, the gleam in his eye drew the attention of everyone in the room. He began moving from table to table as he spoke, bringing everyone into his eyes' embrace.

"As much as we have chosen this moment," Boniface said, "we are also *being chosen* in this moment.

"Your rank has brought you wealth beyond the needs of mortal flesh. It has brought you fame and deference. It has brought you the power to judge and to execute justice in your counties and realms. Few rooms in the world hold such power and authority as this one. Fewer still bring such power and authority together for such noble purpose." Boniface held his chin in his hand, dramatically pondering the moment. Carloman heard his father grunt his disapproval.

"I said before that we are 'being chosen.' Now what could that daft old priest have meant by that?" he asked himself and waited for the chuckling that followed. "Power without purpose is self-serving. You are being chosen because you are men of power who have faith. You are being chosen," Boniface paused for effect, "because you serve God.

"You have a duty to your Lord, of course," the bishop said, bowing to Charles. Boniface must have sensed that Charles was not pleased, for he stumbled through his next line. "If Charles says, 'Lay siege to Narbonne,' you lay siege to Narbonne. If he says, 'Stop,' I'm sure you all would know what to do. But in your daily execution of justice, in your arbitration of dispute, in your never-ending pursuit of security for the realm, you also have a responsibility to ensure that your actions *and your behavior* live up to the will of God.

"What does that mean?" he asked himself again. This time, however, he did not wait for the laugh but plunged into his subject with vigor. "It means that you have a responsibility to be an example of Christ to those around you, to teach the gospel of our Lord. You have a responsibility to oppose those who seek to seduce the people away from Christianity. And let there be no doubt, there are many, and their forces are strong.

"Today and every day, there are human sacrifices made to pagan gods on your lands. Today and every day, there are orgiastic rites being performed where three or more lay naked and fornicate shamelessly together under the moonlight. The teachings of Christ are undermined by pagans in our marketplaces, in our fields, and even in the ranks of your armies. If you want to know why lawlessness exists in your lands, it is the pagan influence that drives it. If you want to know why the women in your villages give birth to the crippled and feeble-minded, it is because of the pagan manner in which their children were conceived. If you want to know why there are never-ending wars on our borders, it is because the one true religion, Christianity, is challenged in the land.

"You have the power to combat this influence and so are being chosen by God, this day, this morning, this moment, to do His will. As His chosen, I know you will bend the power of your sword to do His bidding. As men of responsibility, I am confident you will know what to do."

Boniface held up his hand in blessing. Heads bowed across the room.

The Knights in Christ knelt. Boniface made the sign of the cross, saying, "May God bless you, the Father, the Son, and the Holy Ghost. Amen."

"Amen," came the chorused reply.

Carloman did not immediately rise from his chair. It was not the first time that the bishop had shown him the will of God, but rarely had Carloman seen it so clearly. He held on to this vision, reluctant to return to his duties as host. He said a silent prayer of thanks and made the sign of the cross. Charles cleared his throat. Carloman stood.

He thanked the knights and nobles for their attendance. He recognized his half brother, Gripho, and acknowledged his brother's commitment in Christ and announced that Gripho would fast and pray for the twenty-four hours leading up to his elevation. This brought the boy a round of applause from the room. Gripho waved and smiled, albeit uncomfortably. Carloman then thanked his father for his support of their breakfast. This brought the room to their feet, with cheers for "Charles" and "The Hammer" echoing through the room.

Charles rose and bowed to receive the praise. He raised Gripho's hand, and the applause grew louder. He kissed Carloman on both cheeks and repeated the gesture for Boniface. Putting his arm around both of them, he smiled for the crowd.

"That was much farther than I would have gone," Charles said under his breath.

"We were only speaking to the faithful," Carloman said.

"Next time, I'm going to the hunt."

When the ninth morning bells rang at the Chateau of Pierre de Solon, only a few of the knights had straggled in. An early morning rain chilled the early arrivers who, led by Liutfred of Alemannia, began to drink and welcome the rest of the arriving knights with shouts and toasts. As each group meandered in, the gathering grew not just larger, but more boisterous.

Hunoald and Waifar stormed the gathering on horseback, circling the group and holding their spears aloft. They screamed their war cries and drove their warhorses at the revelers. This caused a number of those nearest the edge to move instinctively into a defensive position. Just steps away from the group, the two Aquitainians brought their charge up short and dismounted. Both of them laughed loudly at their jest and clasped their peers in greeting. They were welcomed by laughter in return. Odilo thrust cups into their hands.

Just past the tenth morning bells, Sunnichild and Trudi appeared on horseback to more cheers and toasts. They dismounted. Odilo bowed with a dramatic flourish and made a great show of presenting the Lady Sunnichild and the Lady Hiltrude. The two wore matching white cloaks. An aide produced a small table where Odilo quickly unfurled maps of the chateau grounds. Three sections were outlined in red.

In a loud voice, Odilo announced that the hunt would be competitive. Two individual winners would be chosen based on the number of boars killed and on the largest killed. There would also be team awards for the greatest number of boars or venison brought to the feast.

"Hunoald, Waifar, and the knights of Aquitaine will join Radbod and the nobles from Frisia," Odilo announced. Cheers greeted this decision. Hunoald embraced Radbod, and the two shook their spears and roared at the remaining knights. "Liutfred and the Alemannians will hunt with Ateni and the knights of Provence." More cheers followed as the knights rearranged themselves based on the pairings. "And I," Odilo said with an impish smile, "will join the Austrasians—" The Austrasians raised a cheer before he could finish. Odilo held up his hand for quiet. "Led by the fair Hiltrude."

The knights fell silent.

"A cunt?" The slur was just loud enough to be heard. It floated over the gathering. A considerable amount of grumbling followed.

Odilo had expected some resistance to taking a woman on the hunt. He raised his hand to quiet the protest. Before he could speak, however, he heard Hiltrude mutter, "Horseshit."

Turning, he saw her throw off her cloak to show her plated armor and leap to horse. Grabbing a spear from an unsuspecting Alemannian, she thrust it aloft and shouted, "Austrasia! Austrasia!"

The Austrasians immediately responded to her battle cry, shouting,

"Austrasia! Austrasia!" They too leapt to horse. Catching the moment, Odilo's knights echoed the call, shouting, "Bavaria! Bavaria!"

Soon all of knights gathered were laughing and cheering Hiltrude's audacity.

As the three parties set out, Odilo and Trudi accompanied Sunnichild and the knights of Austrasia and Bavaria to the northeast sector. The morning rain turned to a drizzle and then stopped altogether. Odilo chose a path that led their party alongside the River Oise. It followed a wide swath of green grass, bordered on the right by leafy shrubs, which after a mile led into a wood of birch trees and maples. Odilo set a leisurely pace so that he and Trudi could talk.

"That was a marvelous performance."

"I thought you might like it," Trudi said. "At least I didn't have to challenge any of them to fight."

Odilo laughed. "I would have paid to see that."

"With this group, you may get your wish."

"Oh, I think you made your point. The fact that you are Charles's daughter was not lost on anyone."

She reined her mount. "You think they backed down in deference to my father?"

Odilo reined in as well. "No, my young knightess. All of the nobles here have faced Charles on the battlefield. He's beaten every one of us. Let's just say your display back there seemed familiar. Men of war respond well to acts of defiance and audacity."

"That's better." Trudi spurred her mount forward.

Again he followed her lead. "I couldn't help but notice the pendant you wore the other day," he said.

Trudi glanced around them, taking in the nearness of the knights riding with them, and squinted her eyes. "Did you like it?" She smiled up at him.

"I found it beautiful and intriguing."

"It is a bit exotic, don't you think?"

"Around *your* neck, it is definitely exotic. Such pendants are rare in these parts."

"So I've heard." She laughed.

"May I ask how you came by it?"

"It was a gift from Sunni. She said it might catch your eye."

"I am always drawn to exotic beauty. It is a weakness of mine. Such beauty has power. But power," he paused, "often has consequences."

"I am learning about power," she said. "Would you like to see it again?" she asked with a direct look.

"Very much so."

"Then I will wear it for you tonight at the roasting party."

"I am honored at your generosity." He bowed.

He was still amazed that Trudi would give herself over to pagan ritual. But he could not dismiss her offer to wear the pagan fertility charm tonight. And he could not have made it clearer that there could be consequences. She had brushed it off without a thought. His eyes searched out Sunnichild. When they found her, she simply smiled and flashed him a hand signal that said, *All is arranged*.

The path forked southward, and the party turned into the wood. At Odilo's signal, knights fanned out in a *V* shape, ten men on each side. They marched forward, banging their shields to flush the boar out from the brush and funnel him into a killing zone, where the knights on either side of the *V* would hurl their spears at the charging beast.

Much larger than its brother, the pig, the boar is a killing machine with sharp tusks and a ferocious charge. The most dangerous spot on the field was at the bottom of the *V*. Should the flanking knights miss their mark, the bottom of the *V* would meet the rushing animal head on. Not only was the animal harder to hit from this angle, the consequences for a miss could be deadly.

As was the tradition for hunt leaders, Odilo and Trudi took the position at the bottom of the *V*. Sunnichild moved outside the formation alongside two knights Odilo had assigned to ensure her safety.

The hunters pressed forward, spears out and eyes wary. Occasionally, they beat their spears against their shields. Half an hour turned into an hour. An hour turned into two. No boar charged out of the wood. No one threw a spear. And still they marched.

The morning came to an end, and the party had nothing to show for its effort. Odilo called a halt and ordered a meal served of cheese, cold meat, and wine. A few knights grumbled over the choice of hunting ground, and Odilo laughed.

"Enough complaining. Remember you could have been at the prayer breakfast!" he called. Everyone laughed and nodded in agreement.

When the meal ended, they took up the flanking *V* formation again and again headed south, away from the river. The knights banged their shields and plodded through the wood, their heads swiveling from side to side. As before, they walked without incident, relaxing over time as the thought of a charging boar grew remote in their minds.

Without warning, one crashed into their midst. A few hearty throws were made, and the beast fell with a spear protruding from its neck. Shaking its head to lose the spear, the boar regained its feet and charged the nearest knight. More spears flew. All missed their mark. As the boar kept on unchecked, a knight raised his spear and plunged it into the boar's back, throwing all his weight into the blow. The boar's momentum lifted him off his feet, and the beast crashed into him, tearing a gash in his thigh.

Odilo watched the knight attempt to rise, only to fall back to the ground beside the fallen animal. Blood soaked his leg. Knights on either side bent to his aid, applying bandages and a tourniquet. One or two dragged the animal away to be field dressed, and several bent to retrieve their thrown spears. Most leaned on their spears to watch those tending to the fallen knight.

No one saw the second beast charge. It too followed the path of the *V*, although this time no shields were banged, and no spears were thrown. The large animal crashed through the wood unchecked, heading directly for Odilo and Trudi. They, like everyone else, had been watching the fallen knight and remained unaware of the danger until the boar lunged at them.

Without a word, Odilo stepped to the right. Trudi spun away to her left. Then, in a fluid motion, their arms lifted and fell together, impaling the beast between them. It twisted under their spears, thrashing wildly as neither blow was a killing stroke. Odilo leaned down on the shaft of his spear, trying to drive its point further into the animal's shoulder. As he pushed into the animal, it surged forward in an attempt to gore his leg.

Trudi, having lost hold of her spear, drew her sword. The blade flashed above her head. She brought it down on the beast's neck with both hands, severing its head in one stroke.

The hunters were stunned into silence. Blood spewed over Trudi's legs and pooled at her feet. With a visceral shout, Odilo swept Trudi into his arms. Then setting her down, he raised her hand high above their heads. The knights cheered and banged their spears against their shields. Odilo bowed theatrically to Trudi, and the cheers grew louder.

He had never seen a woman wield a sword like that. Her strength and speed surprised him. She laughed, embarrassed at the applause, and he found it oddly compelling that she could be both strong and vulnerable. He studied the lines of her face and the curl of her hair. He took in the fullness of her lips and the light in her eyes. She was powerful, he realized unexpectedly, and quite beautiful.

One of the hunters stepped forward and put his foot on the animal's carcass to remove Odilo's spear. Liberating it, he shoved the tip into the base of the boar's neck. With a shout of defiance, he lifted the boar's head high above Odilo and Trudi in celebration. Blood rained down over both of them.

After the morning rain ended, Pippin and Bertrada rode from the villa with a basket for lunch and made their way to their favorite hiding place. She could not have been happier. Pippin had been gone four months fighting Charles's war in the south. At twenty-seven, he was, thankfully, his own man and had refused to attend the prayer breakfast. It was, she told herself, her turn. And at nineteen, she wasn't getting any younger.

Just off the north road, the path meandered to the right and grew difficult in its disrepair. Over time, the two had made it more difficult by moving logs and boulders onto it to discourage passersby.

Farther along, the path forked. The left climbed up craggy terrain, and the right worked its way downhill to an abandoned house. Pippin had told her that twenty or thirty years ago it had been a groundskeeper's home. Its roof had partially caved in, and its walls were full of holes.

As usual, they took the path to the left. Once over the rocky hill, the path angled sharply down and threaded through the woods to a small stream, measuring about fifty hands across. The stream led to a bed of boulders that formed a small waterfall that filled a natural pool.

Once across the stream, Pippin tethered the horses, grabbed the lunch basket from her hand, and they scampered down the path to where the boulders sheltered the pool. Without a word, Pippin stripped naked and dove in, surfacing after a moment in the middle of the pool with a shout at the water's cold. He whipped his head to clear the hair from his eyes and leaned back in the water. He smiled at her.

Bertrada laughed. "You look like a Spartan!" she called.

He laughed and surface dived into the water. She saw his buttocks lift out of the water and giggled, knowing he was showing them to her on purpose. At the other end of the pool, he surfaced again and began to climb the rocks up to the waterfall. He was not tall, like most of Charles's kin. The warrior training he had undergone for twenty years defined his body. His shoulders and arms were knotted with muscles. His chest and back were scarred and bruised from battle. One scar in particular stood out. A diagonal slash from his right shoulder down to the middle of his back, the scar was ghost white, irregular, and constantly reminded her of his mortality.

Although his ascent was meant, she was sure, to further display his backside, Bertie had to laugh as his flaccid penis and hanging stones flopped helplessly with each step of his climb. Of all his features, she liked his hindquarters the best.

Pippin gained the top of the falls, spread his arms wide, and fell forward. Bertie caught her breath as he plunged headfirst toward the rocks. He kept his cross-like posture until just before he landed, when he tucked his body and flipped right side up to land in the pool just beyond the boulders.

He came up laughing. Bertie's stomach relaxed, but her laugh was nervous. He swam to the edge and splashed her.

"Okay, okay, you silly oaf. Don't get my clothes wet."

In moments, she was naked, diving in beside him, screaming at the cold just as he had. Then she was in his arms, feeling their bodies slip against each other. His kiss too was wet and slippery as she entwined her legs around him.

She loved being with him. She loved the tautness of his body and the pure strength of him. Their kisses became more passionate, and she grew hungry for him. When he moved to thrust into her, she raised her hips to his.

But he couldn't get the rhythm right. He struggled in the water to keep his balance on the rocky floor of the pool. She laughed at his ineptness, and eventually he laughed with her. He let her lie back in the water. She floated away, drifting off his erection, letting the water's coldness fill her. After a moment, she stood and walked toward him. With her eyes half-closed, she kissed him and gently pressed herself to him.

Smiling, she gripped him in her right hand and walked to the edge of the pool, pulling him along by his hardness. She climbed out of the pool without letting go of him and lay back against a large boulder warmed by the morning sun.

He kissed her, and his fingers invaded the warm wetness between her legs, and he buried them deep inside her. She groaned, and he drew her hands over her head and pinned them against the rock. Using his right hand, he lifted her left leg and slipped inside her.

She gasped as his thrusts slammed her against the boulder. He leaned back to allow her to adjust her pelvis. She wrapped her legs around him, and he sank into her again. Arching her back, she heard him groan. She looked at him with half-closed eyes and moaned, "Oh, Pippin."

Now he was groaning with every stroke, and she felt him full and ready to burst.

"Come into me," she said.

His semen exploded into her. She squeezed her legs with the spasm of his release and kissed him lightly as his body relaxed.

Afterward, they splashed in the pool, playfully touching and kissing each other. When they had cooled off, Bertrada circled her legs around him, this time to hold herself afloat while they talked.

"I just can't get enough of you," she told him.

"That's what they all say."

"Pig!" She splashed him.

"Bertie," he said, suddenly serious, "this is all I want. You and me, here, now, like this. I can't stand to be away from you. All throughout the campaign, I dreamt of you, of being here with you, of being inside you."

"And the women of Provence?" she asked.

He splashed her.

"Will your father mind that you missed the prayer breakfast and the hunt?"

"They don't care if I show up or not. They only need me when there's fighting—then I'm important. All the ceremony and secret meetings aren't for me."

"But won't you too be mayor?"

"You watch." He looked at her in earnest. "When they split the kingdom—and they will—I'll get the short end of it. I'll get all the fighting and none of the wealth. Carloman will get all the wealth and none of the fighting."

"And Gripho?"

"Gripho will get nothing. Charles will set him up nicely with a county, at most with Bavaria, to ensure that he is a landed nobleman. But Gripho's too young to be mayor. And by the time he is old enough to take on more responsibility, Carloman's son, Drogo, also will be of age, and Carloman won't let Gripho surpass him."

"None of it matters, my love, as long as we get to be together." Bertie released her legs and stood to embrace him. The conversation had taken him someplace else, someplace away from her. His body was tense and rigid. Putting one leg behind his knee, she shoved him down into the water. Spluttering, he came up for air, and she leapt upon him, driving all her weight down on his shoulders to dunk him again under the water.

This time he rolled under her weight, using her momentum against her. Finding his feet first, he had more control and dragged her from the water with both hands. Playfully, she squealed in fear.

"What are you going to do to me?" She smiled suggestively. "As I recall, you still have some work to do."

He dunked her.

Gripho, in full armor, knelt alone at the altar rail while Boniface droned on in Latin. Burning incense wafted across the chapel, nauseating him. He was seven hours into a fast that would end at noon on the next day when Charles knighted him. Boniface said there would be prayers every six hours. As if Gripho wasn't bored enough.

Of course, Carloman was there, along with thirty of his Knights in Christ, dressed in their red-and-white vestments. After the midnight prayers, only a few would bother to remain. Gripho couldn't wait until they left him alone.

Sunni had told him that the fast and the mass were unavoidable.

What Gripho couldn't understand was why Sunni had allowed it. Wasn't she Charles's wife? Couldn't she have interceded? He hated this. All she had said was his time would come and to be patient. They must think of him as Christian for him to succeed.

So for now, he was Christian. He prayed. He stood at the appropriate times and knelt at the appropriate times. He looked pious when Boniface turned to face the congregation and looked serious when he did the readings.

But he hated the stink of incense.

When Boniface and the others left, Carloman approached him at the altar rail and knelt beside him. He urged Gripho to reconsider his decision against being a Knight in Christ. "In time, you could lead them," he said. "In time, they would become a force that knows no geography."

Gripho pretended to be deep in prayer.

"Think about it." Carloman left, his knights with him.

As soon as he was sure he was alone, Gripho stood, took off his armor to the waist, and found his food cache beneath a pew in the back of the chapel. He decided that when he became a knight, he would tell Carloman to go fuck himself. Pippin, on the other hand, might have to wait. Pippin might beat him till he shat himself.

If I become mayor, everything will change. I won't need the Church. I won't need their ceremonies. I will just rule. As a son of Charles, I will have it all. Of course, I'll have to fight Carloman and Pippin, but by that time, I'll have others to help me. With a little imagination, it shouldn't be too hard. He wondered what his mother had planned. Sunni always had a plan. But why she wasn't letting him in on it?

When Gripho finished his bread and cheese, he sipped some wine and returned his cache back to its place under the pew. Then he climbed the altar steps to sit in the priest's chair. Once seated, he leaned back and farted. "That, at least," he said aloud, "smells better than the incense."

A score of bonfires circled the reunited hunting parties. Spitted boars and flanks of venison turned slowly over the flames while the revelers whetted their appetite on bread, cheese, and wine.

Waifar had speared the largest boar. The knights from Provence and Alemannia had killed the greatest number, so they too would receive a prize. News of Odilo's boar being beheaded only served to increase Trudi's reputation. She and Odilo had cleaned themselves up before the roast, but dried blood still streaked their garments. Trudi found herself surrounded by nobles, each toasting her bravery and skill.

Odilo sought out Hunoald, Godefred, Ateni, and Radbod. Without Charles or his sons in attendance, he could meet openly with each of the nobles without raising any concerns. Sunni complimented him on his day and teased him about the evening ahead. He queried her about how and where Trudi's rite would happen, but Sunni gave no details. He would have to wait and see what the night would bring.

Most of the knights were well on their way to drunkenness. Finally the roasts were done, and the knights tore into the animals. Ateni of Provence insisted on using a knife while most of the guests simply pulled the meat off with their hands.

Odilo sought out Trudi and Sunnichild to share the boar the two had killed earlier. Someone had stuck the boar's head on a pole behind Trudi's seat.

"To a worthy opponent." Odilo raised his cup, toasting the beast.

"To a worthy opponent," Trudi echoed.

They spent the evening learning more of each other. Trudi explained her years in training with the knights. Odilo told her of his youth in Bavaria, how he had fought with his uncle against Grimoald, how Charles had intervened.

As the fires waned, the revelers either passed out on the ground or made their way back to the chateau. Sunnichild rose to excuse herself and kissed the two of them. She whispered something into Trudi's ear and disappeared into the night with her two armed escorts.

Trudi waited until Sunni was well out of sight before asking him to escort her back to the chateau. When they had left the glow of the campfires, she reached out to grasp his hand. She led him toward the chateau for a short distance and then turned westward across the lawn to a path that appeared out of the moonlight. It was easy to follow because the grass had been worn down by cartwheels. Two parallel strips of earth pointed their way into the woods. Without warning, Trudi pulled him off the path, through the trees, onto a smaller pathway. From the sound of water in the distance, he tried to determine where he was in relation to the chateau.

"How do you know where to go?" he asked.

"Shhh."

He let her lead. His excitement, the darkness, her hand, the secret path—it made his heart pound. He felt foolish. He had been through this before. He knew the ritual. She should be nervous, not him. But while she looked calm, he could not quell the hammering in his chest.

The ground became harder, and they began to climb. Past a group of boulders, they ducked under a tree that leaned across their path. There, without warning, Trudi bent in the moonlight and disappeared. She pulled him after her.

It took every ounce of Trudi's control not to just tackle Odilo in the moonlight. The day had been so *magical*—the stab of panic at the boar's rush, the thrill of spearing it, the rush at severing its head. *This is what men must feel after battle,* she thought. *This is power.*

All day long, she had wanted to laugh out loud. She drank ale with the men and felt at home in their company. More than that, she reveled in their attention as they feted her success. For the first time in her life, she felt beautiful.

At dinner, she had flirted with Odilo by the fire and watched the hunger build in his eyes. She could feel the heat inside him every time she touched his hand or his arm. She felt more than beautiful with him. She felt glorious.

But as the evening progressed, her hand strayed regularly to the amulet at her throat. She became impatient for the feast's end. When she had finally led him away from the fire, her breath was short from the excitement.

Ducking into the cave, she noted with satisfaction that Sunni had spared no detail in preparing it for the rite. A small fire burned near the opening, and its smoke ascended through a small hole at the top of the cave. Blankets had been laid, wine poured, and bedding stowed. Near the fire sat a polished mahogany box, about two feet wide and a foot deep. An earthen decanter lay near it.

Trudi made Odilo sit on the blanket and went to the box. From it, she took three candles. While she lit the candles, she kept her back to him to hide the shaking in her hands. She could barely breathe. Carefully, she placed the candles in a triangle around the blanket. She next took a handful of herbs from the box and threw them onto the fire. A sweet aroma filled the air while a smoky haze gathered at the roof of the cave and then slowly descended upon them.

She brought the box next to Odilo, opened it, and turned to him, kneeling before him on both knees.

Surprisingly, he looked nervous. He was as eager as a young boy. She began to smile. She felt surprisingly in control. She reached for his two hands, lifted them to her lips, and kissed them.

She took a deep breath. "This is a rite of passage into womanhood. I have elected to share this rite with you. Do you wish to share it with me?"

"Yes." It was his turn to smile.

"This I do of my own will," she said. "Not of yours. Not of my father's. This I do of no one's will but my own."

Odilo nodded. In this rite, he was required to move only at her bidding. He could not touch her unless she asked him to. She could tell it was driving him frantic.

"Then let us begin," Trudi said.

She stood and removed her robe, her vest, her tunic, and lastly her underclothes. She took her time, folding each garment and placing them in a pile. She delighted in how such a mundane thing could become so sensual by having a man watch. The tension between them built with each abandoned piece of attire. His eyes never left her.

She liked it. She liked his watching her. When she was finally naked, she stood before him, letting his eyes have her. She felt but a moment's hesitation—a hint of timidity that sent a shiver down her spine—but the hunger in his face restored her sense of power.

The heat of the fire beat against her skin. Her blood raced. The smoke made her dizzy. Everything inside the cave looked blue and black from the smoke and the undulating firelight flickering against their skin. Trudi held her shoulders back, her head high, and looked directly at him. She realized she had stopped breathing.

"Undress," she said.

Odilo shucked his boots and stood to take off the rest of his clothes. Far less deliberate than she, he pulled his chemise over his head and hopped up and down to remove his pantaloons. Trudi couldn't help but smile. When he was finally naked, he stood before her, expectantly. His body was lean but lacked the youthful skin she had seen on boys her own age. His skin was dark and covered with scars. A thin layer of sweat covered him, making him gleam in the firelight. He was already erect. This too made her smile.

"Lie down," she commanded. He lay on the blanket. She knelt beside him. Her hand touched the skin of his chest experimentally. The heat of it resonated within her. Her hand moved over his chest, barely touching him. She felt her own skin flush and withdrew her hand.

"We are of the earth," she said and bent to grasp a handful of dirt from the floor. It was a reddish clay mixture and moist. She spread it from the base of his neck, down across his chest and stomach to the top of his pubic hair. His stomach trembled and clenched under the touch of her fingers.

"We are of the earth," he replied, following the forms of the ritual.

She grabbed a second handful and smeared it from her left shoulder down over her breast and stomach to end similarly in her pubic hair. She grabbed a third handful and repeated this act with her left hand so that a *V* shape covered her torso. Her nipples stood erect under the reddish mud.

"Our blood is of the earth." She reached for the decanter and poured a small portion of the liquid into her hand. She smelled boar's blood for the second time that day as she wiped some of the liquid on his lips and on each of his cheeks. She then took the flagon and poured the fluid into a small pool on his belly and along the length of his erection.

"Our blood is of the earth," he said as she marked her face and stomach in the same manner as his and poured the blood over her pubic hair. She returned the decanter to its place beside the box.

"Our breath is of the earth." She drew to her one of the candles and, from the box, a dried plant Sunni had given to her. She held it to the candle and, as it burned, breathed in its smoke.

"Our breath is of the earth," he said, and she leaned over him to blow the smoke into his mouth. He inhaled it from her lips. As she did this, her lips brushed his.

The cave swirled with colors as the light of the fire and the candles bounced wildly off the dark and white patches of their bodies. She was looking at him intensely now, watching him wait for her. Groaning, he arched his back. She waited for him to compose himself.

"This I do now, I do alone." She pulled from the box a carved piece of polished wood with a figure of a woman cut into its shaft, the same figure that adorned her pendant. The phallus gleamed in the firelight. She straddled his stomach and positioned the phallus between her legs.

"I am a woman of the earth." With a sharp push, Trudi shoved the phallus head into her, rupturing her hymen. Gasping, she waited for the pain to subside.

"My blood is the earth's blood." She let her weight down again, taking the phallus completely inside her.

"They are joined," he whispered.

Odilo lay beneath her, his body taut with anticipation. After a long moment, she leaned forward to kiss him on the mouth. In a fluid motion, she pulled the phallus out of her and reached back for his manhood. Slowly she sat back, taking him inside her. She straightened until she, again, had her full weight on him. She threw her head back and paused to regain her composure. She looked down at him. His eyes were pleading with her.

"Now." The smile returned to her face. "You can touch me."

CHAPTER 3

For Want of a Nail

The first sounds Gripho heard from his position behind the platform supporting Charles's chair were those of knights and guests assembling for his elevation. Swords and armor clanked. Loud voices acknowledged other voices. Horns practiced their trills. The heightened murmur of the expectant crowd swirled through the courtyard where Charles would receive Gripho's hands.

An ancient symbol of vassalage, commendation or "the laying of the hands" was the critical rite of knighthood. It was the ultimate gesture of both submission and honor. Charles took few vassals directly into his hands. Those who could boast of it were men of power, allies of great stature, or fearsome enemies he had conquered. Each of these men too had taken the clasped hands of lesser men into their own.

Some men were bound to the large monasteries. Some to families from landed estates. The laying of hands pledged one's life and position to one's lord.

The knights attending Gripho's elevation were great and terrible warlords, representing the collective might of the Franks. Many had supported Charles and flourished. Others had opposed him, been vanquished, and restored to power only after hostages had been taken and fealty pledged. All had one thing in common. They had submitted their clasped hands to Charles and so committed their fortunes, their might, and their lives to him.

Now it was Gripho's turn to join their ranks.

From his position behind the platform, Gripho could see little. He heard the crowd quiet at the appearance of his family, their footsteps echoing through the platform. Sunni would be positioned to the left of Charles's seat while Carloman, Pippin, Hiltrude, and Carloman's son, Drogo, stood to the right. Once they were in place, a polite applause greeted them. The courtyard again grew quiet as the crowd turned its attention to Charles's empty chair on the platform.

Horns announced him. Loud, fat, base notes, one overlapping another, created the sound of an imposing and never-ending presence. Middle tones layered on top of these, rising in chords above the base, bringing a heightened sense of expectation. At exactly the same moment, all the horns paused. And in the lull that was left, a high horn began to trill. A second joined in, then a third, and a fourth until a rolling fanfare cascaded down upon the crowd. At an unseen signal, these too quieted. Charles had arrived.

At a barked command, the Knights in Christ snapped erect in a clipped note of metal striking metal. As Charles passed through their ranks, knights on each side of him slammed fist to shield, echoing his progress toward the platform. Gripho heard Charles's footsteps ascending, and again, all was quiet.

It was time. Gripho checked his armor, held his head high, and waited. The drums began. In a rhythm known to marching men everywhere, big bass drums boomed and echoed off the walls of the villa. Gripho emerged from behind the platform, and the pace of the drums quickened. When he reached the platform, it doubled. By the time he climbed the stairs and turned to face the crowd, the drums were frenzied. He looked into the expectant faces of the crowd, and the drums stopped.

With just one beat of hesitation, the knights and celebrants erupted into a shout of acclamation so great that Gripho felt its force.

In that moment, he understood all the care and caution his mother had taken to ensure he reached this platform. This was power. It was for this he had waited all his life. He would no longer stand in the shadow of Carloman and Pippin. Now he was their equal. Surveying the room, Gripho saw the hope brimming in the eyes of the knights from pagan territories. He realized he was their hope. He drew his sword and held it aloft. The acclamation grew louder.

He turned back to Charles and knelt. The crowd quieted and knelt with him. Gripho placed his sword at Charles's feet. He smiled up at his father and raised his clasped hands. Charles, with a small smile of his own, took Gripho's hands into his. The crowd erupted again.

Charles waited for silence. "You will honor my commands and prohibitions," he said, his smile gone.

"I will honor them."

"You acknowledge my right to punish the transgression of my commands and prohibitions."

"I acknowledge your right."

"You commit yourself and your vassals to my military service."

"I so commit."

"You pledge tribute."

"I pledge tribute."

"You pledge fidelity."

"I pledge fidelity."

"You will not place the life of your sovereign in peril."

"I will not."

"You will do nothing to endanger him."

"I will do nothing to endanger him."

"You will introduce no enemies to the realm."

"I will introduce no enemies."

"You will not abide the infidelity of another."

"I will not."

"On your life, you pledge."

"On my life, I pledge."

Charles rose from his throne. "Rise, Gripho, vassal of the realm."

The crowd roared its approval. Gripho stood, turned to the crowd, and waved. Cheers and shouts greeted him. With Charles's leave, Gripho bowed and descended the stairs. The knights lining each side of the walkway repeated their gesture of fists on shield to salute Gripho's exit. The crowd continued roaring until after Gripho disappeared.

From Pippin's perspective in the courtyard, the silence had been ominous. No horns, no cheering—just he, Carloman, Drogo, and Sunni making slow progress through the crowd to the platform. And although he knew that the ceremony had been designed to honor Gripho, Pippin couldn't help but feel awkward, walking through a silent crowd. It was strange. The smattering of applause the family finally received only emphasized his misgivings.

Ominous too was Charles's entrance. Although he arrived with great fanfare, Charles looked a little disoriented. Pippin's father made his way down the aisle with gauntlets thundering but climbed unsteadily to the platform. Up close, there was no question, Charles looked peaked. Pippin tried to catch his eye but failed.

Even Carloman's Knights in Christ gave him pause. The show of gauntlets slapping shields had Pippin reevaluating their purpose. When Carloman had formed them, Pippin thought of them as little more than a prayer group—knights from different regions getting together to celebrate their faith. But their display today showed them as a force, and a formidable one at that. Did they serve Charles or Carloman?

What startled Pippin most, however, was the crowd's reaction to Gripho. Although it was obvious that many of those cheering loudest were from Bavaria and Alemannia, where Gripho and Sunni had kin among the Agilolfing clan, the strength of the crowd's acclamation was surprising. Gripho was a boy. He had barely fought in battle. What had he done to deserve such adulation? Pippin glanced at Sunnichild. She was beaming.

Gripho knelt before Charles and, looking up, smiled at their father. When Charles smiled back, Pippin's stomach clenched, and he began to sweat. Charles did not smile at his sons. He demanded of them. This was not the father he knew.

Looking around the room, Pippin realized his world had changed.

Charles had grown old. Carloman had built an elite force of religious fanatics, loyal only to him. Gripho had the support of Sunni's family as well as the knights in the east.

Where are my allies? Pippin thought. *Who will follow me?*

He had been away too long, too long with the Lombards in Rome, too long on campaign with Charles, too long with Bertie—just too long.

Although no one was looking at him, Pippin's face flushed with embarrassment. He had been foolish. Power might be won on a battlefield, but it was kept in rooms like this. His disdain for politics had led him to squander all he had won through the force of arms. Trapped in his supporting role, he watched the rest of the ceremony, smiling a wooden smile. By the time the Knights in Christ gave Gripho the same salute they had given Charles, Pippin's embarrassment had turned into fury.

"Milady?" The cleric looked up at her questioningly.

"Good afternoon, Brother David." Sunni would have been more comfortable if the palace clerk were not a priest. Although she had no proof, Sunni always felt that Boniface had staffed the position to gain inside information about palace business. Unfortunately, there was little she could do about it. The Church was the only reliable source for literate workers, and Charles had made it clear that this was the way it would be.

Being literate, Sunni was a vital link to Charles in the administration of palace business. So often was he out on campaign that Sunni had been forced to take over responsibility for signing many of his charters and missives. She was so accustomed to this role that she continued in it even when Charles was back in the palace.

Sunni held out her hands, and Brother David handed her the day's documents. A wiry little man, he reeked with a foul odor that made Sunni nauseous. It was the smell of something rotting, sickly sweet and musty at the same time. She was certain the man didn't bathe, and she had never seen him in anything but the same stained grayish robe and sandals. On many days, she had left the clerical room with the brother's stench on her clothes. Sometimes it stayed for hours.

On the afternoon of Gripho's elevation, Sunni had sought out the tedium of the clerk's office to take her mind off Charles. At the ceremony, he had looked ghastly. She worried that his health was worse than he had let on. She took the reports from the clerk and began her customary review.

She checked the receipts of the tax she had imposed on the Paris Fair. The tax had produced a minor windfall to the treasury as well as a flurry of complaints. She had ignored the latter for the benefit of the former.

She picked up a newly drafted charter that Boniface had penned for Charles's signature. It concerned the donation of the villa at Clichy to the monastery at St. Denis. Sunni raised her eyebrows and whistled softly. The villa at Clichy was one of the loveliest in the realm. It was a kingly gift, so kingly that it had to be the price for something equally significant. Sunni's forehead creased. What could Charles want of the Merovingian priests? Why would he ask Boniface—

Sunni could no longer breathe.

With a certainty she could not describe, Sunni knew Charles was dying. She also knew where he was to be buried. Charles would be buried in the Merovingian crypt of St. Denis, as if he were king.

To Sunni, this vanity could only be Charles's idea. He would thus proclaim that he was as much a king as any Merovingian who ever sat on the throne. St. Denis was the family church of the Merovingians. To bury Charles in their crypt—the very man who for the past twenty-seven years had usurped their sovereignty—would be sacrilege to the St. Denis priests. She was surprised that Charles hadn't had to pay more to buy their souls.

He was dying. The thought struck her as impossible. He was dying. She pictured his face in her mind and tried to imagine it gone. She started to tremble. She could no longer focus on the document. She couldn't even read it. She watched her hands take up her pen. She watched them dip it in ink and sign the charter. Then she watched them apply wax to the parchment and affix her seal. She stood while her hands gathered the documents and presented them back to the clerk.

"Milady?" Brother David asked in exactly the same tone he had greeted her.

"Thank you, Brother. I feel the need for a walk." Sunni watched herself walk the length of the corridor to where it met the staircase, and then watched herself descend to the villa's main hallway. There she met several women and stopped to thank them for their help in organizing the fête for Gripho. She nodded to passersby and walked straight through the main entrance, out its doors, and into the fresh air of the courtyard.

Acknowledging curtsies and bows with a polite smile, Sunni took the path that led down to the water. She discovered that she was running. When she reached the water's edge, she found a secluded spot and stopped to collect herself.

"Charles!" she said out loud. A small tear trickled from her right eye. She raised a gloved hand to wipe it away. A second appeared. She wiped it as well. More fell. She found a handkerchief. The trickle soon surpassed the capacity of such a small piece of cloth.

"Stop," she commanded herself, but her breath caught in her chest, and she quietly began to sob. She tried to shake her head clear, but the sobbing grew inside her until she could no longer contain it.

"No," she pleaded. But this word too worked against her and soon became a lament she could not stop.

She tried to run, but her feet refused to move. She doubled over. Her knees gave way. A howl forced its way past her lips, and she lay on the grass weeping. She wept for Charles. She wept for Gripho. And after a time, she wept for herself.

A handmaiden found her much later sitting by the water, disheveled, face streaked, and staring blankly at the river. When she could get no response from Sunni, the maid sent for Charles and the doctors.

After failing to agree on which potion would restore Sunni to herself, the doctors had left three for her to try. The stewed snakeskin gave the room a wretched stench, a smell only outdone by the mustard and garlic poultice the doctors had applied to Sunni's chest.

Sunni waited until she was alone with Charles before she removed her robe and the poultice and began washing away its residue. When she had finished, she summoned a handmaid and handed her the robe and the tray with the three potions on it. "Throw these out," she said. She picked up a white robe with a blue collar and blue cuffs and cinched it with its belt. She stood before her husband, who was sitting on her bed, watching her curiously.

"Why didn't you tell me?" she asked.

"Sunni—"

"How long have you known?"

"Known what?"

"That you are going to die." Sunni said it almost matter-of-factly. Only a slight hesitation before the word "die" betrayed her emotions.

"Sunni—"

"Don't insult me, Charles. I saw the charter for the villa at Clichy. I know what it means for you to be buried at St. Denis. I know how hopelessly vain and stubborn you are. How long have you known?"

"We all die, Sunni."

She threw a goblet from the table at him. It glanced off his shoulder and hit the wall with a sound of metal denting. As she went for another, he crossed to her and caught her in his arms.

"Narbonne," he said quietly, hugging her to him. "I've known since Narbonne."

"You think that I'd be the one person you'd tell." She looked up at him, her eyes brimming, but her arms struggled to free themselves. "Instead you told Boniface."

"Ah, my love. He's a priest."

"I'm your wife." One arm broke free from his grasp. "I'm your wife," she repeated, hitting his chest for emphasis when she spat out the word "wife." "Have I failed you in some way? Have I lost your trust? Have I mistaken your love? Just nights ago, you said, 'I'll be fine, Sunni. I've been resting, Sunni. It's time for me to be mayor, Sunni.'" She looked at him. "Liar."

Charles tried to recapture her in his arms, but she pushed him away.

"Sunni."

"Liar."

"Sunni, listen."

"Who's speaking? The mayor or my husband?"

"Today, I'm both."

"Yes, milord. How may I serve you?"

"Sunni, enough." Charles picked her up by her arms and sat her on the bed. "I do love you." Charles knelt before her. "I should have told you. I didn't want anyone to know." Seeing her begin to protest, he held up his hand. "I told Boniface because he is a priest. He cannot break the confidence.

"I am dying, Sunni. Of my three sons, only one is ready to rule. And that likely means war. How will they stand up to the Lombards, the Saracen, Hunoald and Waifar, the Saxons? Do you want me to go on? How about the Church? Or Theudoald?"

Sunni couldn't stand the thought of that dilettante prig being mayor. When Pippin of Herstal had died, his wife Plectrude had tried to name Theudoald mayor, but the boy was eight years old. Civil war broke out, and Charles, although a bastard, had stepped in to seize control.

"So you see, it isn't just a discussion between a dying man and his wife. You have a stake in this. Our son, Gripho, has a stake in this. The greater the number of people who know about it, the less control I'll have over the outcome."

Sunni laid her hand against his chest to stop him. "Charles, you didn't even give me a chance."

He folded her into his arms. "I'm sorry, my love," he said. "I'm sorry." Sunni surrendered to his embrace and wept quietly. After a time, she lifted her head from his chest to kiss him. His kisses and touch grew more passionate. Sunni's became frenetic. Soon, she was pushing him back against the bed, pulling his clothes from him, desperate in her need for him.

"I could help." They were still in bed, lying naked to cool their bodies.

"I'm sure you could." Charles chuckled.

"I want to."

"Sunni, once I'm dead, your every action will be seen as a move to benefit Gripho. You'll be a partisan."

"I've got relations with Plectrude's family. I could help forestall Theudoald. I can rule for Gripho until he's of age and keep Carloman and Pippin from fighting."

"Gripho will get Thuringia and the tribute from Bavaria. Carloman will get Austrasia, Alemannia, and the tribute from Aquitaine. Pippin will get Neustria, Burgundy, and Provence."

"If Gripho has Neustria, it may prevent some of the nobles from backing Theudoald's claim," Sunni said. "It could prevent a civil war."

"Or cause one," Charles said. "If either Pippin or Carloman believe that you have unduly influenced me, they may challenge his claim. Austrasia and Neustria are the keys to the kingdom. Giving Neustria to Gripho could pit brother against brother."

"On what grounds?"

"They don't need much of an excuse. Although I do like the idea of forestalling Theudoald's claim. Perhaps it could be only a part of Neustria. I'll have to think on it."

"What about Trudi?" Sunni asked.

"Ah, good news. I had a long talk with King Liutbrand. He is proposing Aistulf."

"Aistulf?" Sunni's body turned cold. While Charles went on about "balance" and "keeping the border safe," her mind turned to Odilo. "Trudi has met someone."

"Who?"

"Odilo. She is very taken with him, and from what I can tell, he with her."

"They found each other on their own?" Charles frowned. "Trudi barely looks at men. She'd rather fight one than meet one. No. You brought them together. Now you can separate them. It has to be Aistulf.

Liutbrand and I have agreed to terms. She will live near Rome. The dowry is set."

As he spoke, Sunni again felt herself detach as she had in the clerk's office. This time, however, when she tried to imagine the world without Charles, she could see it unfold before her. The orders and proclamations and missives he made today would not carry over into that world. In that world, she could not draw strength from him. She would have no power to wield in his name. She would lose the physical security he had built around their family and the wealth that secured their status. His family would turn against her and her son. The starkness of the world without Charles appalled her. When Charles finished talking, Sunni just nodded her head. "I love you," she said.

"I know you do, my love."

She kissed her husband on the forehead and on each one of his eyes. When Charles left, Sunni sent two messages. One went to Odilo, the other to Trudi.

When Pippin finally tracked down Carloman, his older brother was in the vestibule of the church having a heated argument with Boniface. Pippin stood to the side to let them finish. The bishop's face was nearly scarlet, and his attempts to keep his voice at a whisper were far from successful.

"This is unacceptable," Boniface fumed. "Charles can't just postpone Gripho's high mass. That is a Church matter. And that woman is not ill. She has bewitched him!"

Carloman held up his hand in caution. It did little to calm Boniface.

"Yes, Carloman. I use the word intentionally. No God-fearing woman would undermine her own son's mass. I will not abide it."

"It is done, Boniface. Charles has sent word throughout the residence. I've tried speaking with him. He is adamant."

Boniface took note of Pippin's presence and frowned. "I will have to see to this myself." He waved in Pippin's direction. "You clearly have other affairs to attend to." The bishop hoisted the hem of his robe and stormed from the vestibule.

Pippin took two minutes to relay the concerns he saw illuminated by Gripho's elevation.

"Are you simple?" Carloman turned on Pippin, just inches from his face. "Of course the elevation was about politics. Of course it was about succession. Do you think Charles is going to live forever?"

Pippin bridled at the rebuke. This was how his older brother always spoke to him. He lectured. He scolded. He berated.

"You spent half your life on the Roman peninsula," Carloman continued, "lying in the sun, and when you come back here, you spend the rest of it lying with your girlfriend. And you're surprised that you're being left out? Yes, I created the Knights in Christ to be a weapon. We're going to need them. Yes, Boniface and I are trying to move the Church to support our claim. We're going to need that too. These old bastards are not just going to fall into line."

As overbearing as his brother was, Pippin had to admit Carloman had a point. He too was worried about support for their claim. Charles had defeated most of the nobles at court. His sons had not. There would likely be at least one challenge to their claim.

"Our strategy is to avoid civil war," Carloman said, touching off fingers as he listed each point. "Work through the Church to amass an army that will forestall any questions about our right to rule. In return, we give back some of the land Charles took from the major monasteries. Then we help Boniface consolidate the local churches, and in return, he supports our claim to the throne."

"Do we need the Church?" Pippin asked.

"I am a Christian knight, Pippin. I intend to be a Christian mayor. We do need the Church. But the Church also needs us. And I, for one, will support her."

"And if there is war?"

"Any trouble, we use the Knights in Christ as our early mobilization force and back them up with the support we have from Austrasia and Neustria. If we can't quell the uprising, and it looks like civil war, we'll have to raise a Merovingian to the throne."

"No," Pippin said.

Stating the obvious, Carloman lectured him about their role as mayors serving the Merovingian kings. He recounted the portion of the fealty pledge that included "allegiance to the king." He explained that the nobles would not accept their claim to the throne as legitimate and would demand they raise a Merovingian.

"Father didn't make war on the entire realm just to return it to the Merovingians," Pippin said. "He means for us to be kings."

"Unless he names himself king, that won't happen. Even if he did, he'd still have to back it up with force," Carloman said. "After Narbonne, I thought he had the perfect opportunity to clear the way when Pope Gregory asked for his aid against the Lombards." Pippin looked up at this. "But he turned us down, cold. There must be something we don't know."

"Or maybe he just waited too long. Did you see him at the elevation yesterday?"

"He didn't look himself."

"What about Gripho?" Pippin asked.

"Sunni will make sure he gets something in the succession. Charles has three choices. Make me mayor of the realm. Divide the realm between the two of us and give Gripho landed estates. Or split the kingdom into thirds and make each of us mayor."

"Gripho's not ready," Pippin said.

"That doesn't mean it won't happen. Sunni can act in his name until he comes of age. I wouldn't count him out."

"The nobles won't support him."

"Who, my dear brother, is going to support you?"

Pippin's face reddened. When he began to make a mental list, there weren't as many on it as he had hoped.

The next day, Charles held court for petitioners and held private meetings with nobles in preparation for the following day's assembly. Sunni held a breakfast for the ladies of the court but adjourned it in plenty of time for them to prepare for the evening festivities. Carloman's wife, Greta, was seemingly everywhere, fretting over arrangements, arguing with chefs, chasing down musicians, and placating dignitaries.

Sunni had hoped to find Trudi at the breakfast, but the girl never appeared. Seated at the head table with Carloman's wife, Sunni had to sit through endless speeches by noble women who took every opportunity to refer to the military achievements of their husbands or the strength of their family bloodlines. Many found a way to talk about both.

She also had to acknowledge a horde of well-wishers and accept the sympathies and ministrations of countless women who chastised her for leaving her bed so soon after her "attack." This, of course, meant she had to listen to them recount their own maladies even if they had nothing to do with Sunni's perceived problem.

"Thank you so much. It was nothing," she would say. "No, no. It was not a reaction to the food. I just had too little to eat." Or, "Bless me, no. I'm not pregnant! I'm much too old for such things." And, "You are so kind!"

When at last the tables were cleared, she went to Trudi's room. The girl was not there. Frustrated, she sought out Odilo.

She found him in the main hall watching Greta lord over the preparations for the fête. Sunni frowned. She flashed him a hand signal. Odilo waited a moment and then ducked into a service corridor for the kitchen. She gave some encouraging words to Greta about her decorations, and when the woman was distracted, followed Odilo into the corridor. Her eyes had to adjust to the darkness, and she stumbled.

"Here," Odilo called. He was huddled in an alcove made for storing ale. The stench of it reeked from the walls.

"Did you get my message?" she asked.

"Yes. But it was very cryptic. What did you mean, 'Now is everything'?"

She outlined what she knew of Charles's health, what his plans were for both Gripho and the kingdom, and guessed that announcements would be made at the assembly.

"And Trudi?" Odilo asked.

"It's to be Aistulf," she said.

"It can't be."

"Charles would brook no argument." She looked up at him, trying to gauge his reaction in the dim light. "It solidifies the southern border and surrounds the pope."

"What does Trudi say?" Odilo asked.

"I have not seen her. Have you?"

"She stayed with me again last night but left early this morning. She's quite a girl, Sunni. I cannot let Aistulf have her."

"It may not be up to you, Odilo. And from what I've seen, you can't afford a war with the Lombards."

"This is intolerable. How could you get me into this?"

"It's up to Trudi, Odilo. If she leaves of her own free will, Aistulf will have no grounds to come after you."

The two talked through the different scenarios that could arise from Charles's death. None of them looked good to Sunni.

"You think there will be war?" she asked.

"It may be unavoidable," Odilo said, his face grim. A footstep in the corridor surprised them, and they fell silent while a servant made her way from the main hall into the kitchen. "Carloman will press the Church's ambitions. And if there is no king to hold the realm together, there will be challenges to the boys' right to succession. They will have to back it up with iron. They are good fighters, but none of them is Charles. I will speak to the nobles from Alemannia and Bavaria, those who will support Gripho. Though his youth will be perceived as a weakness, if several stand for him, he may survive unscathed."

"There may be a challenge from Theudoald," Sunni said.

"I wouldn't be surprised," Odilo said. "That would keep Carloman and Pippin busy."

"What if Gripho got part of Neustria?"

"Charles will never agree to that." Odilo frowned. "Neustria is at the heart of his power. Besides, it would push the older boys into a war."

"Maybe not. If we can pull Neustria into an alliance, it may help us to carve out a middle kingdom for Gripho."

"Be careful. You don't want war with the older boys. Let them fight everyone else. Gripho's young. Give him time to grow up."

"Now is everything," Sunni said.

"Trudi is everything," Odilo said. "I've got to find her."

The two searched for an hour but could not find her.

It was a cool night, the air heavy with moisture. In the main hall, six great fires blazed in braziers around the room. Minstrels strolled, jugglers juggled, and magicians performed their tricks in a room filled with banners of red, green, blue, and yellow. Tapestries depicting battles long past had been cleaned and repaired. Large candelabras and candleholders were placed strategically to light the room. Along several walls, large tables were laden with food and drink.

Had she been in a different frame of mind, Sunni would have loved this. There was much to celebrate. As guests arrived, they joined a colorful procession through the main hall, greeting every member of Charles's family. Gowns of blue and white and red swished in a series of half circles, clockwise around Sunni and Charles, and then counterclockwise around Greta and Carloman, and on to Bertrada and Pippin until all hands had been touched, all greetings given, and all introductions made.

After an hour or so, when the talk of politics had lost its zeal, minstrels and jugglers masterfully redirected dying conversations and broke apart well-formed cliques. Servants carried large trays of ale, wine, and mead, and soon laughter and song carried through the hall. A musical sextet captured guests' feet in one corner of the room. The colorful gowns swirled and bowed and floated in time with the music. Cups were raised to Charles and to Gripho. Stories were told, memories recalled, and intimacies shared.

Occasionally fights erupted. These were quickly subdued before swords could be drawn and blood spilled. Several corners of the hall sporadically broke into song, some with bawdy lyrics more appropriate to the battlefield.

"To the ball came ten virgins, in all their gentleness …

And when it was all over, there were ten virgins less …"

Pippin and Bertrada moved through the room gracefully. They

lightly inserted themselves into one conversation after another until they had engaged most nobles in the room. Bertrada's youthful, fresh looks made this possible. Older men gave way willingly to engage her in their conversation. Pippin, usually more cautious and deliberate, seemed more sober in his demeanor. He took advantage of Bertrada's reception by group after group and found a way to engage a least one person in every conversation. *A nice couple,* Sunni thought. *People like them.*

Sunni had spent the better part of the evening avoiding King Liutbrand and his son, Aistulf. They had agreed early in the evening to talk later, but as far as Sunni was concerned, it couldn't be late enough. She used the room to keep her distance and worried over what she would say without first talking with Trudi. By the twenty-second bells, however, even Sunni could no longer put off the moment. After a deep sigh, she made her way across the room to speak with Liutbrand and his son.

"King Liutbrand." Sunni extended her hand.

He took it in his, raised it to his lips, and kissed the top part of her knuckles. "Milady. May I present my son, Aistulf?"

"It is nice to see you again."

"Milady." Aistulf took her hand and bowed.

If Trudi couldn't have Odilo, Sunni thought to herself, she certainly could do a lot worse. Aistulf was taller than she remembered, lithe, and powerful. His face was narrow, like his father's, but darker and less open. *He looks like a warrior.* "I hear we have much to talk about."

"Yes, although much has already been discussed," Liutbrand said. "We were hoping to meet Hiltrude but have not yet seen her. I thought Charles might make his announcement."

"Unfortunately, she has taken ill with a stomach ailment. I, myself, fell victim to it yesterday."

"So I was informed. I hope you are feeling better."

"Yes. Yes, I am. Thank you."

"Please give Hiltrude our compliments and—"

Liutbrand stared across the room, puzzled. Aistulf followed his gaze. Sunni turned to see what had so grabbed their attention and found her answer. Trudi had arrived.

Dressed in a long white gown, Trudi wore no jewelry, no ribbons, no bows, no powders. Her hair was pinned up but poorly. Several strands hung down by her face. Taking tentative steps, the girl swayed visibly and stumbled five steps into the room. Her face strained above her newfound entourage, clearly looking for someone.

Sunni excused herself and waded through the crowd to Trudi's side. She took Trudi by the arm and walked her back the five steps to the door.

"No!" Trudi wrenched her arm away and turned to the room.

"Trudi, listen to me."

"Liar," she hissed.

Liutbrand and Aistulf arrived at just that moment.

"Well, King Liutbrand! So nice to meet you." Trudi leaned toward the king with her hand outstretched. He made to take it, but Trudi lost her balance and had to grab his arm to stabilize herself. "Excuse me," she whispered.

"Trudi!" Sunni tried to intercede. Trudi brushed right by her.

"And you must be my betrothed, Aistulf." Trudi threw her arms over Aistulf's shoulders. Aistulf held her off as best he could. Trudi laughed and slipped her arm through his. "Don't we look regal?"

Liutbrand looked furious. "I expect, Sunnichild, that you will get her under control," he said. "I will not be delayed by some foolish girl." He walked off. Aistulf followed.

"Trudi!" Sunni grabbed the girl by both her arms.

"Liar," Trudi whispered. "Where's my power now?" Trudi tilted her head back. Tears brimmed in her eyes. "You whored me. You had me lie with Odilo. You made me believe I had a choice. You made me a whore." She looked directly into Sunni's eyes. "I hate you."

Sunni's palm flew across the girl's face. "Listen to me, little girl. Do you think power is given? It is taken. Stop sniveling in front of all these people and become the woman you wish to be. If you want to be with Odilo, make the choice." Sunni stormed away from her.

Ten steps into the crowd, Sunni reconsidered. The girl needed her. Sunni turned to find Trudi still standing in the doorway, the outline of a red handprint beginning to form on her left cheek.

"Trudi?" Odilo had come to the girl's aid.

Trudi held up her hand to ward him off. "No," she pleaded. "No. Please, Odilo. No." She turned her head away.

Distantly, Sunni heard musical instruments calling the crowd's attention to another part of the room. Looking up, she saw Charles on a small platform with King Liutbrand and Aistulf. As the crowd quieted, the two seemed to be disagreeing with Charles. Charles shook his head vigorously.

No, thought Sunni. *Not now*.

"Good nobles and gentlewomen," Charles called out over the quieted room. "As many of you know, there is a long friendship between my family and the Lombards of the Roman peninsula. My son Pippin," Charles pointed out his second son in the crowd to a smattering of applause, "lived with King Liutbrand for many years and was adopted as his son. Today, that relationship grows ever stronger as my good friend Liutbrand's son, Aistulf," Charles placed his hand on the boy's shoulder, "has agreed to take as his bride my daughter, Hiltrude."

The crowd erupted with applause. Charles waved his hand ceremoniously to turn the crowd's attention to where Trudi stood by the door. Five hundred pairs of eyes turned to her. Sunni saw Trudi look to her father and then look to Odilo. She tried to stand up straight and compose herself. When she spoke, all she could manage was, "I—" Then Trudi did the one thing she had sworn to Sunni she would never do in front of her father. She burst into tears.

By tradition, Charles should have met with the nobles he had summoned for assembly over several days to map out military plans for the season, air grievances, make judgments, resolve land disputes, and grant offices. This assembly was different.

By Charles's command, the September assembly began on the large parade grounds near Quierzy, with the nobles in rank alongside their men. There would be no preliminary meetings with Charles. The nobles would receive their orders with their men.

Across the parade ground, the troops amassed in ranks, representing every region of the realm. Several hundred of the lesser nobles were on horse while several thousand fighting men stood alongside them, shield and spear at the ready. They were the elite fighting force of the Franks. They were not, however, all the troops Charles had at his disposal. Each of the nobles also had regional forces garrisoned throughout the realm that could be called upon to support specific military campaigns.

Charles rode to the parade ground on his black warhorse, followed by Carloman, Pippin, and Gripho. Charles acknowledged each of the nobles as he passed before them.

"Ateni."

"Huh-yah, milord."

"Radbod."

"Huh-yah." With each acknowledgment, the troops from that particular garrison slapped spear to shield and stood at attention. They remained so until Charles had reviewed the entire assembly.

When they were finished, Charles and his three sons rode to the pavilion, dismounted, and climbed onto a platform. At a signal from Childebrand, a score of men ran out onto the parade ground and positioned themselves one to a garrison. These were criers. They would repeat Charles's words so that all the troops could hear.

Charles looked out over the assembled might of the Franks. Drawing his sword, he raised it high above his head.

"To the glory of the Franks!" he called.

And in one voice, the assembled force shouted in return. "Huh-yahhh!"

"To the glory of the Franks!" he called again.

"Huh-yahhh!" they answered.

"Huh-yahhh!" Charles shouted.

"Huh-yahhh!" they echoed.

Charles sheathed his sword and began to pace back and forth across the stage.

"We are soldiers, you and I," Charles began.

"We are soldiers, you and I!" shouted the criers. Charles looked up at the interruption but continued on.

"We are men of war. And we have been at war for as long as I can remember. We wage war against foreign enemies: the Vikings in the north, the Saxons to the east, and the Saracen to the west. But too often, we are at war against each other, region against region, family against family. The cost of this is always high. Our sons and brothers perish, our treasuries are spent, and our common faith and fealty challenged.

"The time has come to forge a lasting peace among the Franks. With the conclusion of this last campaign in Provence against the traitor Maurontus and the Saracen plague, we are at last united under one Frankish flag. Let us turn away from historic grievances and feuds to claim a brotherhood amongst the Franks. Let us turn our swords against the Vikings, the Saxons, and the Saracen, but not against each other.

"To build this brotherhood among the Franks, let us start with brothers. On the day I was born, there were three mayors of the palace, so again shall there be three. These three." Charles swept his arm to indicate his sons. "These three brothers will unite the Franks as mayors of the palace."

Charles paused for the criers.

"Huh-yahhh!" the Alemannians and the Bavarians shouted.

"Huh-yahhh!" echoed the Austrasians. Some of the Knights in Christ began beating their swords against their shields. Others joined in until the entire field was in an uproar.

Charles put up his hands to signal for quiet. When he received it, he spoke again.

"I hereby elevate Carloman to mayor of the palace for Austrasia, Alemannia, and assign him tribute and fealty from the duchy of Aquitaine."

"Huh-yahhh!" shouted the troops.

"Pippin shall be mayor of the palace for Burgundy, Provence, and Southern Neustria."

"Huh-yahhh!"

"Gripho shall be mayor of the palace for Thuringia and Northern Neustria and will receive tribute and fealty from the duchy of Bavaria."

"Huh-yahhh!"

Charles waved to an attendant, and three chairs were brought onto the stage. He bade his sons to sit. "Today on this field, a new brotherhood of the Franks is born, forged in battle but united by blood. I call upon the nobles here today to pledge their fealty by commendation."

With that, Childebrand rode forward before the troops and called out the first name. "Ateni of Provence."

Ateni clearly was startled when his name was called. He rode his horse forward, and after a moment's hesitation, dismounted, climbed the stairs, and knelt before Pippin, laying his hands in those of Charles's son.

"Liutfred of Alemannia," Childebrand read.

Showing a similar set of emotions, Liutfred rode his horse forward, dismounted, climbed the stage, and placed his hands in those of Carloman. Childebrand continued reading the list until all were accounted for and then placed his own hands in Carloman's.

Charles remounted his horse to watch the procession of nobles pledging fealty to his sons. He drew his sword and, standing straight in his stirrups, shouted his war cry, "Francia! Francia!"

War cries from every region responded.

"Austrasia! Austrasia!"

"Neustria! Neustria!"

"Burgundy! Burgundy!"

Holding his sword out with its blade flat, Charles spurred his warhorse and let his weapon slap the shields of his soldiers, mounted and foot alike. He galloped the length of the gathered troops.

They began to chant.

"Charles! Charles! Charles! Charles!"

"Huh-yahhh! Huh-yahhh! Huh-yahhh!"

When Charles had completed his romp among the troops and the shouting had died down, Childebrand took the stage and announced that the nobles would meet at the pavilion on the next day at the tenth bells. With a great grin on his face, Charles dismissed the nobles.

"Northern Neustria?" Pippin fumed. "He gave Gripho Paris? He gave him St. Denis, Quierzy, Laon? He gave him the keys to the kingdom."

Childebrand could do little to console Pippin. His nephew had cornered him immediately after the assembly. "Pippin, I'm not the one you should question. I'm just an old dog of a warrior. Talk to your father. He must have had his reasons."

"I know what his reason is," Pippin said. "Her name is Sunnichild. I just don't understand why I've fallen so far out of his favor. The men follow *me* in battle. He relies on *my* strategies for victory."

In truth, Childebrand didn't understand it himself. Pippin was a pillar of Charles's army. He fought like a madman. And Charles relied on him heavily. No, Childebrand could not understand Charles's decision at all.

As a stepbrother of Charles, Childebrand could have, in his own right, made a legitimate claim to being mayor, but he had little interest in it. He was a soldier. He liked being a soldier. He liked being around soldiers. Nearing fifty, with one eye taken from him in a knife fight, Childebrand had to admit that life on campaign was more difficult now than it had been when he was younger. But if Charles could go on campaign every year, so could he.

Pippin was pacing back and forth. Childebrand watched him, seeing the echo of the boy's father.

"So be it," Pippin said. "I don't need Paris. I'll do fine in Burgundy and Provence. I'll be happy with the Rhone Valley. There's great hunting, good wine and fine weather. What else could a man want?"

He is angry, thought Childebrand. *And hurt.* "And your father?" Childebrand asked.

"He's made his decision. Carloman and Gripho can figure out what happens next. They've got all the power. I'm going to Burgundy."

"Now?" Childebrand asked.

"We had a dispatch about trouble there. I'll take twenty men on horse. Send two hundred foot soldiers to follow. We'll travel light. That should be enough to handle it."

"Won't you at least say good-bye to your father?"

"I won't whine in front of him," Pippin said. "I won't contest Gripho's claim. Charles made his decision. It is clear that I've lost my father's faith.

But I don't have to stay around to be humbled by every noble in Quierzy. Today was embarrassing enough."

"Who will you take with you?" Childebrand asked.

"You for one, old man, assuming Carloman will give you leave."

Childebrand smiled at that. He was never one to ask permission. To signal his assent, he removed the small metal orb he used in place of his lost right eye. There was no need for such decoration out on campaign. He liked to tell people that he could see better without it.

"Your family in Burgundy can help," Pippin said. "I'll also need you to marshal the nobles from Provence and Burgundy and to locate some supplies. Ateni will likely stay here for the meeting, as will Patrice, but we should be able to leave with a suitable force by nightfall."

"I'll get started." Childebrand patted the ax he wore at his hip.

The gesture caught Pippin's eye. "Why do you wear a Saxon ax?"

Childebrand looked down. It was an elegant weapon with a curved edge, counterbalanced on its opposite face by a small hatchet. "I was always tripping over my sword."

"I'll leave word for Carloman. Do me a favor—don't speak of this to my father. He'll want to stop me."

"Huh-yah."

"Now," Pippin said almost to himself, "all I have to do is convince Bertrada to go with me."

Childebrand couldn't help laughing.

They weren't ready by nightfall. For this, however, Pippin could hardly blame Childebrand, who had his twenty men of horse ready, the men of foot waiting, and six carts of supplies. It was Bertrada who caused the delay.

"You can't expect me to pack and leave without notice," she fumed at Pippin. "I'm not one of your soldiers. I have attendants. I have to close up my house. I have to provide for the servants. You have all that taken care of for you. I have to do this myself."

"I want to leave by nightfall," Pippin said. "I'll help you pack."

"No!" Bertrada put her hands up. "Don't help me so much. I'll be fine if you just leave me alone. I'll meet you at the gate at eighteenth bells."

Pippin waited. Eighteenth bells came and went. Nineteenth as well. Pippin stood just inside the gate while Childebrand and his knights tried vainly to be discreet in the shadows by the main gate. The rest of his small army waited outside near the camping grounds. Pippin would meet them once Bertrada arrived.

At almost the twentieth bells, Bertrada came down the path from the stables, leading her white mare by its reins. Three handmaidens followed with horses. One led a mule packed with saddlebags and bedrolls.

"Milord Mayor." Bertrada bowed formally with a wide grin on her face. "We leave at your pleasure."

"Get on your horse, Bertie. If we're lucky, we can reach Laon by midnight. If not, we sleep under the stars." He smiled in return.

"As milord commands," she said and put foot to stirrup.

Pippin led the troop out the gate and circled the villa to take the southern road to the camping grounds. Dusk was turning into darkness, and Pippin had trouble seeing the small group of soldiers that made up the rest of their contingent. When the road sloped downward, Pippin had a broader view of the landscape and saw his men collected by the side of the road.

"Gunther?" Childebrand called out.

"Huh-yah."

With that acknowledgment, Pippin continued past them down the road. The soldiers fell into line behind them. Once they were in formation, Pippin spurred his horse and picked up the pace.

They turned onto the western road, heading for Laon along the River Oise. The road was well kept on their side of the river, and they made progress, helped considerably by the light of a half-moon that reflected off the water to their left. They rode quietly for a long time, and Pippin began to relax to the rhythm of the horses and the murmuring sounds of the river.

It was good to be out in the night air, good to be away from the court, good to be on his own. Pippin knew he would not return soon. He could not suffer the embarrassment. He would not suffer the betrayal.

Pippin had always felt close to his father, despite the time he had spent away with the Lombards. When he and Charles were on campaign, they were almost like brothers. They thought alike. They fought alike. They enjoyed each other's company. Pippin believed he had earned his father's trust and respect. And he knew that Gripho had not. Why Charles had chosen Gripho, Pippin could not understand.

"Hello, brother." Seemingly out of nowhere, a soldier appeared to his right, riding a brown horse and wearing a leather helmet and small plates of armor.

Although startled, Pippin recognized the voice. "Trudi?"

"A fine evening for a ride. I hope you don't mind my joining you." Trudi took off her helmet and shook her hair loose. She smiled at the surprised comments coming from the soldiers behind them.

"What are you doing?"

"You weren't the only one disappointed today, Pippin. I need to be away from here—and quickly."

Pippin rode for a while, considering his sister's plight. "You have to go back."

"I'll go back no sooner than you."

"Charles will come get you."

"Not if I marry first."

For the second time that day, Pippin felt out of touch with the turn of events. "Is there something wrong with Aistulf?" he asked.

"Oh, he seems like a fine man. He's good looking enough. And I hear he's good with a sword." She paused. "I just have other plans."

Pippin blushed. Someone had taken her heart and probably a whole lot more. "Who is he?"

"Brother, I came with you because I trust you. And because I know you find yourself in a similar position."

"My situation is different."

"Is it? Then why are you leaving so suddenly in the night? The nobles meet with Charles in the morning. From everything I've heard, the mayors are to be there to map out the fall campaign. I think I read your situation correctly, Pippin. It is the same as mine. We both had different plans. We both need to go."

"Who is he, Trudi?"

Trudi looked at him. "Tell me you will help me, Pippin. Tell me you understand."

"Trudi, I know Aistulf. I know the Lombards. He will make a fine husband. He's a little arrogant, I know. But you will love the court there. Rome is within a day's ride. So is the Mediterranean Sea. You have to go back."

"Could you live without Bertie?"

Pippin did not respond.

"It is a simple question. You and Bertie aren't yet married. What if Charles pawned you off to someone else? He spoke to Liutbrand about you and his daughter. Did you know that, Pippin? Could you go back to Rome? Could you abandon Bertie? Now that you are mayor, would you let anyone dictate whom you married?"

"It's not just about love, Trudi. This could start a war. Do you think the Lombards will sit by quietly and do nothing?"

"If I marry, it will be too late."

"Who is he, Trudi?" Pippin pushed, more gently this time.

"Tell me you will help me, Pippin. Tell me you understand."

"I will help you, Trudi. I don't agree with what you're doing, but I understand."

"Thank you." Trudi laid her hand on his forearm. They rode together in silence for some time. She breathed a heavy sigh. "Odilo. I'm going to Bavaria. I will marry Duc Odilo."

Pippin whistled. The political implications of such a marriage were enormous, particularly after Gripho's elevation to mayor. With Trudi marrying into the Agilolfing family, Gripho would lord over a middle kingdom within the realm. Suddenly, Pippin saw the political puzzle in his mind fall into place. "Sunni knows about the two of you," Pippin stated rather than asked.

"She knows I love him. She doesn't know that I am leaving with you."

After a moment's reflection, Pippin chuckled. Then he laughed.

"What is it?" Trudi asked.

"Carloman is going to have his hands full." Pippin shook his head and flashed a hand signal to Childebrand. Without hesitation, the older warrior called out orders for doubling the pace. There would be no stopping in Laon that night.

Sunni busied herself by closing the drapes, putting the wine away, and straightening the blankets around Charles.

"Are you going to tuck me in?" he asked.

"You're not well, Charles."

"I'm not. But I'm not a child either." He took hold of the belt on her night robe and pulled her next to him by the bed. She looked down to see the smirk on his face and found herself grinning in return.

"You are every bit the child, Charles Martel. You always get what you want."

"And now I want you, my love." He opened her robe and cupped her breasts in his hands, feeling their weight. With his right thumb and forefinger, he pulled her left nipple toward him. She followed it and climbed onto the bed. She straddled his blanketed form and leaned over him. Her hair fell around his head so that their two faces were cut off from the world.

She inhaled the smell of him, felt the warmth of his breath, and kissed him lightly. The kiss became more urgent. She opened her mouth for him, and he teased her. At first, his tongue played around the edges, touching her lips and her teeth. She played back, touching his tongue lightly and retreating, encircling it and retreating, pushing into his mouth and retreating. With a moan, his tongue pushed deep inside her mouth, and his arms circled her body. He pressed the length of her to him, pulling her down by her hips to grind them against his.

He tried to roll her over but was hampered by the bed sheets and blankets that lay between them. She laughed as he struggled to win his freedom. She moved to help by rolling off him and pulling the blankets off his legs. Unencumbered, Charles rose to his knees above her, a warhorse rising to his hind legs, and pulled the nightshirt over his head.

She raised her hands to touch his body. He became still above her, watching her. Some of the old wounds were whitish and indented, as the holes and rents in his skin never completely healed. Tears came to her then. She blinked them away and moved her hands playfully lower while his erection fought to rise. They met above his abdomen, and she circled him with her hands.

She led his erection down her torso until it lay between her legs and then changed direction, pulling him inside her. When he could go no further, he stopped.

"This is how I want you to remember me," he whispered into her ear. "This intimacy. This moment." He kissed her softly. Her tears came again, and this time she could not deny them. They fell lightly down her temples into the pillows below.

"I love you," he said.

"I know," she said. "I love you too."

They began to move against each other slowly and with great tenderness, savoring as much of each other as their bodies would allow. In time, passion overtook them, and their thrusting and taking grew more heated and frantic. Their bodies arched and convulsed in wave after wave, until at last they came together and lay quietly in each other's arms. Sunni had never stopped crying.

"I don't want to watch you die," she said, struggling not to whimper.

Charles looked at the vial at his bedside. "Christians believe," he said, "that we go to meet our maker. Death is but the beginning of a new life in heaven."

"Pagans believe you return to the earth, that the power of your life is returned to be used again. You have great power, Charles. The earth will rejoice and welcome you home." Sunni's eyes filled again. "I just can't watch you die." They lay together, her body conforming to his as it had for countless nights during their sixteen years together. Sunni nuzzled her cheek into its place between his ear and his shoulder. A small tear escaped one of Charles's eyes and trickled down into his ear.

"It will be when the sun rises tomorrow," he said, stroking her hair.

Sunni looked up, and Charles put up his hand to stop her question. "I've enlisted the help of someone who knows her craft well.

"At first my stomach will grow warm, and then my limbs will go cold." Sunni didn't breathe. "My vision will fade, and my breath will become short. In the end, there will be pain, and then my time on this earth will end. I'm not sure who will meet me—my god, the earth, or the devil—but I go on my own. You can't go there with me. It will be fine if you go for a stroll early tomorrow morning. You will be with me in my last moments no matter where you are."

"I'll always love you," she said.

"I know."

Although she woke before sunrise, Sunni never took her early morning stroll. Instead, she sent for Charles's children and his grandson. And those who came said their good-byes and received his blessings. Sunni stayed with Charles through the warming in his stomach, the coldness in his limbs, the fading of his vision, the shortness of his breath, and the pain they both suffered for his passing from this world into the next. In the pagan fashion, she closed his eyes, kissed his forehead, and then kissed each of the eyelids she had just closed.

"Good-bye, my love," was all she had the power to say.

CHAPTER 4

The Mourning After

Carloman was finding it difficult to concentrate. He had not slept well. Since his father's death two days before, he had cancelled the rest of the assembly and asked Boniface to handle the funeral services. Besieged with requests for meetings, decisions, and guidance on the most trivial of matters, he tried to buy time. He avoided the nobles, thinking that without Pippin, it would be fruitless to see them. He begged their indulgences and announced he would take a day to fast and pray, hoping that by then Pippin would return.

One decision Carloman *had* made was to promote one of his Knights in Christ to serve as his family's "champion." Their history was so rife with assassination and murder that Carloman felt it necessary to create a special detail from those most loyal to him to protect his family. And he had found the perfect man to lead them.

With Saxon-blond hair and piercing gray eyes, Johann of Cologne had an arresting presence. And Carloman took great comfort in the man's absolutes. Johann was the type of man who would forgive no sin, tolerate no transgression, and give no quarter. He rarely left Carloman's side.

Carloman's eyes returned to Charles's bier. The man had been invincible. Even beside his father's corpse, he felt small and unworthy. Fortunately, Boniface was there to guide him, and Johann to protect his flank. *If not invincible,* Carloman thought, *at least I am well fortified.*

Boniface stayed with him throughout his all-night vigil but insisted that Carloman meet with the nobles, with or without Pippin. "Faith is one thing," he said. "Weakness is another."

Knowing well the havoc a death such as that of Charles could bring, King Liutbrand was first to visit Carloman in the family chapel where Charles's body lay awaiting the funeral at St. Denis. He came to offer the young man his help and to ensure that the betrothal of his son and Hiltrude was secure. He found Carloman praying over his father, clutching his prized relic, the finger of St. Martin, close to his chest.

Charles's body lay in a low, open stone casket. A lid bearing a carved likeness of Charles adorned the bier. Charles had been dressed in a purple cloak, a white shirt and vest with gold buttons, and black pantaloons. He wore soft leather boots that Liutbrand knew could serve no purpose other than decoration. A gold crucifix lay at his throat, and a matching gold wreath, made to look like ivy, circled his brow.

Charles's face was a ghostly caricature of the man who had conquered a continent. Pasty white skin hung slack from his facial bones. His closed eyelids were sunken and dark, his lips a purplish blue. Although his body had been washed and perfumed, its lurking odor of decay penetrated the smell of the autumn flowers decorating the chapel. What startled Liutbrand most, however, was the utter stillness of the body. Charles had been vibrant, dangerous. His presence had filled every room he entered. Now his corpse seemed insignificant, a frail thing, easily discarded and ignored.

Boniface was at the altar, leading Carloman in prayer. Liutbrand bowed his head. He could wait. Several Knights in Christ stood near Carloman, eyes methodically watching the room. Liutbrand smiled at this, thinking at least the young man knew his family history.

Carloman would need his help. Charles had been the power. Despite the mayor's show of pageantry days before, no one would readily accept his young sons as mayor. Charles had beaten the realm into submission. If his sons were to rule, they would have to follow suit. Yes, Carloman and Pippin would need help. And Liutbrand meant to give it to them. Of course, help always had a price.

As Boniface finished the prayers, Carloman let go of his relic and made the sign of the cross. He stood, approached Boniface, and knelt to receive the priest's blessing. With his thumb, Boniface traced the sign of the cross on Carloman's forehead and placed his palm on his godson's head. To Liutbrand, the two froze for a moment into an odd tableau. Blinking, Liutbrand realized that Boniface was now the father. He would have to be taken into greater consideration, particularly when it came to matters concerning the pope. All would have been much simpler were Charles alive.

"Mayor," Liutbrand said when Carloman finally turned to him, "I am sorry for your loss. Your father was a great mean." Liutbrand offered the young man his hands, which were readily taken in friendship.

"Thank you, King Liutbrand. You have always been a great friend and ally. I appreciate your condolences." Carloman looked at him gratefully, his eyes sunken and red. Next to the altar, Boniface was putting away his vestments and listening to every word.

"I understand that the burial will take place next Sunday at St. Denis," Liutbrand said.

Carloman nodded distractedly. "Yes, it was quite extraordinary that the priests there granted the family such a boon. Their support has not always been so generous."

Boniface moved behind the young man's right shoulder, and Liutbrand watched for Carloman's reaction. The young man clearly accepted the priest as his counselor. Liutbrand saw an advantage and quickly changed tack.

"And your brother, Pippin? I have heard he is no longer in Quierzy."

"Unfortunately, there was little warning of my father's death. Pippin left for Burgundy the night before Charles died. We had reports of an uprising."

"And Hiltrude?"

Carloman shrugged. "Apparently, she went with Pippin. I assume Charles gave his blessing, as she didn't leave word with either Sunni or me. I've sent messengers to ensure their return for Charles's funeral."

"Given her display the other night, I hope nothing is amiss with her betrothal to my son, Aistulf. Your father and I had an agreement. I expect that it is still in force."

"If I may," Boniface interrupted and then waited for Carloman's permission to join the conversation. Liutbrand frowned, but the young man nodded, and the priest continued. "The betrothal caught a number of us by surprise. And while we are all delighted with the union between your son, Aistulf, and our fair Hiltrude, no one has any understanding of the agreement between you and Charles. Given his recent death, it may be worthwhile for us to discuss the conditions."

"I would expect the son to honor the word of his father," Liutbrand said.

"I am sure that we will find an honorable solution to this dilemma," Boniface said. "It is just that you have us at a disadvantage."

Carloman's eyes kept drifting to his father's corpse. He thought it somehow appropriate that he and Liutbrand discuss affairs of state with his father's body in the room. As Liutbrand detailed the marriage arrangement between Aistulf and Hiltrude, its import penetrated Carloman's distracted state. The longer Liutbrand spoke, the more alarmed Carloman became. When Liutbrand spoke casually about his troops stationed outside Rome, Carloman flushed.

"Am I to understand," Carloman said, "that you won't invade Rome if your son marries my sister? That's the crux of the arrangement?"

"Crudely put, but yes."

"And we're to look the other way while you effectively imprison the pope and confiscate the Church's land?"

Liutbrand raised his hand at this. "Recognize, my young friend, that I have no desire to see any harm come to the pope. My grievances are purely related to land—land my family has laid claim to for centuries. And given your predicament and the emperor's lack of support—" Liutbrand shrugged and opened his arms. "The distance from Constantinople to Rome these days is great, both geographically and spiritually. Someone must see to protecting the Holy See."

"I doubt the pope will see it that way." Carloman moved closer to the Lombard king, towering over the shorter man. "And as if that weren't enough, we are also committed to raising Aistulf and Trudi's son here in our court and donating enough grain for you to feed a small kingdom?"

"Yes."

"No." When Liutbrand sought to interrupt, Carloman overrode him angrily. "If you invade Rome, we will throw you out. If you so much as threaten Rome, we will send legions there to ensure no one is harmed." A rivulet of mucus appeared under his damaged nose. "I don't have to barter Trudi to keep you out of Rome. I have other ways of doing that. I will show you how to protect the Holy See." Carloman had to interrupt himself to wipe his nose with his sleeve. "What do you mean by 'my predicament'? What predicament is that?"

"It seems clear that you have your hands full with your own family's problems," Liutbrand said. "The kingdom is split. Your claims to being mayor certainly will be challenged. And even if they stand, Gripho's 'middle kingdom' creates certain problems, don't you think? With his family ties in Bavaria, he now controls much of your way to Rome and the Mediterranean. There is even talk that he will lead as a pagan, uniting all the former pagan regions." Liutbrand paused and repeated his gesture—arms spread wide, palms facing up. "And I haven't even mentioned calls for raising a Merovingian king. My guess is that you will have more important things to do than to 'throw me out' of Rome.

"No, my young friend," Liutbrand continued, his eyes cold now, "you need a peaceful southern border. You need access to the Mediterranean. You need an ally on the Roman peninsula, not an enemy. When Hiltrude marries Aistulf, I will have every incentive to support your family. The pope will be left alone, save a minor loss of land, and he will be grateful for your sister's presence in my court. And once you are firmly established, you and your brothers may have, with my help, the means to remove the Merovingians forever. Refuse, and I may have to protect my own interests to your south."

At a signal from Boniface, Carloman asked Liutbrand's indulgence and the two retired to one of the chapel's vestibules.

"I will chop him to pieces," Carloman said.

"You are far too good a strategist to make that kind of error," Boniface said. "This is not a new situation, Carloman. This is why your father chose not to help the pope."

"What do you mean?"

"Your father knew he was dying. He knew there might be civil war. He knew you would need the army here. That is why he refused the pope's request. That is why he agreed to the marriage with Trudi. It keeps Liutbrand at bay and the pope safe."

"Why didn't he tell me he was dying?" Carloman's voice choked.

"Your father told me." Boniface put his hand consolingly on Carloman's shoulder. "It was my burden to bear."

Carloman took a moment to gain his composure. He didn't like Liutbrand's logic, but he couldn't argue with it, just as Charles had not. The talk of a pagan uprising was ridiculous, but if their claim to the office of mayor was challenged, they would have few troops available to send to Rome. Fewer still if Gripho didn't comply. He would need to talk to Sunni and to Pippin. He wondered why Pippin had gone off in the night. Carloman's eyes strayed to the casket. Not for the first time in the last two days, he felt very much alone.

Carloman had always prided himself on knowing the best course. In this case, he knew instinctively that Liutbrand had just outlined it. There were few alternatives. He looked to Boniface and saw his mentor nod.

"Very well, King Liutbrand," Carloman said when they returned. "Trudi will marry Aistulf. I will send an armed guard to ensure her safe return. But know this, should you break faith, I will hound you no matter how 'full' my hands are. There will be no invasion of the Holy See, and the pope is not to be touched."

King Liutbrand bowed. "It is the least I can do for family."

Trudi rose before dawn to find their camp already beginning to wake. A makeshift breakfast was being prepared. Two of Pippin's men had begun to strike tents and stow packs.

"Plenty of time," she said to herself, rubbing her hands together to ward off the chill. She rolled up her small bed rug and gathered her cache of herbs. A twinge of guilty pleasure nestled itself in her stomach, and she caught herself grinning stupidly. She hurried outside the tent. Stopping only to light a small taper in one of the camp's smoldering fires, Trudi walked to the river alone.

She waved to the pickets standing guard, pointed to a large cluster of trees to indicate her intentions, and, receiving nods, found a place to pee privately. When she finished, she quietly moved deeper into the woods. In a small clearing well hidden by trees, she spread her rug on the ground. She placed the lit taper carefully on a broad, flat stone and drew from her cache a twig with dried leaves. She touched the leaves to the taper and watched them catch fire. Leaning forward, she inhaled the smoke and held it in as Sunni had taught her. The smoke seemed to seep into her body through her lungs. After several repetitions, she ground out the burning twig and the taper and let the darkness subsume her.

When her eyes adjusted to the moonlight, Trudi stepped back to her rug, took off her robe, and stood naked in the clearing. Feeling foolish and somewhat giddy, she knelt, sat back on her heels, and folded herself into the *S* shape that Sunni had shown her. She laid her arms alongside her legs with her hands facing up beside her feet. She touched her forehead to the ground.

"What is here is everywhere," she intoned. Nearby, the river lapped the shore, and she slowed her breathing to match its rhythm. She let her thoughts drift, imagining herself at the edge of the river, water lapping quietly over her body in small, warm, soothing waves. In moments, she was afloat, the current carrying her along its path. Then she *was* the current, its power flowing through her body and driving her further downstream.

"We are of the earth," Sunni had told her. "All the power and substance of the earth is here within us. It is in all things. What is here is everywhere. What is not here is not at all." When Trudi had looked puzzled, Sunni had explained. "The earth gives our bodies sustenance. We eat and drink her bounty every day. Everything that makes up the earth is within us. This is also true of the earth's power. All that sustains us: the plants and animals that nourish and clothe us, the trees and stone that provide our shelter, the sacred water that sates our thirst are alive. The earth gives us the spark of life, and in that spark, we are connected to everything."

With Sunni's help, Trudi had become *conscious* of that power. She had spent every evening in Sunni's chambers preparing for her fertility rite, attempting to sense the earth's spark, and becoming aware of the life in all things. Her sessions always began with water and its flow. Only once had Trudi made the transition between feeling her body in the current and *being* the current. But Sunni had said that was enough. It only took the one time to be *conscious*. It should be easy to return, now that she knew.

Other than her fertility rite of passage, the two had not had time to go further in her instruction. There were more levels, Sunni had told her. Trudi was only an initiate. Although she had become *conscious*, she had not yet understood her *connection* through time. After that came the sacred act of *creation*.

Knowing she had limited time for her meditation, Trudi released the power of the current from her mind. But instead of returning to her place on the shore, she found herself hovering in the mist over the water. Trudi let herself float in its upward-drafting currents and eddies.

Curious, she let her mind shift and *became* the mist. She drifted high in the air above the river. Looking down, she could see the pickets standing guard in the moonlight next to the copse of trees that hid her. Drifting higher, she could see the campfires from their camp. She saw

Pippin's men saddling horses, and when she looked east, she saw the orange glow of the morning sun cresting over the horizon.

"Enough," she said aloud, trying once more to return to her place on the rug. But again, she found she could not return. She stayed with the dawn and felt its warmth wafting over the horizon. The heat lifted her higher still, and soon she looked down on the earth from a great distance. The surrounding landscape fanned out beneath her on both sides of the river. She could see the deep forests to the north and east and far in the distance, the River Rhine. To the northeast, she saw the Quierzy Road. To the south, their path wound through fertile countryside and farmland as far as she could see. It led through Reims and Châlon sur Marne into the heart of Burgundy.

Attempting to see more, Trudi stretched to climb even higher, venturing near the small wisps of cloud high in the morning sky.

"Trudi?" Trudi teetered and fell the great distance back to earth. Her mind reeled back inside her head. Someone was near. Very near. Disoriented, she tried to pull herself up. She scrambled to find her robe.

"Trudi," Pippin said again. This time more softly. He was standing in the clearing, holding out her robe for her. "I think this is what you're looking for."

Trudi looked up at her brother. Thankfully, he was alone. Despite her initial embarrassment, something about Pippin struck her as odd.

He stood several paces away, holding out her robe in front of him like a curtain to block out her nudity. When she took a step forward, he took one backward. And he clearly had no idea what to do with his eyes. One second he'd avert them, and the next she'd catch him peeking at her breasts.

"Pippin," she chided him. His expression was a cross between shameful curiosity and a plea to her for assistance.

Trudi couldn't help laughing. He looked so helpless using her robe as a shield. His battle armor only added to the irony. She put one hand over her mouth in an attempt to control herself, but her giggling continued. Taking pity on him, she took the two steps between them, turned, and slipped her arms into the robe. She pulled the robe around her and cinched the belt. She allowed herself one more giggle before turning to meet his eyes.

"So how long were you standing there?" she asked.

"Not long." As Trudi bent to roll up her rug and pick up her herbs, her brother kept talking, filling the silence she left between them. "We started to break camp, and I came looking for you. The pickets said you had been in here for quite a while. I thought something had happened. And then I found you like this," he said, motioning to the ground where he had found her. "Trudi, what were you doing?"

"Nothing worth the worry on your face, brother." Trudi smiled. "But thank you for coming to my rescue." She kissed him on the cheek and started for the edge of the clearing.

"Seriously, Trudi." Pippin hadn't moved. "What were you doing?"

Trudi never missed a step. "There are some things, my dear brother, that a man should never ask a woman. This," she said, "is one of them."

Carloman struggled for composure. Boniface was not giving him a chance to grieve. When Carloman refused to leave the side of his father's corpse, the bishop had brought the realm's nobles to the vestibule, insisting that further delay would undermine Carloman's strength and leadership. Carloman, however, did not feel very strong, and he was sure that he didn't look much like a leader. After King Liutbrand, Theudoald was next into the chapel. He arrived with two Neustrians: Ragomfred the Younger, son of Charles's early nemesis, and a tall gray-haired man named Maurice, whom Carloman had always respected for his acumen as a merchant. Carloman was, in fact, surprised to find Maurice in this company.

Theudoald strode through the chapel with the gait of a man taking charge. His blue coat and breeches were impeccably clean. Tapered at the waist in the latest fashion, they gave him the look of someone incredibly fit. He also wore a white shirt with a lace collar. This too was a new trend among the nobles at court. As he approached the casket, Theudoald pulled a perfumed handkerchief from his sleeve to ward off the smell of the corpse. The man did not kneel or bow or pray next to Charles's casket. He regarded the body briefly and turned his back on it to face Carloman and Boniface.

Johann, with hand on the pommel of his sword, stood in his way.

"My respects, Carloman," Theudoald said over the young knight's shoulder.

"Thank you." Carloman nodded to his protector and Johann gave way.

"Of course, Charles's death raises a number of questions worthy of discussion," Theudoald said.

"Confronting death always does," Carloman said.

For just a moment, Theudoald seemed confused by this response, but he plunged on.

"The first revolves around the division of the kingdom into three parts." Carloman looked at the man, as if recognizing him for the first time. This too distracted the nobleman, but again he continued. "Historically, there is precedent for this, of course. There have been mayors of Austrasia, Neustria, and Burgundy before, but never has Neustria been split in such a fashion. Neustria is the key to power in the kingdom. Even Charles understood that. Although he was my grandfather's bastard son, he knew that his power stemmed from combining the might of Austrasia and Neustria. He spent seven years fighting to control both of them."

Carloman's eyes searched out Ragomfred. He understood the reason Theudoald had brought the nobleman along. The young man's father had been the architect of the Neustrian resistance to Charles. The implied threat of their combined interests was obvious.

"Despite your father's dramatic show at the assembly," Theudoald continued, "the current division of the kingdom cannot stand. It is clearly the work of that witch Sunnichild. She manipulated your father to benefit Gripho and her family's power. The result is an abomination. Aligning the northern end of Neustria to Alemannia and Thuringia is like mating a prize horse with a dog. The match won't take. The boy's too young to be mayor, and Neustria should be ruled by someone who can protect its interests."

"And you, I am sure, have thoughts about who that should be," Boniface said.

Theudoald looked to Carloman. "I'm not here to bargain, boy. Split the kingdom in thirds. Leave Neustria whole and to me. You take Austrasia, let Pippin have Burgundy, and we'll divide up the rest of the pieces later."

"You laid your hands between Gripho's just days ago," Carloman said.

"Don't be naïve. Do you want civil war? I have the troops." He nodded to Ragomfred. "I have the resources." He nodded to Maurice. "And I have the legitimacy that your father could only dream of. I *am* the grandson of Plectrude and Pippin of Herstal, not a bastard son. I *was* named mayor before Charles seized my grandfather's treasure and lay siege to the kingdom. I *will* be mayor of Neustria. Your choice lies with how. My way, everyone gets what they want except the witch's son. Any other way, and there will be war. And if there is, I may not just settle for Neustria. I've got just as much Austrasian blood as you."

"My father made his wishes clear," Carloman said, looking at the casket. "I see no need to renounce them."

"Your father took my rightful place as mayor and took the throne as if he were king," Theudoald said. "I mean to right both wrongs. Join me in this, and we will have peace. Oppose me, and I will make my claim with iron."

Boniface stepped in. "This is a time of great family grief, and Pippin is away on campaign. Perhaps you could wait a few days until he arrives and can be consulted."

"You have until the funeral."

Carloman fought to clear his head. He tried to count the number of nobles who might back Theudoald. When he reached a dozen, he stopped counting. Looking at Ragomfred, he saw nothing but anger in the man's face. Clearly, the son had inherited the family's feud from the father. *Theudoald is not bluffing,* thought Carloman. *No one is bluffing today.* Carloman's eyes sought out his father's casket. He felt his face flush with embarrassment. If there was going to be a bluff, he realized, it would have to be his own.

"That's a nice coat," Carloman said to Theudoald without looking up.

The noble looked at him warily. "Thank you."

"I would hate to have to bury you in it."

Theudoald stiffened, and Johann took a step forward. Nodding to his two companions, Theudoald strode out of the chapel, much as he had strode in.

Outside the doorway to the chapel, Sunni stood in the vestibule. She hadn't intended to eavesdrop. She had intended to join Carloman in the chapel, both to grieve for her husband and to participate in the political discussions surrounding Gripho. She knew that no time would lapse between Charles's death and the political maelstrom about his succession. Frankish nobles were known for their plots and secret deals. "Nary a friend among the Franks," the saying went. She had seen Theudoald stride into the chapel and had meant to join the discussion with Carloman and Boniface, but some instinct held her back.

When Sunni heard Carloman's response to Theudoald, she left the shadows and hurried down the hall. Her grief for Charles would have to wait. She had too much to do in too little time. She had messages to send, clothes to pack, and as she made her way back to her chambers, she too started counting nobles. She didn't stop at twelve.

"You're joking!" Bertie laughed.

"I'm absolutely serious," Trudi said.

"He is quite good looking. And from what I hear, quite *experienced,*" Bertie said with a sideways glance and an evil grin. "To be truthful," she whispered, "I've always had a crush on Odilo myself. He's so—" Bertie's face flushed. Shaking her head, she said, "How did this happen? It is all so sudden."

"I'm not really sure what has happened," Trudi said. "I left before I spoke to him. He doesn't even know I'm gone."

"The whole court knows you are gone by now," Bertie said. "Even the cooks."

"I had to leave. I won't be sold or bartered."

"Then you had better stay one step ahead of your father and King Liutbrand," Bertie said. "They will come looking for you."

"Do you think Odilo will have me?" Trudi asked.

Bertie looked at the warrior girl with some sympathy. She was an innocent, and Odilo was not. But would he marry her? He would be a fool not to. The girl was a prize, and the politics were obvious. With Sunni, Gripho, and now Trudi, the Agilolfings would be a force. She reached over and patted Trudi's hand.

"I'm sure he'll have you. How will you send him word?"

"I plan on waiting for him in St. Vitrey. If he'll have me, we'll travel east to Bavaria from there."

"And if he won't?"

"I can't go home."

"Charles will always welcome you home."

"I wish I could believe you," Trudi said.

For a time, the two rode in silence, enjoying the quiet of the countryside. As they made their way south, the number of houses lining the road increased, and the road became more crowded. Gunther said they were within two days of Reims. Bertie couldn't wait. She'd sell her soul for a bath.

Remembering Pippin's description of Trudi's odd behavior, Bertie asked, "And just what were you doing down by the river this morning? You nearly frightened Pippin into the priesthood."

"Oh, it was a pagan exercise Sunni showed me," Trudi said. Bertie couldn't keep the shock from her face. Trudi added quickly, "She said it helped with lovemaking."

After a moment, Bertie blushed. "Is it something you can teach me?" she whispered.

Trudi laughed. "We'll have to find someplace a little more—um—private."

"I should hope so." Bertie giggled. "It would have been much harder to explain if Pippin had found the two of us."

Carloman rubbed his eyes. Although he had confused a few names in the parade of nobles and lost track of the conversation at times, for the most part, he had kept his composure and avoided making any obvious mistakes. Save, perhaps, the threat to Theudoald.

The bishops and priests had come offering condolences and prayers from their churches and monasteries but had taken the opportunity to remind him of his promise to return the churches' lands. Ateni of Provence had paid his respects, as had Liutfred of Alemannia, the latter seeking assurances regarding Gripho's claims. And while Liutfred hadn't threatened him, he had come close. The Alemannian had made it clear that he expected Gripho to be treated fairly despite his young age. He seemed disturbed when Carloman offered only vague assurances.

Everyone had asked about elevating a Merovingian king to keep the peace.

Even at this late hour, a number of mourners had crowded into the small chapel. Boniface had again stepped to the altar to lead them in prayer. Carloman knelt. Without hesitation, all the congregants fell to their knees. The Latin words droned above him and around him, but he could not hold them any longer in his mind. He felt himself nod briefly into his folded hands.

When he looked up, a new retinue had joined them. Odilo stood to the side of the chapel, his head bowed and his arms folded in front of him. Carloman nodded to him and waited for an end to the prayers. After the room's final amen, Carloman stood and made his way toward the Bavarian.

"My sympathies," Odilo said.

With a slight nod, Carloman indicated an alcove off to their right and waved off Johann. He and Odilo pushed through the mourners into the relative quiet.

"Your father was a great man."

"Thank you." Carloman held a handkerchief to his nose.

"Perhaps this is not the appropriate time and place," Odilo began.

"No one else has hesitated."

"It's just that, one hears things."

Carloman stopped wiping his nose and looked at the Bavarian. "Such as?"

"Parisian nobles holding midnight meetings. Sunni sending dozens of couriers scurrying throughout Neustria. The Alemannians grumbling to the Frisians. Will there be war, Carloman?"

"There is no reason for war."

"But there may be a challenge."

"There is always that possibility."

"And if so, with whom will you side?" Odilo's face was calm. He might have asked if it would rain tomorrow.

"There is no good answer to that question, Odilo. A declaration from me one way or another could start the war you fear. By taking a side, I force everyone's hand."

"One could also argue that your declaration could avoid war. A clear signal from you might dissuade those susceptible to pressure."

"Perhaps," Carloman said, but he didn't offer anything more.

After a few moments, the Bavarian shook his head. "I shall be clear, Carloman, even if you will not. The Agilolfing family will defend Gripho's claim. As will the Alemannians. And I would not underestimate Sunni. She is not without support." Odilo sighed. "Brother warring against brother is no way to start your reign as mayor, Carloman. Put down the challenge. Let us all go home to our families and mourn the loss of your father rather than curse his passing. Put down the challenge and keep your father's family intact."

Odilo never raised his voice. No hint of a threat tainted his tone. Yet the ultimatum had been delivered.

"One more thing," Odilo said. "A piece of friendly advice. If Theudoald makes his challenge and backs it with force, be the first to raise a Merovingian king. Don't leave that to him. He'll use it to undermine your support. Nobles are skittish when it comes to attacking a king."

"Thank you for your concern," Carloman said.

Odilo put his hand on Carloman's shoulder. "I am sorry for your loss," he said. "I will be leaving shortly after the funeral. I had hoped to give my condolences to your sister. Is there any word of her return?"

Carloman shook his head. "Unfortunately, not." The handkerchief returned to his nose. "She left with Pippin, who was taking the southern road to Reims. I sent some knights to ensure her return. I expect we will see her shortly after the funeral."

"Perhaps our paths will cross on my way back to Bavaria," Odilo said carefully. "She's not in danger?" Carloman looked up quizzically. "The knights?" Odilo offered.

Oddly, the question gave Carloman pause. He had ordered one of Trudi's friends, Ansel, to lead a group of knights to find his sister. But the knight had reacted strangely to the order. Rather than being honored at the task, Ansel had tried to suggest he was unworthy. And stranger still, when Carloman dismissed the knight's modesty and ordered him to leave immediately, the young man broke into a profound sweat.

"No danger at all," Carloman said. He blew his nose, tucked his handkerchief back in his sleeve, and looked toward the growing crowd in the chapel. "If you will forgive me." He gestured toward the chapel.

"Of course." The Bavarian bowed. "May honor strengthen your sword."

"And may truth guide its way," Carloman replied.

"We are ready, milady."

Sunni nodded, dropping the veil over her face, and braced herself for the long procession taking Charles's body to St. Denis. She hated the notion of grieving in public. She hated wearing black. It was a Christian tradition. Pagans wore white. And without Charles, she did not feel at all like pretending anymore. She also hated leaving. She, like Charles, would not be returning to Quierzy, although few but her closest confidants knew it.

She had arranged for her personal items to be sent discreetly to Laon during the funeral festivities. Other precious gifts and artifacts would be left behind to avoid suspicion. As she exited her chambers, six Bavarian knights of her choosing fell in beside her. There would be more among her retinue in the procession. She didn't believe she would need them, but her instincts pushed caution, so she was cautious.

They made a small parade through the villa, Sunni, her handmaidens, and her armed escort. Not a word was spoken as they descended the broad staircases and advanced through the halls. She nodded to the servants and attendants as they passed. When they reached the main hallway, the bulk of Charles's court was waiting. Several hundred voices hushed in an instant upon her arrival, and in near unison, all heads bowed.

Gracefully, Sunni bowed in return and swept her entourage through the crowded hall to where Carloman, Gripho, and Boniface were waiting. Greta stood nearby with her arm around her son, Drogo.

Sunni went to them first, kissed Greta on each cheek, and hugged Drogo to her chest. She felt him stiffen beneath her embrace. Remembering that he was no longer a boy, she let him go, smiled, and mussed his hair. He managed a small smile in return.

Turning next to her son, she kissed him more formally, like Greta, once on each cheek. His eyes were red-rimmed and puffy. "May honor strengthen your sword," she whispered to him. He bowed, unable to speak the rejoinder. Finally she turned to Carloman and Boniface. Much to their surprise, Sunni curtsied before them.

"Milord," she addressed Carloman. "Your grace," to Boniface.

Carloman took her hand to raise her to her feet. As she pulled herself erect, Johann and several Knights in Christ advanced to the party from both sides. Startled by the intensity of the young man, Sunni looked to Carloman, who immediately raised his hand to stop their advance.

"Forgive me, Sunni," he said. "The road can be dangerous even for mourners."

"Of course." She smiled at Carloman without showing a trace of suspicion and turned to her stepson's knights. "Thank you, Johann. But as you can see, I have given today's honor to the sons of my native country. Perhaps I will have the pleasure of your men's company at another time." She nodded her head in dismissal. Johann's reputation named him a

Christian of the most intolerant kind. Sunni had no doubts that if Johann knew of her pagan beliefs, he would strike her dead on the spot.

Johann looked to Carloman, who nodded his assent. In unison, Johann and his knights bowed to Sunni and stepped away.

"It's time," Boniface said.

The party advanced to the great doors of the hall where an open-bed carriage carrying Charles's casket awaited them. As tradition called for Sunni to accompany the body, Carloman helped her into the seat beside the driver. Stepping back, he motioned for the doors to be opened. Sunni had hoped that Gripho could accompany her on this journey, but the carriage did not allow for two passengers. Sunni took her seat next to the driver, an elderly man with wisps of white hair falling around his face. He smiled a broad smile with broken and brown teeth. Sunni nodded a silent salutation.

"Milady." He paused for a moment. "Samson," he said, introducing himself. "Like from the Bible."

Sunni nodded again, and they left the villa, making their way down to the river. As they exited, scores of Frankish nobles lined up behind them on horseback. Armored and carrying their banners aloft, they struck Sunni as a haunting echo of their recent return from the campaign in Provence. *There's just no one to lead them,* she thought.

"Different without the mayor," Samson said.

"Excuse me?"

"Different without Charles ... to lead them, milady."

Sunni stared at the driver for a long moment and then shook her head. She must be more exhausted than she knew. She would have to be more careful. She could not afford to speak her thoughts aloud. Much depended on the next few days.

A crowd had formed at the entrance to the eastern road. Sunni thought there was something odd about them; fifty or sixty strong, they blocked the procession's access to the road. They weren't hostile, just quiet. No one among them spoke. They stood together in the chill of the morning, warding off the cold and waiting.

Led by her six Bavarian knights, the carriage approached them. They parted, politely backing away to provide access to the road. She heard mixed and muffled voices calling out to her from the gathering.

"… for your loss."

"God bless you, ma'am."

"… a great man."

"So sorry …"

A young girl stepped forward into the road and laid a bouquet of fall flowers beside the road. As she stepped back, another took her place to lay a second bouquet. Hands with flowers reached from the crowd, and soon the side of the road was covered with bouquets and flowers. Sunni nodded to her well-wishers, suddenly thankful for their good-byes.

Once they reached the main road, however, Sunni was startled to see that the crowd was not limited to the small group at the entrance. People lined both sides of the eastern road. Five and six deep, their number stretched out as far as she could see. Those closest to the road were nobles or wealthy gentry. Farther back, villagers and servants strained to see. Several children had been lifted high on their parents' shoulders. Their gaze followed the outstretched arms beneath them, pointing to her carriage.

Sunni's sense of intimacy shattered. Thinking their curiosity ghoulish, she scowled beneath her veil.

"Ah, milady, no. More, they're feeling part of something large," Samson said. "A big part of their lives, Charles. One of their own, passing on. Many of 'em scared. Many grieve." Samson pointed to an old woman kneeling beside the road, rocking back and forth, her face contorted in anguish, a strangled moan escaping her lips.

More flowers lay along their path. Some placed a wooden crucifix, others the branch of a tree. Sunni smiled at this; the branch was a symbol of the tree of life, a pagan belief. The priests had tried to say it was a local custom symbolizing the palms honoring Jesus. She knew it to be a symbol of one's life force returning to the earth.

On both sides of the road, fighting men came forward at her approach, bowed, and plunged their sword point down into the earth.

Sunni nodded her head. *They too grieve.*

As the carriage moved east, Sunni noticed that the crowd lining the road wore simpler clothes; some came in rags. Their faces and hands were smudged from toil. *Paysans,* she thought to herself. *People of the country.*

"Charles was a savior to them," Samson offered. "Not Jesus on the cross, mind you, no. Did his saving here in this world. Saved 'em when it mattered. Saracen came over the mountains, and none could stop 'em. At Poitiers, Charles did, surprised 'em at midnight. Killed their Sultan. Run 'em off like wolves in the pasture."

Several peasants stepped forward as the carriage passed. First their heads bowed, and then their knees bent. Others followed, and the gesture spread like a wave until all were on their knees. As if in prayer, silence took them. The carriage continued to roll, its wheels creaking in contrast to the quiet. To Sunni, it was almost reverent.

Among the branches and flowers, there were few crucifixes here in the countryside. She noticed the peasants closest to the road were laying something different alongside their path. Sunni couldn't make out what the new tokens were.

"Hammers," Samson said before she could ask, "to honor his passing."

Looking up, she saw hundreds strewn along their path.

It was Trudi who first noticed the odd odor. It was morning, and she and Bertie were riding together as had become their custom. Despite their differences, they enjoyed each other's company. Something about the burning-wood smell, however, nagged at her. "There's another scent," she insisted. "Something sweeter."

She saw Gunther's head tilt up, and his eyes grow wide. He spurred his horse. Arriving next to Pippin and Childebrand, Gunther quickly engaged the two in urgent conversation. When they were done, he ordered the party to pick up its pace.

As they advanced, the sweet aroma grew more pungent, and Trudi rode forward to join Pippin. Bertrada followed. The knights' faces were grim and stern. They straightened in their saddles, checked their weapons. Childebrand fingered his ax. Pippin ordered Gunther and a team of scouts forward. The air was thickening with smoke.

"What is it?" Trudi asked.

"Fire," Pippin said.

"We know that," Bertrada said. "*What*'s on fire?"

"A village."

"Oh, my God," Bertie said, her eyes moistening.

"What's that sweet aroma?" Trudi asked.

Pippin said nothing.

"The people—" Trudi urged her horse into a gallop to chase the departing scouts.

Childebrand moved his horse to cut her off, forcing her to rein in. He spoke in a lowered voice. "We don't know what's going on yet, child. Let's just wait for the scouts to carry out their orders."

"I'm not a child," Trudi said.

"No, I suppose you're not," Childebrand said, "at least not to most of these boys. But to me, you'll always be my niece." He softened his tone. "This is an army, Trudi, not a hunting party. If you are going to dress like a warrior, you should act like one. Nobody goes off like that unless they are ordered to. And nobody does any ordering save your brother, Gunther, and me."

Trudi's angry stare softened under his gaze. "I'm sorry, Uncle," she said.

"We'll hear soon enough. And we'll get to the bottom of it."

It took just more than an hour for one of the scouts to return. It was Arnot. Pippin had always liked the man. He spoke little, traveled well, and had the uncanny ability of going unnoticed.

"Huh-yah," Pippin said.

"It's the village of Loivre," Arnot said. "The town's been looted and burned. No fighting men in sight. Gunther is searching for survivors. Way's clear."

Pippin ordered them to ride at a gallop. As they drew near the village, the sky grew dark with smoke. Twenty homes or more were aflame, and some already had burned to the ground. The sweet pungent smell hung heavy in the air. Bertrada put a handkerchief to her nose. She was crying.

Gunther and his men were helping the local peasants gather valuables and livestock into a field some distance away from the fires. Some had been dispatched to prevent the house fires from spreading into the fields. Pippin shook his head. None of the houses would survive. But if the fields could be saved, the town would rebuild.

Pippin again sent Gunther and Arnot forward with a scouting party, this time to track the marauders. All others were assigned tasks helping the surviving peasants douse fires, gather wood for temporary shelter, find lost horses, and bury the dead. Bertrada sent her handmaidens to shred her packed undergarments for bandages. She saw to the wounded.

Pippin approached Childebrand. "Report?"

"From what I can get from the survivors, and there aren't too many of them, they were attacked for their women. The marauders arrived at midmorning, rounded up the residents, and lined them up along the main street." He waved at the path between the houses. "They put all the women in one row, the men in another. Children, they ran off into the forest. They ushered the men into one of the houses and then lit it on fire. Twelve bodies were found. They took some of the women with them."

"How many?"

"Six."

"How many marauders?"

"They say twenty on horse."

"Does anyone know who they are?"

"It was Bradius, Pippin."

A fierce and brutal warrior, Bradius had been a lieutenant of Maurontus. Carloman had captured him once in Burgundy, but Bradius managed to escape to fight again in Provence. He had been one of the last to be defeated at Narbonne, long after Maurontus had been captured. On the battlefield, he was a monster. It took the sheer force of far superior numbers to defeat him. Even then, it was at great cost. He had laid his hands between Carloman's and swore fealty on the day they left for Quierzy. He and his men had obviously moved north.

"We'll give chase in the morning," Pippin ordered.

Pippin's small army camped near the village and broke bread with its residents. Peasants from nearby farms found their way into town to offer solace and support. Families grieved far into the evening. Campfires burned late.

An hour past midnight, Arnot returned to camp and made his way to Pippin's tent where Pippin and Childebrand were out front talking quietly and watching the stars.

"They're in Reims," the scout said.

"How many?"

"Thirty. Sixteen on horse."

"Are the women alive?"

"Yes. They're all at the Knight's Inn."

"Are the men drinking?"

"More than their fair share."

Pippin looked at Childebrand. "Break camp," he said.

Pippin asked Bertrada and her handmaidens to stay behind with a couple of soldiers to help the village recover. Trudi insisted on going with him to Reims. They were there before dawn.

Situated between Paris and Luxembourg, Reims was a traveler's city. At this hour, however, it was dark and quiet. The gate stood at the north end of the city. Built by the Romans centuries earlier, its towering arches rose thirty feet in the air. Pippin woke the guards to open the gate, and his men passed through without disturbance.

Moving through Reims as quietly as seventeen armed men on horse could move, they found inns on every corner and eateries on every street. They passed through open markets where empty stalls awaited the morning's merchants. One could find everything in Reims, from perfume and spices to the mysteries of the holy land.

Arnot led them on a meandering path through the merchant's district to streets that were somewhat dirtier and the buildings in greater need of repair. At a broad intersection of two thoroughfares, Arnot brought them to a halt. A figure stepped out of the darkness.

"Huh-yah, Pippin," came a whisper.

"Which is it, Gunther?"

"Across the street on the right. They have the top two floors. Three are still in the common room, passed out from drink. The women are upstairs."

"How many men are there?"

"Fifteen, I counted."

"Arnot said thirty."

"I counted but fifteen."

"Where are the others?"

"We tracked them all to the gate, then lost 'em. These here, we found by searching the taverns."

Arnot and Gunther quickly described the layout of the inn. Three stories tall, it had two entrances, the front door and a servant's entry through the stable in the back. Two stairways, one near each door, led to the rooms above.

"Three bedrooms on each floor," Arnot concluded. "Two men, one woman, each bedroom."

Pippin counted out three teams of five and mapped out the attack strategy. "Knives only," Pippin hissed. Turning to Trudi, he pointed to two of his men. "You stay here with them. No one, save us and the women, leaves the inn alive." Trudi nodded, and they melted into the night.

Pippin led his team in through the stable. One of the horses stirred but then quieted when Arnot produced an apple. The party moved to the rear of the main house and came to the kitchen door. It was locked. Pippin tried the window. It too was locked. They peered around the corner—no windows or doors. Arnot signaled for Pippin to wait by the door and disappeared around the corner. After several minutes, they heard the latch pull back from the inside. The door swung open to reveal a ghostlike figure standing just inside. It was Arnot. He was covered from head to foot in ashes. Pippin shook his head. Arnot had squeezed through the chimney's cinder chute.

They moved quietly through the kitchen into the common room. Three inert forms sat by the small fire, their upper bodies splayed across the eating tables. Two still clasped near-empty mugs of ale. At Pippin's signal, three of his men moved into position behind them. In near unison, they grabbed handfuls of hair, lifted heads off the table, and drew blades across their throats. Arnot stepped to the front door to let the others inside. Pippin and his men crept up the back stairs.

"Who's there?" a loud voice demanded. Everyone froze. A stout man in muttonchops and a nightshirt stood at the top of the front stairs with a lit candle in one hand and a nightstick in the other.

"Ah, good sir," Arnot said as if he had been looking for the innkeeper all along. "Sorry to disturb your rest." Pippin heard Arnot climbing the stairs and signaled his men to wait while he moved down the corridor. He counted three doors. "I know it is late," Arnot was saying, "but these gentlemen and I wish to inquire about rooms for the night." He was nearly at the top stair. "Are you, by chance, the innkeeper?"

"We've no rooms." The man lifted his candle to better observe his unexpected guests. His eyes grew wide upon seeing the ash covering Arnot's hair and face, and he lifted his cudgel in alarm. He stopped when he realized that the point of a knife was pricking the soft underside of his chin. Arnot put his hand on the innkeeper's lips. Pippin edged closer. They would have to improvise.

"Perhaps the stable then?" Arnot continued in a normal voice. Pippin signaled to Childebrand and the others. They began to climb the stairs. "Surely you have room in the stables?"

Gunther moved behind Arnot up the front stairs. The door nearest Arnot opened a small crack. One eye peered into the hallway, and the door closed quickly. Without hesitation, Arnot slammed his forearm into the face of the innkeeper, who crumpled under the blow.

"Go!" Arnot hissed and threw his shoulder to the door. Before it struck, the door swung wide and Arnot fell into the room. Pippin heard swords being pulled from scabbards and threw himself into the chamber. Slamming his left shoulder into the one nearest the door, he drove his right hand, blade first, deep into the man's midsection. The bandit collapsed around the blade. Pippin used his momentum to spin on his right foot, almost in pirouette, and slashed backward with the blade in his left hand. The blow caught the second man in the throat, just as he was raising his sword. The three froze for a moment while Pippin watched the recognition of death creep into their eyes. They fell where they stood. Shouts were coming from upstairs and from other rooms.

"Thanks," Arnot said and ran back into the hallway.

A naked woman of middle age lay tied, spread-eagle on the bed. She had been beaten brutally. Pippin wanted to go to her aid, but he knew he didn't have time. He followed Arnot into the hall.

The passage was narrow and crowded with combatants. Pippin was blocked from the fighting by the backs of his own men. Stepping back, he saw that the marauders were trying to push their way through the attack by the weight of their numbers. One of Pippin's men went down and then another. Knives slashed faces. Fingers gouged eyes. The narrowness of the hallway prevented either side from avoiding blows. Using knives, Pippin and his men had an advantage over the marauders who had grabbed swords. The narrow corridor gave no room for more than one thrust of a sword. Once the blade hit home, the man wielding it became vulnerable.

Childebrand had the other end of the corridor blocked, and men on both sides were going down, their bodies making the hallway impassable. Arnot fell, and Pippin threw himself into the battle. He was the last between the marauders and escape. He fought with two blades, blocking and slashing, his left hand held high, and his right low.

Pippin rolled right, moving away from a sword thrust, and jabbed upward with his knife under the arm of his assailant. As the man fell, Pippin slashed down with his left, catching another near the neck, high on the back of his shoulder. Looking up, Pippin saw Childebrand, bloodied and smiling, stabbing the last in the hallway through the throat.

In the end, Pippin and his men had the advantage of surprise and numbers. Too many of the marauders had been killed in the first attack to rally effectively. Pippin, Gunther, and Childebrand cleared the hallways and searched the rooms. There were thirteen dead in all, including the drunks in the common room.

To Pippin's chagrin, there was no one to question. All the marauders had been killed. He and Childebrand went to free the women hostages. Most were found tied to the bedposts in each chamber. Face up or face down, they had been raped repeatedly, their bodies welted and bruised, the beds covered with blood and semen. When the women were untied, those conscious became frantic, clawing at any who approached. Childebrand tried to ensure that their bodies were covered but could get nowhere near them. Pippin sent one of his men into town to find a doctor.

Gunther reported that four of Pippin's men had been killed in the struggle. Two, including Arnot, had been wounded. Childebrand applied field dressings and announced all were capable of riding.

"Where's Trudi?" Pippin asked.

Seeing nothing but blank looks, Pippin rushed outside and found the two men they had left with Trudi unconscious in the street. There was no sign of her. Pippin stood over the bodies, death filling his eyes.

"Close the gates," he ordered. "Wake the town." He threw his knives deep into the earth.

The smell of incense was overpowering. Ten priests, wearing the finest ecclesiastical robes that Sunni had ever seen, circled the altar at St. Denis with smoking thuribles. They *chink-chinked* their way around Charles's surviving family, each pausing before Carloman in their small parade. One by one, they swung the smoking vessels back and forth on golden chains over his head until a small cloud of incense hovered over the entire chapel. There were, Sunni noted, more priests on the altar than mourners.

Heaps of flowers had been arranged around the casket to blunt the smell of decay. Charles's face had lost some of its flesh. Only the skin remained to cover the bones. A pale milky color, it too was decaying. The corpse's lips had frayed and pulled partially back to reveal gray-brownish teeth.

The lid had been left open to allow the priests to bless Charles's forehead with holy oil. One by one, each of the ten priests ceremoniously approached the altar, bowed, and moved next to the casket. Whispering Latin prayers, they dipped their thumbs in the holy font, reached into the open space of the casket, and traced the sign of the cross on Charles's forehead. Boniface, his golden robe sparkling in the candlelight, was to be last.

From her vantage point on the altar, Sunni was the first to see the doors at the back of the cathedral swing open, fast and wide, spilling sunlight into the darkened nave. Two armed men stood silhouetted in the brilliance of the arched doorway. They stepped into the cathedral and strode toward the altar, swords and body armor clanking above the murmur that followed them down the aisle. One step from the altar, Hunoald and Waifar stopped. Holding his head high, Hunoald turned to face the congregation. He stilled the room in an instant.

Carloman rose from his prie-dieu at the altar. Hunoald turned to face him.

"I renounce my vassalage," Hunoald said in a loud, clear voice. He thrust the stump of his right arm in Carloman's direction. "I renounce you as mayor. I denounce your succession as a sham. I owe my fealty to a king," he said, slamming his stump against his chest. "And you are no Merovingian."

Sunni was just two steps behind Carloman. She could see her stepson shift his stance to balance his weight and saw his hands drift to where his sword would have been, had he not been attending his father's funeral.

Hunoald stood before Carloman, his eyes angry and malevolent. Long moments passed, and no one moved. A small movement caught Sunni's eye, and she recognized the real threat. Waifar. The man stood behind his father like an angry bear leashed to a tree. His face was flushed, and his eyes rolled with a glare that she had seen only in fanatical priests.

Without warning, Waifar stepped up to the altar and strode directly toward her. It took Sunni a moment to realize that she wasn't the object of his ire. Waifar crossed to the casket and spit. His sputum hit the corpse on the forehead and ran down into its eyes.

Sunni hadn't seen Carloman move, but he was suddenly behind Waifar, one step to his side, still facing forward to watch Hunoald. With his back to Waifar, Carloman placed his left foot midway between the brute's feet and grabbed him by the collar of his armor and pulled forward. Waifar's left knee buckled on Carloman's leg, and the giant toppled backward to the floor.

Hitting the floor, Waifar rolled to his right and attempted to regain his feet. Carloman kicked him in the face before the Knights in Christ descended on them. They seized Hunoald and wrestled with Waifar, trying to pin him to the floor. Johann pulled Carloman clear. With a roar, Waifar found his feet and threw off his attackers. But the effort also threw him off balance. With his back to Charles's casket, he stumbled sideways and fell to the floor. Johann closed on Waifar, his sword in hand.

"Stop!" Boniface ordered.

Johann continued to advance. Boniface broke into the circle and threw himself on the fallen knight, covering Waifar's body with his own. His golden cope billowed over them. The Knight in Christ froze.

"This is the house of God!" Boniface shouted. "You are men of God! Put away your swords." Johann backed away and lowered his weapon, but he did not return it to his scabbard.

Boniface rose to his feet and turned on Waifar. "We blessed this corpse with holy ointment. Who are you to defile it? Who are you to defile the holy ground of the church? You are a disgrace to your faith. Take your anger outside to the streets. And you, Johann." He turned on the Knight in Christ. "You dare draw your sword in this place?"

Johann bowed his head but left his sword in hand, his eyes never leaving Waifar. Boniface suddenly looked exhausted. His shoulders slumped. He drew from his sleeve a handkerchief and began wiping the face and eyes of Charles's corpse. "I should excommunicate you all."

Hunoald shook himself free from the knights who held him, and with a nod to Waifar, he turned and strode down the aisle. Waifar followed, scowling, his eyes never lifting to meet any others in the congregation.

Boniface dipped his thumb into the font of holy oil and retraced the cross on Charles's forehead. He then bent, kissed the spot, and whispered, "Good-bye, my old friend." Straightening, he motioned to the other priests, and together they hefted the casket's lid into place.

CHAPTER 5

Après Charles

"Open the gates," a voice echoed from above.

Bertrada waited for the wooden doors to open. As unusual as it was for the gates of Reims to be closed at midday, it had required little more than mentioning Pippin's name for the guards to let her pass. Not so for the crowd of forty-odd travelers also waiting to get into the city. From what she could gather, they had been waiting all morning.

The walled defenses of Reims were minor compared to those of most cities its size. Since it was a trading center, the city elders had made the decision long ago to acquiesce to strength rather than to fight it. Invaders came and went. The merchants cared little, as long as their shops and stalls were left intact and they could continue to trade their wares. Bertrada was sure that closure of the gates was not a good sign.

The gates opened enough for Bertrada and her two companions to move forward. They nudged their horses under the arched gateway and rode into the broad courtyard beyond. Once inside the city, Bertrada felt her heart began to race. The news brought by Carloman's courier was dire, and she feared for Pippin. He would be devastated by Charles's loss.

The gates closed behind them, and a roar of outrage arose from those left outside. Oddly enough, the first thing Bertrada saw upon entering the gate was another crowd on the inside, waiting to get out.

She had expected to inquire after the constable of Reims to locate Pippin. Although it was not a large city, she thought it would take some effort to track him down. But there in the middle of the courtyard just inside the gate stood Pippin. Gunther was to one side giving orders to men from the city garrison. Childebrand stood nearby, reviewing maps on a small table. A long line of people snaked through the courtyard waiting to speak with him. And there were armed men everywhere. Even from this distance, Bertrada could tell Pippin was angry.

She led her companions to the table and waited for him to finish. The news from the courier required his full attention.

"And you did nothing?" Pippin queried a short, balding man with a medallion that named him as Charles's emissary.

"Please understand, my lord," the emissary said. "We have only a small garrison here. We could not stand up to such numbers. I spoke with the city's elders, and the consensus was to accommodate them as best we could until they moved on."

"And your accommodations include allowing murder and rape?"

"Until today, there were no such problems." The emissary shook his head. "No one was murdered. There was no bloodshed. I will admit that, on occasion, a few of the local girls from the countryside received the gentlemen's attention." The emissary lowered his voice in confidence. "But you must agree that such behavior would not require our intervention. As noblemen, one should expect to see a certain amount of *droit du seigneur.*" His eyebrows arched, seeking agreement. When he received none from Pippin, he looked insulted. "You can hardly expect us to have interceded!"

"That's where you're wrong." Pippin ripped the emissary's medallion from his neck. "You are relieved." Surprised, the man hesitated, looking for further instruction. Pippin simply said, "Go."

"Of course, my lord." The former emissary bowed, and Pippin turned away.

Seeing Bertrada, Pippin abandoned the line of waiting nobles. He kissed her, but his eyes fixed on the horseman who had accompanied her, a messenger from Charles's court. "Do you have something for me?"

The messenger nodded but made no move for his pouch. He looked away, as if something on the horizon held his attention. Then he looked to Bertrada, fidgeting with the reins in his hands.

She stepped forward and put her hand on Pippin's chest. "Charles is dead, Pippin. He died the morning after we left Quierzy."

Pippin's eyes flickered but never left the messenger. When he did finally return her gaze, his eyes plead for refutation. When she offered none, he looked away. Like the messenger before him, his eyes searched the horizon. Underneath her hand, Bertrada felt his body coil and flex.

"Give it to me." Pippin held out his hand to the messenger without looking at him. The man handed him the sealed letter. Pippin took it, stared down at the familiar seal, but made no move to break it. Looking up, his eyes sought out Childebrand. The older man's one eye looked down on his nephew sympathetically. He put his hand on Pippin's shoulder and took the envelope from his hands.

"We must go back, Pippin," Bertrada said, filling the silence. "I know you wanted to leave all that behind. I know you wanted to start over in Burgundy. But this changes things. We have to go back."

"I can't," he said.

"You must," Bertrada said. "Carloman needs you. Your presence is expected."

"Trudi's been taken," he said, color creeping into his face. He took Bertrada's arm and walked to the edge of the courtyard to recount the events of the night. Her eyes filled when he told her what had been done to the peasant women. They widened in alarm when he described finding the two bodies outside the inn with no trace of his sister. "We shut the gates and searched house by house until we were sure that none of the bandits remained inside the city walls. A large party was seen taking the road south toward Châlon sur Marne. I'm readying the men to give chase." He looked back at the horizon. "They can only be half a day ahead."

"Find her," Bertrada said with more heat than she intended. "Bring her back." Although he nodded, for a sliver of a moment, she saw his anger falter, replaced by a sudden stab of pain and doubt. He looked away, and it was gone. She could have wept then, but Pippin did not have time for grief. "I will wait here for you," she said.

"Stay with Childebrand," he said.

Gunther had gathered their company at the city's gates. Several new men from the local garrison filled in for those who had fallen. Pippin returned to speak with Childebrand, ignoring the long line of petitioners. Bertrada watched as the two argued. On several occasions, Pippin gestured toward her. In the end, he proffered Childebrand the emissary's emblem, which Childebrand, with his head bowed, reluctantly accepted.

Bertrada watched Pippin mount the horse next to Gunther. Childebrand waved for the guards to open the city's gates, and Gunther signaled for the party to ride. Pippin took the southern road in a cloud of dust. He did not look back to say good-bye.

Carloman prayed. He asked forgiveness of his sins. He asked guidance in his daily trials and blessings on his family. He arrived at the point in his ritual where words should have been unnecessary. But he did not feel the presence of his Savior. His body didn't flush with fervor. His mind didn't clear of worldly concerns. For some reason that Carloman could not grasp, the Lord's holy touch eluded him, leaving him with a vast emptiness where the ecstasy of his faith should have been.

Carloman lowered his outstretched hand. He let go of the holy relic he wore around his neck, crossed himself, and stood. *Maybe tomorrow,* he thought. *Maybe I'm just too tired today.*

He had moved the court to the family residence in Paris on the Ile de la Cité. Of all the residences, this was his favorite since it was where he had spent the best moments of his youth. There was a monastery across the Seine, St. Germain des Prés, where he had received his first communion and was married. Early each morning, he rose and, surrounded by Johann and his knights, made the short pilgrimage across the bridge and along the river to the church. There, he attended mass and then returned to conduct the business of the day.

For days now, he had been meeting with Neustrian nobles, trying to shore up support against a challenge from Theudoald. Ragomfred and Maurice had been very busy and very clever in undermining the basis for his succession. By echoing Hunoald's call for the elevation of a Merovingian king, they provided a convenient excuse to nobles who didn't want to give their allegiance to Carloman. And the idea was gaining support.

Nary a friend among the Franks, Carloman thought ruefully.

Everywhere Carloman went, people were talking about Hunoald's renouncement. It had plagued him now for days. Division among the Frankish nobles implied weakness. It invited discussion. It legitimized dissension and alternative proposals.

"Damn him!" Carloman said aloud, surprising himself. Realizing he was still in church, he hurriedly made the sign of the cross and started back to the Île de la Cité. His walk was brisk. Images of Waifar spitting into his father's face haunted him. He could still see the spittle on Charles's forehead. He could see Hunoald's stump extending toward him like a sword as the Gasçon renounced him. *Hunoald will die,* thought Carloman. *Waifar as well.*

Surrounded by Johann and his Knights in Christ, Carloman crossed the bridge onto the Île de la Cité and turned right toward the residential compound. *It was time to talk to Sunni,* he thought. He had seldom seen her since the funeral; she had been campaigning to gain support among the Neustrian nobles. Using a distant family tie to Charles's stepmother, Plectrude, Sunni had rallied nobles against Theudoald's claim with appeals of her own.

Carloman had spent much of his time since the funeral focusing on gaining ecclesiastical support. He had moved quickly to put the plan he and Boniface had crafted into place. God knew, he needed a show of support. He had Boniface ask the bishops attending Charles's funeral to stay in Paris. A council was offered to discuss increased Church support in exchange for confiscated Church land. Bishop Aidolf of Auxerre had agreed to come. So had the bishops from St. Denis and Rouen. Carloman was not sure that it would be enough. He prayed it would be.

Greta was at the gate waiting for him. For a woman in her late twenties, she carried herself like a queen. Several women stood with her, chatting casually, clearly enjoying the morning sun. There was not a guard in sight. Carloman turned on Johann, fury in his eyes. The young blond knight was already moving knights into place to protect Greta.

"Good morning, my love," Greta called to Carloman.

"Greta, you must not leave the residence without a guard."

She made a show of examining her spot just inside the gate. "But I haven't left the residence." She laughed. Carloman frowned. She enjoyed mocking him in front of her friends.

"Please, Greta, there is danger. Remember—"

"Yes, yes. I know all about your family history," Greta interrupted. "I just am sick of constantly being under guard. You would think that I was Johann's prisoner."

"Better than someone else's," Carloman growled.

Greta laughed. "You can be so *lordly,* sometimes, Carloman. Anyway, I'm glad you're back. You're just in time to see Sunni off."

"Sunni?"

"Yes, she's heading back to Quierzy."

Carloman was stunned. No one had told him. Again, he turned on his blond protector. "How could I not have been forewarned of this?" he barked.

"I am sorry, milord. I have no knowledge of it," Johann said, his eyes furious with embarrassment.

He turned back to his wife. "I don't understand."

Sunni's carriage appeared from behind the carriage house. Unlike the cart she had taken from Quierzy, this one was worthy of a queen. A small sitting room on wheels, its black polished wooden doors rode high above wheels as tall as a man. Drawn by six white horses, it bespoke wealth, nobility, and power. Behind the carriage rode Gripho and Odilo with his contingent of Bavarian knights.

They were an impressive group with their armor clean and their horses well groomed. They sat straight in the saddle and moved with a calm assurance. Only Gripho looked ill at ease.

The carriage stopped at the gate. Sunni opened the carriage door and waited for the driver to place a small wooden staircase outside her door so she could descend to greet them.

"Thank you, Samson," she said to the driver. She turned her head to Carloman and Greta.

"How lovely of you two. Thank you so much for seeing me off."

"I … uh … didn't know you were leaving," Carloman said.

"It is rather sudden," Sunni agreed. "But my uncle was leaving for Bavaria and will be traveling the road to Quierzy. He offered to accompany me home. And I have to say, I am ready to go home."

Every instinct in Carloman's body screamed at him not to let her leave. "Yes, I know the feeling," he said. "But I would like you to stay. There is much to discuss, and I hope when Pippin arrives to better clarify our areas of responsibility."

"I'm just going down the road, Carloman." Sunni chuckled. More soberly, she asked, "Have you heard from Pippin?"

"No. But he should return any day now."

"Come see me when you're ready, Carloman," Sunni said. "I've been through enough of late."

A long silence followed while Carloman thought through his choices. He had no real authority to tell her to stay. Gripho was a mayor in his own right, and she, acting as regent, could decide where and when they came and went. He could not use force. Odilo's men would stop anything but a full assault, and even a minor one could trigger a civil war. Reason had not worked. He was hamstrung.

"At least you're in good company," he said with a nod to Odilo. The Bavarian nodded in return.

"Stay close to Quierzy, Sunni," Carloman said. "Greta and I will be returning soon. Once the conclave is done and Pippin returns, the issue of the challenge will be settled. Then it will be time to talk."

"I wish you well, Carloman," Sunni said, with a sad smile on her face.

"Farewell, my brother," Carloman called to Gripho as Sunni regained her seat in the carriage. The boy's nod was somewhat insolent.

From his saddle next to Gripho, Odilo called out to him. "Remember what we discussed, Carloman. Keep your family intact."

Carloman nodded to the Bavarian. "May honor strengthen your sword, Odilo."

"And may truth guide its way, Carloman."

Carloman and Johann stood aside to let the procession pass. Twenty Bavarian knights moved in pairs to the gate to lead the black carriage with the high wheels out onto the avenue. Twenty more followed behind. Each pair saluted Carloman with perfect precision as they passed, and Carloman took care to salute them just as precisely in return.

When they were gone, Carloman noticed that Greta was crying.

"Why the tears?" he said, putting his arm around her.

"I don't know," she said. "I looked into the carriage to wave good-bye to Sunni and saw that she was crying. So I started crying too."

"They're just down the road," Carloman said, trying to reassure her. He only wished that there were someone to reassure him.

Trudi's wrists hurt. Struggling to massage the pain there, she found more in her shoulders and her ankles. When she moved, she discovered the pounding in her head. It lanced through her with each jostling of the horse and made her nauseous. She tried to speak, but in the way of dreams, she could not.

It took several minutes to figure out that she was lying face down across a horse's back as if she were a sack of flour. Her hands and feet were tied and held together by a rope under the horse's belly. The only thing she could see was the horse's flank and the muddy ground that passed under her eyes. She watched it roll by distantly. The ball of cloth stuffed in her mouth made even groaning difficult.

The gag brought home the reality of her situation. And with that reality came all the horror of her helplessness. She started to panic. Screaming against the cloth in her mouth, she bucked wildly against the horse, trying to throw herself free. Her stomach landed hard on the pommel of the saddle, and pain stabbed through her as the air rushed out of her lungs from her clenching diaphragm.

She couldn't breathe. She lay helpless for long moments, struggling to inhale. Her heart pounded in her ears. Blood rushed to her head, and her eyes started to bulge. Just as she began to lose consciousness, her diaphragm loosened in a spurt of pain, and Trudi sucked in air through her nose in long strained draughts. She stopped struggling to free herself, all her attention focused on breathing and staying conscious.

"I don't suppose you'll do that again," a male voice behind her said. Trudi tried to scream through the cloth gag. He laughed at her.

They rode for hours. The pain in Trudi's head stabbed against the back of her eyes. Her wrists chafed raw and started to bleed. Several times, she lost consciousness, always awakening to the shock of her situation. Wracked with pain, she couldn't help but long for the end of their journey, but she knew instinctively that the night would be worse. She tried not to think of the women of Loivre. When it started to get dark, Trudi began to cry.

She had fantasies of Odilo coming to her rescue, or Pippin. But each bruising jolt of her horse undermined her hope. She wasn't even sure that Pippin was alive. The last she had seen of him, he was storming into the inn. What if he was ambushed? What if he had been killed? Her fears rose unchecked within her, and she could not set them aside.

They rode for hours without stopping. Trudi abandoned herself to the pace and let the pain wash over her. Just before the last light of day disappeared, the party turned off the road. Riding single file, they entered a forest that quickly shut out most of the remaining light. After another half hour of riding, they stopped to make camp. Her horse was tethered to a tree. They left her there. No one came to untie her. She began to fear they might leave her there all night.

When they did come for her, two sets of rough hands unbound the cord holding her hands and her feet. She cried out through her gag as the ropes cinched tighter so that the knots could be loosened. They left her wrists bound but undid her ankles. Then with little in the way of care, two men lifted her off the horse and stood her on her feet. Her legs wouldn't hold her. Grabbing her by the elbows, they dragged her into the camp.

Two fires had been lit in the middle of a broad clearing. One large fire stood at the center of the camp, and a second, smaller version, sat at the top of a small incline away from the trail. Both were situated under trees to disperse the smoke from their flames. A crowd had gathered around the larger of the two, where a large pot was cooking stew.

The two men took her up the incline to the smaller fire. A man lounged there with his back against the tree, staring at the fire. He was alone, pouring wine from a skin into an earthenware cup. Without looking up at the threesome, he waved with the cup hand, gesturing that Trudi be seated near him. He tilted the cup and smelled the wine before he sipped. Then, swirling the liquid around his tongue, he closed his eyes to savor its flavor. The men took off her gag. She spent the next few moments working her tongue and spitting out pieces of cloth.

What she noticed first was the thin white scar running from his left ear to the left-hand corner of his upper lip. He appeared to be about thirty years old with short dark hair and a tired, worn look about him, like a blade in want of a stone or armor dented from too many blows. His clothes too looked disheveled and haphazard. Trudi imagined that they probably looked that way even before the day's ride.

When he had finished tasting the wine, his eyes opened, and he set the wine cup down. Only then did he turn to look at Trudi. Her sense of danger soared the minute she saw his eyes. He regarded her as one would an object, an object in which one had little interest.

"Who are you?" he asked.

"My name is Trudi."

He waved away her response. "That is a little girl's name, not the name of someone wearing armor. Armor such as that requires a far grander name."

Trudi thought of how Sunni would respond to such a man. She tried to straighten her shoulders. "Hiltrude," she said, looking directly into his eyes. "Hiltrude, daughter of Charles, son of Pippin of Herstal."

For the first time, a glint of emotion touched the man's eyes. Trudi saw a flash of anger in his gaze along with something else, something eager.

"A grander name, indeed," he said.

In her bravest voice, Trudi said, "You have me at a disadvantage."

"Yes. Yes, I do, Hiltrude, daughter of Charles, son of Pippin of Herstal," he said. "I certainly do have you at a disadvantage."

"I meant your name," she said.

"Who was with you at the Knight's Inn?" he asked. "Your father? Was it your religious-fanatic brother, Carloman? Or that son of a bitch, Pippin?"

"It was Pippin," she said.

"And I suppose he has Childebrand with him?"

"My uncle was there as well, yes."

"They'll follow."

"They will," she said, with more confidence than she felt. It unnerved her that he smiled.

"Forgive me for being a terrible host." He leaned forward with a knife to cut the bonds holding her wrists. She began rubbing the life back into them. "You must be thirsty." He poured more wine into his cup and held it out to her. "Tell me, Hiltrude, why do you wear armor? And what were you doing watching the door of the Knight's Inn? That seems hardly the behavior of a lady."

"We were saving six girls from Loivre," Trudi said. As she spoke, her fears dissipated into anger. "They were being raped at the Knight's Inn. Men of arms took them by force from their homes and burnt their village to the ground. The men of the village were gathered together under one roof and burned alive. I saw their bodies. I helped bury them." Trudi looked up into the blank eyes of her captor. "I came to the Knight's Inn to stop the rape. I came to watch those murderers die."

"From the looks of it, you got your wish," her captor said. "I doubt that anyone staying at the Knight's Inn last night saw the break of day. When it comes to violence, your brother is a thorough man, Hiltrude, very thorough. Of course, he was stupid to leave you so unprotected."

"You are Bradius," she said.

He bowed his head.

"Those are your men."

"Those *were* my men," he corrected her. "I hired them in Tours. A bad lot." He shook his head. "I released them from service when I could no longer afford to pay them. They came north. Apparently, to help themselves. When I heard they were in Reims, I came to investigate. As luck would have it, I found you."

"You claim no responsibility for Loivre?"

"Your family absolved me from responsibility well over a year ago." Bradius spat into the fire. "They murdered my family and took away my home, the home my family has held since the days of the Romans. Your brother gave it to one of his men. He took my hands in his and named me his vassal and rode away thinking all debts were paid." Bradius look at Trudi with his blank green eyes. "I can assure you, they are not."

Boniface had hoped to keep at least twelve bishops in Paris for the council with him and Carloman. Twenty had stayed. Among them, many of the leading voices in the Church. They were seated by rank at a long rectangular table—the more powerful bishops at the center of the table, and the less powerful at its ends. An argument had broken out between Bishop Gairhard of Paris and Bishop Aidolf of Auxerre that threatened to distract the council from its purpose.

"Perhaps I'm not the most chaste of bishops," Bishop Gairhard said from the corner of the room. "But at least I'm no hypocrite. How many young peasants have lost their virginity to your monks, Aidolf? How many are here today in your entourage?"

Boniface knew that no one else would stand up to Aidolf of Auxerre. The bishop had responsibility for the monasteries of Orleans, Troyes, Nevers, Avallon, and Tonnerre. He held warrants on the lands of over a hundred nobles and had fighting men in numbers that rivaled Carloman.

"Your charges are baseless, Bishop," Aidolf said in a calm and reasonable voice. "Of course there are monks who stray from their vows. Who among us is not a sinner? I can assure you the monks of Auxerre hold their vows as dearly as do any in this room. Any indiscretions of the sort you describe are merely isolated incidents, unworthy of your attention."

"I have seen it with my own eyes!" Gairhard stood, trembling as he addressed the conclave. He was an older man, stiff with obstinacy. "We preach abstinence. We vow chastity. Yet the monks of Auxerre openly flaunt their sexuality. Two of your men visited our monastery in Paris and sodomized our stable hand. I demand atonement."

Bishop Wido of St. Wandrille stood. A short man with an ugly mole on the side of his face, Wido was across the table from Bishop Aidolf. Wido had been an ally of Charles, and Boniface was relieved at his intercession. Wido folded his hands in prayer and walked to stand beside Bishop Gairhard. Motioning for the elder bishop to bend, Wido whispered into his ear in a low soothing voice.

Gairhard's eyes jumped to Wido's face in surprise, and the color drained from his face. Wido whispered again, and Gairhard abruptly crossed himself and sat down. Wido next moved to Aidolf. Again, whispering in earnest, he drew a nod from the bishop of Auxerre.

Wido turned to face the group. "With the permission of Bishop Aidolf, I have promised Bishop Gairhard that I would personally investigate this matter." Aidolf nodded in assent. "Should there be need of further repentance," Wido continued, "I will ensure, with Bishop Aidolf's assistance, that repentance is made."

Boniface did not wait for further discussion. With a hearty "Let us pray," he ushered Bishop Wido to his seat so that the council could officially get under way.

As one, they turned their attention to Carloman. He stood and outlined his plan to return lands taken by his father in exchange for the Church's spiritual and financial support of the succession. He detailed the number of troops he would need, the amount of treasure and resources, and asked for a public proclamation of their support from their pulpits.

When he finished, no one spoke. Carloman looked to Boniface for support. Clearing his throat, Boniface thought he could strengthen the case for Carloman's demands, but Bishop Aidolf interrupted and spoke first.

"Please recognize, Carloman, that your father had a strained history with the Church." Aidolf waved away the young man's protestations. "Yes, yes, we all remember that he stopped the Saracen in Poitiers many years ago and again these past few months in the south. But he also ruthlessly deposed many of our brethren—some sitting at this very table. He took the Church's lands and its wealth. He bullied our priests. And now that his quest for immortality has failed, you come to our doorstep seeking support.

"It is ironic that the son brings to us the same lands that his father stole, to ask for our assistance in carrying on his legacy." With a smug smile curling the corners of his mouth, Aidolf sat back and motioned for others to comment.

"We've had twenty-five years of this!" began a portly bishop from Rouen at the end of the table. And for over an hour, the prelates rose to tell stories of their abuse by Charles. With each telling, the room grew louder. Boniface feared that the meeting was teetering on disaster. When he tried to interrupt, Aidolf overruled him. The bishop was content to let the group inflate the record to oppose any offer Carloman could make.

As the passion faded from their discussion, Boniface stood to address the group and began to circle the table, touching the shoulders of those seated at the banquet table.

"Yes," he began. "Charles Martel was a brutal man, particularly during those early years when his success was in doubt. And yes, he often rewarded service to his family and friends. But should the sins of the father fall to the son?" Boniface stood behind Carloman. "Here, we have a truly religious knight." He put his hands on Carloman's shoulders. "He wears a relic from St. Martin of Tours close to his heart. His knights have dedicated themselves in the service of our Lord.

"For twenty-five years, we have faulted the father for his treatment of the Church. How can we refuse the son who seeks to make restitution and to beg forgiveness?"

Many of the bishops around the table were nodding in support. Boniface, sensing he had succeeded in swaying the group, called for a vote of support from the conclave.

"There are two issues that remain," Aidolf interjected. "You have asked us to commit to you Church resources, Church wealth, and armed support for your succession. We are inclined to do so. You and your brother Pippin are men of God and were raised as Christians by your mother, Chlotrude." Aidolf frowned. "We are less supportive of your brother Gripho. His mother was pagan. We are concerned that his 'middle kingdom,' as it is being called now in Paris, could be aligned with Alemannia and Bavaria. If he is pagan, it could split the kingdom geographically and religiously.

"We favor Theudoald as mayor in Gripho's place. He is Christian. His claim has legitimacy. Although he opposes the very land policy you have offered us, we see him as less of a threat to the kingdom than your half brother. We will support your succession if you support Theudoald."

Boniface saw Carloman's face redden. The young man placed both hands on the banquet table and rose to his feet. "If I renounce my brother, there will be war. And it won't be small scrapes in the far corners of the kingdom. It will be civil war on a scale that will touch every part of the kingdom." Carloman's punched the table with his fist. "There is no way to avoid it."

"Which brings us to our second issue," Aidolf said. "You must raise a Merovingian to be king. It will quell calls for war and force the factions to petition the new king to resolve grievances. Your family serves as mayor, owing fealty to the king. The current absence of a king begs for war." Aidolf sat back, his eyes on his hands, which formed a steeple in front of him. "Those are our two conditions."

"And if I refuse them?" Carloman asked.

Aidolf shrugged. "Then we, regrettably, cannot accept your offer."

"We will need some time to consider this," Boniface said.

"You may have until the day after next," Aidolf said. "The council will end its deliberations then at sundown."

Trudi couldn't help watching his eyes. So green and so opaque, they were startling to her. But where they had been devoid of feeling earlier, there was now a deep sadness to them that threatened to overwhelm him—a great loss, perhaps. Something else was there as well; resignation, she decided. *Bradius grieves.*

He sat with his back against the tree, drinking his wine. On occasion, he kicked the logs in the fire or added new ones to it. When he finished one wineskin, he opened another. She began to think he had forgotten her. She tried not to move, tried not to draw his attention, tried not to breathe. But her legs began to cramp and soon lost their feeling. She leaned to one side to stretch them. The movement caught his eye. And for a long moment, he stared at her legs, as if waiting for his thoughts to catch up with his eyes. His eyes took the rest of her in slowly, savoring her body the way he savored his wine. When at last his eyes met hers, they had lost their melancholia.

"That's Saracen armor," he said with a slight slur to his words.

"Yes. It is."

"I fought with the Saracen." He looked away. "Against your father at Narbonne. They're a priggish lot, but they fight well." He gestured at her armor. "They would be surprised to see a woman wear those plates."

Trudi did not respond.

Again his eyes stared at her body, and again another long moment passed. He got to his feet, came to where she sat, and squatted down before her. He leaned in, close to her face.

"Take them off," he whispered. His voice was thick, and his eyes clouded. He reeked of wine.

"No," she said with all the courage she could muster

"I don't think you understand your situation." He was definitely slurring. "It is not a request." He drew a knife from his boot. Looking into her eyes, he placed the tip of his knife at the base of her throat. She tried to pull away.

"Don't move," he commanded, taking hold of her hair with his left hand. "One must be careful around such keen objects." With the smallest motion, he flicked the blade gently, and Trudi felt her skin part under its sharpness. A trickle of blood rolled down her chest. Her heart quailed.

"I said, take them off."

She pulled the leather strap holding the armor in place, and it released off her shoulder. His eyes never left hers. She felt them penetrating her courage. She drew the strap across her body and reached for the second clasp below her armpit. When this had been freed, she shrugged her shoulders, and the armor fell off her body like a summer gown.

She trembled, watching him survey her body. His eyes absorbed the outline of her breasts, locked as they were inside her battle leathers. When he looked up into her eyes, she saw the hunger she had seen in Ansel before him. Standing, he used his knife to force her to stand. Stepping away from her, his eyes swept from her feet up to her neckline. Suddenly, a look of confusion crossed his face. His eyes grew wide, focusing on a place just below her neck. Exerting light pressure with his blade, he lifted her chin skyward.

"What is this?" he demanded. With his left hand, he grabbed hold of the amulet Sunni had given her and ripped it from her neck. "Where did you get this?" he asked.

"What do you mean?" Trudi said, beginning to cry.

"This." Bradius shoved the pendant into her face. Anger poured from him. "Where did you get this?" He was shouting.

Trudi wept. "It was a gift."

"It's pagan," he said.

"I know." She cringed from him.

"What are you doing with it?"

"Sunni was teaching me. I am an initiate."

"No!" he cried. "That can't be. No daughter of Charles would be pagan."

"I am *conscious*," she said.

With a guttural cry, he lashed out at her with a backhanded blow. It took her in the face and knocked her from her feet. "This will not deter me," he growled at her. He stood above her, his body taut, his eyes filled with anger and lust. "It's a lie."

Trudi was frantic. She searched her mind, desperately seeking something that would appease him. "What is here is everywhere," she said.

Bradius roared his anger at the heavens. Several men from the nearby campfire scrambled to their feet and rushed to ascend the small hill.

"This is some sort of trick. You can't be pagan. Charles would never allow it."

"He doesn't know," Trudi said. "Sunni guided me in secret."

The men rushed into the firelight, circling the pair and searching for what had caused the alarm.

"Your father drove me from my home because I would not kneel before his cross." Bradius seethed, his eyes wild. "He took everything from me because I am pagan. And now you dare mock me with this?" He threw the pendant to the ground.

"Sunni was pagan," Trudi said, pleading. "Charles accepted her."

"She prostrated herself before his god." Bradius turned on her. "I would not. I rebelled. I took up arms against him. I drove him back. We fought like madmen for days. Good men," he said, sweeping his arm to indicate those standing near him, "came to my aid. When it was clear to Charles that we had won the day, we sued for peace. We begged for tolerance. And then your brother, Carloman—" his emotions choked off his words.

"Your brother arrived with his Knights in Christ," Bradius continued. "They tortured the peasants. They discovered our sacred tree." His eyes welled. "Did Sunni speak of the tree? Did she teach you that it links this life to the one that came before us and the one that comes after?" Bradius turned from her to look into the fire. "We learned that Carloman meant to burn it," he said in a quiet voice. "I split our force in two, leading one half to save the tree. The move exposed us to attack. Your father's column fell on our rear guard like vultures. By the time we reached the sacred tree, it was already destroyed."

Trudi still lay on the ground where she had landed. She sat upright and wiped the blood away from her swollen mouth. Bradius stared into the fire.

"And the other half?" she asked.

Bradius did not answer. "Outnumbered three to one," one of his men offered. "Killed to a man."

"They took my son hostage," Bradius said. "They used him to bring me out of hiding. I came with Auguste." He glanced at the man who had just spoken. "They told me to kneel before their cross. They told me to place my hands between Carloman's." Bradius looked down at his hands. "They bound my son. They beat him. He was so brave." His face twisted in anguish. "I knelt before their cross. I placed my hands in Carloman's. I betrayed my faith and humbled myself to save my son." His voice found an edge. Anger crept back into his face. "And they killed him."

"No!" Trudi shouted at him. "Carloman would never kill a child."

"The boy was thirteen," Auguste said. He put a hand on Bradius's shoulder. "His name was Unum. Roused with youthful anger, he would not suffer his father to shame himself. Though his hands were bound, he cursed your god, spat on Boniface's cross." Auguste spoke as if in a trance. "One of the Knights in Christ, a blond man with cold eyes, drew his sword and, in one stroke, beheaded the boy. His body stood for a time as if nothing had happened. Then the knees buckled, and he fell forward. His head rolled to my feet. His blood covered their cross."

Bradius wept by the fire. He stared into its blaze while tears ran down his cheeks. "In the night, we were rescued. We rode south to join Maurontus and the Saracen. I never got to bury him." With a sigh, he turned to face her. He did not bother to wipe his tears. Trudi wept with him.

When he next spoke, the edge returned to his voice, but with sadness and exhaustion. "So you can see why your presence here offers me such opportunity. I always meant to return you to your father," he said. "But my intention was that he would find you somewhat … damaged."

His eyes held hers, challenging her to denounce him. Then his shoulders slumped, and his head bowed. Bradius sheathed his knife. Turning to Auguste, he said, "Bind her." Looking at Trudi, he said, "Your pendant has saved you tonight, Hiltrude, daughter of Charles. Tomorrow, however, will decide tomorrow."

Sunni's carriage didn't slow down when it passed the entrance to the villa at Quierzy. Gripho laughed as the servants who lined the road watched in confusion as her carriage passed by. Somewhat comically, he bowed to them from his horse, enjoying the baffled looks he received as he and the Bavarian host followed.

Many hours later, they arrived at Laon. Although the defensive fortifications of the ancient Roman city were sound, it was the land that made attacking the city formidable. Laon stood atop a high ridge that looked down over a wide and open plain. The steep incline leading up to the city made attack extremely difficult, if not impossible. The hill was so steep that its one road had to loop back and forth upon itself, repeatedly, to permit ascent.

It took the better part of an hour for them to make the long trek up the road to the city gates. When they arrived, the gates were open, and the compte de Laon stood waiting their arrival. Several dozen Neustrian nobles, grinning broadly, stood with him inside the gates.

Samson scrambled down to place a small step beside Sunni's carriage, and Odilo dismounted to open her door and to offer her his hand as she descended.

"You are most welcome, mistress," the compte said. "All the preparations for the family villa have been made per your instructions. And," he looked to the nobles surrounding him, "your other … guests have arrived as expected."

Sunni swept into the gathering, thanking the compte and allowing him to kiss her hand. She greeted the nobles individually and warmly by name, thanking them for coming to her assistance.

"And the Thuringians?" Sunni asked of the nobles gathered. "Where are the Thuringians?"

"Here, milady!" a shout came from the interior courtyard. A dozen more nobles rode forward and dismounted just inside the gate. A robust man with long gray hair and a sweeping mustache led them. He strode forward with a confident gait, although it was somewhat encumbered by a limp favoring his right leg.

"Heden," Sunni said, hugging the older man. "I knew you would come."

"I wouldn't miss this for the world," the big man said. "I am sorry for your loss, Sunni. I know that you loved him." He motioned two younger boys forward. "You know my sons, Petr and Bart." Gripho estimated that the two boys were twelve and thirteen. The younger of the two, Petr, looked weak.

"Of course," Sunni said, kissing them three times on alternate cheeks. "You both look so much like your mother." At this, all three fell silent. Sunni looked to Heden. "Something happened to Hilda?"

"She took ill," he said. "Couldn't keep down her food. There was nothing anyone could do. We buried her months ago but grieve for her still."

"You poor boys," Sunni said, hugging them. "Well, there's plenty to do here to keep you from your grief. Gripho will see to that." Sunni turned to look to him. Gripho looked away.

Heden next turned to Odilo. "May honor strengthen your sword, Bavarian."

"And may truth guide its way." Odilo bowed in return.

"I suppose all this is your doing," Heden said, clasping his arm.

"Some of it," Odilo said. "Charles's death leaves much to question. I just wanted to help offer a few answers."

"Will you stay here in Laon with us?"

"No," Odilo said. "I'm going to solidify the lands to the east. I want Carloman and Pippin to know that a challenge to Gripho would meet with great resistance."

"Are you sure such a direct confrontation is wise? Carloman won't abide a pagan uprising."

"He'll be alone, Heden. Pippin and Carloman will be alone in a world where every part of the kingdom is a threat. They can't fight us all."

The older man frowned. "Their father certainly did."

Chapter 6

Sunni

The horizon was black. Sunni waited patiently on the villa's broad balcony. Wearing only a long blue robe that fell to the floor, she faced east. A hint of crimson touched the darkness, framing the landforms at the end of the world. With each passing minute, it pushed back the night. Gold followed red, and still Sunni waited. At last, a spear of light crested the horizon and spread across the broad plain below, casting long shadows over the landscape.

From her pocket, Sunni pulled a small bag of herbs, untied the string that cinched it, and dipped in three fingers to draw out a pinch of the crushed leaves. She tossed them over the balcony. A small breeze picked up the herbs and dispersed them into the air below.

"We share in your bounty," she said quietly, "as we share in all life. I bless the earth from which all things come."

Footsteps sounded behind her, and she instinctively clutched the bag to her chest. When she turned, she found Samson shuffling toward her down the length of the balcony. He bowed and looked out over the balcony to the north. The plain spread out below them in breathtaking colors and stark shadows. Gold and red hues splashed green and brown groundcover. The plain was vast and flat and stretched to every horizon.

The only objects to snag the eye were a swath of trees and brush that invaded the valley from the northeast.

"You're late," Sunni said.

"I am." Samson nodded, his white hair tangled and swirling in all directions at once. From his pocket, he produced his own bag of herbs and quickly performed the same ritual that Sunni had just completed.

When he finished, the two watched in silence as the morning sun banished shadows across the valley. Sunni enjoyed being with Samson. He radiated confidence and surety. She would have kept him in service even if he had not been a lore master.

He had revealed his calling to her in Paris several days after Charles's funeral. He was from Alemannia and had spent his life moving from town to town to heal local peasants, divine their future, and teach them the lore of their faith. For the past ten years, he traveled with a sibyl, a female lore master known for her visions and portents.

Two months earlier, they had slaughtered a goat in a foretelling and dipped their hands into the animal's blood to draw the runes of power. The sibyl had recoiled from the liquid as if she touched fire. She shook from head to foot. Then, in the rune stones, they foresaw the death of a Christian king in the west. The sibyl declared that Samson's destiny was linked to the man's widow. The next morning, Samson started his journey west. When he heard of Charles's death, he came to find Sunni.

Samson did not know what kind of help he could offer her. He just insisted that he was destined to be here with her. She had taken him in service and was glad of her decision. Through all the turmoil of the past weeks, he was the one person she knew who didn't have a political or personal agenda. She enjoyed his company. He was comfortable.

A wretched scream startled them from the courtyard below. Sunni's heart leapt, and her face flushed. It was the cry of a woman, wounded and angry. Frantically they searched the shadows. "There!" Sunni barked, pointing out a cat stalking a tall tree in the corner of the courtyard.

Hissing, it arched its back and raced toward the tree. It leapt and scrambled up the trunk, clamoring toward the lowest branch. Its claws scratched furiously against the smooth bark, trying to catch hold. Just as it came near its goal, a flurry of wings descended from the tree to beat the cat around its head and shoulders. The feline lost its grip and fell back to the ground. It let out another wretched scream to match the first they had heard. The bird flew back to its nest, high in the tree, chirping protectively into the morning air over her nestling. The cat renewed its hissing, arched its back, and circled the tree once again.

"An omen," Samson said.

Sunni nodded. "I hate cats."

After a moment, she pointed toward the southwestern horizon of the plain below them. "If Carloman comes, he will come from there. He will bring as many as will follow, thinking to cow us into submission with the size of his host. He will use numbers to hide his fear. He won't be thinking about how to feed so many mouths during a siege."

She shook her head. "Charles would never have allowed Theudoald to bully him. He would never have let his thoughts be guided by the Church. Few people understood that Charles used Boniface as much as the bishop used him. Unfortunately, Carloman believes whatever the man says. In the end, Carloman's religion will blind him. He will tell himself that he is doing the Lord's work."

She sighed again. "If he comes, it will be because he thinks himself weak. He doesn't realize how much power he has."

Heden circled the ancient city atop the ridge. He ordered walls reinforced, holes patched. He had soldiers build pointed impediments outside the walls to slow the advance of attacking troops and had trenches dug on the north side of the walls to trap attackers within arrow range. Inside the walls, he inspected fallback positions and had rocks and tar and buckets of water carried up to stash behind the ramparts. Earlier, he had sent Petr and Bart with Gripho to gather stores from the city to support the newly garrisoned troops. They would need food, water, bandages, but most of all bodies. They needed help to defend the city. Heden had told the boys to bring him as many able-bodied men as they could muster. He sent several soldiers with them to help with the requisition.

His men, along with the Neustrians, drilled in the courtyards, preparing for siege. The women cut up cloth for bandages. They polished armor. The blacksmiths sharpened weapons, and young boys trained to carry water, arrows, and spears up the stairs of the ramparts.

Heden was not surprised Sunni had sent for him. In fact, he had expected as much as soon as he had heard the news about Charles. She would need a champion to protect her son's interests and to lead her allies. She would need someone she could trust. She had many who could fill that role, including Odilo, but she had only one who had been betrothed to her.

It had been many years since Charles had spirited Sunni away from Heden. They had been in love long before the Hammer had fallen on Bavaria. Heden had showered her with gifts, and she delighted in his attentions, always teasing him about his age and stoking his fire with innuendo. Her presence overwhelmed him. He was besotted, unabashedly besotted, and she knew it. He had courted her, wooed her, and won her. Had her cousins not made such a mess of things, Charles would never have intervened, and Sunni would have been his.

While he had understood the political realities at the time, he rebelled against her decision. He ranted at her intransigence and threatened to steal her away in the dead of night. In the end, he could do nothing. Charles had already broken much of his hold on Thuringia, and Heden was impotent against the military strength of the Austrasians. He was also impotent in the face of Sunni's decision to leave him. In the wake of her departure, Heden's life grew very dark.

Returning to his stronghold in Würzburg, Heden let himself be swept into the inertia of his old life. He took a wife, Hilda, a good woman of twenty-five who loved him and bore him two sons. But his affections never matched hers. He kept Sunni's place in his heart, intact, sacred. For years, he spent his days ruling what was left of his native Thuringia, raising his children, caring for his family, and dreaming of a woman he could not have.

One night, Sunni arrived at his palace. Only nineteen and on her way home to Bavaria to visit her family, she asked to spend a few days resting and enjoying his company. She had come alone with a small retinue of soldiers, handmaidens, and one lone priest to see to her "continuing religious instruction."

It was in May on a night of pagan revelry, when fires were lit in the fields and the people combined their fertility with that of the earth. Great poles were sunk into the ground by the fires, and women of childbearing years took hold of ribbons tied to the top of the poles and danced in the firelight. The men danced in the opposite direction in a circle around them, singing a rhythmic chant. As the women circled the pole, their ribbons grew short, and the circle of men closed on them. When at last the ribbons were wound completely around the pole, the women stopped and turned to face the circle of men.

In such a way, they would pair off. If there were more women than men, or men than women, the group would divide in threes to accommodate. All would make a mad dash to the fields within the light of the bonfires to add their fertility to that of the fields. Pagans called this rite "communion," much to the frustration of the Church priests.

Arriving on such a night, Sunni's intentions could not have been more obvious. She was asking to join them at the fires. Although it was rare for a duc and his wife to participate in such ceremonies, it was well regarded among the peasants when they did. Nobles often attended, sometimes to officiate and sometimes to participate, but always disguised by a mask to avoid later questions about progeny. Heden turned to his wife, raising his eyebrows, and waited for her decision.

"It seems we're to make a time of it," Hilda said, smiling as she ushered them into the house. The lone priest followed them into the house with a confused look on his face.

At dinner, Sunni provided Hilda with a small vial for the priest's wine. After he nodded off and was put to bed, the threesome dashed off for the fields. The duc and his lady were robed for the ceremonial benefit of the peasants, and Sunni's face was painted for anonymity.

Sunni danced with the peasant women and reveled in the light of the fire. Heden and Hilda "officiated" over the ceremonies and lit the bonfire to the cheers of the locals. But when the chanting stopped, and the couples moved into the light between the fire and the night, Sunni found Heden and Hilda. She came to them naked, her painted face reflecting the ever-changing firelight. She did not rush to them but luxuriated in the effect she was having on them. When she reached Heden, she took from him his robe and stepped back to look at him in the moonlight. Her hand touched him lightly on the shoulder and traced a line down his chest, across his stomach and down to the hardness between his legs.

Without letting him go, Sunni turned to Hilda and kissed her lightly on the mouth. She kissed her again, this time hungrily, and the two Thuringians folded Sunni between them, losing themselves in her passion.

She never again returned to Thuringia. But that one time had been enough for Heden. He kept the joy of that night in his heart and lived for years in the comfort of his family's arms.

When it came, Hilda's death hurt him terribly. He wept when he closed and kissed her eyelids. He wept as her body was lowered into the ground. And although his boys needed a father then, more than ever, Heden lost himself in the blackness of his mind and mourned the passing of his second great love. He drank. He ignored his children. He ignored his duties.

The darkness kept him until the news of Charles's death woke him from his melancholia. Looking into the mirror, he saw a shadow of his former self. He bathed, shaved his beard, combed his great mustache, ate a great meal, and went to find his children. Days later, word came from Sunnichild. "Meet me in Laon," was all the message had said. Heden donned his armor.

Now he stood on the battlements filled with purpose. His blood quickened in anticipation of battle, and his heart pounded at the thought of Sunnichild. The puissance of life had returned to him tenfold. And as with all men afforded a second chance, he had the vigor of a man half his age. He lorded over preparations for the siege, whipping the ancient city into readiness. *Let Charles's whelp show his face here,* Heden thought. *I won't let her go again.*

When Heden had ordered him to go with Bart and a troop of soldiers into the city to requisition men and supplies, Gripho bridled at the command. He didn't like taking orders from Heden. And he didn't like his mother deferring to the old bastard either. *Am I not the mayor? Shouldn't I be in command?* Yet he accepted the role eagerly. *At least I get to do something important.*

If asked, everyone in Laon would acknowledge Gripho's title, yet the power of the office eluded him. Even the Bavarian nobles who supported him deferred to Heden when it came to defending the city. Gripho wanted to *stab* someone. At least he could lord it over Bart and Petr. Whatever indignities he suffered at Heden's hand, Gripho would redouble on the man's children. *That* gave him some solace.

But he had to admit that he liked Bart. The boy would be a good lieutenant and, once his father was out of the way, a valuable ally. But the younger brother, Petr, was a weakling. That one would be more comfortable hiding behind a woman's skirts than riding with men into battle.

Gripho led the men into the city, barking orders and admonishing the men to look sharp. He enjoyed being in command. It was a job he felt born to do. He took them into a broad square in the oldest and most affluent part of the city. Large homes, some two stories high, surrounded a well-kept park on three sides of the square. A large church and its cemetery occupied the fourth. Bells were ringing the hour, and Gripho noted the late-arriving parishioners making their way through the large open doors of the church.

"Hah!" Gripho kicked his horse. "I think we've just found a whole troop."

He led the soldiers to the front of the church and urged his horse up the short flight of steps to its doors. Although an acolyte had begun to close them, the boy stopped when he saw Gripho's approach. Gripho rode past him and into the church. The rest of the men on horseback followed.

Gripho made his way to the altar where a furious priest awaited him.

"How dare you defile a house of God!" the priest demanded. "We have begun His holy mass."

Without so much as a glance, Gripho turned his horse and his back on the man to address the congregation.

"All able-bodied men present will come with me at once."

Some rose to their feet. "Where are you taking us?" one asked.

"Just get in line," Gripho said.

A man bolted for the door only to face drawn swords. The priest stormed in front of Gripho, grabbing the reins of his horse.

"Take your men from here at once. You will not interrupt the holy mass."

Gripho signaled for the men in the congregation to continue and leaned down to address the priest. A knife appeared in his hand, and it went to the priest's throat. "Do you know me?"

The priest's eyes grew wide at the blade.

"Do you know me?" Gripho insisted. The priest hesitated, clearly not knowing.

"I am mayor," Gripho said. "Never tell me what to do, priest. I am sick of you robe-wearers thinking you serve a higher power. I am the higher power. I am the law. Never make that mistake again." He put away his knife. "Let's move along there," he called to the men in the congregation. A well-dressed man near the front of the congregation was trying to say good-bye to his wife. He put a fat purse in her hands and gave her instructions about their house. "Now!" Gripho interrupted them. The man scrambled for the line.

As the two-dozen men filed from the church in two lines, flanked by riders on either side, Gripho followed them out, thinking how much he liked being in command.

"Devil!" the priest shouted after him.

Gripho turned his horse to look back at the priest and smiled.

Heden has done well, Sunni thought as she finished making a tour of the battlements. She was amazed at the progress he had made in preparing for the siege. Approaches to the city were blocked, battlements fortified, troops garrisoned, and stores stored. She hoped that it all would prove unnecessary but was impressed that Heden was so well prepared.

She found him on a rampart with Odilo, looking down over the plain. A map drawn on sheepskin lay unfurled between them. They nodded to her briefly and returned their attention to the map.

"I've already sent sorties to requisition food here, here, and here," Heden said, pointing. "Carloman won't find an egg within a day's ride."

"How about the cattle?" Odilo asked.

"They should start arriving here during the next two days." Heden smiled. "Although I must say, I've become quite unpopular among the local population."

"And the wells?"

"It's too early to poison them. We'll wait until our scouts bring word of his army. We don't even know if Carloman is definitely coming."

"Oh, he's coming," Sunni said.

"You have word?" Odilo asked.

Sunni kissed her uncle on the cheek. "None," she said. After an exchange of looks, Sunni added, "I've heard nothing about Trudi either."

"You've done well, old man," Odilo told Heden. Heden bowed to acknowledge the compliment.

"How long can you stay?" Sunni asked.

"I must leave," Odilo answered. "I've sent word to the Frisians and the Alemannians. If Carloman does war against Gripho, there must be a response."

"Your presence here would be significant," Heden said.

"We'd just be more mouths to feed." Odilo smiled, clapping Heden's shoulder. "You have more than you need to defend Laon. What you need is a diversion. If the rest of the kingdom rebels, Carloman can't sit here in siege for long. He'll have to respond."

"I hope you're right," Sunni said. "Everything hangs in the balance."

"Milady?" a voice called from the bottom of the stairs. "Milady!"

The disheveled head of the compte de Laon appeared on the stairs and was quickly followed by the rest of him. He was a plump man with large jowls and a puffy face. Although slightly out of breath, he quickly straightened his coat to restore a modest degree of dignity. He bowed to Odilo and then to Heden before continuing.

"My good Compte," Sunni said.

"Milady, this situation is growing intolerable," the compte said. "When I welcomed you to Laon, I had no idea that this, this foreigner would be commanding my troops and taking control of my city. We have citizens being conscripted into service, and the surrounding towns and villages stripped of their cattle and food stores. These people won't have enough food to survive the winter."

"My good Compte," Sunni interrupted, in an effort to placate the man. But once started, the compte would not be so easily deterred.

"Your man here," he indicated Heden, "has turned the city into an armed camp. He has put in place curfews, limited merchants' ability to sell their wares, and displaced families from their homes to house his soldiers. Are we at war? If so, the news hasn't reached my ears."

"No war has been declared, Compte," Sunni said. "However, the risk of one is very high. My apologies for involving your fair city in this, but the die is cast. Our success is now your success. If Carloman breaks with my son over his rights to succeed their father, we could be under siege within a week." Sunni's eyes bored into the red-faced compte. "Have you ever lived through a siege?"

The compte shook his head.

"This man has." She indicated Heden. "And you would do well to support him in his preparations."

Heden described for the compte the rigorous steps necessary for defending the city: the storage and rationing of food and supplies inside the walls; the spoiling of resources Carloman might find outside them; the spikes outside the gates to slow Carloman's attack, the archers on the wall to thin his ranks, and for close-in work, the burning tar, cinders, and rocks needed to pour over the walls.

As Heden spoke, the price of defending Gripho's claim came to life around her. Sunni saw hundreds dying of hunger and disease behind blockaded walls as catapults and rock-throwers pummeled Laon's defenses. She saw the walls breached and thousands more slaughtered in relentless attacks to take the city, bodies heaped outside the wall as defenders poured flaming pitch and cinders over the ramparts. She paled at the cost.

"Once into the breach, there is no way back," Heden was saying. "You either win or die. The fighting is ferocious. Men who survive—they rape, kill, and steal without remorse. No one is spared. Carloman will wait for a day or two, to ensure the appetites of his men are sated, and then enter the city to restore order." Heden looked at the compte with deadly serious eyes. "That's what you should be worrying about, Compte."

The compte's face flushed.

"Can't you just fight him?" he asked.

"No," Sunni said. "He has too many men. Our best bet is to stay here."

The compte stared out onto the plain below them and took a long moment to gather his composure. He straightened his coat and faced Sunni squarely.

"Although it has been many years, milady, I am no stranger to combat. I fought with Charles against Ragomfred. My brother was killed at Charles's side. I know the costs of war. But I beg you to reconsider, milady. This fight is between you and Carloman. Leave the people of this city out of it. The cost to them will be high whether you win or lose. There must be a way to negotiate."

Sunni looked to him with compassion. Perhaps it was because he was Bertrada's father, and she knew she had put him in a delicate position. No one knew where Pippin stood. But she had heard the truth in his words. "If there is, I will find it," she said. "But until then, I must have your help and support."

"I am sworn by your late husband to protect these people. I will honor my pledge. You will have whatever support I can find."

"I understand there has been some resistance to our requests for men," Heden said.

"Perhaps if you didn't send armed men into church during mass to conscript soldiers, you might find less resistance" replied the compte.

Sunni raised an eyebrow.

"No offense, milady," the compte continued, "but your son has made a habit of impressing men during mass. Our priest has taken great offense to his violation of the church's sanctity."

"I can assure you that such behavior will stop," she said.

"Thank you, milady."

"Is there anything else?"

"Yes, I believe there is," the compte said, turning to Heden. "If there is to be a siege, might we not evacuate the women and young children? It would cut down on the number of mouths to feed."

"I agree. The elderly and sick can go too," Sunni said.

"I will send word about time and place," Heden said, frowning. "All departures must be orderly and controlled. I will not tolerate panic. No able men will be allowed to leave, and no one will take their belongings or food. My men will inspect everyone leaving. You will have two days. No more."

The compte bowed and turned to go. Just as his head was about to disappear down the stairs, he turned to address Sunni one more time.

"Milady, for the sake of us all, if there is a way to avoid this siege, I beg that you find it."

"You have my word," Sunni said.

With a quick nod to Heden and Odilo, he turned and disappeared down the stairs.

"I'd watch that one," Odilo said.

She nodded but thought he might be the only sane one among them.

Father Martin genuflected before the tabernacle and hurriedly touched his right fingertips to his forehead, his sternum, and his two shoulders. Muttering to himself, he made his way to the confessional at the back of the church. While serving under Monsignor Beaulieu had its merits, the sacrament of confession was not one of them. The monsignor had made it clear from the beginning that he refused to hear confession, leaving it to Father Martin to carry twice the load. Father Martin hated confession.

Listening to one parishioner after another recount one sin after another had become an unholy burden to him.

At first, he had enjoyed the discreet window into the souls of his congregation. Knowing their secrets, knowing their lusts and lies, had a euphoric effect on him. He had felt powerful for the first time in his life. But the feeling of power soon gave way to the burden of responsibility for those secrets. And the burden eventually gave way to the boredom at their repetition. One lust led to another as surely as one lie spawned a second. He hated his parishioners' pettiness. He hated their greed. Most of all, he hated the never-ending repetition. No matter how many times he had counseled repentance and been reassured that they would not sin again, they always did. No wonder that Monsignor Beaulieu avoided the duty.

A line of parishioners wound its way from the confessional along the far wall of the church, down to the fourth station of the cross. It was far more people than he expected for the middle of the week. Typically he would have seven or eight parishioners. There must have been thirty or more lining the wall, clutching rosary beads, and mumbling their Hail Marys. He hadn't noticed that they all were women until he opened the confessional door. Looking from face to face along the line, he saw that they were, to a person, afraid.

"What is going on here?" he asked an old woman who stood first in line. "What has happened?"

"They're taking out the women and children," the woman said. She was heavily wrinkled and had but three teeth in the front of her mouth. "For the siege, Father. We're leaving, come morning. The men, they're staying."

A chill ran down Father Martin's spine. He had heard talk about a siege when he went to complain about the interruption of his mass. He had discounted it as rumor, of course. Civil war in Neustria had been unknown for over a generation. It was a thing of the past. Everyone said so. Besides, the succession had gone smoothly. Charles had three sons. The kingdom had been divided and the nobles pledged. What could cause a civil war? Father Martin could think of no good reason. Yet if they were evacuating the people …

He had been horrified to learn that the knight who had invaded his church had indeed been one of Charles's sons, the "boy mayor." He could still see the malevolence in the young man's eyes. They held no fear, no remorse. It was as if he enjoyed the confrontation. A trickle of sweat ran down the back of Father Martin's neck.

He was desperate to ask what the old woman knew about the evacuation plans. Were priests to be included? He prayed it would be so. Maybe he could offer to minister to those being relocated? He would ask the monsignor. He knew he should be reassuring his frightened parishioners, but all he could manage at the time was a thin smile for their benefit. He tried to hide the slight tremble in his hands by putting them behind his back.

Muttering something about the evacuation being "a precaution," he opened the door to the confessional and entered the small chamber the monsignor called "the box." He sat heavily on the wooden seat built into the back of the confessional, leaned forward, and pulled open the small window to the compartment next to him. He placed his head in his hand and sighed.

"Yes, my child," he said.

"Bless me, Father, for I have sinned," the supplicant, said. "It has been three days since my last confession."

A loud crash interrupted them. It sounded like the huge oak door of the church had fallen off its hinges. Father Martin could hear a flurry of movement and gasps outside the confessional box. He started to excuse himself so that he could go investigate when a second crash sounded. Father Martin stood and reached for the door.

"Priest!" a harsh and threatening voice called. "Prieeeeesst!"

Father Martin's hand froze at the door. He knew that voice. It had haunted him since the day the boy mayor had entered his church on horseback.

"Where are you, priest?"

Father Martin could hear his parishioners scurrying away from the confessional. He could hear Gripho's steps drawing near. Father Martin's hand started to shake. He began to pray. *Hail Mary, full of grace, the Lord is with thee. Blessed art thou amongst women, and blessed is the fruit of thy womb, Jesus.*

The head of an ax splintered through the door of the confessional inches from his face. Father Martin stared at the curved edge of the ax dumbly as if its presence made no sense. The ax head twisted in the door and disappeared. Father Martin peered through the crack only to see the ax fall again. He jumped to the back of the confessional just before the door exploded.

"There you are," Gripho said. His features were young, and his frame was short, but the boy's body was massive. With one hand, he grabbed Father Martin by the collar and dragged him out of the confessional. The priest scrambled to gain his feet, but the young knight's grip held him down. He was being dragged to the front to the church. Once there, the boy mayor dropped him at the foot of the altar.

"No, please," the priest whimpered, hiding his face. "Please."

Gripho kicked him in the head. The blow caught him on the temple, and bright flashes crowded Father Martin's sight. When they disappeared, the priest found himself staring up the length of a long blade. Its point rested against the soft spot at the base of his neck. He started to cry.

"Shut up, priest," the boy mayor said. "Did I not say that I am the law? Did you think that running to that pitiful Compte de Laon could protect you from me?" He let the weight of the blade sink into the soft flesh of Father Martin's neck. The priest felt the tip of the blade puncture his skin, and his bowels released. A moment later, he fainted.

When he awoke, Gripho was gone. Lying back against the cool of the floor, Father Martin thanked God for his life. He touched the place on his neck were the sword had cut him. Although his fingers came away with blood, he knew he was not seriously injured. Gripho had only meant to frighten him.

Father Martin decided to speak to Monsignor Beaulieu about ministering to those being evacuated. The thought of being imprisoned inside a city under siege with that monster was more than he could take. He would have to find a way to leave.

Struggling to his feet, he found the church empty. He was relieved that no one had witnessed his humiliation. The smell of his own waste assaulted his nostrils. Disgusted, he turned toward the door that led to the sacristy. It wasn't until he reached the door that he also smelled smoke. It was a subtle smell. He almost hadn't caught it.

Frantically, he searched for its source. He found his answer behind him on the altar. A lit candle lay on its side, fueling flames that rose lazily from the altar cloth. They rolled along the length of the altar and licked the wooden reredos that rose behind it. The flames began to curl through its ornate, hand-chiseled wood lattice, surrounding the cross and the statues of the Virgin Mary and Michael the Archangel in halos of flame.

Father Martin began to panic. *The Holy Eucharist!* Already transformed into the body of Christ, he could not let it burn. He ran to the altar, fumbling for the key to the tabernacle. Ignoring the flames around him, he inserted the key into the latch that locked the two small wooden doors housing the Eucharist. Springing the lock, he threw open the doors and thrust both hands into the dark enclosure.

He found the chalice that held the Eucharist, just as the flames leapt to the sleeves of his cassock. In a second, both were aflame. Screaming, he reeled backward, holding the chalice aloft. The flames flew up his arms until they engulfed his hands and swirled around the chalice. He stared at his arms in disbelief. Despite his pain, he was transfixed. A sign from God. He was sure of it.

He heard a gust of wind blowing next to him and turned to see the entire reredos plume into flame. In seconds, it spread to the wall and up to the ceiling. The church was on fire. Father Martin did the only thing he could think to do. He ran.

Buried in her maps, Sunni barely heard the knock at her door.

"Come in," she called without looking up.

The commotion at the door, however, required her attention. Standing, she investigated and found the door partially open with only a man's buttocks backing their way into her chamber. *Fortunately,* she thought to herself, *he's fully clothed.*

When she opened the door wide to reveal the buttocks' owner, he had turned. Now the doorway was filled with pigeons. Dozens housed in four or five containers cooed and fluttered in discordant pandemonium. Sunni stepped back. The man straightened. She finally recognized her mystery visitor. It was Odilo.

"Forgive me, Sunni, but I was hoping you would keep these for me," her uncle said. "It's only for a little while, and they are really no trouble at all. You just have to feed them."

Carrier pigeons! Sunni thought.

Without invitation, Odilo strode through her chambers, carrying the flapping cages out onto her balcony. "I brought them along for Gripho's elevation," he said, lining them up along the wall. "I assumed I would be gone for a while but now believe you will have greater use for them."

Sunni noticed that each cage was marked with a different colored ribbon. Odilo fussed with their organization so that every cage could be easily accessed. Once satisfied that all was in order, he returned to Sunni to greet her more properly.

She kissed him three times on alternate cheeks and laughed at his ever-present grin. "I don't know if we can feed them," Sunni countered. "We are, after all, expecting a siege."

Odilo responded by producing a large bag of seed that he handed to her. This was followed by a number of tiny canisters meant for attaching to the legs of the pigeons. Looking up, his face sobered.

"The white cage," he said, "is for keeping in touch. There are six birds. I will send them back with news from Bavaria so you will never run out. The blue cage is to announce Carloman's arrival. Those birds already have canisters attached to their legs and messages already written. Release all the birds at once. The same is true for the green cage. But only release these if Carloman leaves. The red cage signals that Carloman has breached the wall, and defeat is imminent. Again, release all the birds at once. Their messages are already written.

"Use the white cage birds to provide details, if you have time."

Sunni looked perplexed. "Why different cages?"

"The white cage is for me. The others are for our allies. If Carloman declares war, this is the fastest way to inform the rest of the kingdom and mobilize a response. Carloman won't be able to maintain a siege if everyone else rebels."

"Unless we accidentally burn down the city."

"Yes, avoiding that would help." Odilo cleared his throat. "What did Gripho say about the priest's charges?"

"It was the same priest who went to the compte about Gripho earlier this week. Gripho said that he wanted to teach the priest a lesson but only threatened him. He claimed the priest fainted so quickly that it was pointless. Gripho left. He said the church was intact at that point."

"You should let your son know we don't need anymore 'lessons,'" Odilo said.

"Believe me, I have." She shook her head, exasperated. Looking up at Odilo, Sunni asked, "How can I convince you to stay?"

"You can't. I must go, or there won't be an eastern front. I would also like to see if I can find word of Trudi. I was upset that she hadn't reappeared by the time we left."

"If she is with Pippin, I'm sure she is safe."

"I hope so." Odilo's face turned dour.

"Exactly what are your intentions for her?" Sunni asked. "She is betrothed to Aistulf. When she returns, Carloman will pack her up and send her off with him and King Liutbrand."

Her uncle seemed to wrestle with this. His casual manner was replaced by one more urgent and intense. He started to respond to her question twice, but each time checked his words.

"I didn't expect this," he said, "and I'm not really sure how it happened. I was intrigued by the politics of such a marriage. She is a unique girl. And I'm not some foolish boy who gets swept away by a woman simply because she throws me a smile. Yet, for some reason, I cannot stand the thought of her marrying Aistulf. I cannot stand the thought of her being with anyone at all." He looked exasperated. "Were this a different time ...," he started. "I'm not even sure how she feels."

"What will you do if you find her?" Sunni asked.

"I'll ask her to go with me," he said.

"Will you marry her?" Sunni's voice was almost a whisper.

Odilo nodded, as if to himself.

Sunni took Odilo in her arms and hugged him to her chest. Looking up into his face, she smiled a broad beatific smile. "She will be a lovely bride," she said. "And you will have beautiful children."

Odilo laughed. "All mothers are the same," he said.

"What will you do about Pippin?"

Odilo looked at her questioningly.

"Pippin's not going to let her leave with you," Sunni said. "And both of them will want to come back to mourn their father. If Trudi returns to Paris, she'll leave with Aistulf, not you. If you find her, you'll need to take her from Pippin."

Odilo nodded.

Sunni laughed. "I'm not sure which of us has the easier task."

"Speaking of love," Odilo said with a glint in his eye. "What are your intentions with Heden? That mustachioed man seems to have quite a bounce to his step."

Sunni reddened and then laughed some more. "Oh, I don't know, Odilo." She laid her head on his shoulder. "I was so young then."

"He wants to be more than your champion," Odilo said.

"Yes, yes, I know." She sighed. "He has already pressed his advantage."

Odilo raised his eyebrows.

"It was nothing." Seeing the doubt on his face, she added, "It's a long story."

He raised his eyebrows further.

"Stop it." Sunni laughed, shoving him with her hand.

"Sounds like you are under siege both inside the city walls and out." Odilo chuckled. "Be careful, niece," he warned.

Sunni's face sobered. "Will you return to aid us?"

Odilo shook his head. "It's a long way to Regensburg. And bringing our armies this far west would leave us vulnerable. We do better by giving him reason to abandon the siege and come east where he will have to fight a growing rebellion. I would prefer to fight on our ground." He kissed her lightly on the forehead. "I'm sorry, Sunni. But you and Heden are on your own."

It was already late when Samson snapped the neck of the chicken and let it run around the courtyard, its head flopping from side to side. Children doing chores nearby stopped to point at the dangling head and laughed when the bird ran toward them. They scattered before its random fury, howling when it chased the littlest boy. When the fowl finally collapsed, Samson grabbed its legs and stuffed it into a large sack.

Making his way to the western end of Laon, Samson passed the ancient walls that had once fortified the city. The walls had been extended to enclose fields and pasture so they could prolong its food stores during a siege. Using a shoulder-high walking stick covered in runes, Samson followed the old wall north until he found the footpath Sunni had described to him. He took the path west and then north again to a pasture that sat high on a plateau.

Sunni, Gripho, and Heden waited for him there with three soldiers. They stood at the center of the field on a broad flat stone that was blackened from many fires. Samson nodded to Sunni and smiled.

"The rite is held here?"

"Yes," Sunni said. "That is what I have been told."

"Small to hold a fire," he said.

"They would try to be discreet."

Samson frowned. Handing Sunni his staff, he paced off the stone by length and by width, three paces by three. He shooed his companions off the stone, stood at its center, and faced east and then north. He shook his head as if disappointed. Then he began to pace again, but this time away from the stone to the north.

"Is something wrong?" Heden asked.

Samson stopped, kicked the turf two or three times with his toe, and smiled. "Shovels," he said.

Heden dispatched his soldiers for shovels, and when they returned, Samson set them to digging into the soft ground that surrounded the stone. Each blade sank just a knuckle into the turf before it hit stone. Samson urged them on. One by one, the soldiers unearthed eight large square stones of equal size. They surrounded the one on which Samson stood. Together, they formed a grid of nine, three rows of three. The center stone, the one blackened by fire, was slightly raised in comparison to the others.

"Better," Samson said, satisfied. "Better."

Sunni too was smiling. "A rune square," she said. Heden nodded.

Samson stood on the center stone. "The stones are of the Eternal Ones," he declared, his voice resonating with authority. "To Wilbet belong the first three." He pointed to the northernmost row. "There the future will be." With a wave of his hand, he indicated the second row. "To Barbet belong the second three. There the present be." He gestured behind him. "To Einbet belong the last. There what lies is past."

As the sun began to descend over the city to their west, Samson instructed the soldiers to build a small fire on the northern edge of the center stone. Stepping back to the last row, he began to empty the contents of his large sack.

He produced a large wooden bowl, which he set upon the stone. Next he withdrew the chicken carcass and a knife. With a swift but sure stroke, he severed the chicken's head from its body and cast it aside. He held it up by its legs until its blood filled the bowl at his feet. The sweet, pungent smell of fresh blood mingled with the smoke of the lit kindling. Discarding the carcass, he reached again into his sack for a large bag of stones and an ox pelt. Stepping forward to the center square, he unfurled the ox pelt. A painted version of the same nine-square rune grid filled the skin. This he placed at the center of the stone. He next positioned Sunni to the east of the grid, Gripho to the north, and Heden to the west.

Facing the fire and Gripho, Samson sat cross-legged before the pelt and set the bag of stones beside him. From his belt he took a twig with dried leaves, which he lit from the fire. He brought the smoldering leaves toward him, surrounding his face in smoke. He inhaled deeply several times and then cast the twig into the fire. The smoke seemed to swirl through him, lifting above the nine squares.

Closing his eyes, he began to hum, his upper body swaying before the fire. He circled one way for several minutes before retracing his path for several minutes more. The moment the sun touched the western horizon,

Samson stopped. Without opening his eyes, he lifted the bag of stones, opened it, and cast its contents behind his back.

Each of the twenty-four smooth, water-worn stones had a rune painted on its face. Reaching behind him, Samson found one stone after another. Each stone he touched, he placed on the grid before him. When the grid was complete, he collected the unused stones and returned to Sunni to retrieve his walking stick. Holding it at arm's length before him, he walked to the bowl of blood and dipped his staff in it. On each of the nine great stones, he traced the same rune that was placed on the rune grid before the fire. The last to be drawn was the center stone.

He touched the edge of his staff to the flames of the fire and in a soft voice intoned, "The Eternal Sisters have spoken. He pointed his staff to each of the three stones behind him, the stones of the past. "Einbet calls 'Ansuz, Sowulo, Ken,' naming Yggdrasil, the sacred Ash, the Tree of Life. Our link to the other worlds is strong, giving us strength to overcome our trials."

He pointed to the second row, the stones of the present. "Barbet calls 'Jera, Raidho, and Thurisaz,' naming JorTh, the earth. Our presence here is favored but is not in harmony with the world. The course of events cannot be changed."

He tapped the final three stones, those of the future. "Wilbet calls 'Uruz, Naudhiz, Hagalazm,' naming strength, adversity, delay. Our path, though strong, will be waylaid. So the sisters speak."

Samson slumped against his staff. Sunni moved to help him. Heden followed. Gripho stood alone, still to the north of the rune grid, hands on hips. "What does that mean?" he demanded. No one acknowledged his question. Sunni and Heden tried to make the lore master sit, but he insisted that he must leave the stones. They helped him to the grass where he sat on a nearby stump.

"What does it mean?" Gripho repeated. He rushed to the old man and leaned into his face. "The course of events cannot be changed? Our path will be waylaid? Waylaid by whom?"

"Gripho," Sunni cautioned.

"I need to know!" he shouted. "Tell me, old man. How is our path waylaid?"

Exhausted, Samson looked up into the boy's eyes. "Betrayal," he said distinctly. "You will be betrayed."

"Who?" Gripho shook Samson by the shoulders. "Who will betray me?"

Samson shrugged as the sun lost its last light in the west. "Your past," he said.

CHAPTER 7

Carloman

"*Fiat voluntas tua sicut in caelo et in terra.*" Kneeling beside the bed, Carloman took his face in his hands and tried to block out the day through prayer. Unconsciously, he used the heel of his palms to rub the weariness from his eyes. The pressure caused his sinuses to run. A familiar trickle of mucus ran down his right nostril and onto his upper lip. Fumbling for a handkerchief, he tried to sustain his concentration. "*Panem nostrum quotidianum da nobis hodie.*"

Boniface had used his influence with the bishops to purchase another three days, but they had found no alternative to the ultimatum given by the council of bishops. In less than two days, Carloman had to decide if he would make war on his brother Gripho. The idea appalled him. "*Dimitte nobis debita nostra …*"

"I have had the most frustrating day," Greta said, striding into their bedchamber. She swept past Carloman's kneeling form and dropped into a chair before her table, the one filled with creams, lotions, powders, and brushes. At twenty-five, Greta had no need for such accouterments. Yet she spent most evenings primping before the large mirror on the wall.

"First, that *vache* Eileen had the nerve to suggest that her son was 'clearly' the best warrior his age. She acted as if Drogo wasn't even a consideration—"

"*... sicut et nos dimittimus debitoribus nostris ...*"

"She said he had won every competition for sword and ax. Is that true? Carloman?" After a moment, Greta shrugged off his silence and began brushing her long blonde hair. "Then Jeanine promised Hélène that we would attend her social gathering tomorrow night. I just couldn't turn her down, Carloman. I know you find the Lady Hélène a bit strange, but I really think it would be good for us to go out. You've been so absorbed with your 'succession,'" she said, imitating his voice and rolling her eyes. "I hardly get to see you anymore."

"*Et ne nos inducas in tentationem ...*"

"Most of the court will be there. But it's to be very informal. Without Sunni or Gripho or Pippin or Trudi, we're all the family that's left. That is, unless you count Theudoald, of course. So, you see, we really have to go."

"*Sed libera nos a malo. Amen.*"

Crossing himself, Carloman glared at the mirrored image of his wife. "I was praying," he said.

She continued to brush her hair. "You're always praying. If I had to wait until you were finished praying every night, we'd never have a conversation."

"That wasn't conversation. It was a monologue."

"No, dear," she said. "I just filled in your parts. Someone has to."

"I was talking *to God.*"

"Oh, and was *He* listening?"

"Damn it, woman!"

"Don't be so dramatic," she said without looking up. "You spend far too much time on your knees, Carloman. You won't find Theudoald waiting for God to give him answers."

"What did you say?"

"Don't look so shocked. He's a man who knows what he wants. Everyone's been talking about him."

"And just what has he ever done to deserve such talk?"

"They say he was born to be mayor. They say he's a different kind of leader. One who leads with ideas, not threats."

"They're forgetting Gripho."

"They think you've already decided against him. Theudoald acts as if your decision has already been made. Most of the Neustrians are beginning to believe him too."

"And what do they have to say about me?" Carloman asked.

"The Church crowd is happy." Greta applied lotion to her hands. "Everyone else is waiting."

"Waiting for what?"

"Waiting to see if you're Charles's son," she said. "They were afraid of Charles. They don't seem to be afraid of you. It's time to get off your knees, Carloman. You are nearly thirty. Decide who will be mayor. Lead."

"It's not so simple. I won't condemn us to war so easily."

"There will be war either way."

"But if I renounce Gripho's succession, I renounce mine as well. And if I do that, Theudoald, as well as every noble in the Frankish Kingdom, is open to challenge my claim. I'll be fighting for the next twenty years, just as Charles did."

"Unless you and Theudoald strike a bargain to divide the kingdom."

"I'd never trust him. Once the damage was done, I'd be at a permanent disadvantage."

"Assurances could be made."

"Why are you so strongly for Theudoald?" Carloman asked. "I always thought you were close to Sunni."

"What happens after you're gone, Carloman? What happens if you split the kingdom as Charles has split it? Austrasia and Neustria will be divided into pieces, and Gripho will have the heart of the kingdom. I can't imagine that the Neustrians will accept that. The moment you are gone, Drogo will be forced to fight Theudoald's family all over again, and he won't have the army you have to survive such a challenge. And you can be damn sure that Drogo's Uncle Gripho won't come to his aid. If you don't redistribute the kingdom to keep Neustria and Austrasia intact, you're simply leaving the battle for your son to fight."

"So you think I should just declare for Theudoald?"

Greta nodded her head. "I'm just repeating what everyone else is saying."

"Well, stop it." Carloman began to pace. He could not stand the thought of Theudoald being mayor of Neustria. The man was an ass. Carloman hated his lace collars and lace cuffs. Carloman hated his presumption. He hated the condescending airs and affected manners. He had been stunned by the support the nobles had shown Theudoald so far. Theudoald had never joined them on campaign, had never once defended the kingdom. Now the Church was supporting Theudoald. It was a slap to his father's face. It was a slap to his.

"You know, he's really not so bad," Greta said.

"Who?"

"Theudoald. He is very well educated. Distinguished, gray hair. He writes. He speaks several languages."

"You've spoken with him?"

"It's hard not to. He's everywhere I go. And he is very good looking."

"Are you in jest? If you are seen with him, the court will think you are my intermediary. It's no wonder that the nobles believe it is already decided."

"That's ridiculous, Carloman. This isn't my doing."

"He will not be mayor." Carloman seethed. "He will not." He slapped the table. Vessels with lotions and creams lifted off its thin wooden top and came down again with a clatter.

Greta rose from the table, straightened the collar on his robe. Her touch reassured him. "I'm sorry, love," she said.

His anger, however, wouldn't abate. "If I pick Gripho, there will be fighting right here in the streets of Paris. And I'm not sure that I'll have the resources to defeat Theudoald. If I pick Theudoald, I'll have the treasure, but there will be civil war from one end of the kingdom to the other."

Greta started to kiss him softly and repeatedly on his cheek and neck.

"The man's a buffoon," Carloman said. "I cannot believe he has such support."

"It is his hair," Greta said into his neck. "He has nice hair."

"Do you mock me?" Carloman grabbed her by the arms and shook her. Her cheeks blotched red. Carloman was surprised at the sense of satisfaction this gave him. He wondered what had made him want to wound her pride so. She looked up into his eyes for a long moment and then sighed. She crossed the room, found a flagon of wine, and returned with a goblet for him.

"I'm sorry, love," she said. "I should have left you to your prayers. It's just that … I've been so alone these last days."

Carloman struggled to comprehend.

"Sunni's gone, so is Bertrada, so are Pippin and Gripho and Charles," she said. "And you are either preoccupied by Boniface or your prayers. There's been little room left for me."

He stood before her, wondering how he had gotten so angry and why it had left him so quickly. A gap now stood between them.

"I'm sorry too," he said. "I shouldn't have gotten so angry. I'll go to Hélène's 'gathering.' But I'm not interested in Eileen's assessment of Drogo's skills with a sword."

"I knew you were listening," she said, hugging him. When she let him go, she stayed in his arms and playfully pressed her body against him. He put his arms around her, and she kissed him on the lips, and her eyelids lowered. When she spoke, her voice was low and whispery.

"You *were* getting ready for bed, weren't you?"

Startled by her quick change in emotion, Carloman could do little more than nod.

"Well, perhaps I can help you with that," she said, reaching for his robe. She slid it off his shoulders and let it sink to the floor and began to pull his shift over his head. This required her to stand on her toes to reach over his shoulders. As she did so, she let her breasts push into his chest and touched her lips to the side of his neck.

He should have felt something. A quickening of pulse, an ache to touch her, heat where her skin had touched his, something. Confused, he took her into his arms and kissed her mouth. He watched his hands caress her body and struggle against the clasps and ties that kept her clothes in place. He watched as her kisses became more urgent. He watched as she pulled herself from her clothes, letting them fall to her feet while her hands traveled his body and her mouth kissed his nipples. She ground her pubis into him.

Nothing stirred. He threw himself into their embrace, but his body remained detached. She pushed him back against the bed. She untied his pantaloons. Her mouth descended on him, her head rising and falling with him between her lips.

High above her, he looked away. He felt her hesitate and then start anew. Again he felt her pause, this time longer. She rocked back on her heels and used her hand to try and pump life into him. Carloman's cheeks flushed. She stopped altogether.

He lay naked on the bed with his pantaloons around his ankles. His penis lay long and flaccid on his thigh. She looked up at him, her eyes still hooded with lust. Then she too looked away.

Kissing him lightly on the tip of his penis, she rose to her feet. Circling the bed, she returned to her table, sat naked in the chair, and took up her brush. She began to stroke it through her hair in long, languid strokes.

"I think I'll wear my blue dress to Hélène's tomorrow night," she said. "You know, the one with the white collar? I think it will look nice with those earrings you gave me and the boots I bought today."

Carloman lay inert on the bed for several moments before rising to his feet to put his clothes away. Drawing on a nightshirt, he said, "Yes, that would be lovely."

Liutbrand waved away the fly. This late in the year, the insect was hesitant and slow. The king of the Lombards was tempted to catch it in his hand and crush it for its impudence. At the moment, however, he was preoccupied. He let the creature escape.

He was ready to leave. He had been in Paris too long, with too little to show for it. Although he had a commitment from Carloman that

Aistulf's betrothed would return, he had seen no evidence to assuage his doubt. A messenger brought news of Pippin, but Liutbrand doubted the account of Trudi's disappearance. It was too convenient. Given her performance the night before she left, Liutbrand was convinced that the story of her abduction was a lie. Her reluctance for the match with Aistulf was obvious. Pippin's support for her was also painfully clear. He had hoped for more from his adopted son. It was time to leave.

Carloman had, of course, attempted to placate his concerns. Twice he had let the young man persuade him to stay longer in Paris, awaiting Trudi's return. Liutbrand liked the pragmatic young man. Carloman had a gift for strategy. He understood consequences. His only flaw was his slavish devotion to his faith. It would be his undoing. Pippin had no such predilection; Liutbrand chuckled to himself. His only predilections were for women and winning. That boy was all instinct, a pure fighter.

Liutbrand shook his head. Trudi was the key to his plans. With the pope under his protection, Liutbrand could already exert influence over the Church and all its holdings. By linking his heirs with Charles's progeny, he placed the Lombards in line to inherit Charles's legacy. With boldness and luck, his family could rule the continent within two generations. Trudi's children would be in direct line for succession. With the Merovingians so weak, his grandson could even be king of the Franks. His plan could survive without Trudi, but it would require waiting another generation, maybe two. Liutbrand was too old to wait that long.

He sent for Aistulf.

When his son arrived, Liutbrand closed the door behind him and motioned for Aistulf to take a chair. Instead, Aistulf casually walked to the window.

"How may I be of assistance, Father?" his son asked.

"I'm going home," Liutbrand said.

That seemed to get his son's attention. "And I'm not?"

"I want you to find your future wife and bring her back to the peninsula."

"Ah, yes, Father, your grand plan. And if Charles's warrior princess refuses to come?"

"It isn't up to her to decide. Take the bulk of our military contingent, find her, and bring her home. I've got other things to do."

The young man's eyebrows lifted.

"I'm going to Rome," Liutbrand said. "My agreement with Charles and Carloman was Trudi's hand in exchange for my restraint. Until she shows her face in our court, I'm not inclined to be restrained when it comes to invading Rome."

"You're willing to risk a war with them?" Aistulf's eyes returned to the window.

Liutbrand grunted. Sometimes his son could be so detached. "There is no risk. Carloman hasn't got the troops or the time to deal with us. He needs everything he has just to hold onto the kingdom. You take care of getting Trudi. I'll take care of the pope.

"We'll leave together," Liutbrand told his son, "pay our respects to our host, and ride out by the southern road. Once outside the city, I go south, you go east. The messenger said Pippin was in Reims. Start there and find her."

Aistulf made no response.

Liutbrand's eyes began to blink rapidly. "What is it?"

Aistulf turned to him. "Why we are wasting our time on these barbarians? It is inconceivable that they are as important as you think. For centuries, the only threat to our power on the peninsula was the emperor in Constantinople. Yet here you are casting our lot with these," Aistulf crinkled his face with disdain, "glorified peasants."

Liutbrand started to speak, but Aistulf cut him off.

"You know the type of people we're dealing with. When was the last time you saw anyone interrupt a funeral to spit on the corpse?" Aistulf shook his head.

"And have you taken a good look at Charles's daughter? I'll grant you that there is something dynamic about the girl, but she dresses in armor! It's as if she is going to do battle with the next man she sees.

"She will never fit in at court. And if I force her to come with me, she will skewer me in the night while I sleep. It was intolerable that you dragged me to this pigsty from the peninsula in the first place.

Now you want me to rope in the sow and bring her home to court." He shuddered.

"Grow up, boy." Aistulf's face reddened. "This is not about wedded bliss. This is about power."

"Am I to rape her to produce your heirs?" Aistulf asked.

Liutbrand stood very still. He let his silence speak for his anger. When he finally did speak, his voice was a menacing whisper.

"She is the key to hegemony. Find her. Bring her back." When Aistulf attempted to interrupt, Liutbrand slammed his hand down on the table.

"She has been promised! Hiltrude may be unwilling, but she's not stupid. She is the daughter of Charles Martel. She understands power. Marry her, and the Roman Empire will be restored. Your son may be king of the Franks as well as king of the Lombards. Bring her back, and Hiltrude will become your wife and the mother of your children. But first, you must find her."

Aistulf reddened, bowed formally, and left the room.

"Good boy," Liutbrand said. "Good boy."

It took three flights of stairs to reach the guest rooms at the rectory of St. Denis. Bishop Wido was out of breath and sweating by the time he reached the landing. His short legs had made the ascent particularly difficult, but his need was urgent. He banged on the door to the quarters given to Bishop Aidolf.

"Yes?" Aidolf's muffled voice called.

"They are seeking to completely undermine the council." Wido burst into the room. "They have gotten side agreements from Gairhard and three other bishops for—"

He stopped in his tracks.

Bishop Aidolf stood at the center of the room, stark naked, sinking his penis into the anus of a young man of twenty bent before him. Aidolf's eyes were glazed, half closed in lust. The shock of his naked flesh held Wido stunned. The man was incredibly fit, and despite Wido's best intentions, he stared openly at the man's penis. He was stunned by its size. It took him a moment to realize that Aidolf had stopped midthrust. When Wido finally met Aidolf's eyes, the bishop stared back with disdain. He began pushing himself once more into the young man.

With an effort, Wido regained his composure and turned his back on the lurid display.

"So they aren't so easily intimidated," Aidolf said. Wido could hear the sound of flesh slapping flesh. As Aidolf spoke, the pace increased.

"No … no, they aren't," Wido croaked. "They are coming to the council to reject our ultimatum. They believe they have enough support without us."

"They're wrong," Aidolf said. A low groan escaped from his paramour.

"Please, pull yourself out of that man," Wido said. "This is hardly proper."

The only response he received was heavy breathing.

Pulling a handkerchief from his pocket, Wido wiped the sweat from his brow. He didn't know what to do. He wanted to leave but needed Aidolf's support. He heard a gasp behind him that was quickly followed by a clenched groan. After that, he heard nothing. When Aidolf appeared at his side, he was still naked. He took the handkerchief from Wido's hand and wiped off his penis.

"I need a drink," he said to Wido. "Want one?"

"Yes." Wido was drained. "Yes, I believe I would."

Aidolf walked across the room to a table filled with liquors as his young man scurried from the room. Aidolf poured himself a goblet of an amber liquid and a second for Wido.

"What I don't understand about you, Wido, is that you were always Charles's man. Why switch sides? What has Theudoald promised you?"

Wido took a long pull from the drink in his hand. It burned on the way down. He was relieved that Aidolf had picked up a robe to put on. He took his time, however, shrugging into it. Wido forced himself to look away from the man's nakedness. He knew Aidolf was trying to intimidate him. Unfortunately, the man was succeeding.

"Who could stand up to Charles?" Wido said. His voice sounded shrill even to him. This wasn't going well. He took another drink that burned less this time and started again. "I was a joke to Charles," he said, looking into his cup. "He called me 'Bishop Dwarf.' And while he let it be widely known that he took me hunting, what most people didn't know is that he made me carry his spears. He never took me seriously and never stopped raiding the coffers of St. Wandrille. He took our land, our wealth, and our resources. The humiliation never stopped.

"Theudoald, on the other hand, calls me 'friend.' He treats me with respect. Nothing," he looked up at Aidolf with hard eyes, "nothing would make me happier than to see him displace Charles's sons."

"So it is personal," Aidolf said with a smile. "Revenge is my favorite of motives. What is it then that you want from me?"

"The bishops are afraid of you. You must bring them into line."

"Are you going to threaten me again?"

Wido's face reddened.

"You were astute to recognize my vulnerability," Aidolf said, waving toward the door through which the acolyte had disappeared. "I can't afford for Boniface to interfere with my passions. He has the pope's ear, as you know. But you underestimate me, Wido." His voice had gone cold and hard. "Threaten me again, and you will understand what revenge can really mean.

"You are fortunate that I agree with your strategy. I have no interest in helping Charles's sons. The weaker they are, the stronger we will be. We will put a Merovingian on the throne. That much is certain. If we can make Theudoald mayor of Neustria, so much the better. Now, my little Bishop Dwarf." He leaned over Wido. "I trust that your investigation on behalf of that hypocrite Gairhard will result in nothing?"

"It might help if your monks were more discreet," Wido said, stiffening against the threat.

Aidolf smiled. "Oh, we will be discreet," he said. "Of that you can be assured, but what of you, my small friend? I noticed your intense interest in my initiation of that young acolyte. Perhaps you would care to join us next time?" As he spoke, Aidolf's robe parted, and Wido could see the white of the man's penis dangling in the darkness.

Wido's stomach clenched, and his face flushed red. He stood frozen while the heat from Aidolf's body wafted toward him. Aidolf opened his robe further and took hold of his penis and began to stroke the length of it. Stumbling backward, Wido tore his eyes from the sight and fled the room.

He heard Aidolf's laugh follow him down all three flights of stairs.

Carloman had never felt comfortable around Lady Hélène. The widow of a prominent Austrasian nobleman, she was now in her thirties, lived in Paris, and was most notable for throwing lavish parties. Carloman had been to several of her soirées, and this one was no different. There was good Burgundy wine and even a flagon or two from Bordeaux that she had reserved for him and Greta.

But he always found Hélène odd. She was beautiful in a mysterious way. She had piercing blue eyes, which was rare except among the Saxons. Her hair was dark brown, but closely cropped, which was never in fashion. She had a slight accent that was hard to place. To Carloman, it had echoes of Aquitaine. Widowed for four or five years, she had never taken an interest in another man, though many had tried to court her.

Greta had once told him that Hélène was rumored to be having an affair with Charles. There certainly had been a connection between them, but Carloman refused to believe it was sexual. When Charles and Sunni were together, they exuded sexuality. Charles and Hélène were something different. Exactly what, he had never figured out.

As he circulated through her apartments, he ran into several noblemen and knights he had needed to see. For that, at least, the night was not a complete waste of time. He was feeling cheered after hearing Boniface's news that Bishop Gairhard had agreed to petition his fellow bishops to reconsider supporting Theudoald as mayor. Carloman was confident that with three or more bishops siding with them, they would have enough gold and troops to gain the council's support and settle the question of succession.

Now he could not wait for the council to meet. The land would be back on the table in exchange for a commitment of gold and soldiers. He would concede to naming a Merovingian but draw the line on Theudoald. That ass would never be mayor. If the bishops didn't agree, he would walk away. No Merovingian, no land, no Theudoald. Carloman felt very good about his prospects. He accepted another goblet of Bordeaux.

Greta had deserted him early in the evening. She seemed to be very taken with Lady Hélène. A clique of sorts had developed among the women of the court after Charles's death. They seemed to be sorting through the social implications of the succession. Carloman didn't bother to follow any of it. He had plenty to do all by himself. He watched his wife chatting with a cluster of women. She had worn her hair back in an elaborate braid that made her look tall and elegant in her blue dress. She was very beautiful.

"She's very beautiful," a voice said. Theudoald stood next to him holding a goblet of wine. "Your wife, of course. A beautiful woman. You are a very lucky man, Carloman."

Carloman noticed that Theudoald again wore the lace collar and cuffs. He had nothing to say to the man.

"Don't you think this is excellent wine?" Theudoald ventured.

Carloman could feel the rest of the room watching them.

"This Bordeaux. It is very good, don't you think?"

"No matter how many people see us together, Theudoald, I will not consent to you becoming mayor. If you plan to contest the succession with arms, you had better get ready."

"Oh, I don't think that will be necessary," the tall man responded. "I have some information."

"I doubt you have anything I'm interested in hearing."

"I'm sure that the council will be. It involves your youngest brother and a priest."

Carloman turned toward Theudoald.

"Oh, so you *are* interested? Good. It seems there is this priest in Laon. Sounds like the start of a good joke, doesn't it?" Getting no reaction out of Carloman, he frowned and continued. "The priest was minding his own business, tending to his flock in old Laon, when Sunni arrived with a whole host of renegade nobles, Thuringians, and of course, your half brother Gripho." He had said the word Thuringian as if it were a curse. "You do at least know that she is in Laon?" Carloman nodded. "Good. Well, it seems that your dear half brother harassed this priest by conscripting soldiers during holy mass—took his horse right into the church—then attacked him for complaining to the good Compte de Laon. There was one more thing ... what was it? Ah, yes, he burned the church."

Carloman could feel the blood drain from his face. "I'm sure you are mistaken. It is certainly a rumor. Gripho would never do such a thing."

"In this particular case, I'm afraid you are wrong." Theudoald was enjoying himself. "The priest was burnt horribly but survived to flee with the women and children. He made his way to Paris with the aid of his monsignor, and they already have had a preliminary meeting with the council. I heard they've told their story from Laon to Paris. By tomorrow afternoon, it should be the talk of the court. I'm surprised you haven't heard this before, Carloman."

"I don't believe it."

"He is very convincing, very convincing, I'm afraid. I'm sure that when you hear their eyewitness account, it will change your mind. I've heard the council is meeting early tomorrow to review his testimony. Isn't that the same day you are to meet with them? I wonder what kind of impact that might have on your proposals."

Carloman's stomach began to churn.

"I'm sorry to interrupt, but it is simply unfair to have the two best-looking men in the room talking to each other." Lady Hélène appeared between them and grabbed each of them by an arm and steered them toward the circle of women nearby. "The ladies are already complaining. If you keep it up much longer, people will talk. You both know my house rules. No politics, no religion, no money lending. All other vices, of course, are welcome." She positioned Theudoald in the circle of women and said, "Theudoald, Eileen asked about your idea to build another bridge across the Seine. Why don't you tell her about it?"

Theudoald chuckled and turned to the woman to expound upon his bridge idea. Hélène recaptured Carloman's arm and led him away from the milling crowd.

"Thank you," Carloman said.

"You are entirely welcome. He must have told you about the burned priest. He's told everyone in the room since he got here."

"Yes, he did. Is it true?"

"Apparently."

"He is such a shit." Frowning at his indiscretion, he immediately apologized to Hélène.

"Oh, don't worry. I quite agree. The man's a shit." She laughed, and he felt the tension easing a bit. He began to laugh with her.

"Other than him, you've thrown a very nice party, Hélène."

"Thank you. I try to please."

"Why *did* you invite him?"

"I wanted to see how you would react to him."

"You are a strange lady, Hélène. You've always been a mystery to me."

"Tell me, Carloman. Will you be king?"

"Such talk could be taken for treason, my lady."

She leaned closer and spoke in a more conspiratorial whisper. "Will you be king?"

"From the look of it, that path now appears to be blocked. I know my father had wanted his sons to be kings. He just didn't live long enough."

"No, he didn't," Hélène said. Carloman saw emotion fill her eyes and was unexpectedly moved.

"Perhaps this is an indiscreet question, my lady, but I've always been curious about your relationship with my father."

Hélène shook her head and tried to recover her earlier playful mood. She smiled, the coquette once again. "I was his assassin."

"Oh you were, were you?" Carloman chuckled.

"Yes, Charles found me quite helpful at times." Her smile was now radiant.

Enjoying the banter, Carloman played along. "And just how did you dispose of your victims?"

"Oh, an assassin never reveals trade secrets. But you would be surprised how easy it is for a woman to move about freely during the night." She chuckled. "Everyone always seems to want to look the other way."

"Well, if you could take care of that one for me," Carloman said lightly, pointing to Theudoald, "I'd consider it an enormous favor."

"Consider it done." Hélène smiled. She leaned close to him, her voice taking on a seductive quality. "Would you like it to be slow or fast?"

Surprisingly, Carloman found himself attracted to this woman with the short hair and the blue eyes. "Slow," he said. "He deserves it to be slow."

"Very well then," she beamed. "Slow it is."

Carloman performed a mock bow to seal their agreement, and they both laughed.

Greta joined them, smiling as if she had been part of the joke. "I'm so glad to see you two having a good time," she said, grabbing each by the arm.

"Greta," Carloman said. "I'd like to introduce you to my new a—"

Hélène placed her hand lightly over his mouth. "No, Carloman. You mustn't spoil the game." She turned to Greta and said, "Carloman has asked me to be his messenger of sorts."

"Really," Greta said. "What kind of messenger?"

"One who only delivers bad news." She laughed.

Carloman found himself laughing right along with her.

Led by a dozen of his Knights in Christ, Carloman and Boniface made the trip to St. Denis on horseback. As they approached, pedestrians massing in the narrow streets began to impede their progress. Frowning, Carloman hand-signaled Johann to quicken their pace, and they cantered into the square outside the church. It was filled with people, and the crowd there was already unruly. In the distance, a drum beat with military precision.

Carloman and Boniface started for the church doors when a new procession arrived. Led by the drummers they had heard, it promised to overwhelm the already-packed square. At their front, a tall, bearded priest dressed in white carried a cross. Unlike many of the crosses present in the square, however, this cross was too large to be carried aloft like a banner. A large wooden monstrosity, the cross was life-sized and overwhelmed the priest. He shouldered his burden and dragged it as Christ had dragged the implement of his death to Calvary. Carloman looked to Boniface for an explanation.

"It is has two related meanings. It reminds each of us of how great a burden Christ carried on our behalf and reminds us how great is the weight of our responsibility to the Church."

"Death to pagans!" the procession chanted to the rhythm of the drums. "Death to pagans!"

"Let Gripho burn!" someone shouted in return.

Several fistfights broke out around them. The crowd seethed like turbulent water. Waves of people shoved and pushed, trying to find space. Some had fallen to the ground and struggled to avoid being trampled. The drums and the chanting never stopped.

"We better get inside," Carloman said.

Led by Johann and the Knights in Christ, Carloman and Boniface waded through the crowd toward the church door. Curses and shouts greeted them as they drove a wedge into the crowd. Carloman was shoved several times, forcing the Knights in Christ to surround him. As they climbed to the church, Carloman saw a burnt effigy of Gripho lying on the steps. He made it to the top before he was recognized.

"It's the brother! It's Carloman!"

"What will you do, Carloman?"

Several voices booed. The crowd surged toward them but was restrained by the Knights in Christ. Before Carloman and Boniface could gain the church doors, the crowd parted to Carloman's left, and the priest with the large cross carried his burden up to the church. Standing in front of Carloman, he stopped. The drums fell silent, and the crowd hushed.

Carloman met the priest's eyes and realized the man was exhausted. Sweat streamed down his face, and his lungs heaved inside his chest. The priest tried to take another step forward and faltered. Carloman watched the huge cross lose its center of balance. Tilting to one side, the cross threatened to fall off the man's shoulder into the mud of the square. The priest tried to compensate but was too late. The cross began to fall.

Instinctively, Carloman stepped to the man's side and threw his shoulder under the cross. Its weight was enormous. He staggered beneath it, trying to counter its momentum. Straining, he straightened his legs and took the full weight onto his right shoulder, accepting the whole burden from the priest. Looking for a place to set the cross down, Carloman decided to lean it against the church beside the two large wooden doors. He started to drag the behemoth up the steps. Hands reached out to steady him. As he gained the top of the steps, he struggled to push the cross erect, and several of his Knights in Christ lifted the burden with him. The base of the cross found solid stone, and the crucifix stood of its own accord to the left of the church doors.

Unburdened, Carloman straightened his clothes, which had cinched under his arm, and turned back to the crowd. An eerie silence had taken the square. A polite circle of space enveloped him where the crowd had retreated. He stood alone on the steps of the church next to the cross, his head high above the crowd. No one in the square uttered a word. All eyes were on him. The priest in white advanced to the step below Carloman.

"Like Simon of Cyrene," the priest exclaimed, "you are willing to risk yourself to shoulder Christ's burden. Are you willing to shoulder his burden in Laon? Are you a true man of God, Carloman, son of Charles?" He knelt before Carloman and bowed his head. "If you are willing to bring those to justice who have desecrated God's church, I offer you my service in this hour of need."

Like ripples from a stone striking water, the gesture spread behind him in an ever-widening circle. In moments, the entire square was kneeling. Carloman pulled the priest to his feet. Standing next to him, Carloman looked out over the crowd. They would expect something from him now, he thought to himself. He had to address them, say something.

"I am Carloman, son of Charles, son of Pippin of Herstal," he said in a voice that carried over the crowd. "I have come to the church council today to raise an army. My intent is to keep the peace and keep our land from civil war. I do not know what has happened yet in Laon." Some grumbling surfaced to his right. He raised his voice. "But I promise you this, I will right this wrong. I will see justice done. This deed will not go unpunished."

The crowd surged to its feet with a roar.

"Death to pagans!" A voice shouted. The chant swept through the square, the crowd leaping to their feet. "Death to pagans! Death to pagans!" The drums picked up the beat.

Carloman raised his hands to quiet the crowd. It wasn't what he had meant. He wanted to correct them, explain that death was not the only answer. But they wouldn't quiet. They were caught up in their own euphoria. Boniface appeared next to him. He had thrown off his cloak to reveal his cassock and had donned his stole. He held his right hand aloft, and in moments his gesture had its desired effect. "Let us pray," he intoned. The crowd quieted. Heads bowed. Hands folded, and knees bent.

"Oh, Holy Father, who has given His only begotten Son for our sins, bless these good people for their piety. Bless them for their holy rage against the desecration of your church. And bless your servant Carloman, who takes up this burden in Your name ..."

There was more, but Carloman wasn't listening. He had bowed his head with the others, but his mind reeled with implications. He needed some space to think. He was desperate to go inside, but as long as Boniface prayed, he would have to remain.

After what felt like an eternity, Boniface ended with the blessing, "In the name of the Father, the Son, and the Holy Ghost."

"Amen," the crowd said in unison.

The priest in white lifted Carloman's hand aloft. "To Carloman!" he cried.

The crowd roared its approval. Carloman nodded and raised his other hand to wave. The crowd cheered louder. Thinking of how to exit, Carloman clasped the shoulder of the priest, turned to the crowd, and bowed. Although he didn't think it possible, the cheering doubled, again. Pulling himself erect, Carloman executed a military turn and made for the door of the church. Boniface and the Knights in Christ followed. As if by magic, the door opened at their approach. A pair of monks had stood at the ready inside the door, waiting for the appropriate moment to push it open.

Four of the knights preceded him into the church. Boniface and the rest followed while Johann and two others kept back to hold off the crowd. As the huge door closed behind them, shutting out the early afternoon light, Carloman was stunned by the sudden shift to the calm, quiet darkness of the church.

Boniface clasped Carloman on the shoulder with one of his blacksmith hands. "This is an enormous opportunity. The people are whipped into a furor. Lead them! Strike a blow against the pagans. This was God's house. Show them that even a mayor cannot burn God's holy church. As a man of God, you cannot abide that.

"You must renounce Gripho, Carloman. Demand that the council give you the money and men you need to war on your pagan brother. Deal with Theudoald later. Unite us all in this cause and become God's lightning bolt of fury."

"You condemn me to a lifetime of war, Boniface."

"Your brother has condemned you. So must you condemn him."

"What if it isn't true?"

Boniface sighed. "This priest's story has become the truth. His burns are visible whereas Gripho is not. No one will believe your brother's story, even if he has one."

A bell in the church tower tolled the hour, and a messenger arrived to take them to the council. They followed the messenger to a large meeting room located adjacent to the sacristy. Inside, more than a dozen bishops faced them at a table meant for twenty. On the right side of the room near the table sat a portly monsignor and the burnt priest.

The priest was bandaged across most of his upper body. Both hands and arms were completely covered, as was his torso, save one shoulder, and much of his face. His lower body seemed to have suffered less from his tragedy.

Carloman searched the faces before him until he found that of the Bishop Auxerre. "Your Eminence," he said, nodding to Aidolf. Before anyone could speak, Carloman strode to the bandaged priest. The man stood at his approach. Carloman reached out to touch the bandages covering the man's face. He hesitated, awaiting the man's permission. With a nod from the priest, he began to unwrap the white linens. When the last wrap fell, the priest stared at Carloman defiantly. His face was an oozing pinkish version of flesh. Gaping sores bled openly. The damage was hideous.

Carloman reached for the bandages on his arms and then his torso. With each layer, Carloman's hesitation dissipated. At times, the linen lifted what was left of the skin with it. The priest struggled against the pain to remain erect. At last the man stood naked to the waist. A ghoulish figure, disfigured for life.

"Who did this to you, Father?" Carloman asked in a whispered voice.

"It was your brother Gripho." The tortured figure spat out his words.

"If I may—" began the rotund monsignor beside him. Carloman cut the man off with a gesture of his hand.

"How did this happen?" Carloman asked the priest.

"He attacked me and burned the church. I was inside."

"How was he provoked?"

"Your brother?" The priest winced in pain at the effort to talk. "He threatened me. I complained. He dragged me to the altar and threatened to kill me. He wasn't provoked."

Carloman peered into the man's eyes. "Did you see him burn the church?"

"Sir, I must protest—" interrupted the monsignor again.

"Silence!" Carloman wheeled on the man. Turning back to the priest, he said, "Did you see him burn the church?"

"Yes. He set fire to the altar."

"Why did you not leave?"

"I tried to save the Eucharist."

Carloman sighed. It was something he would have done. He shook his head remorsefully. "Do you have family?"

"The Church is my family."

"Then I will see to it that the Church is well compensated to care for your needs." Before the priest could reject the offer, Carloman held up his hand. "Peace, Father. May God take pity on your pain. I am not your enemy. Though it seems," he said, turning to the council, "that I must become my brother's keeper."

Seeking out Bishop Aidolf, he said, "I leave tomorrow to bring Gripho to justice. Here are my final terms. Whatever men you plan to send should meet me in Quierzy. What gold you plan to give, give now. Those who declare for me will receive the lands we discussed. Those who refuse get nothing. I will deal with the subject of Theudoald when I return."

"And the king?" Aidolf asked. "We will not support you without a commitment to restore the Merovingians."

Carloman searched the eyes in the room for room to negotiate. He saw little. His eyes flickered over the hideous torso of the priest from Laon.

"You have my commitment."

Bishop Aidolf of Auxerre looked for and gained the silent assent of the council. He turned his attention back to Carloman and Boniface. "So you have ours. The council is ended. Go with God, Carloman."

CHAPTER 8

Trudi and Pippin

Save for a few short stops to rest, Pippin and his men had not left their saddles since the last day they saw Reims. They were haggard, disgruntled, cold, and frustrated. Pippin had pushed the men far beyond their limits, ignoring their obvious exhaustion. Bradius was just ahead, and until he was caught, Pippin refused to eat and refused to sleep.

Bradius was clever. Pippin would give him that. The man knew he was being followed. He used the woodlands bordering the southern road to frustrate their search. Repeatedly, Bradius had hidden, backtracked, and laid false trails to fool them. The only consistent thing he did was to move south. And while Bradius had hidden camps with stores of food, Pippin's men had to scavenge or send men to buy supplies from nearby farmhouses and villages. The bastard stayed just beyond their reach.

On the fourth day of their search, the afternoon sky turned gray, and the air was heavy and wet. It grew cold and began to rain.

Pippin caught Gunther's eye and turned away. They both knew a hard rain would wash away the tracks they were following.

At first, just a few large drops fell. They landed hard, announcing their presence on impact with a quick staccato sound. After a slight hesitation, the skies opened, and the air became thick with water. With no wind to interrupt its course, the rain fell directly from above, overwhelming everything in its path. Its sound drummed off their armor. Water streamed off the road. In an instant, the trail left by Bradius was gone.

"Shit," Gunther said. Pippin turned away from him and rode on.

Knowing they were being followed comforted Trudi. Bradius had led the small party south along the river road for most of the day and then doubled back through the wood to throw off pursuit. Someone was coming despite Bradius's tricks. All she needed to do was wait. Any hour might bring relief.

It was her second day since the confrontation over her necklace. Bradius had set a relentless pace, taking little time for rest or food. Fortunately, her head had begun to feel better, and the nausea had passed. She also was allowed to ride upright with only her hands tied. Far more important, however, was the fact that Bradius was ignoring her.

She had been brought to his fire the previous night only to watch him drink with Auguste. She hadn't said a word. To her relief, the men treated her as if she didn't exist. She had survived the night untouched.

In the saddle, her fantasies of rescue grew ever more elaborate: Odilo descending on her captors to save her; Odilo and his men waiting in the brush to ambush them; Odilo and his men barring the road to meet Bradius in a frontal assault. Always it was Odilo who won the confrontation, and always it was Odilo who took her in his arms. She imagined his kiss, the press of his body, the rich smell of him.

In late afternoon, they camped. As before, Bradius sat at a separate fire on a small rise, away from the men. As before, he sent for her to sit with him. He had chosen a spot below a large tree and was busy fashioning a lean-to with a canvas cloth he had pulled from his saddlebag. Expecting rain, the men at the fire below did much the same.

"I've never before met a girl in armor," Bradius said. Trudi started at his voice. "Have you been in battle?" His tone was casual, curious.

She was wary. "No," she said.

"What were you doing in Reims?"

"I told you—"

"Yes, yes, 'the rape of Loivre.' How noble." He waved off her indignation. "But why were you riding with Pippin in the first place?"

Trudi hesitated. "We had heard that there was trouble, an uprising of sorts. Pippin was named mayor of Champagne and Burgundy, so ... we came."

"Felicitations," Bradius said. "But you've avoided my question. Why are *you* here? It was clearly a hostile mission. You've never been in battle. Why would you go along on a sortie that would likely require hand-to-hand combat?"

"I insisted."

Bradius looked at her. "That's not it," he said. "Either you're lying or there's something more you're not telling me."

She didn't answer.

"Trouble at home?" he asked with a smile. Trudi averted her eyes, blushing.

"Let me guess," he said, clearly amusing himself. "A young girl of marrying age—perhaps even a little older than marrying age—dressed in armor, an important but dictatorial father ... hmmm. Whom did he pick to marry you?"

Trudi didn't answer. He continued.

"Let's see, who might be available for a woman as grand as Hiltrude, daughter of Charles? There's Ateni of Provence, a nice catch if you like old farts with bad teeth. There's Heden of Thuringia. But he's pagan. Charles would never accept that. There's Patrice of Burgundy. Now *there's* a catch."

"It was Aistulf," she said.

Bradius seemed confused. "Aistulf? The Lombard? The swordsman? That Aistulf? What could be wrong with Aistulf? He's young. He's good looking. He's from a powerful family."

"I'm in love with someone else."

"Ah, I should have known. It's always love. And just who is this lucky fellow?"

"Odilo of Bavaria," she said, her chin rising.

"And may truth guide his sword," Bradius said, chuckling. "But I heard he was pagan. Does Charles know?"

Trudi shook her head.

"Does Odilo return your affection?"

"I think so," she said. "I hope so."

"You don't know."

Again, Trudi shook her head.

"One should know before running away," he said.

They ate a sparse meal, having had no time to hunt for game. Bradius broke out rations of hard bread, cheese, and, of course, his wine. He opened the wineskin, poured the red liquid into his cup, and swirled it around as if he were at court rather than on the run in the woods south of Reims. This time he gave her a cup.

Saluting the sky as if in toast, Bradius declared, "It's going to rain."

And it did. A deluge. Their spot on the high ground worked to their advantage as the rain washed down the hill away from them. Bradius moved under the canvas tarp of his lean-to and waved for Trudi to join him.

She refused. Bradius shrugged and focused his attention on cutting another slice of cheese. When he had succeeded, he recaptured his wine and leaned back against the tree. Seeing her standing in the downpour soaked to the skin, Bradius chuckled again and raised his wine to her in salutation.

It took less than a minute for Trudi to realize she was being foolish. If Bradius wished to do her harm, there was little she could do to stop him. Standing in the rain gave her little protection from him and none from the downpour. Angry in embarrassment, she crowded into the lean-to with him. Bradius refilled her cup with wine and gave her some cheese. Together, they watched what was left of the fire sputter and die. Darkness began to fall. Despite the canvas lean-to, they were getting wet.

Bradius offered her room to reposition herself away from the leakage. He kept the wine dry and ensured they both had full cups.

"I'm not sure I like drinking with Charles's daughter," he said. "It is against my religion."

She smiled despite herself.

"He is a butcher, you know." Bradius's voice turned serious. "He's had blood on his hands since the day he named himself mayor."

"He was challenged!" Trudi retorted. "Every sector of the country rebelled."

"That should tell you something. Charles seized power from Plectrude and Ragomfred. It would be tolerable if he had left it at Neustria, but Charles had to subjugate the entire continent. How many people had to die for your father to rule?"

Bradius drank as deeply as he grew passionate.

"He didn't need to come to Provence. He doesn't need to rule in Aquitaine. Bavaria and Frisia would be separate countries but for your father's butchery."

"Bavaria was at civil war. My father stepped in to stop it."

"And conveniently abducted the royal family and took over."

"That's not what happened!"

"It's not? Tell me, Hiltrude, why does your family butcher the Saxons?"

"They raid our countryside and attack our people."

"Who attacked first?"

"I don't know what you're talking about."

"Those people are pagan. They have different beliefs than Charles and his precious Church. He attacks the Saxons because they won't kneel to his cross."

"It's not that simple," Trudi said. "Every year, more Saxons show up at our borders. Every year, they take over more land. They've pushed to the Rhine." The heat of her argument and the wine brought a flush to her face.

"And what about you?" she said. "You fought *with* the Saracen. My father had to beat back the Saracen before they took over *our* land and imposed their religion on us. How is that any different?"

"At Poitiers? That was Abd ar-Rachman, a very different Saracen. And though your father fought to protect Christianity, no religion need dominate. When I fought with the Saracen, my beliefs were tolerated. You can't say as much about your father."

A long silence followed. Bradius drank more, Trudi less.

She had no answers to his accusations. He was right that war was almost an annual event for her family. She had roamed the kingdom with her father from the time she could walk, watching him put down one rebellion after another. It had never occurred to her that Charles might be anything other than the rightful ruler.

She thought of Carloman and Boniface and their obsession with the Church. She thought of their efforts to either convert or banish the pagans. She thought about Sunni hiding her faith and her own dabbles in it. Why did the Church consider it so wrong?

Trudi stared at this strange man sitting next to her and tried to understand him. She felt no threat emanating from him. The violence she had sensed in him had been replaced by a casual, condescending tone she could not reconcile. His melancholy remained, but his manner was more passionate. She watched him staring into the rain.

"How long will you run?" she asked.

"Until I figure out what to do with you," he said without looking up.

"That won't end it," she said, shivering.

Shaking his head in agreement, Bradius said, "No. It won't."

He pulled a blanket from his pack and began to wrap it around her. She stiffened at his touch. Chuckling, he pulled it around her and returned to his place. It took her a few minutes to realize he had no blanket for himself.

"Tell me about Sunni," he said into the dark. "Tell me about becoming pagan."

The next day, Bradius rode them hard. Several times, Trudi begged him to stop, only to be cautioned into silence. She could barely sit in her saddle, and her wrists were bleeding again from the ropes that bound her.

When they camped and she had been unbound, she slumped by the fire, exhausted. Although the rain had ended that morning, her clothes had never dried. She was covered with mud, her hair was tangled and wild, and she shook from the cold. She clung to the fire for its warmth.

Bradius too seemed exhausted. Dark circles had formed under his eyes, and his movements were hurried and angry. Despite his concern for discovery, he built up the fire and handed her what was left of their food.

Rummaging through his horse's pack, he found another skin of wine and poured himself a cup. This time, however, he didn't perform his ceremony. He upended the cup and drained it. He poured himself more. Leaning back against the tree, he stared into the fire. Melancholy poured from his eyes. Trudi began to worry for his sanity. She needed to engage him, to draw him away from his darkness.

"Tell me about your son."

His eyes flared, anger seething through them. When they met hers, however, they softened. So did his words.

"He was a troubled boy," Bradius began, looking down into his cup. "His mother died young, so I raised him alone." He grunted a little laugh and looked up for a moment. "Unless you count Auguste. Unum would count him, so I suppose I should. Auguste and I raised him." He smiled crookedly.

"When he was very young, Unum was quiet and sensitive. There was a sadness about him that I could never touch."

"Maybe he missed his mother," Trudi ventured.

Bradius looked at her and nodded slowly, his eyes misting. "I'm sure he did." A long silence ensued while he looked back into the fire. "I used to take him fishing, to a small eddy where fish in the river would congregate. He had a real knack for netting the most. It was the only time he would ever smile. That and when he was with Auguste. They were a pair. They rarely spoke, so they both felt right at home. The two would hunt together. Most times, they came back without any game. I always accused them of failing to raise a bow. They were just taking very long walks in the woods."

Although he was clearly talking to her, Trudi felt as if she had been forgotten. She was afraid to speak for fear of stopping his tale. Something, however, did stop him. He pondered the fire as if in a trance. For a long while, he said nothing.

"Why do you say he was troubled?"

He sighed. "When he was eleven, he killed another boy in warrior training. It was judged an accident, but it was not. The boy was huge, much larger than Unum or any of the others. He was fond of bullying and taunting the boys. One day in knife practice, he surprised Unum by head butting him just as their contest began. Unum went down, and the bigger boy kicked him between the legs.

"The instructor applauded the move, cautioning the other boys not to focus solely on their opponent's weapon. Unum lay on the ground humiliated. To make matters worse, he wept before the other boys. For days, they taunted him. Unum swore he would never cry again."

Bradius slopped more wine into his cup as if he were angry at its emptiness. He drank deeply, wiping his mouth on his sleeve. He never once looked at her.

"Later that week, they were in sword practice. Again the instructor paired him with the larger boy. Unum was so afraid and angry that his hands shook. They confronted each other, wooden swords aloft. The bigger boy rushed Unum, trying to knock him down. At the last possible moment, Unum sidestepped and put his sword between the boy's legs. The bully went down hard, and before he could get up, Unum lifted his wooden sword high above his head. With both hands, he drove the point into the other boy's testicles.

"Screaming, the bully grabbed his crotch. Unum lifted his sword again. Before the instructor could intervene, Unum had crushed his windpipe. He lay at Unum's feet, eyes wide. He turned red and then blue. He died within minutes."

"That's horrible," Trudi said.

"It changed Unum," Bradius continued. "He carried an anger with him that he could never put down. He didn't say anything for weeks. When he did, it was always hateful and arrogant. Yet, beneath this, I could see he was nervous. He would never speak to me about it. He just looked at me as if I knew his malady and could provide a remedy. I never could. Neither could Auguste. After a while, the few friends Unum had, he lost."

Bradius grew quiet and stared off into space. To rouse him, Trudi picked up his discarded cup and held it out for some wine. Bradius filled it for her; she drank and then held it out for him to finish. When he took it, their hands touched. He looked away.

"He became sullen and defiant," Bradius said, "insolent and cruel. After a year, I brought a lore master to see him. He took the boy into the woods for three days. When they returned, Unum was exhausted. He had not eaten or slept. But his nervousness was gone. So was his anger. A darkness still clung behind his eyes, but Unum was restored to me."

She touched his wrist with compassion. He withdrew from it, taking a long stick from the fire. Bradius drew three symbols in the dirt. "The boy's skin was marked with three runes: Uruz, for inner strength; Thurisaz, for defense against harm; and Ansuz, the god rune, the divine breath of the ash." Seeing Trudi's questioning look, he elaborated. "The lore master said that taking a life so young had tainted Unum with the life that comes after. He had broken his barrier to the next world. The lore master explained that the barrier could never be healed, but it could be strengthened.

"They fasted for three days. They inhaled the smoke of the sacred herbs. More than that, he wouldn't say. The runes are wards to strengthen the barrier: Uruz, to give him strength; Thurisaz, to defend him against the taint; Ansuz, to restore the barrier between his life in this world and the next."

They sat quietly. Trudi knew Bradius would offer nothing further.

"You must have loved him very much," Trudi said.

"All men love their children," Bradius said, as if from a distance. "That's what makes them vulnerable."

"That's what makes them valiant," Trudi whispered.

Odilo was running out of time. If he was going to be of any help to Sunni and Gripho, he needed to move east to rally the eastern provinces. The trip to his capital city of Regensburg would take him at least two weeks of hard riding. Any further delay would be disastrous.

But Odilo didn't start out for Bavaria. Instead, he went to Reims to seek news of Trudi. When he arrived with his contingent of Bavarian knights, he found Bertrada and Childebrand lording over the city. He suffered through a host of questions concerning Charles's funeral and its aftermath before he could casually inquire after Trudi.

Bertrada reached out to take his hand. She described the rape of Loivre and Trudi's abduction. He was shocked. The news that had been reported in Paris had been far less ominous. He felt Bertrada's eyes watching him and struggled to maintain his composure. He offered his men in assistance, but Childebrand thought more men would be an encumbrance. So Odilo waited.

Fortunately, Bertrada proved to be a gracious hostess. Childebrand had commandeered a small villa so Bertrada could establish a guesthouse for those from Quierzy. She provided rooms for Odilo and his senior officers, had dinner prepared, and kept him company during his anxious vigil.

Although Odilo had met Bertrada several times at court, he had had few opportunities to actually speak with her at length. He was surprised to find her both intelligent and entertaining. She was so charming that he found himself reevaluating Pippin. The young man must harbor more than skill with a sword to attract such a dynamic woman.

As the eldest daughter of the Compte de Laon, Bertrada had intimate knowledge of the region. She took him on a tour of Reims. She showed him the grand arch built by the Romans in the first century and took him into some of the vast tunnels they had dug beneath the city. There she showed him endless rows of the area's wine being stored in the cool temperatures below ground. After dinner on the first day, she sat with him by the fire, and they talked late into the evening.

He was surprised to learn that Bertrada, much like Trudi, once had her hand promised in marriage. At the time, she had been happy with the choice; he was the son of the compte in the neighboring city of Soissons. Bertrada chuckled when she described his gangly arms and big ears.

Meeting Pippin had changed everything for her. He was nothing like anyone she had ever known. Within days, they had become lovers. Within weeks, she had broken her engagement, left her father's house, and moved to Quierzy. Bertrada's face fell as she described her father's reaction to the news. The compte had been furious, but Bertrada was in love and had a lifetime's experience having her way with the man.

Three of Carloman's Knights in Christ arrived at the house in Reims, and Bertrada made them welcome. Odilo tried to engage them in conversation but had little success. They were close-lipped about their reasons for being in Reims and suspicious of his. One was named Ansel, a brute of a man who had acquired a peculiar malady that Odilo found oddly disturbing. Something caused him to sweat profusely. Since the man's companions seemed to take no notice of it, Odilo, out of politeness, did not inquire.

After another night of waiting, however, Odilo became concerned. If he stayed, waiting for Trudi, and Carloman declared war on Gripho, Odilo would be trapped in the west. If he left, he might lose Trudi forever. Desperate to make a decision, Odilo decided to confide in Bertrada his feelings for Trudi.

He was surprised to find that she already knew. And while he was delighted to learn that Trudi had fled Quierzy and her betrothed to wait for him, it did little to change his situation. He told Bertrada that he would have to leave in the morning.

"You should stay," she said. "She came for you. You should be here when she returns. Who knows what condition she will be in when Pippin finds her. She will need you close."

"Unfortunately, I cannot," he said with some difficulty. "Events have overtaken us. If Carloman renounces Gripho, there will be civil war. If there is, I cannot be found here. I am exposing myself to grave risk delaying here as I have. I must move east."

Bertrada seemed to weigh this. "What of Trudi? What if Pippin finds her?"

Odilo drew from his cloak a sealed letter. "Give her this and tell her I await her in Bavaria. I will leave four knights to escort her."

"Pippin may not let her go."

Odilo nodded. "My men have been instructed not to force the

question. They're here only to protect her if she comes east." He held Bertrada's eyes. "Tell her I love her. And pray she returns soon."

Several times, Bradius doubled back on their trail or laid false trails for their pursuers to follow. *He must think they're close,* Trudi thought. Otherwise he wouldn't work so hard to throw them off his trail. To Trudi, her captor looked haggard and exhausted. Bradius was barely holding on.

He had been silent since telling his son's tale by the fire. His eyes had become dark and haunted. Several times during the day's ride, she had caught him looking her way with an emotion somewhere between anger and need. Each time their eyes had met, he averted his gaze.

When they camped, they did not untie her. "We won't be here that long," Auguste had said. As was their habit, the men set up two fires, some distance apart. Bradius sat near his without a word. He cut a small slice of cheese for himself and pulled out his wineskin. Instead of his usual ceremony for savoring his cup, this time he drank directly from the skin. *He looks ready to weep,* she thought. He leaned his head back against the trunk of the tree.

"I'm going to close my eyes for a moment," Bradius said, his eyes already closed. Within seconds, a soft snore purred from his mouth.

Trudi sat very still. The men at the other fire were still drinking and awake. Her eyes searched the camp for something sharp. She spied the small knife Bradius had used to cut his cheese. He had left it by the wineskin.

Crawling as quietly as her bound hands would allow, she picked up the knife and fumbled with it between her hands. It took her some time to invert it to press against the rope. She tried sawing with the blade but couldn't find enough leverage. Frustrated, she propped it on a broad flat stone and pushed her bonds down on it, moving her wrists back and forth. The blade turned sideways. Fumbling, she tried again. And again.

She held the blade between her teeth and then her knees. Finally, she positioned the knife between the heels of her boots, sawing gently back and forth. At last, the blade bit into the ropes that held her. She worked at the bonds for several minutes and then rested to save her strength. When the last strand parted, she wanted to shout in triumph. Instead, Trudi rubbed her wrists and surveyed the camp to find a path to escape.

It was not completely dark, though the trees of the wood blocked out most of the moonlight. From what she could see, she would have to cross through the other campsite to regain the path leading back toward those who followed. Like Bradius, many of his men had fallen asleep. She would have to go now.

Pocketing the small knife, she went through Bradius's sack and found a small square of cheese. This too found its way to her cloak. Satisfied, Trudi backed away from the fire. Bradius still snored.

Inside the cover of the trees, she circled around the other campsite. She moved from tree to tree, stopping at each to listen for any sign of alarm. Staying just outside the camp, it took her less than an hour to gain the path. She stayed to its side, hidden in the wood. She hadn't yet seen the picket. She would have to be careful.

Moving away from the campfire, she found him. He was on the opposite side of the path, facing south. Taking great care with every step, she continued to advance. She held her breath. Despite her best efforts, her left foot snapped a twig. The picket turned and saw her among the trees. She stood frozen, praying that she blended into the fading day. It took him a moment to discern who and what she was. He shouted and sprinted across the path toward her. Trudi turned on her heel and bolted into the woods.

She ran blindly, which she knew to be a mistake. But the picket was so close there was nothing else she could do. The trees seemed to fly by her. Her right shoulder caught a small sapling that had blended into the darkness. She careened into a large oak on her left. She started to fall but kept her balance by dropping her left hand to the ground. Instinctively, she flipped over her hand and felt her shoulder scream with pain. She needed to stop. She needed to hide.

Her near fall had oriented her to the left of her pursuer. She pushed hard to find some place ahead in which to hide. She saw a patch of undergrowth. She dove for it and struggled to control her breathing.

Her pursuer halted at the silence. He called again to the camp and began to walk in ever-widening arcs to find her. She knew she would have to move before his methodical search found her, but for the moment she had to stay put to catch her breath.

A forward scout waited in the road. "They turned into the woods," he said.

Pippin moved his horse into the brush to examine what was left of the tracks. Climbing back onto the road, he sat for a moment and then rode south without explanation. When he returned, it was at full gallop.

"It's a false trail," Pippin said. "Real one's up ahead."

Gunther ordered scouts into the woods to be certain the first trail was false and signaled the rest of the men south down the road.

When they arrived at the spot Pippin had explored, Pippin pointed out the distinctive marks left by the horseshoes of Bradius's party. Several clear and deep hoof prints with the telltale signs appeared in the mud just below the tree line.

"We're close," he said to Gunther. "We've always been one step behind them, and I think this is that step. Send Arnot. He knows how to be quiet."

Gunther signaled for Arnot to scout forward. With a nod from Pippin, Arnot dismounted and melted silently into the woods.

Pippin met the eyes of his men to acknowledge the pending action. Their respiration grew heavy in anticipation, and its vapor curled in the cold to shroud their faces. Bodies tensed. Hearts thundered. "Easy," Pippin whispered.

Arnot was back. He knelt before Pippin and Gunther to map the landscape. A long road in. Ten men. No pickets he could see. No sign of Trudi or of Bradius. No ground advantage. No archers. Pippin was suspicious. Bradius would leave pickets.

Pippin motioned for them to dismount and remove all armor to increase their speed and reduce the potential for noise. With almost no sound, his men complied.

Bringing them in close for instructions, Pippin singled out the six archers into two groups of three. The rest of the men were divided into three squads. One knight would stay behind with the horses. The two groups of archers would enter the woods in north- and south-flanking motions, circling the camp to position themselves slightly west of the outlaws on both sides of the camp. He drew a circle in the dirt with an *X* through it. Each of the three squads would be responsible for attacking one quadrant of the enemy camp—north, east, and south—the three closest to their position. Archers taking the west would attack first and drive any remaining outlaws east into the main body of their attack. Pippin signaled for knives and hatchets only and sent the flanking archers into the woods. As they left, he flashed them the hand signal for "luck."

When her pursuer followed his search pattern away from her, Trudi slipped further into the woods. She heard calls from the camp behind her and turned left again, hoping to circle back to regain the path behind her pursuit. She came to a small clearing and waited at its edge, struggling with the thought of being so exposed. She decided to risk it, ran into the clearing, and stumbled. Rising to her feet, she found Bradius standing at the opposite edge of the clearing, waiting for her.

She froze. His face was contorted with anger. Voices and the sounds of pursuit grew behind her. She sprinted left. Bradius moved to intercept her. He caught her before she reached the woods, throwing himself forward to trip up her legs with his arm. She rolled left out of his grasp and scrambled to her feet.

She threw a kick at his head. He blocked it with his left arm. She spun left and kicked, hitting his rib cage. He grunted and turned to face her. He seemed to reevaluate his quarry. A coldness descended over him. He looked detached, unreachable, murderous.

He walked right at her, standing straight, leaving himself wide open to attack. When he came within striking distance, she kicked, punched, rolled, and kicked again. Somehow, he blocked every blow. She feinted with her left hand to set up a spin kick with her right leg. He waited for the kick to develop and then blocked it easily. *God he is fast*. She threw a punch; he countered and somehow pinned her right arm to his side. Swinging his right leg and hip under her, he took her to the ground.

He clasped her wrists in his hands and wrapped his legs over hers. She struggled underneath him, straining to throw him off with her hips. She found the nearness of him suffocating. The tension and intimacy of their struggle touched something raw and familiar. Images of Ansel pushing against her flooded her thoughts. She felt the heat rise within her.

Surprised at her body's reaction, Trudi stopped struggling altogether. For long moments, their breath mingled in the growing darkness, shrouding their faces in white clouds. She looked up into his eyes and saw the coldness in them melt away. In its place rose a look of pain and lust. His face flushed, and his lip began to curl.

"Don't," she said.

He bent to kiss her lips. She turned her head. His lips found her neck.

"Bradius!" She renewed her struggle beneath him, but this just drove her hips into him. She felt his hardness through their clothes. Again she stopped, short of breath. He moaned and ground himself against her.

She did not want this. Not this. "I beg you in the name of your son," she said. She felt him hesitate.

His green eyes bore into her. Doubt flickered behind them.

"This is not revenge," she said. "Not anymore. You cannot take me like this. 'This, I do of my own will.'"

He looked at her with surprise.

"I am a woman of the earth," she said.

A great sadness clouded his eyes. He rolled his weight off her to lie beside her on the ground. "Ah, Trudi," he said, his voice reeking of dejection. "I thought I could do this. I *wanted* to do this. I have lost so much—my wife, my son, my lands, the tree, and now, my soul. I beg your forgiveness."

Pippin was wary. There were no pickets. Bradius would never make that kind of an error. He and his men moved into position. They stopped within twenty steps of the main campfire, hiding among the trees and underbrush. He waited several minutes for the archers to circle the camp. When he was confident that they had time enough, he gave a short whistle and signaled for the men to advance.

Silent as ghosts, they waded into the camp. Pippin could see four men near the fire. Moving past the nearest, he sliced backward with his knife to sever the man's throat. His hatchet took the next. The outlaw looked down in horror at the ax head, half-buried inside his chest. Pippin was already on to the third. He drew a second knife.

The man slashed first. Pippin blocked it with one blade and buried the other in the man's abdomen. With barely a moment's hesitation, he drew the blade upward, gutting him to the sternum. Hearing someone behind him, Pippin spun to his right and dropped into a crouch, looking for the attack.

It never came. A lone figure stood with an arrow protruding from the center of his neck. It had punched its way through the man's Adam's apple. Pippin's eyes searched the camp. There was no one else to fight. It had taken less than a minute. Each of the three parties met at the fire.

"Clear."

"Clear."

"Clear."

"Bodies?"

Two hands were raised. Each held up three fingers. "That makes ten," Pippin said. "Any sign of Trudi?" All heads shook no.

"Pippin," Arnot's whisper came from the woods. "This way."

Pippin nodded to Gunther and followed Arnot into the night.

Trudi heard Pippin's roar before she saw him. Scrambling to their feet, she and Bradius separated. Bradius crouched to await the attack. Pippin burst from the woods at full sprint, aiming straight at Bradius.

When Pippin reached him, Bradius feinted left and spun right. Two knife blades flashed in the moonlight. Neither bit. Both men turned, circling, blades up, seeking advantage.

Trudi couldn't bring herself to believe that Pippin had finally come. She stood to the side, watching dumbly as the men circled. Gunther, Arnot, and a dozen others spilled into the small clearing. They too went for Bradius.

Pippin raised a hand to them without taking his eyes off Bradius. "He's mine."

Realizing that she was finally safe, Trudi doubled over in relief. Gunther came to her side. "I'm all right," she said. "I just can't believe you are here."

"This will be over in a second."

Pippin and Bradius closed on each other, blades blocking blades, elbows flying. Bradius head butted Pippin. Pippin stepped back, his nose starting to bleed. With a growl, Pippin closed again, and a flurry of metal again shone in the moonlight. This time Bradius backed away bloodied. His face was cut, just below the eye.

"Stop!" Trudi shouted. No one paid any attention to her.

Pippin advanced again, and the two exchanged blows once more. Pippin's blade caught Bradius's shoulder.

"Pippin! Stop!" They continued to circle.

Trudi advanced toward the fighters. Gunther grabbed her by the arm. Without thinking, she spun toward his grasp and wrested her arm away from him. She sprinted toward the combatants. The men closed again.

"I said, stop!" Trudi stepped between them just as blades began to descend.

Bradius's knife caught her in the right shoulder. Pippin's blade arced toward her chest with all his weight behind it. Trudi raised her fists to ward off the blow, but her arm gave way under Bradius's knife. Pippin's blade descended just as she collapsed. He tried to turn the blade, but it sliced into her arm. The blow took her to her knees.

Both men stood back in horror.

"I told you to stop," she said weakly.

Gunther was there. He pulled off her jacket and ripped off the back of her shirt to probe the wound.

"Trudi?" Pippin was clearly at a loss. "You know about the women in that inn."

"It wasn't him, Pippin. They weren't his men. They were mercenaries."

"Did he? Did he?" Pippin sputtered

"He didn't touch me," Trudi said.

Arnot and several men seized Bradius and took away his weapons.

"It doesn't change anything, Trudi. This ends here. Arnot!"

"Huh-yah." The three men holding Bradius dragged him before Pippin and pushed him to his knees.

"No, Pippin." Trudi said. "No, please."

Pippin slid the point of his knife under Bradius's chin.

"No!" Trudi struggled to her feet and stumbled toward them. She pushed Pippin's blade aside. "There's been enough killing."

"He must be held accountable."

"We have enough blood on our hands."

"I won't just let him walk away, Trudi. There is no other way."

"Give me your hands," Trudi demanded of Bradius. He looked at her dumbly. "Give me your hands!" Furious, she shoved Arnot in the chest. He let go of Bradius's arms, and the man held out his hands.

Trudi took his hands in hers. "Will you honor my commands and prohibitions?" Bradius looked at her as if she were insane. "Will you acknowledge my right to punish any transgression of my commands and prohibitions?"

"Trudi, no!" Pippin said.

Light dawned in Bradius's eyes. "I honor your commands and acknowledge your right."

Pippin swore and threw his knife into the ground. It sank to its hilt.

"You commit yourself and your vassals to my military service."

"I so commit."

"You pledge tribute."

"I pledge tribute."

"You pledge fidelity,"

"I pledge fidelity. On my life, I pledge."

Trudi looked at Pippin and then back to her subject. "Rise, Bradius, vassal of Hiltrude, daughter of Charles, son of Pippin of Herstal."

Then she collapsed.

"She let him go?" Bertrada rounded on Pippin. "And you let her?"

Pippin stood in the corner of Trudi's room and shrugged his shoulders. He didn't seem to care about Bradius. His only interest was Trudi. Bertrada gave him an exasperated look and sent him back downstairs. She needed to bathe her patient and replace her bandages. After a moment of grumbling about it, Pippin complied and left the room.

On the face of it, the rescue of Trudi had been a complete success. Trudi had been found unmolested if not unharmed. None, save the two men guarding Trudi, had been killed. And they had completely routed Bradius and his brigands. Nonetheless, she was worried.

Something was wrong.

They brought Trudi into the villa and sent for doctors to tend to the girl's wounds. Fortunately, Gunther's field dressing had been clean and sound. After feeding Trudi the broth from a stewed chicken, Bertrada let her sleep for the night and an entire day.

Pippin was something else altogether. At first she had thought him exhausted. But after a full night's sleep and a hearty breakfast, he remained withdrawn. He tended to his men and his horse but did little else save watching his sister convalesce.

It was Gunther who relayed the story of the chase and Trudi's bizarre acceptance of Bradius's hands. Pippin had listened to the tale without saying a word. Why had Trudi spared Bradius? No one had answers. Why had Pippin let him go? Why was he so distant? She needed to get him alone. But first she needed to bathe Trudi.

"God, help me," Trudi moaned.

Bertrada stroked the girl's hair. "Careful, Trudi. You've been hurt. No, don't try to sit up."

"Oh, Bertie." Trudi's eyes welled.

"I know, dear." Bertie leaned forward, taking the girl in her arms. "You're safe now. No one will hurt you." She rocked her, letting Trudi weep. She stroked her hair and cooed her name. When Trudi's tears were exhausted, Bertie laid her back on the bed and dried her eyes. Some color had returned to her cheeks, but Trudi looked pasty and weak. Dark circles shadowed her eyes, and a large bruise colored the left side of her face.

"Bradius?" She looked around her.

"He's gone, Trudi. He can't harm you."

The girl sighed and closed her eyes. "He won't harm me."

"What happened, Trudi? Why did you let him go?"

The girl shook her head, her eyes still weepy. "We've got enough blood on our hands." She took Bertrada's hand in hers. "Charles killed his men, took his land, and destroyed his place of worship. Carloman … Carloman … murdered his son right in front of him. I thought our family had done enough harm."

"How can you be so sure he won't try again? How do you know he won't come back to take you hostage?"

"He wanted revenge," Trudi said. "He hates Charles. He wanted to take his revenge but couldn't do it. He didn't have it in him. By letting him go, I forged a temporary peace." Trudi chuckled.

"What?" Bertrada turned, grasping at hope that the girl could smile.

"Charles is going to kill me," Trudi said, shaking her head.

"Oh, honey." Tears sprang to Bertie's eyes. "Of course you don't know."

"What is it?"

Bertie laid her hand on the girl's shoulder. "Charles died just after you left Quierzy. Sunni, Carloman, and Gripho were with him. The burial was over a week ago."

Trudi seemed to crumple in on herself. Her hand went to cover her mouth. The gesture had little impact as a howl of despair poured from her. She wept in huge racking sobs that left barely enough time for her to inhale. Bertrada tried to take her back into her arms, but Trudi refused her, shying away into the recesses of her bed. Burying her face in her pillow, she waved for Bertrada to leave.

Pippin appeared in the doorway and rushed to Trudi's side. Seeing him, Trudi reached for him. He took her in his arms. She tried to speak but could not. She looked into his eyes, and her hand rose to his face in a silent plea. Pippin shook his head slowly, and his sister hid herself in his arms. In moments, they both wept openly. Bertrada moved to Pippin's side and put her hand on his shoulder. There was nothing more she could do. She left the two of them to their sorrow.

For three days, Bertrada refused to entertain any notion of a return to Quierzy. She insisted that Pippin stay with his sister. She forbade any political or military discussions and twice had to stare down Childebrand when news arrived of Carloman's pending siege. She let them heal. Slowly, Trudi's color returned, as did her strength. When she was able to get out of bed, Pippin took her on short walks through the city. Bertrada fed them well, watched over them, and to her great relief and satisfaction, eventually saw them smile.

When at last Bertrada acknowledged that they could return to the world, she announced a great feast to celebrate Trudi's recovery. All her out-of-town guests, Pippin's men, and Childebrand were asked to join her in celebration before finding their way home. She accepted no refusals.

Early, the morning of the feast, Bertrada slipped into Trudi's room alone. "We need to talk." She handed Trudi a letter. "I've been waiting until you were well to give you this."

She watched as Trudi's hand caressed the edge of the letter and turned it over to check its seal. Her finger played with the brown melted wax. It had run a little to one side and was thinner in some places than others. It was crudely done, but the seal was clearly Odilo's. Trudi handed her back the letter.

Bertrada couldn't hide her shock.

"I can't read," Trudi said, frowning. "Could you do it for me?"

Bertrada smiled in relief and sat on the edge of the bed. Trudi sat down next to her to look over her shoulder.

"My dearest Trudi," Bertrada began.

"I hope this letter arrives in your hands and that you are now safe and

well. I am haunted by the nightmare of your abduction. I will never be at peace until I know you are safe and with me. I came to Reims to find you and learned that any effort on my part would only increase your jeopardy.

"As you can see, I cannot be there to welcome you. Events have overtaken us. Carloman is preparing to make war on Gripho, and should I stay in the West, I would likely be imprisoned. I must go east.

"I must tell you the simple truth. I love you and want you to be with me. I have left four of my best men behind. They are there to escort you on the road to Bavaria. They are there to bring you home to me.

"Our lives are forever intertwined. Odilo."

Bertrada was crying by the time she finished the letter. She wiped her eyes with the back of her hand and looked up at Trudi expectantly.

Trudi wasn't crying. She looked very small and frightened on the bed.

"Don't you want to go?" Bertrada asked.

"I don't know," Trudi said. "It seems so long ago. Is it real?"

Bertrada folded the letter and gave it to Trudi. She put her hands over the girl's. "Only your heart can tell you that," she said gently. She leaned over and kissed Trudi on the forehead. "*His* heart is in this letter."

Candles stood in all the windows, and small white carved angels lined the mantels. Wreaths hung on every door, and garlands framed the windows. A fire snapped in the hearth and filled the villa's main room with the rich scent of burning oak. Trudi lifted one of the angels, admiring how delicately it was made. Bertrada's decorations held her enthralled. It was something Trudi would never think to do. All her life, she had dismissed such things as silly. But today, Trudi was touched by them.

The feast began early in the afternoon with boar's head paté and quail's eggs. As soon as Bertrada had the wine poured, Childebrand began the toasts.

"To Pippin, the ghost who never sleeps."

"Huh-yah!" Cups upended, only to be refilled by waiting servants.

"To Trudi, lord of the outlaws!" Pippin quipped, laughing. And again, cups were raised. By dinner, most of the thirty-odd guests were drunk on the region's fine wines. The room was boisterous, thought Trudi, and just a little dangerous.

Ansel was there. He had come with Monty and Brand. There could only be one reason for his presence. He was sent by Carloman to take her home. She refused to meet with him. But Bertrada had invited him, and now he stood across the room staring at her. His eyes were strange and nervous, and he was sweating. She avoided him.

She had been arguing all day with Pippin, who wanted her to return home. He said they needed to rejoin their family. She countered that Carloman had already left for Laon to lay siege to Gripho.

"Maybe we can stop it," Pippin said.

"It's too late," she said. "Besides, what about Odilo?"

Pippin frowned at this. "You know he will likely lead the independent duchies to rebel. He may declare war against Carloman and me."

"Don't war against Gripho. Stop Carloman. Odilo won't rebel if there is nothing to rebel against," Trudi said.

They had reached a truce. Trudi promised to consider returning home. Pippin promised to consider letting her leave with the Bavarians.

Bertrada wouldn't discuss it. "Your heart should decide this," was all she said.

The feast roiled with laughter and exuberance. Pippin's men feted their success in avenging the town of Loivre while Childebrand seemed to beam in his newfound role as the mayor's emissary to Reims. He wore the medal around his neck and Trudi was sure that the man would never take it off.

One of the men started to sing "The Widow's War," a doleful song of great sorrow, valor, and loss. One by one, each of Pippin's men took up the ballad, and soon the whole room was singing. The sadness of the widow's story filled Trudi with emotion. When the song was finished, a respectful silence followed as each guest pondered its significance. A soft voice called, "Huh-yah!" and cups were upended again. Trudi wondered how much she had had to drink.

Later, after the meal had been served, Gunther again took up the toasts. He slurred the words so badly, however, that no one understood what he said. An awkward silence followed, and he glowered at the crowd for their temerity.

"Huh-yah!" Trudi shouted, giggling.

"Huh-yah!" the room shouted, and all was forgiven.

Bertrada stood, and the room quieted, as much as could be expected at that time of night. "To Trudi, may she find her heart, wherever it may be, at home or in Bavaria." As before, cups were raised and drained. This time, however, one cup remained full.

"Bavaria? What nonsense is this?" It was Ansel. He stood, cup in hand, with a perplexed look on his face. "Trudi is going home." The room fell silent around them.

"I haven't yet decided," Trudi said.

"It isn't up to you," Ansel said. "I have orders from Carloman. I don't know what all this talk about Bavaria is, but you're coming with me."

Trudi flushed with anger. She didn't take orders from Carloman, and she wasn't going anywhere with Ansel.

"It's not up to *you*," Pippin interjected, to Trudi's surprise. His words were slurred, but his tone clear. Pippin stood, his chair scraping the floor behind him.

"My apologies, Mayor Pippin. As a Knight in Christ, I am bound to follow orders from your brother. Those orders take precedence over yours. She's going with me."

Pippin's sword leapt to his hand. Its point was an inch from Ansel's throat. "Get out, knight," Pippin said. "You've overstayed your welcome. My sister goes where she wishes. It isn't up to Carloman anymore than it is to you."

Ansel did not move.

"Get out." Pippin's voice lowered to a whisper.

It was Childebrand who finally had the sense to intercede. "Off you go," he said, wrapping his arms around Ansel's shoulders. He walked the knight to the door. "Think on it, man," Childebrand said. "That was no farmer with his sword at your throat. That was one of Charles's sons. You best be on your way now."

Ansel turned his head to seek out Trudi. "I will be back to—"

"You'll be leaving now." Childebrand nearly threw Ansel out the door.

Trudi had not moved. Her silence and fury infected the room.

"Pay him no mind," Pippin said. "He can do nothing to you. I won't let him."

Trudi shook her head, her eyes distant. He didn't understand. How could he? "What if you're not there, Pippin?" she whispered. "What if you're outnumbered?"

"No one would dare touch you," he insisted.

She continued to shake her head, finally knowing what to do. "I have to go."

Pippin's eyes were brimming. "Don't," he said. "You and I are all that's left."

"No, Pippin. Find Carloman. Make him stop this nonsense. You're the only one who can. I'm going to Bavaria." Trudi took her brother's face in her hands and kissed him on the forehead. "You have the power to save us all," she whispered to him. "It will have to be you."

Pippin stared at his sister for a long time. Finally, he shook his head with a self-deprecating, wry smile and raised his cup to her. "May honor strengthen your sword." His voice filled the room.

"Huh-yah!" their guests shouted.

They squandered the morning. And Trudi, for one, was grateful. Bertrada had surprised them all by having her cook prepare an elaborate breakfast. Each of her guests was offered a large omelet tailored to his or her tastes. The cook rolled out a table filled with ham, bacon, sausage, onions, and several kinds of cheese. Trudi laughed when Gunther, unprepared for such largesse, had simply said, "Yes," when the cook had shown him the table. After eating their fill, they lingered in Bertrada's great room by the fire.

It was then that Trudi delivered her surprise. She descended from her room dressed in the armor her father had given her. Gunther had recovered most of its pieces during their hunt for Bradius, and Bertrada had ordered them repaired and polished. She had added a green cape, Pippin's color. Trudi thought it added a touch of femininity. With the exception of the need for a sling to hold up her right arm, Trudi felt as if she had been made whole. She acknowledged the whistles and applause she received by performing a mock pirouette for the room. The metal of her armor gleamed in the firelight.

Like a good general, Bertrada swept in to announce that it was time to leave. Outside, the sky was a bright blue, and the air crisp with the chill left by the last of the morning dew. They made their way to the city gate and split into two groups, Bertrada joining Pippin and his men to head north, Trudi joining the Bavarian knights to go south.

Outside the gate, Pippin's men dismounted to say good-bye. The discomfort they had felt around Trudi during the early days of their journey was gone. During her convalescence, Trudi had forged a growing intimacy with the unit. She had used the time to seek them out, one by one, and thank them. She asked about their families and learned the names of their children. At the gate, she hugged each knight, whispering her thanks.

As a group, she joked with them, knowing that they were more comfortable with such banter. They laughed when she made fun of Arnot's sheepishness around women and Gunther's inability to smile. She found herself lingering with them, not wanting to let go of the security they represented.

She choked up when she came to hug Gunther. The gruff, short man blushed at her show of affection and stammered until she laughed in spite of her emotions.

Childebrand kissed her on the forehead and tousled her hair. "Your father loved you, Trudi," he said, "even if you always pissed him off." He smiled then and let her go.

The four Bavarian knights sat in their saddles, waiting.

She went to kiss Pippin. And even before he hugged her, she started to cry. As he began to pull away, she clutched him to her and buried her face in his chest.

"I never thanked you," she said.

"There's no need."

"There is," she said, looking up at him. "I always imagined that Odilo would find me. I believed that his love," Trudi rolled her brimming eyes at the word, "would bring him to me, that he would save me. But it was you. You found me. You saved me. It wasn't his love that stopped Bradius." She was crying openly. "It was yours."

Pippin hugged her again. Several of the men turned away to provide them some privacy. The Bavarian captain's horse nickered and stepped out of line until the man yanked in his reins to regain his position.

"Take care of our family," she said, trying to compose herself. "Save Sunni and Gripho." With her one free hand, she tried to wipe away her tears. "Stop Carloman, and when you are done, come visit us in Bavaria." She laughed. "I've heard they make good beer."

He laughed at her and used his thumbs to wipe away her tears. "Are you sure you want to do this?" he asked.

Trudi nodded. To avoid further discussion, she kissed him and turned to mount her horse. Pippin lifted her so she wouldn't strain her shoulder. She put her left foot in the stirrup and swung her right over the horse's back. The four Bavarians spurred their mounts forward, and Trudi followed them out onto the southern road. Before they had gone ten paces, Trudi turned to wave to Pippin. But he and his unit were in their saddles heading north. At the last moment before she lost them to a bend in the road, Bertrada turned and blew her a kiss.

Trudi heard a final "Huh-yah," and they were gone.

CHAPTER 9

Laon

Sunni knew he would come. She was on the wall when he arrived. And while she had seen armies from many different ramparts throughout her life, this was the first army that had come for her. No amount of anticipation could have prepared her for the visceral threat of Carloman's army. A chill took her when his red banner first appeared on the horizon. It seeped through her skin, descended her spine, and found a home in her extremities. She drew her cloak around her. Carloman had come.

She sent for Heden. The two of them watched the vast army's inexorable march across the horizon. It was a parade of manpower, malevolence, and might. Drums led them into the valley. At the front were knights, vassals to Carloman and his commanders, who grouped themselves according to their liege lords. Next came their men of horse, who rode with shields draped over their backs and lances anchored to their right stirrup. Each unit carried its own banner so that across the field men could identify their regiment. Red, green, blue, and gold splashed against the reflecting light of their armor.

"How beautiful," Sunni said.

Legions of men on foot followed those on horse. Organized into perfect squares, ten deep and ten across, the columns funneled onto the plain in pairs, moving across Sunni's vista from left to right. When she had counted twenty such pairs, the columns halted. As one, they turned to face her. As one, they advanced. One hundred paces later, they came to an abrupt halt, and two new columns of men in perfect squares entered the field behind them. When these had mirrored their predecessors across the plain, they too turned as one. Together, the combined columns advanced another hundred paces. Again they halted, and more squares joined the field. And more. Next to her, Heden groaned.

"Six thousand," she said when the full contingent was in the field.

"Enough," he said.

It was noon before they saw the machines.

"Trebuchets," Heden said. "I count six."

Dragged by teams of mules, the massive one-armed slings towered over the soldiers on foot. Carts carrying rock-throwers—smaller versions of the catapults—and massive stone missiles trailed behind.

"How will they get them close enough to do any damage?"

"That's their challenge," he said. "If we weren't so high on this ridge, such machines would reduce our walls to rubble within a week. Drawing them up such a steep incline, however, leaves them vulnerable. They have to get close enough to do us harm."

Behind the war machines, a less disciplined procession followed Carloman's army. Wagonloads of supplies as well as shepherds guiding cows, sheep, pigs, and goats made their way onto the field.

"Carloman came prepared," Heden said.

At the rear straggled what appeared to be an army of civilians. These wandered onto the plain throughout the afternoon and evening, haggard and desperate in their appearance. Several carried crosses. Few were dressed for the journey.

"Who are they?" Sunni asked.

Heden shrugged. "It is not unusual for civilians to follow an army, particularly one preparing for siege. Wives, lovers, prostitutes, children, and merchants all follow armies for their own reasons. But this is different. There are too many. There is almost a small city traveling with Carloman." Heden shook his head. "I don't understand it."

Gripho joined them. Thankfully, thought Sunni, the boy had been more subdued since the burning of the church.

"That must be the entire army," Gripho said. He scanned the banners slowly, looking for something in particular. "Where's Pippin?" he asked.

"Our reports still have him south of Reims trying to find Trudi," Heden said. "This is just Carloman."

"Maybe Pippin doesn't support him."

"Maybe," Sunni said. "But that's not the same as opposing him." She looked at Heden. "How long has it been since Odilo left?"

"Only a few days. He's still a long way from Bavaria."

The army filled the plain below them, marching toward the base of the ridge. Sunni shuddered. It was not the sight that chilled her. It was the sound of six thousand boots pounding the ground at the same instant. It was the sound of drums and horses and armor banging and prancing and clanking in unison, marking the army's progress toward them. It rolled up off the plain to their vantage point high on the ridge. Sunni drew her cloak tighter around her shoulders.

"Our only hope," she said, putting her hand on Gripho's shoulder, "is to hold out here and wait for the rest of Francia to rebel. If Carloman splits his army, we'll have an opportunity to defend our claim."

Her son shrugged off her hand. "My claim," he said. Gripho looked first at his mother and then at Heden. "We'll have the opportunity to defend *my* claim."

Heden scowled and took a step toward the boy. Without taking her eyes from her son, Sunni reached out a hand to soothe her former lover.

"Of course," she said, "it's your claim."

Although Heden had halted at the touch of her hand, his weight shifted from foot to foot, and his hand tugged on the ends of his great mustache.

Far below them, six thousand troops, several hundred mounted cavalry, and all Carloman's knights on horseback stopped moving at the same instant. The drums stopped. The horses stopped. The clanking of armor stopped. Everything stopped. The plain fell silent. It was an impressive display of discipline. Sunni could not breathe.

Very near to Carloman's banner, a new flag was unfurled and placed on a standard. A single knight rode forward carrying it in his stirrup. At an unseen signal, he stood in his saddle and raised the flag above his head. He waved it three times.

Gripho looked to Heden.

"Parley," the Thuringian said. "They want to talk."

"I'll go," Gripho said.

Heden grunted.

"We'll all go," Sunni said. "But first there is something I need to do."

She strode from the ramparts and took the steps down from the wall. By the time she reached the courtyard, her pace had hurried. In the privacy of her villa, she broke into a sprint. Running up the stairs and through her rooms, she burst onto her private balcony and lifted the pigeon cage marked with blue. Opening its latch, she pulled one bird after another from their temporary home and released them into the afternoon sun.

Standing in his saddle, Drogo waved the banner again high over his head in a broad sweeping motion.

"That's enough, son," Carloman said behind him, his voice almost conversational, as if they were at home playing in the courtyard.

Drogo sat down and anchored the banner pole in his right stirrup. He turned his horse back to the line and took his place by his father's side. "Who do you think will come?" he asked.

"I think they both will," Carloman said. "Sunni to negotiate, and Gripho because he, like you," he smiled at his son, "will be curious."

"Do you think they'll fight us?"

"Hopefully not. But from the looks of it, they are prepared to."

"How do you know?"

His father pointed to the trenches and defensive fortifications outside the walls. "You wouldn't put up obstacles like that if you didn't plan to defend."

"Maybe they'll listen to you."

"Maybe."

"Or maybe we could just grab them when they come out?"

Carloman laughed. "That sounds like my father."

"Why couldn't we? Then no one would get killed."

"They will come with enough men to conduct an organized retreat," Carloman said. "It would also be bad form. The parley should never be violated lightly, especially among countrymen." After a moment's thought, he added, "And family. You never know when you might need the courtesy yourself."

A flag was waving high on the rampart. They both strained to see it over the steep angle made by the ridge.

"They're coming," Drogo said.

His father nodded.

Drogo couldn't help but be excited. He had been waiting so long for his father to treat him as a knight. He couldn't count as legitimate the battles with Charles at Avignon and Narbonne. He had stayed behind the lines for most of the campaign and had been allowed to fight only when the battle had been decided.

This time would be different. This time, he was in his father's retinue. And everyone knew Carloman's banner was always in the thick of the battle. Drogo shifted in his saddle. He couldn't get comfortable. His armor didn't fit quite right. He had grown since the summer, and the plated girdle he wore was too tight. When he shifted his weight, the leather squeaked, and the metal scraped. He caught some of the amused looks from his father's men. His face flushed red. He'd show them when it counted. His horse shied a step or two. *Damn*.

"You might as well get used to waiting, Drogo," Johann said, sitting protectively close by. "This is a siege. Waiting is part of the strategy." A few of the men chuckled. Drogo was furious with himself.

A cavalry contingent made its way down the ridge. For the most part, it followed the winding road down the incline. The horsemen, however, often deviated from the path to descend more rapidly, as if they all knew a secret way down the ridge. Drogo saw Gripho's purple banner with its hawk next to one he did not recognize.

"Heden," his father said, answering the unasked question, "the Thuringian."

When the Laon contingent arrived at the base of the hill, they formed a cavalry line one hundred paces from his father's. Carloman nodded to Drogo, and the two of them rode forward with Johann. Mirroring their movement, three riders separated from the opposing cavalry and closed the distance. Sunni and Gripho accompanied an older man with a long mustache. They stopped just paces from Carloman and Drogo.

"Hello, Carloman," Sunni greeted them. Drogo smiled in response. "Welcome to Laon," she said. "I would invite you up, but," she looked out at his vast army, "I didn't anticipate that you'd bring so many extra guests."

"Sunni. Gripho." From Carloman's tone, the three of them could have been strangers. Carloman looked to the Thuringian. "Heden." The older man inclined his head in acknowledgment. "A curious time to be in Laon, don't you think?"

"I have always been a hopeless romantic," the Thuringian said.

"Hopeless is an appropriate word."

"Why are you here?" Sunni asked.

"A priest arrived in Paris. He was horribly disfigured by fire. He claims that Gripho set fire to him and his church. His monsignor backs up the story."

"And?" Sunni asked.

"I'm here to investigate and address this heinous act."

"You have no authority here," Sunni said. "Gripho is mayor, and I am his regent. If there is to be an investigation, it is mine to hold. Not yours."

"This was a house of God," Carloman said, his voice growing louder. "Given your upbringing and the fact that Gripho is your son, I doubt you could grant this matter the gravity it deserves."

"You could have sent a messenger," Sunni said. "Or you could have come alone. You didn't need to bring an army to get my attention. Why are you really here, Carloman? Why do you need six thousand knights camping outside my door? Certainly they're not here to 'investigate.'" Sunni's voice rose in anger. "This has nothing to do with that pitiful priest. The fire was an accident. This," she said leaning in, "is about the succession. This is about the division of the kingdom. This is about you and Gripho."

"I come on behalf of the Church," Carloman retorted.

"You've come on behalf of yourself."

"He," Carloman pointed at Gripho, "desecrated the house of God."

"He desecrated nothing."

"This is about justice," Carloman shouted.

"This is about power," Sunni said.

"I suggest you get your things together and come with me willingly," he said.

"What about Pippin?"

Carloman stared at her in silence.

"Does he support you in this? Or are you taking advantage of his absence?"

"If you don't come with me peacefully," Carloman said, "you'll come by force of arms." Carloman pulled on his reins and began to turn away. Johann turned with him.

"Carloman!" Sunni's shout made him pause. He turned his head. "You are not your father," she said, holding his stare. Carloman turned his back on his family and rode to rejoin his army.

Confused, Drogo looked from Gripho and Sunni back to his father.

"That's it?" he whispered to Sunni.

"That's it, Drogo," Sunni said. "You should go now with your father."

He looked to Gripho. His uncle nodded in agreement.

Drogo took his banner of truce and turned away from them, joining Johann, who had stayed behind for him. He followed his father toward their cavalry line. A sinking feeling took him, and Drogo wondered whether he would ever see Sunni and Gripho again. He turned in his saddle and looked over his shoulder. Only Sunni remained. Gripho and Heden had started back up the ridge. She sat stoically, her body erect and rigid. But when her eyes caught his, they softened. Sadness filled them until she shook her head as if to banish an unwelcome thought. When she next looked at him, she smiled. It was a loving smile, the one he had known all his life. And she waved to him. It was a small gesture, but in that moment, it was all he could see.

With a shiver of guilt, Drogo smiled and waved back. He turned and joined his father in line.

The next day, Gripho watched from the rampart as a lone archer worked his way up the hill outside the city walls. The man was a fair distance from the gate. Behind him, a long line of soldiers snaked its way up the winding road from the plain below. The archer notched an arrow and let it fly at the wall of the city. It fell short of its mark. He advanced, and the line of soldiers advanced with him. Fifty paces up the hill, he stopped, and the line stopped with him. Again he notched an arrow, again he let it fly, and again it fell short. They continued to advance.

At last the archer seemed satisfied that his position was as close as he could get to the rampart without being within arrow range. Burying an arrow in the side of the hill, he waved at the men behind him and pointed to the arrow as his marker.

The soldiers advanced to the arrow and split into two lines, one moving east, one moving west, and both moving parallel to the walls. Within little more than an hour, they had encircled the city. They began to dig. Using the steepness of the slope to their advantage, they cut into the side of the hill to form a wall. The dirt was shoveled onto the high side of the bunker, toward the city, and packed into mounds several feet thick.

Gripho was surprised to find Heden standing next to him. He had been so engrossed in the earthworks that he failed to hear the gray-haired bastard approach.

"What are they doing?" Gripho asked.

"Carloman's building a wall around the city," Heden said. "The battle ground will lie between. With that wall, he can keep anyone from coming or going."

Gripho came back to the wall every day after that, and always Heden was there, watching the earthen wall rise around Laon. Carloman's army carried planks of wood up the steep hillside to hold the wall into position and to lay stable flooring for the trench that lay behind it. Opposite each of the city's three gates, Carloman erected a makeshift wooden gate. He built the walls there higher to face the city's ramparts. Scaffolding had been built up around these, and soldiers were stationed there to stand watch.

"He can defend his troops from our sorties using those ramparts," Heden said, pointing to scaffolding being built near the gates. "They will set up rock-throwers there to disrupt any attack coming out of our gates. And anyone entering the field between the walls is within range of their archers. Given enough preparation, they could destroy any force we might send outside our walls before we could get into position."

Gripho was impressed by how thoroughly his brother Carloman prepared. "What can we do to stop him?" he asked.

"Attack before they're ready." Heden pointed out several platforms being built behind the dirt wall on the far side of the gate. "He will have a hard time getting his catapults close to the walls. That's why he's building the ramparts. If we can prevent his catapults from getting too close, Carloman will be in for a long and difficult winter."

But much to Gripho's dismay, Heden didn't attack. Instead, the old fart waited. Two days went by, and the Thuringian continued to let Carloman dig in unmolested. The dirt wall now stood three feet high and housed a labyrinth of fortification, walkways, storage facilities, platforms for the rock-throwers, and arrows for the archers. Heden did nothing to stop the never-ending line of soldiers moving up and down the winding road from the plain below. The man was content to wait.

Gripho was not.

"When are we going to attack?" he asked on the third day. "You said yourself we need to attack before they're ready. If we wait much more, they will be." But Heden showed no interest in answering his question. Like Carloman and Pippin before him, Heden had dismissed Gripho's concerns. Gripho even called the old fuck a coward, and Heden ignored him. The Thuringian simply pretended not to hear.

On the fourth day, Gripho was first to the eastern wall. He could see the pulleys and winches lining the hillside and the mules and horses being driven downhill to bring the machines up. Progress was slow since the wheels of the trebuchets were small and solid. Progress was further hindered by the wide base the trebuchets needed for stability. But they were drawing close. By evening they would be in place.

Gripho waited for Heden to climb up the steps to the rampart. "You waited too long, Heden. They've finally come," Gripho said.

"The catapults?" Heden's eyes seemed to twinkle when he said the word.

"Yes."

"How many?"

"They're bringing up three."

"How far up the ridge are they?

"About a third of the way."

"Good boy. Send for the captains. We attack in the morning."

Gripho wanted to kill him.

At dawn the next day, Heden led one hundred men on foot streaming through the city gate. They veered right and headed for the lowest part of the dirt wall. They marched quickstep in formation with shields on their arms. Some of the men carried torches. Others brought buckets of pitch. Shouts erupted from behind the dirt wall, and within seconds, archers and rock-throwers appeared.

"Shields!" Heden shouted from the front of the column.

Without breaking stride, the soldiers raised their shields above their heads to form a metal and leather roof to deflect the falling arrows. Wooden missiles rose and fell but were too few in number to have much effect. Heden knew there would be more next time.

A whooshing noise came from the wall, and a rock slammed into the side of the column, cutting one man in half and crushing the legs of several others. As the men went down, those behind them in formation stumbled over them, breaking their line.

"Close up!" Heden shouted. More arrows fell. More rocks were thrown. More men went down. "Close up! Close up!"

As they reached the low dirt wall, long wooden pikes shot out from behind it, skewering several in the front row in the groin and in the stomach. Soldiers behind the wall had rammed them forward trying to break the onrushing wall. The ploy had worked. The pikes gored many and hampered most. With their shields over their heads, Heden's men had left their bodies vulnerable from below.

"Forward!" Heden shouted. He batted away a pike and pulled men forward between the poles. "Over the wall!" he cried. He led them up over the short dirt wall, and they dropped into the trench behind it, using their shields as battering rams. They arose into hand-to-hand combat. With his shield to his left, Heden elbowed the soldier to his right in the face. A sharp pain sliced into his side. He hacked down on the man with his sword, and his blade caught flesh and bone. Throwing his shoulder behind his shield, he shoved left into the men clustered there, knocking several down. He kicked one in the groin and thrust his sword into the abdomen of the other. With a practiced motion, he slid his arm through the sling of his shield, and it slid onto his back. He drew his knife with his left hand.

More men came from his left. He waded into them. Slicing through the eyes of the first with a backhanded slash, Heden thrust his sword past the man into the stomach of the next. He continued forward, struggling to maintain his feet on the blood-soaked wooden planks lining the trench. He twisted and slashed, moving from one opponent to the next. Suddenly, he was free. Looking back, he saw his men running through the trench toward him. Bodies from both armies littered the wooden walkway.

"To me! To me!" Heden shouted, pounding his chest. He gathered the men behind the closed gate, forming them into two lines, and led them straight for the catapults. With a furious intensity, they cut a swath through late-arriving Frankish soldiers who ran into the attack rather than forming a defensive line. The mistake cost them their lives. They were slaughtered to a man.

Nothing stood between Heden and the siege engines. He raced down the hill to the platforms that held two of the machines in place. The third was still being pulled up the hillside. Heden called for the pitch. Only two men who carried buckets remained. He signaled for them to be poured onto the two stationary machines. Within moments, the torches were applied, and the flames licked up the wooden shafts of the catapults.

Rallying to defend them, a number of Carloman's soldiers formed a line at the gate and began an organized advance. Seeing them, Heden threw his weight against the side of the burning catapults. Thirty hands joined his, and with a groan, they toppled the machine from its perch. It began to roll clumsily down the side of the hill. Within twenty paces, its wheels caught a rock and the behemoth flipped over, somersaulting toward the plain below. On its second flip, the machine broke apart and became a wave of fire sweeping down the hill.

Seeing the battle line approaching, Heden knew he didn't have enough time for the second catapult. The fire would have to suffice. He blew his horn—two short blasts followed by one long—and they ran down the hill deeper into the enemy's territory. Carloman's soldiers closed behind them, cutting off their escape. Ignoring the peril, Heden cut a path straight down the hill to the third catapult. While several men hacked at the thick cords with their blades, Heden formed a rear guard to protect them from the impending charge. He ordered the men into two lines, shield overlapping shield, to create a defensive wall across the road. Each man assumed a well-practiced position with his left shoulder behind his shield and his right foot behind his left. In the second row, each man positioned his shield in the gap between the two men before him, creating a wall behind the wall and fortifying the strength of their position.

Carloman's line slammed into them. Although Heden's men gave way a step or two, they held. Shield against shield, the first rows of each line strained against each other, trying to force a break. Having the higher ground, Carloman's line had the advantage.

Heden blew his horn, one long blast. His men, with practiced skill, used their swords in a series of orchestrated thrusts into the faces and feet of their opponents. This was desperate work as it made the attacker vulnerable. Any exposure from behind the shield provided a target for the other line. While many of these blows proved futile because of the size of the shields, the wounds once inflicted were debilitating. Many men were blinded or crippled in the line. Carloman's line responded with complementary skill, and the two lines locked in an orchestrated dance of furious deadly thrusts.

Behind them, the last strand of the rope holding the catapult was severed, and the huge machine fell away. Its speed was startling. Within seconds, it was airborne and flipping down the steep slope. Pieces of the equipment flew in every direction. On the second bounce, the catapult exploded into a rolling heap of detritus. After a brief cheer, the men turned and threw themselves into support of their cohorts on the line.

Heden again blew his horn. Two long blasts.

Cavalry thundered from the gate of the city. Led by Gripho, they numbered more than forty. They made straight for the gate in Carloman's dirt wall. Defenders of the makeshift rampart called for archers and set to launching the rock-throwers. They came to this late, however, since their attention had been diverted by the fate of the falling catapults. Much to their surprise, their own gate opened before Gripho's charge, letting the cavalry hurtle past their defenses.

Heden's line held.

"Hurry, Gripho," Heden whispered to himself.

Gripho swept into the backs of the Frankish line. Even the men who had heard the attack coming had little chance to defend themselves. The cavalry waded into them, hacking downward with their swords, sinking their blades into the heads, necks, and shoulders of the foot soldiers before them. The cavalrymen were drenched in blood.

With long elegant sweeps of his sword, Gripho severed Frankish heads from their shoulders. They seemed to float off their decapitated bodies as if they had never been joined. Gripho spurred from one to the next, laughing as one ghoulish ball after another hit the ground. Blood spewed upward from their wounds. It was slaughter. He and the cavalry kept at it until all the Frankish line was dead.

Heden's horn blew. Three long blasts. His remaining foot soldiers regrouped into formation, flanked by Gripho's cavalry. They turned back to the gates. The cavalry rode ahead and swept behind the wall, forcing the archers to flee before them. The men on foot advanced through the makeshift gate and made for the city. The cavalry closed behind them. Several stray arrows harassed them back to the wall, but none did any damage. The last of the cavalry rode through the city's gates, and its heavy wooden doors closed behind them.

A crowd cheered them as they reentered the city. Gripho raised his sword in salute. When the crowd saw how few returned and how saturated they were with blood, they muted their enthusiasm. Of the hundred men on foot that had left the gate at dawn, fewer than twenty remained. None of the cavalry had been lost.

Heden marched the men to their barracks and, with his duty complete, collapsed.

"You're too old for this," Sunni chided him.

"You knew that when you sent for me." Heden groaned.

He was in his bed. Sunni sat next to him, washing his body with a sponge. He had no idea how he had gotten there. He was weak and feverish. He watched Sunni bend to her task. The sponge was cool on his body. Her hands were gentle.

"I wondered what it would take to get you into my bed," he said with a wry smile.

Sunni reached out to comb his hair with her fingers. Failing at this, her hand cupped his face and then came to rest on his chest, palm down. Her eyes were sad. She dunked the sponge in water and resumed washing away the grime from his body.

"How bad is it?" he asked, somewhat alarmed.

"Bad enough." She lightly touched a bloodstained bandage on his right side. "You'll live, but it will take some time to heal. I'll have to sew it shut, of course."

"One of the doctors can—"

"No," she said. "I will do it."

She made him roll to his left so she could wash his back. She did this efficiently, examining every cut and hole in his skin. When she had completed his upper body, she pulled back the sheet and began to wash his lower body. She cleaned his genitals, moving them from side to side, and then worked her way down his legs to his feet. When she was through, she moved the sponge and water to a nearby table and returned with a needle and thread.

"Are you ready?" she said.

He nodded. Removing the bandage, she probed the wound with her fingers, looking for pieces of cloth or metal.

"Did the blade stay in you?"

"No."

"Did it break inside you?"

He shook his head.

"It looks pretty deep. I'll do the best I can."

Blood was filling the cavity in Heden's side. It brimmed over and began to run down his abdomen to his hip and then onto the bed. Heden watched Sunni maneuver the edges of the severed skin together until they matched and quickly sank her needle through the bottom layer of the skin and up through the top. Her hands moved with assurance, repeating the gesture until the skin had closed over the wound. Blood continued to seep through the stitches. She applied a new bandage to the site and wrapped it around his body to hold it in place.

"Did we destroy the third trebuchet?" he asked her.

"Yes," she said without diverting her eyes from her task. "Their soldiers tried to put out the fire. But by the time they got there, it had been damaged beyond repair. The two you toppled down the hill, of course, are gone."

"There's three more," Heden said. "Carloman won't be caught off guard again."

"How did you open their gates?" Sunni asked. "When Gripho took the cavalry out to cover your return, their gates flew open of their own accord. If not for that, you and your men would have been lost."

"Ah," Heden said, reveling in his secret. "Once inside their trenches, we fought our way to the other side of their gate, then chased the trebuchets." He stroked his long mustache. "Two of our men stayed behind at the gate, pretending to be dead. When Gripho needed the gates opened, they had a miraculous recovery." He smiled up at her. She looked away.

When she was done dressing his wound, Sunni went to get fresh linens. Rolling him first one way and then another, she replaced the wet and bloodied sheets on his bed. She took the soiled sheets from the room and left them outside his door.

"I'm having some soup brought up to you," she said, her eyes still avoiding him.

"Sunni—"

"You shouldn't eat anything solid until your strength returns."

"Sunni," he said, reaching up to take her hand.

She looked at him then. Her eyes were brimming with tears. "Heden, what have I done? I have been so selfish. I wasn't thinking of the cost."

He pulled her to him. She laid her head on his chest, and he felt her tears fall to his skin. Stroking her hair, he said, "Shhh, I'm right where I want to be."

Picking her head up to look into his face, she said, "This isn't even your fight."

"It's one of my choosing," he said. "Besides, there are some things that are worthy of a fight."

She moved to kiss him on the forehead, but he caught her face in his hands and drew her to his mouth. Her lips hesitated at first and then gave in to his embrace. Their soft warmth enveloped his mouth, and he remembered the taste of her. Her warmth spread through him, flooding his extremities. Something happened to him then, something both physical and profound. He could only describe it as "relief." It was as if a tremendous tension lifted from him, a burden removed. His body relaxed, and his blood sang.

Sunni pulled back from him and looked into his eyes. She was smiling and crying at once. She stroked his face with her hand. "You are a lovely man," she said. "I don't deserve such a champion."

"I'll not leave again," he said.

"I know," she said. "You won't have to." Sitting up, she recovered her nurse's voice and said, "You need rest. And I plan to see that you get it. Eat all the soup when it gets here, and I'll check in on you later." She stood to go and bent to pull the blanket up around his shoulders. As she tucked it under his arms, her eyes registered a large lump protruding from the lower end of his torso. She laughed and patted the lump affectionately before turning to leave.

"Maybe you're stronger than I thought," she said.

Pippin took his time though he knew it bothered Childebrand. Despite his uncle's growing frustration, he refused to be hurried. They stopped in Loivre to see to the town's reconstruction. Some of the young girls who had been taken had returned to their mothers' care. Others had not survived. Bertrada checked on each of the women, leaving a silver denarius behind for every household. Pippin insisted that his men help build shelters for the village survivors. Although Bertrada relayed the news of Bradius's capture and their administration of justice on those at the inn, most of the villagers only nodded numbly, as if the news held little meaning for them.

When they regained the northern road, Pippin continued his leisurely pace. They ate well, rested often, and enjoyed the bright sunshine that favored their journey. Each night, they stayed at a comfortable inn. Each morning, he dallied in bed with Bertrada, intent on savoring the last moments of the spell she had woven around him in Reims.

"This is irresponsible," Childebrand said, riding his warhorse alongside Pippin and Bertrada. His face was dark and angry. "You *know* Carloman is at Laon. You *know* the war has begun. And we're wandering around while you dally here with your girlfriend! We're at war, man. War!"

Bertrada patted Pippin's hand and said, "I should probably leave the two of you alone."

Childebrand looked from Pippin to her and back to Pippin, and then blushed. "I'm sorry, Bertie—"

"No need, good sir," she said and laughed. Raising her hand to shield his embarrassment, she pulled back on her reins to let the two men move ahead. "I shall retire willingly."

"I'm sorry, Pippin," Childebrand grumbled, still flustered. Pippin too waved off his apology.

"Why are you in such a hurry?" Pippin asked his uncle.

"Have you not been listening?" Childebrand bellowed, regaining his outrage.

"Yes, yes, I know. Carloman's laying siege to Sunni and Gripho." He paused. "But have you asked yourself, what are we going to do?"

"We can't do anything while we're vacationing here in the country."

"True," Pippin said. "But Carloman brought an army. He has six thousand men. We have less than twenty knights. He's not going to listen to reason. He's not going to leave. Sunni's not going to give in. So what do *we* do?"

"We take Carloman's side," Childebrand said.

"We do?" Pippin asked. "Why?"

"Because you can't take Gripho's! You heard the reports. The boy burned a church. He's creating a pagan state. He's a child! You and Carloman need to take control before the whole kingdom breaks into camps."

"My father named three mayors. What if I could restore the balance?"

"It's too late for that. Carloman would never accept it."

"But what if I could? What if I could end the siege and restore the balance and stop the war?"

"You're no diplomat, Pippin."

"Maybe," he mused.

A long silence followed. "So," Childebrand said, "you *do* have a plan."

"I might be working on one."

"Well?"

"It's not quite ready yet. I need to talk it over with Bertie."

"Bertie?"

"Yes, that woman you just chased away."

"I didn't know you got battle advice from a woman," the big man said.

"She's quite good, actually," Pippin said, his eyes laughing. "But this is about intelligence." Seeing the continued confusion on Childebrand's face, he said, "Her father, you may recall, is the Compte de Laon."

"Little good that will do us," he grunted, "unless she happens to have a secret way into the city."

Pippin smiled and said nothing. Childebrand looked sideways at him, frowning. Pippin let the thought fester in his uncle's mind.

"With that ...," Childebrand said, his one eye flickering. "Maybe we could ..." His lips pursed, and his brow furrowed. "If he could ..." His hand found his face and wrestled with his chin.

"Yes," said Pippin. "We'll need to take some time with it."

"Bastard," Childebrand said. "You knew all along there's a way to intercede."

Pippin nodded to his uncle and grinned.

Pippin and his party made their way down to the plain from the south. He had left Bertrada in a nearby village, lording over the staff of a small inn. In this area, she was better known than he was. The villagers fell over themselves to serve the daughter of the Compte de Laon.

When they reached the outermost of Carloman's pickets, Pippin and his men were held up for several minutes while the soldiers sent for instructions. Although they clearly recognized Pippin, his status was unclear to them. Pippin understood this. If Carloman could war on one brother, why not another? When they finally received instructions, the men escorted Pippin's party through camp rather than allow them to ride in freely. The Knights in Christ seemed to be everywhere and in charge of most regiments.

That's a change, Pippin thought.

A quick look at the troops in camp showed that none of Pippin's men were present. Carloman had brought only those vassals loyal to himself.

Taking all twenty of the knights he had with him, Pippin made his way to Carloman's tent. There they were stopped once again, the guards barring their way with long pikes. Looking around for some authority, Pippin recognized Johann, who was acting as captain. They had fought together several times in the past. Pippin began to push past the picket, moving beyond the raised pikes.

"Hold!" Johann ordered.

Pippin stopped, surprised. Johann strode toward him, his gray eyes cold and uncaring. Pippin continued forward. He could hear swords being drawn.

"Johann, who has ordered you to stand between me and my brother?"

"Carloman said no one was to disturb him."

"That doesn't apply to me."

"Unless he said it doesn't, it does."

Pippin had had enough. "You'll have to kill me then," he said, continuing toward Carloman's tent. He heard more swords drawn, including those of his men. He turned and found Johann's blade pointing at his neck. Pippin stared into the man's eyes, spun on his heel, and walked into Carloman's tent.

He found Carloman standing at a large table, poring over several handsomely colored maps.

"Hello, brother," Pippin said.

Carloman looked up at the greeting. Seeing Pippin, he came around the table and clasped his brother to his chest.

"I'm sorry I wasn't there," Pippin said, his eyes welling.

"He was too," Carloman said.

Johann burst into the tent behind Pippin. Shouts and the clanking of swords could still be heard through the fabric of the tent. Seeing the two men embrace, he turned and left. Outside, Johann called off the guard.

"I heard about Hunoald," Pippin said. "Did Waifar really—"

Carloman nodded. "I was standing right next to the casket." His eyes squinted, distant with the memory.

Pippin felt the fury building inside him. "A pagan curse, that—spitting on the dead … a great insult." His voice filled with certainty. "They should be dead men. I won't let it pass. That's where we should be with our armies, Carloman. Not here. They are the enemy. Not Gripho."

Carloman shook his head, as if dismissing the subject. "Where is Trudi? Is she here?" He started for the flap of his tent.

"She's not here. She's on her way to Bavaria. She's gone to marry Odilo."

Carloman froze. Nothing could disguise the shock on his face. "Father had a pact with King Liutbrand. She's to marry Aistulf."

"Trudi isn't willing. I let her go. She is already under Odilo's protection."

"You fool. Liutbrand will attack Rome. He'll put the pope under *his* protection. You need to bring her back. You should have known not to act on something this important without asking me."

Pippin ignored his brother's insult and moved past him to the table. He picked up the map of Laon and turned it right side up to study it. "What are you doing here, Carloman? Why are you laying siege to Laon?"

"It's a long story, brother. If you had been here instead of gallivanting around Champagne, you would know."

Again, Pippin ignored the jibe. "From what I've heard, you've sided with Theudoald."

"I've sided with the Church."

"You're proving Theudoald's point." Carloman had to know this. If Gripho was not a rightful heir, neither were they. Carloman, himself, was putting the succession in doubt and giving credence to Theudoald's claim.

"I'm doing what has to be done."

"You haven't answered my question. Why are you laying siege to Laon?"

Carloman snatched the map out of Pippin's hands and turned away from him to restore it to its place on the table. "Leave this to me, Pippin. Politics is not one of your strengths."

"Is it yours?" Pippin grabbed Carloman by the arm, forcing him to turn. "I'm not the one who agreed to raise a Merovingian. You've walked into a trap so obvious Drogo could see it."

"Go play with your girlfriend, Pippin." Carloman shrugged his arm free. "I've got more than enough men here to succeed."

Clearly, Carloman had signaled that the discussion was over. Pippin's anger flashed at the snub. It was always like this with Carloman. He never listened to Pippin's counsel. Pippin's voice dropped low, quiet with menace. "You would do well to remember that you were not the only one named mayor." Carloman stiffened. Pippin's tone had registered. "Or are you planning to make war on me too?"

Carloman looked as if he might. His fists were clenched, and his face was red. Mucus leaked from his nose. Carloman pulled a handkerchief from his sleeve to blot the liquid. The movement served to break his tension. Carloman's body relaxed, and when he spoke, his voice was calm. "Gripho burned a church. We can't let that go unanswered."

"I could. I would have left it to Sunni."

"She can't be trusted." Again, Carloman was dismissive. Again, it irked Pippin. "She's pagan! She'll protect Gripho."

"You never took her seriously," Pippin said.

"You're naïve!" Anger flooded Carloman's face. He began pacing inside the tent. "We need the Church. They're withholding their military obligation, saying their duty is to the king. They won't back a pagan mayor and insist we raise a Merovingian."

"Christ!" Pippin stepped in front of his brother, arresting his progress. Their faces were inches apart. "It's everything Father fought against. You *don't* have to do this. As long as we stay together, the Church will have nowhere else to go. Theudoald is no real threat."

"The Church won't support a pagan mayor."

"It's not theirs to decide." Pippin pounded the table with his fist. "You have to stop this, Carloman. You are starting a war that won't end."

Carloman's face bloomed red. "He burned a church, goddammit!"

Flustered at his outburst, he crossed himself hurriedly. Again, he dabbed at the mucus at his nose. "I had to come," he said.

"Let me stop it," Pippin said. "Let me intercede. Call a truce. If I give them my oath of protection, they will come out, and we can work together to divide the kingdom. Sunni will be reasonable."

"Gripho can't be mayor."

"Of course he can be mayor. We just have to decide that he is. Who will contradict us?"

"I will," a strange voice answered.

Pippin turned to find a priest dressed in white standing at the flap of Carloman's tent. Johann stood behind him. Carloman waved the blond knight off. "I will," the priest repeated and stepped into the tent. "There is no room for a pagan mayor. There is no room for Gripho the Desecrator."

"Who is this?" Pippin looked to Carloman.

"I am God's eyes and His ears," the priest said.

"There is an army of support for Gripho's ouster among the Church congregations," Carloman explained. "This man is Father Daniel, their leader. A thousand of his followers have joined us."

Father Daniel held his hand aloft in blessing, awaiting their obeisance. Carloman bowed his head. Pippin stared at his brother and then turned his back on the priest. "Here?" He was nearly shouting. "You brought them with you to a siege?"

Carloman's face was a mask. "I couldn't see a good way to stop them."

"You're feeding them?

"Yes."

"Have you lost your mind?" Pippin shook his head. Then, surprisingly, he began to laugh. It was all so familiar. Liutbrand, the Church, the priest—Carloman was taking care of everyone's interest, except his own. It was as if he were everyone's older brother. "I'm going to end this," Pippin said. "I'm going to go into the city and bring them out."

"We've already parleyed," Carloman said. "They won't come. They've enlisted Heden, the Thuringian. He has proven to be quite effective at defending their interests."

"I can do this."

"No, brother, you're too late." Carloman had restored his composure. He put his arm on Pippin's shoulder. Their eyes met. There would be no more discussion. "I won't turn back. We attack at dawn."

Pippin looked from his brother to the priest and back again. How had it come to this? He shook his head. "*You* attack at dawn, Carloman. I'll have no part in it."

Carloman turned away and busied himself with his maps. "Suit yourself," he said clearly, trying to sound casual. "You'll see when we—"

But Pippin was already outside. He had heard enough.

CHAPTER 10

Stepping into Footprints

On the day of her departure, Trudi spent more than an hour lost in the emotions of her morning. When she returned to the present, she discovered that she and the Bavarians were moving steadily south through the rolling countryside of Champagne. The southern road had dried from the rain, and the day was warming with the sun. Trudi thought it ironic that they were taking the same road she had ridden with Bradius. Unconsciously, she rubbed her wrists.

She tried to engage the captain in conversation, but the man refused to speak to her. Astonished, she looked over her escorts. All were men in their twenties. Each of them had a mustache but otherwise was clean-shaven. She tried to pick out attributes that might help her distinguish one from another but failed. They could be brothers. To make matters worse, each one was as rigid in posture and formal in demeanor as the next.

"Professionals," she said under her breath.

They rode in a diamond formation. The captain took the lead in front, one knight on each side, and the fourth brought up the rear. Again, she tried to engage in conversation, asking questions of the knights flanking her. Again, she received nothing from them. They kept their eyes straight ahead and ignored her inquiries. It wasn't until they had stopped to rest their mounts that any of them spoke. It was midafternoon.

"While on duty, we're prohibited from speaking save on military matters," one of the knights said.

"Then why can you talk now?"

"Hans can guard our position alone," he said, nodding toward the knight standing at attention, watching the road. "When we ride, we are forbidden to speak with you."

"That will make for a very boring journey," Trudi said.

"Perhaps," he replied, "but a safer one."

Trudi decided to test her arm. She removed it gingerly from her sling and tried to let it slowly straighten toward the ground. Gouts of pain shot through her arm into her shoulder and slammed the side of her head. She nearly lost consciousness. Making a move to hold her arm up with her other hand, Trudi felt something tear in her shoulder. She grunted and started to fall until the knight beside her moved to her aid. He helped her to sit on the trunk of a nearby fallen tree and quickly unclasped the armor she wore. She felt blood run down her arm.

"You've opened the wound," her knight said. "It's to be expected. I'll prepare a field dressing." Trudi flexed her hand, marveling at the pain she felt. At least she would be able to use her arm.

"Stop that," the knight said. "You're making it worse." He put a cloth bandage on her wound and took her free hand and placed it on the bandage. "Hold this," he said. "This needs a few days more to heal before you can work it." Although he wound her bandage tight, he surprised her with the gentleness of his touch. Within minutes, he had her wrapped and back into her armor.

"What's your name?" she asked him.

"Juergen," he said.

"So pleased to meet you." She smiled, wondering if he heard the potential for sarcasm in her voice.

"Mount," Hans called from the road. As one, the party swung into their saddles. Trudi stood next to her horse, knowing she couldn't pull herself up alone. With a sigh, Juergen swung down, helped her up, and then regained his saddle. They resumed their formation and guided her back onto the southern road.

"It's going to be a long ride," she said.

No one answered.

After several hours of silence, Trudi decided there was no reason she couldn't hold up her side of the conversation. She chatted about how glorious the new day was. She commented on the rolling countryside and pointed out the colorful flowers and birds they passed on the road south. Recognizing that this might be of little interest to her four armored friends, she told them stories about her training master and how difficult a curmudgeon the man could be.

"With Fulrad, there was no right way or wrong way. There was only his way." She laughed. "At first, he did not want to teach me. He didn't think a woman should be trained for battle. But my father insisted, and my father, he is—was—a hard man to refuse," she said. "Fulrad finally agreed, but had a hard time with it. I wasn't strong enough for the swords he used. He had to find a smaller and lighter blade. Same with the armor," she said. "I couldn't handle the good old Frankish stock. Charles brought me this," she said, indicating her armor. "He got it from the Saracen.

"They fight differently, the Saracen," she said. "Fulrad fought against them with my father at Poitiers. He said they used the shield wall, just like we do. But their sword fighting in melee is much more creative. He said the lighter sword allows for greater flexibility and speed. He had to put together an entire training program just so that I could learn to fight like them.

"One day, I hope to fight against the Saracen myself," she mused. "I want to see whether he really figured it out or just made it up." She laughed again. No one laughed with her. She shrugged, wincing from the pain emanating from her right shoulder.

The knight in front of her, the captain, fell off his horse. His right foot caught in the stirrup. The horse continued forward, dragging him flat on his back. His arms flayed above his head. She could not understand why he made no movement to get up.

Then she saw the arrow imbedded in his chest.

"Wheel!" one of her escorts shouted. Hans, the one on her left, grabbed her horse's reins and turned to his left. Juergen, to her right, turned with them, positioning himself between Trudi and their unseen assailant.

A second arrow whistled by them. A third planted itself in Juergen's shield. They moved to leave the road. From a small copse of trees just ahead to the right, three men on horse appeared. It was Ansel, Monty, and Brand.

Trudi stared stupidly at her childhood friends as the Bavarians moved forward, creating a barrier between her and their assailants. "Ansel," she said.

They charged. Their horses sprang forward, hurtling their riders directly at the attack. With the sound of shield crashing shield and bone breaking bone, the two forces collided.

Ansel and his horse went down. Damaged by the impact, the horse fell across one of Ansel's legs. Ansel struggled to pull himself out from under it. It was left to Monty and Brand to fight the three Bavarians. Blades rose and fell, clanging against metal shields. The Franks stood at the center of the melee, their backs to each other surrounded by the Bavarians.

"No!" Trudi screamed. "Stop!" She wanted to say that these were friends, but the arrow sticking out of the dead captain's chest made her pause. It took a moment for her to remember Ansel's speech at the feast. Caught between fear and fury, Trudi did not know what to do.

The Bavarians were winning. Brand was already on foot and had lost his shield. Juergen and Hans had dismounted to stalk him. Monty was still on horse but bloodied. The third Bavarian closed in on him. Monty swung a mighty blow that glanced off the man's shoulder. The force of it, however, pulled Monty off balance, and the Bavarian punched forward with his shield, catching him in the ear. Monty reeled backward, trying to use his reins to stay in the saddle. His sword arm flailed backward, leaving him vulnerable. The Bavarian ran him through. Trudi watched the blade enter her friend just below the chest and slide out almost between his shoulders. Monty futilely tried to grab at the blade with his hands.

Rage filled her. With her left hand, she drew her short sword from the scabbard in her saddle. She drove her horse at Monty's assailant. A howl of anger screamed from her throat. Monty was falling off his horse, and the Bavarian was struggling to withdraw his sword. With a lurch, the knight yanked backward to free his blade.

Her horse plowed into his, throwing her headlong into the knight, knocking him to the ground. Trudi landed on top of him and rolled to her left to find her feet. Pain coursed through her body. Her shoulder was on fire, the wound reopened. Having dropped her sword, she fought through the pain to pick it up. The knight too had risen to his feet. Recognizing her, his eyes went wide with shock.

"Stop this!" she shouted at him. He looked at her, hesitating. A grunt escaped his lips. He dropped his eyes. Trudi's followed. The point of a sword protruded from his stomach. His knees buckled. He fell forward. Behind him stood Ansel, his sword red to the hilt.

"What are you doing?" Trudi screamed.

"Taking you back."

"Bastard!" Trudi cried as she threw herself at him. "I'm not going back!" With one arm in a sling, she had little balance or momentum, and her blade felt awkward in her left hand. Her swing was clumsy, a wide descending arc, much as if she were chopping down a tree. Ansel blocked it with ease. When her sword met his, whatever held her shoulder together gave way. Blood coursed down her side.

"I don't have time for this," Ansel said and punched her in the face. Trudi went down. Stunned, she sat on the ground and watched as Ansel turned his attention to the remaining combatants. She realized he would be too late to save Brand.

Already bloodied and exhausted, Brand was stalked by Hans and Juergen. With mustered rage, he screamed and rushed Hans in an attempt to narrow the odds. The German parried, spun to his right, and inverted his sword. With his back to Brand, he pulled his blade downward, driving it underneath his arm and into Brand's upper body.

Juergen stepped forward to finish it. He swung his blade in a high arc and severed Brand's head from his neck.

Then Ansel was there. Attacking Hans from behind with a massive overhand blow, he nearly split the German in two.

Trudi stared in horror at the blood and viscera around her. Brand's head lay several feet from his body. She vomited.

Only Juergen and Ansel remained. The two knights circled each other cautiously. Each tested the other, feinting to gauge reaction and speed.

"You must stop," Trudi pleaded, using her sword to regain her feet. The pain in her head was overwhelming. She had trouble seeing.

Compared to the noise of the recent combat, the road was now strangely quiet. All Trudi could hear was their breathing. She tried to move toward them, but she hurt too much. She was behind Ansel, her right side covered in blood. She leaned her upper body toward the pain and cradled her right arm in her left.

"I won't go with you, Ansel," she said. "I'm going with Juergen."

"No ..." He breathed in huge gasps. "Carloman ... orders."

"I won't go." She fell to her knees. The action surprised her.

It also surprised Ansel. As he turned his head toward her, Juergen took advantage, thrusting his sword to render Ansel's left arm useless. Ansel, however, had heard him move. Instead of turning back into the blow, he spun left. He wound up behind Juergen's extended frame. He slammed his left elbow into the Bavarian's face.

Juergen went down.

Ansel stood over him, the point of his sword at the Bavarian's neck.

"Ansel, no," Trudi moaned, struggling to stay conscious.

"I yield," the Bavarian said.

Ansel hesitated, hovering over him, his eyes wild.

"I yield," Juergen repeated, this time urgently.

With a guttural roar, Ansel pushed the point of his sword through his opponent's neck until it caught on his spine. Struggling against the obstacle, Ansel threw his full weight behind the hilt, driving the blade downward until the bone snapped beneath him and his sword sank into the softness of the earth.

Trudi groaned. Ansel dropped his arms. His upper body sagged forward until his hands rested on his knees. From Trudi's position on the ground, Ansel's sword stood like a sentinel against the sweetness of the morning sun. Other than Ansel, it was the only thing left standing. He didn't pull it from the Bavarian. After several moments, Ansel groaned and pulled himself erect. Stepping slowly over Juergen's body, Ansel turned to find her. She could not move.

Like a nightmare, he came for her, a gargantuan, his entire body covered in blood. Whatever strength she had left in her had drained away with Juergen's life. She slipped into darkness just as Ansel bent to touch her. She began to scream.

"Easy, Trudi. You've been through a lot."

The voice sounded familiar and sincere. She opened her eyes, but the room was too dark to see. She tried to rise. Hands lifted her into a sitting position. Lightheaded, she swayed slightly. She found she was not in a room at all, but a tunnel. It took a moment for it to register, but she remembered Bertrada had spoken of places like this. Built in the time of the Romans, the tunnels were often a refuge for bandits and lovers seeking privacy. A small fire burned nearby, its smoke filtering into the upper reaches.

"Here." A hand appeared in front of her face with a small block of cheese. "Try to eat this."

She froze. Bradius.

With a groan, she turned to confirm her suspicion. He sat next to her by the fire, wine in hand. Seeing her discomfort, he raised his cup in mock salute and took a drink.

She searched her wrists and ankles for bindings. There were none. But when she moved, the blanket dropped away. Save for a new bandage wrapped around her shoulder, she was naked. Trudi snatched the blanket to her chin and turned on her captor.

"What have you done?" she asked. Tears stung her eyes. "What have you done?"

His eyes widened at her outburst and then squinted with understanding. "My apologies, milady. I suppose that's what you'd expect from someone like me."

"You're a pig."

"You have nothing to fear from me." He was both wounded and angry. "In fact, a 'thank you' might be appropriate. If not for me, you'd still be in the care of that blood-soaked behemoth who captured you."

"Ansel?"

"You know him?" Bradius looked surprised.

"They were friends … he was my friend," she said.

Bradius grunted in disbelief.

She wanted to argue but was too tired and had too many questions. What happened to Ansel? Why was she naked? She didn't know whom or what to trust.

"My clothes?" she asked.

"Beside you." Bradius pointed. The undergarments had been washed and laid to dry by the fire. "They were soiled and bloody. There wasn't much I could do other than rinse them. You had such a fever you kept sweating through them. Eventually, I got tired of cleaning them, so …" He motioned to the blanket.

"How long have I been here?" she asked.

"Two days."

Trudi groaned.

Bradius threw another log onto the fire. Several sparks lifted skyward and winked out into the darkness. "I found six bodies and an equal number of horses on the southern road." Visions of the Bavarians battling Brand jumped into her mind. She saw Bradius watching for her reaction. "There was … a lot of blood," he said.

"Two horses had left a trail going away from the fight, heading north. Blood marked the tracks. You weren't among the dead, so I followed the living. The tracks turned off the road and stopped at a clearing near a pool of water created by two fallen trees. That's where I found you and the behemoth."

"Ansel." Trudi's throat grew tight.

"You," Bradius said, "were unconscious and almost as bloody as he was. Worse, you were shivering and moaning incoherently. The big knight finally recognized that you weren't well and started to panic. He walked to his horse, then back to you, then back to his horse. He bent down and touched your face. He looked like he was going to cry. He called for someone named Monty. Then picked you up and took you down to the pool of water." Bradius looked up and turned his eyes on her.

"He took off your clothes, Trudi, to check for wounds. But there was so much blood, he laid you in the water and began to wash it away. Then," Bradius hesitated, "then his hands touched your breasts."

Trudi blushed, dread seeping into her.

"His hands snapped back as if they'd been burned. He cursed and shouted something about 'witches' and 'Satan' and thrashed around in the water." Bradius's voice grew quiet, his eyes sober. "Once he started to touch you, he couldn't stop." Trudi began to withdraw into herself. She felt very small. Bradius paused and stared into the fire as if weighing whether or not to go on. When he finally spoke, his voice was low and full of revulsion. "He stood over you, untied his pantaloons, and stroked himself."

Her stomach knotted, and she felt sick. She looked up at Bradius imploringly.

"That's as far as he got," Bradius said, answering her unasked question. "I took advantage of his preoccupation and drew my sword. He was quite unprepared."

"Did you kill him?" she asked.

"No."

Emotions roiled within her, raw, conflicting, and unanswered. She began to cry. She wept for the loss of Monty and Brand and for the violence of their deaths. She wept for their childhood together and the sweetness of its innocence. But she could not weep for Ansel. She felt the humiliation she had suffered at his hands strike her heart like a hammer.

"Where is he now?"

"I left him tied to a tree just off the southern road. I doubt that he will trouble you again."

"You don't know him," she said. "If he's not dead, he won't stop. As soon as he's free, he'll come looking for me again."

"He might need some time to recover," Bradius said. He drew out a small, round ball from his vest pocket. He tossed it to Trudi. It landed on the fold of her blanket. An eyeball. "What is your Christian saying?" he asked. "If thine eye offend thee …?"

To her surprise, this didn't repulse Trudi. Instead, she felt satisfied.

"It was either that or his testicle," Bradius said.

Trudi picked the eye up and examined it. "You can save the testicle for later."

There was something still unanswered. "Why were *you* following me?"

Bradius blushed. It was only for a moment, but Trudi was sure that she had seen it. He rose to his feet, indignant and offended. "Milady, I committed myself to your service. I pledged tribute and fidelity. I don't take such vows lightly." Seeing the confused look on her face, he added, "On my life, I pledged." The bravado was gone. His voice betrayed anxiety.

"But I released you to go."

He looked away. When his eyes returned to her, there was old pain deep within them. "And where do I have left to go?" he asked.

Slowly, Trudi nodded her head. With her left hand, she cinched the blanket under her arm, picked up the eyeball, and tossed it back to him.

"I guess sometimes it pays for a lady to have a champion," she said.

He tilted his head in a slight bow, relieved by her acceptance.

"We've got other problems," he said. "Someone else is chasing you. They look Roman. There are a lot of them on the road, and they stop everyone, asking for information about someone who looks suspiciously like you."

"Aistulf," Trudi said, her eyes welling. Her detachment was gone. "We have to get out of here."

"It won't be easy. We'll need to stay off the main road. There is a 'village road' that goes overland between towns. We won't move as fast, but it's less likely that we'll be watched. If you're strong enough, we can leave in the morning."

Trudi nodded and pulled the blanket to her chin. "I need to get dressed," she said.

Bradius stood. "If you'd like to bathe first," he said, smiling and wrinkling his nose, "and I suggest you consider it, there's a stream nearby. Otherwise, I will leave you to your dressing."

"No, a bath sounds about right." She laughed.

Bradius helped her to stand. She kept the blanket around her while he carried her clothes. When they reached the stream, he helped her into the water and then turned his back while she exorcised herself of dried blood. It had found its way into every crevice of her flesh. She scooped sand from the bed of the stream to scrub her skin. She found a spot to lie back into the water and submerged her head. Her hair was tangled and knotted. She raked her fingers through it, knowing it was useless. When she surfaced, she felt renewed. Although still weak, she had lost the queasiness and lightheaded feeling that had plagued her since she awoke.

When she came out of the water, Bradius's back was still toward her, and the blanket lay folded by the shore. Her clothes were stained beyond recognition. When she finished dressing, she tapped Bradius on the shoulder, and they made their way back to the tunnel.

"Thank you for not watching," she said.

"Oh, I snuck a look," he said.

"You *are* a pig," she said, shoving him. The effort, however, brought a twinge of pain from her shoulder. Seeing her wince, Bradius reached for her.

"I'll need to change your bandage," he said. "It will come off more easily now that it's wet."

Back at the cave, she pulled her shirt off her shoulder, and Bradius moved behind her to unwind the bandage. The action required her to expose part of her breast to him, but she was too tired to argue the point. He set the bandage aside and began to probe her shoulder. She felt a tugging sensation. Bradius threw something into the fire. She felt it again, and again he threw it into the fire.

"What was that?" she asked.

"Maggots. They speed the healing." He reached into his bag and produced dozens of writhing slugs. Trudi recoiled, but Bradius held her. He spread the maggots across her wound and strapped a new bandage into place. She felt them squirm in her wound.

"I am truly sorry for this, Trudi," he said. "You took this blow for me."

"Just don't make me do it again," she said.

He started to laugh. "Now you need something to eat and rest. We'll see if you can travel in the morning." He gave her more cheese and some bread. She took a sip from his cup of wine to wash it down. Looking over the brim at him, she surveyed his disheveled clothes and demeanor. She raised the cup to him in toast.

"To my newest champion," she said, "as surprising as that is. You delivered me from Ansel and have my eternal thanks."

He bowed to her, clearly pleased, and helped her to lie back down beside the fire. Replenishing his cup, he sat against the wall. The fire was hot. She felt surprisingly safe, and within moments fell fast asleep.

"Village road" was a misnomer. What they traveled was more a footpath between peasant communities than anything else. They rode through rolling fields of wheat and barley, passed through pastures for cattle and sheep. Bradius insisted that they keep up a good pace to put as much distance between them and Reims as possible. They slept in barns and grain houses or in the shelter of trees. They moved through village after village making good progress, hampered only by Trudi's periodic need for rest and sustenance.

Bradius insisted that she pack her armor away. He pointed out that she could hardly fight in her condition and that a woman warrior would certainly draw attention. They stopped at one of the larger villages to find clothes for her.

Several people referred them to a matronly seamstress, who at first seemed reluctant to help until Trudi nearly fainted. When she uncovered

Trudi's wound, the woman fussed over her young patron like a long-lost niece. She insisted that Trudi take a hot bath with soap and water and helped her dress with cooing noises that Trudi found oddly reassuring.

There were no new clothes, of course. But with some effort, the woman produced a pair of soft leather boots and a clean and sturdy peasant dress with small white flowers painted on its collar. Trudi also acquired a brown cloak that would be useful in warding off the morning chill. It had the added advantage of covering her shoulders and arms so she could hide her sling. When Trudi emerged from the woman's cottage, Bradius seemed surprised by her appearance.

"Much better," he said, stammering. "I hadn't known ..."

"What?"

"It's just that ..." He looked away. "I've become used to the armor-wearing 'Hiltrude, daughter of Charles.' I wasn't prepared for a young woman wearing a dress named Trudi. It's just a surprise, that's all."

"A good surprise or a bad one?"

"Well, a good one, I suppose."

"You suppose?" Trudi laughed, enjoying his awkwardness. It took a moment for her mirth to infect him, and then he too started to laugh.

"Are you the ones they's looking for?" The question took them both by surprise. Trudi stepped back from their questioner, blushing. He was a tall, gangly man with graying hair and a heavy stubble that covered his neck and chin. He leaned casually against the post where their horses were tethered. His eyes, however, were anything but casual. They swept over the two of them, noting Bradius's armor and Trudi's blush.

"They's said they's to be two of you, man and woman." He chewed on the end of a root and took that moment to spit out its pieces.

"Who was asking?" Bradius countered.

"Soldiers. Not like you, though. Had armored skirts. Sounded strange."

"No one's looking for us," Trudi said.

"Said you'd have warhorses," the man said, looking at their warhorses. "Said you might be hurt." His eyes stared at her shoulder. "Said they'd pay if we found you."

"It's not us," Bradius said. "We're just two travelers heading home. Nobody would pay to find us."

"Said they'd pay." The man stared at Trudi, his eyes cold and uncaring.

"I can pay," Trudi said. She pulled a denarius out of her pocket and held it out to him. Bradius stiffened at her offer but stayed silent. "I can pay you to say nothing."

Without a moment's hesitation, the coin disappeared from her hand and arrived in their questioner's. He smiled at them, bowed, and walked away whistling.

"We've got to go," Bradius said. "You just confirmed for him that we're the ones they're looking for." They mounted up and rode east.

Bradius rode them hard. They rode throughout the day, slowing only to save the horses. Trudi begged him to stop on several occasions. They skirted several villages, avoiding any human contact. He finally relented just outside of Metz and pulled off the road into a small forest of oak trees and pines. The trees filtered out much of their afternoon light. Bradius moved south of the path into a stand of short pine trees.

Dead pine needles covered the ground in a reddish-gold blanket. The forest deadened the sound of their voices to that of a whisper. Once they dismounted, Bradius broke out what was left of their provisions and made Trudi eat a full share. Once he was satisfied that her needs were met, he sat down next to her with his back to the tree.

"How will you know if they are following us?"

"We already know that."

"I mean, when they are close. You knew with Pippin. I remember."

"You never really know until you hear them. Sometimes it's the sound of metal clanking on metal in the wind, or a voice that carries past its owner's intent. I could hear Pippin behind me. He did nothing to hide the sound of his men, until the last." Bradius's eyes looked at the ground. "I have always had a talent for knowing without any evidence."

"A useful skill," Trudi said.

"Of late, yes." His face grew serious. "If they see you, the hunt is over. All that matters then is how long it will take for them to catch you."

Trudi shivered. "Then let's just make sure they never see us."

"I thought we'd go into Metz. We need some supplies, and you look like you could use a decent night's sleep."

Trudi almost laughed at this. "*I* could use a night's sleep?" she asked. Since the day she found her wrists bound and tied around a horse, Bradius had not slept a night. He might have dozed now and again, but the man rarely slept. Trudi would wake in the middle of the night to find Bradius staring into the fire, his wine cup in hand, a haunted look in his eyes. Whatever demons came to him came in the night.

Every morning, she'd discover bags under his bloodshot eyes and wonder how he kept going. He rarely spoke in the morning. When he did, his words often growled behind mucus caught in his throat. What he said usually made little sense. She took the habit of not bothering him until well into the morning.

"Do you have enough money for an inn?" he asked.

She nodded.

"There is one in town. The owner is discreet."

"The town will be watched."

"Unless Aistulf himself is there, who would recognize us? I'm just a soldier of fortune with his mistress, traveling to Selz."

Trudi's eyes flashed at the term. Catching the look, Bradius said, "Would you prefer 'serving girl'? Or perhaps 'wife'?"

"How about 'niece'?" Trudi said. "And we're pilgrims on our way to the holy land," she said. "Your piety will be disguise enough."

Bradius chuckled. "Very well then. I will be your Uncle Otto. And you ...?"

"Your not-so-obedient niece Hildie."

Metz was gray and foreboding. They followed cattle into the town, walking through the wake of the herd's waste. Hawkers sold their wares on the street, relics from the Holy Land, oils from the East, herbs and elixirs to cure every malady from baldness to impotence. Alehouses lined the street, as did their patrons—clusters of men who stared boldly at Trudi as they passed. Bradius nodded to a pair of prostitutes. Seeing Trudi's stare, he shrugged apologetically.

Bradius led them through better and better neighborhoods until the streets they traveled weren't quite so questionable. They stopped at a modest inn named The Pious Widow, which, although spare, was both clean and inviting. The 'widow' turned out to be a woman named Myrna, who had indeed been widowed but could be no older than twenty-five. She greeted Bradius by throwing herself into his arms and hugging him to her breast.

"Oh, Bradius, I thought you were dead." She continued clinging to him, although her eyes registered Trudi's presence and surveyed her from head to foot and back again.

"Where have you been?" she scolded Bradius.

"I had a little run in with Pippin," he said.

"Did you kill the bastard?"

Bradius looked at Trudi and then back to Myrna. "No," he said.

"Did you find your son's body?"

"Yes," he said, his eyes cast down. Trudi stared at him. During their ride, he had said nothing more of his son. Bradius let Myrna go, took a deep breath, and continued. "I found him. There was a mass grave. After Carloman's army moved on, the townspeople came out to bury the bodies of the dead. They said that in the Frank's camp, they found the body of a beheaded young boy. They were so incensed by it that the tale of his murder spread throughout the countryside. Hundreds came to aid the villagers in their task. They buried him last in the mass grave.

"They led me to the field where he was buried, although I could have found it without them. The smell of the place drew carrion and animals to it. A large mound marked the grave. Unum was there. His head was with him."

"Did you bring him back with you?" Myrna asked.

"His death held such significance to those people that no place I could take him would promise more."

Myrna took Bradius back into her arms. Her eyes welled with tears. Trudi had stepped forward, her hand out, but found that she was afraid to touch him. After a long moment, Bradius let Myrna go. They turned in Trudi's direction.

"I need to introduce you to someone," he said.

"Hildie," Trudi said, again extending her hand to the widow. "My name is Hildie."

Myrna took her hand and smiled warmly, but her eyes remained cold. "So nice to meet you." Her eyes returned to Bradius. "There are Romans looking for you," she said.

After lounging in a long overdue bath, Trudi came down for dinner to find Bradius and Myrna huddled in the serving room, whispering to each other. She hesitated, unsure what to do until she smelled the lamb stew wafting in from the kitchen. It made her stomach growl. She took her meal by the fire and ordered ale to wash it down. She attacked the bowl when it arrived and ordered more when she was done.

She expected that Bradius and Myrna would finish their private conversation and invite her to their table. But long after her meal was gone, the two seemed as engrossed in each other as when she walked into the room. Trudi ordered more ale and decided to wait. When that drink was finished, she ordered another. Eventually, she realized they had no intention of inviting her to their table. Angrily, she decided to retire for the night.

The stairway seemed so narrow. She had trouble navigating its turn. Her foot slipped on her way up the stairs, and she had to steady herself on the wall. It took her forever to reach her room. Opening the door, she stepped inside and leaned against the wall. Exhausted, she slid down it until she was sitting on the floor.

She must have dozed. A noise on the stairs roused her, and she cracked open her door to see who was coming. She saw Myrna taking Bradius into the room at the end of the hall. She had guessed this was how the evening would end by the way Myrna touched him. He didn't return these intimacies, but he certainly didn't stop hers.

And he didn't stop at her door. Not that it should matter, Trudi told herself. But the thought of them together made her angry. Why hadn't Bradius just told her? At least she wouldn't feel so stupid. Of course they were lovers. His wife had died many years ago. Why shouldn't he find comfort in the arms of a willing widow? The image of this, however, made her shudder. She shut the door silently and leaned back against the wall.

She didn't know what to do. If Bradius was here with Myrna, what was she doing? She was trying to get to Bavaria. Bradius had said he would accompany her because he had nowhere else to go. But clearly that was false. He did have somewhere to go, or at least someone to go to. And it certainly wasn't her.

That thought rattled around her head for some time stark and alone. Not her. Did she want it to be her? Her stomach began to knot, and she suppressed the idea. What was she thinking? She was going to Bavaria to marry Odilo. Bradius was a convenient ally, a mercenary. How could she care for someone like him? She didn't. She couldn't.

She would leave in the morning. If he wanted to come with her, that was his decision. But she would not wait around biding her time while he dallied here, making eyes and more at "the widow." In fact, she would tell him that now. He should know so that he could have some time to make his decision.

She stood, swaying slightly, and opened her door. Marching down to Myrna's room at the end of the corridor, she raised her hand to knock. From inside the room, she heard a moan. Her hand froze. It was a woman's voice, low and aroused. Trudi heard it repeated twice before it dawned on her what the moan implied. Her hand remained stuck in the air and her feet to the floor.

Her face flushed crimson. She had been such a fool. How could she have let herself have feelings for this man? How could she want him? But she did want him. She did. She wanted to be on the other side of this door, wanted to be in his arms, wanted to be moaning his name in a low and aroused voice. The knot in her stomach sank deep within her, and sweat bloomed from her skin.

Clearly, he didn't want her. Not her. The starkness of that thought pierced her like a blade. Not her. Not her. She couldn't face him in the morning. She couldn't take Myrna's condescending smile. She saw herself standing alone in the corridor, pathetic in her girlish crush on a man who didn't care for her. Not her.

She ran. She ran to her room and shoved the contents of her existence into her two sacks and, leaving a denarius, made for the door of the inn. She strode to the stable, woke the stable boy to saddle her horse, and lit out in the night. She could not stay, she told herself. Not now. Not under the same roof with them. She had to get away. Had to.

It was well after midnight but well before dawn. She left by the main gate and took the Roman road toward Selz. She spurred her horse and rode hard into the night. It wasn't until much later that she slowed her pace and discovered that she was weeping.

Silly girl, she chastised herself, wiping away her tears. *You still have power.* But she didn't feel powerful, and her tears fell nonetheless.

A ray of morning light stabbed its way through the shutters, penetrating his sleep. Bradius stretched out his hands to shield his eyes and reveled in the rest his body had received. Sleep rarely found him, typically only after he had made love.

Although she was no longer there, the bed still held the impression of Myrna's body and her musky scent. He inhaled deeply, remembering how soft her skin felt in his hands and how playful she was. Looking up at the door beside him, he wondered how relentless the day of an innkeeper must be. He was hoping she would return to—

An enormous blow hit the door from the other side, and its frame splintered in front of him. Bradius recoiled at the impact. A second crash destroyed the door, and three Lombard soldiers stood before him, one with a blade pointed at his neck.

"Gentlemen," Bradius pretended to greet them casually, propping himself up on his elbow and pushing away the blade. "Has Myrna taken a husband since I last was here? I swear I had not a clue. I'm not the kind of man who would cuckold—"

One of the soldiers punched his face. Bradius crumpled under the blow, pain lancing through his head. When he sat up, blood poured from his nose. The soldiers clearly did not want to chat, so he waited for instruction. He didn't have to wait long.

A tall, elegant man in Lombard armor escorted Myrna into the room. Without hesitation, he reached into the bed, grabbed Bradius by the hair, and pulled him to his feet. Bradius stood facing the commander, naked and irate.

"He doesn't know that she's not here," Myrna said. "She left last night."

"I need you to tell me where she is going," the commander said.

Not here? Bradius was stunned. Where could she be? Could she have left? Was she hiding? "She's going home," Bradius said. "She's a peasant girl from Nancy. I'm taking her home to her—"

Bradius didn't even see the blow coming. It caught him on the cheek.

"Tell me where she is," the commander said.

"If she's not down the hall," Bradius said, testing out the movement of his jaw, "I don't know where she is."

"Search the building," the commander ordered one of his men. "Get some clothes on," he told Bradius. "I will meet you in the serving room downstairs."

The commander was sitting alone at one of the serving tables. Bradius assumed all other patrons had been chased away. He approached the table, and at a gesture of invitation from the commander sat down opposite him.

"I am Aistulf," the commander said.

"Liutbrand's son," Bradius said.

"And you are?"

"Bradius, formerly of Burgundy."

Aistulf's eyes widened in surprise.

"You fought against me at Narbonne."

Bradius nodded.

"Then you know whom you were accompanying?"

"Yes."

"Was she your hostage?"

Bradius smiled but said, "No."

"Given your history, I am surprised by your presence here. As an enemy of her late father and an enemy of her brother, why are you here with her?"

"I am in her debt."

"You owe her money?"

"My life."

"And now you are escorting her?"

Bradius nodded.

"Where?"

"Wherever she wishes to go."

"You know that is no answer. Please, humor me. I have a right to know. I am her betrothed."

Bradius did not respond.

"You, of course, knew that," Aistulf stated, sitting back from the table. After a moment's reflection, he leaned forward again. "I'm curious about your relationship with Hiltrude. You say you owe her your life. Are you romantically involved?"

The questions took him by surprise. He had never allowed himself to consider it, yet … "You found me in another woman's bed."

Aistulf nodded, his eyes hard. "A fact that has saved you, my rebellious friend." He signaled to two of his knights. "Don't kill him, but make sure he needs a few days to recover." And with that, Aistulf left the room.

Two hands pulled Bradius to his feet and dragged him to the wall behind him. He struggled to free himself until one of the soldiers kicked him in the groin. Pain lanced from his crotch to his stomach, and nausea swept over him. It took every bit of control he had not to vomit. He found himself lying on the ground looking up at his attackers. He watched them kick his body and face until the pain overwhelmed him. In time, his eyes swelled shut. He could no longer see. All that was left to him was his ability to feel the blows hitting his body.

Her hands were raw and stiff and red and chapped. Letting go of the reins, Trudi rubbed her fingers together and cupped them before her mouth. Her breath was warm and wet, billowing white in the afternoon light. It did little, however, to fend off the cold. She shivered and pulled her brown cloak tightly around her shoulders. It was useless in this mountain weather.

Not for the first time, Trudi had second thoughts about her midnight flight from Metz. Maybe she had gotten the wrong idea. Maybe Bradius would have come with her. Maybe he would have left Myrna behind. Maybe …

No. Bradius did not want her. She felt foolish for thinking he might.

Although she left well past midnight, Trudi had found that she could ride without hindrance. She could clearly see the road's broad hard outline in the moon's half-light. It was what she couldn't see that had bothered her.

Everywhere she looked, she saw danger in the darkness. Black against the horizon, the trees, and shrubs became threats to her. At every turn, marauders and highwaymen waited. How could she defend herself with one arm? Dread seeped into her. Her stomach knotted. She found it hard to breathe. No matter that none of these specters ever materialized, her fear began anew with every change in the landscape. She pushed her horse hard through the night.

It was midmorning when she heard the soldiers on the road. It was just as Bradius had said; voices carrying on the wind, gruff words, and a clank of armor warned her that pursuit was close. She hid from them in the forest. Tethering her horse in the trees, she circled back to watch the road. She stayed hidden in the underbrush, sitting with her back against a poplar tree. In truth, she had needed a rest. Her temples pounded horribly, and her shoulder ached. She laid her head against the trunk and closed her eyes.

She heard their search before she saw them. Three warhorses with Lombard soldiers trotted into view, hunting for tracks in the road. All wore similar uniforms, short chain mail that covered their torsos and a mail skirt made in three sections for flexibility. They moved methodically. *Hunters,* she thought. It made her heart skip a beat. She hadn't bothered to cover her tracks. A trickle of sweat formed at the back of her neck and slid down her spine. They moved slowly up the road. One drew near to her hiding place, checking her side of the road. Trudi held her breath.

A lone traveler tried to pass the soldiers heading south. Immediately, the soldiers stopped to question him. Trudi couldn't hear their words but recognized the tone. Their voices rose threateningly. The soldier on her side of the road moved menacingly behind the traveler. The gesture wasn't missed. The man shook his head vigorously and pointed back to indicate where he'd been and then forward to show where he was going. At last, they let him leave.

The soldiers conferred in the middle of the road. One, who appeared to be the leader, seemed to disagree with the other two. The soldier nearest to her pointed to the ground repeatedly. The leader shook his head and pointed north. The argument lasted only a few moments until the leader insisted. The three rode north.

It took her several moments before she could breathe again normally. She would have to leave the road. She didn't have a choice. If she headed north, she would be caught. If she backtracked, she would ride right into their patrols. She groaned and held her head in her hands. An image of soldiers beating their shields to force a boar into a gauntlet of spears thrust into her mind. She had to find another route.

To appease the pounding in her head, she allowed herself a short nap and then regained the road. If she followed the patrol she saw heading north, she would avoid scrutiny for a short time, unless one of them backtracked. She held the horse to a trot. It was not long before the road turned slightly east, and the landscape began to change from woodland to farmland.

She drew up her horse. Since daylight, the forest had hidden her passage. Out in open landscape, she could be seen from a great distance. She would have nowhere to hide. She scanned the horizon. To her relief, no soldiers were in view. The road to the north stretched over a rolling hillside of farms and vineyards. To the east were more mountains.

Her horse pranced, wondering why they had stopped. She looked at the mountains curiously. If the north and south were closed to her, that left only east. This time of year, the mountains might be covered with snow. Even where there were roads, it would be difficult to travel. But she was sure there was a route to Wissembourg. From there, she would have to find her way down into the valley of the Rhine. *At least I'll have a chance,* she thought.

Without further hesitation, she turned off the road and headed east. Two days of uphill riding, cold weather, and poor rations brought her to a mountain perch. Looking out over the horizon, she could only see the road to her past, west to Metz, across the Moselle, down the road to Reims, then north to Laon and Quierzy. The road to her future was just beyond her sightline, down into the valley and across the Rhine, through the Black Forest to Canstatt, across the valley and over the mountains into Bavaria. At Donauwörth, she'd head south along the Wormitt River to the Danube. From there, Regensburg was just a long casual stroll downriver.

I can't go back, she thought. *But do I really want to go forward?*

CHAPTER 11

Trial

When the attack came, they were ready. Despite his hatred for the Thuringian, Gripho had to admit the man knew how to prepare for this. The trenches and barricades that Heden had ordered built outside the walls proved to be critical to their defense. And the mobility he had drilled into their archers became a central asset.

Not that Heden would receive any credit for his preparations. That was always given to the captain in the field. And with Heden still in bed, recovering from his injuries, Gripho knew the day's honor would fall to him. He would finally have a chance to show Carloman what he was worth.

His half brother's soldiers had streamed through their makeshift gate at dawn. They came by the hundreds, heading for the city walls, led by teams of men carrying ladders. Roughly three times the size of a man, the ladders were made of thick sapling trunks lashed together by cord. It took eight men to carry one. Foot soldiers with shields covered their approach to the wall.

Gripho ordered the archers to launch, and dozens of soldiers fell in the field, but the ladders continued forward. As their carriers reached the defensive impediments, they bunched up, waiting for those before them to clear before climbing down into and over Heden's earthworks. Again Gripho's archers took their toll. Down on the field, the soldiers tried to use the ladders to span the trenches and climb the barricades. Some used corpses as human stairs to climb. Neither method was very effective. The steepness of the incline and the awkwardness of the barricades made them an easy target for the archers and, as they drew closer, the rock-throwers.

Massive slingshots capable of heaving huge stones across the battlefield, the rock-throwers were a favorite of Heden. He had drilled the men on targeting the trenches, and the practice was paying off. Boulders hurtled over the wall into the trenches, making them into a killing ground where far fewer soldiers made their way out than had gone in.

But Carloman had numbers in his favor. Once past the trenches and barricades, his men regrouped and lifted their ladders once more. Gripho waited for them at the rampart.

"Hold," he cautioned his men. "Let them climb."

At the wall, the Franks lifted their ladders from the back until they stood upright. In a desperate arc, they closed on the wall while hands and feet on the ground secured them. The bravest clawed their way skyward, knives in their mouths, to meet almost-assured death.

And death Gripho gave them. "Now!" he called. Buckets of burning pitch poured over the wall. Those highest on the ladders caught the worst of it. They fell earthward screaming, their bodies aflame. Many took those on the ladder below with them. Those on the ground dispersed under the threat of the falling pitch. Gripho and his men pushed the ladders off the wall.

More were raised. More pitch was thrown. This time, however, when Gripho ordered his men forward, a swarm of arrows flew up at them. Carloman had sent archers into the field to harry from below. Gripho redirected his own archers toward those on the ground.

Hands clamored over the walls, and then a face. Gripho hurled himself forward, using his sword to skewer the man in the eye. The attacker fell away, taking the ladder with him. Gripho searched the catwalk around him. A pike would be more useful than his sword. He spied one in the hands of a corpse and seized it. Holding it aloft, he shouted to those who manned the wall.

"Keep them off the wall. Keep them off the wall!"

More hands and more faces found the ramparts. Gripho wielded both ends of the pike, skewering those who made it above the wall with its spear and smashing hands and legs with its butt. More came. And more. Gripho and his men hammered them back.

Eventually, the Franks found their way onto a section of the rampart. A great roar rose from below. A wedge had formed where they held the wall. Without harassment from above, their ladders had easy access. More Franks streamed onto the rampart behind them. They were pushing Gripho's men back on both sides of the wall.

Desperately, Gripho tried to rally his men. He ordered a charge, and several of his men threw themselves down the catwalk at the Franks. They weren't enough. He screamed for more. Pulling soldiers up onto the catwalk, he shoved them toward the fighting. *How did they gain such a foothold?* It had happened so fast.

The numbers in the Frankish wedge were growing. *Damn them.* Gripho stood on the catwalk screaming to the soldiers below. "To the wall! To the wall!" He watched as several of his men were thrown over the rampart. He realized that he might not win. Panic began to take him.

A flurry on the opposite wall drew his attention. Heden was there, rallying the men to attack the far side of the Franks. He had set up a short defensive shield wall, much as he had the day before to withstand the Frankish surge. Heden called for archers, and at his command, arrows poured into the Frankish wedge. He ordered one of the smaller rock-throwing catapults turned toward the Franks and used it to hurl buckets of burning pitch into their ranks. The catwalk beneath the Franks caught fire. Soon, many of them were in flames. With the wedge in disarray, Heden ordered a charge. A concentrated force began to push the Franks back on themselves.

Mirroring his attack, Gripho and his men pushed forward. Forsaking his pike, Gripho drew dagger and sword. He stabbed and poked into the main body of the enemy. The space was narrow, the fighting close. A knife cut him in the arm. Then another. He shoved a man off the rampart but didn't stop to see him land. He started screaming. Rage took him as he waded into the Franks. He pushed more off the catwalk. He stabbed and slashed and cut and shoved. He was at the ladder. With a violent push, he launched it into the air.

Heden was with him, screaming for pitch. They poured buckets over the wall along with rocks and boards. Heden called for sand to put out the fire on the catwalk. He ordered men to repair those planks too weak to hold weight.

"They're coming again." Heden's right side was covered in blood.

"I didn't need your help," Gripho said. "You don't need to rescue me."

"Never thought to try. I just like killing Franks."

Despite his anger, Gripho smiled at the old man. "You might want to take care of that." He pointed to Heden's wound.

"I will. I just want to see what's next."

The new attack had a dual focus. More ladders streamed through the gates, behind them a battering ram.

"Take the turrets and the gate!" Heden shouted. "I'll take the walls." He turned and sprinted down the catwalk to cluster the archers.

Gripho ran to the gate.

A battering ram—as wide as a man and as long as four—rolled toward the gate. Ten soldiers, protected by a roof of sand, bent themselves against poles protruding from its sides. The heavy beast made their progress slow. A line of foot soldiers marched behind them with shields held high.

To allow the city's cavalry to sortie, Heden had erected no impediments or barricades in front of the gate, so nothing stood in their way. Gripho's only advantage was his turrets. He let the ram reach the midpoint between the two turrets and then unleashed his rock-throwers.

Many of the missiles bounced harmlessly off the roof of sand. Many never cleared the wall. Several, however, slammed into the men pushing the ram, ripping arms from shoulders and legs from hips. Foot soldiers stepped forward to replace their broken brethren, and the beast rolled forward.

Gripho kept up the barrage. More men felt the sting of arrows and the bite of rocks. More men fell. As the ram neared the gate, Gripho called for archers, and flaming arrows descended but were extinguished in the sand. He called for burning pitch, and finally it began to burn. The men pushing it forward, however, were untouched by the blaze and remained intent on their task. The archers and rock-throwers aimed at their legs but couldn't stop it from coming.

The crash resonated through the city walls. Wood and iron on wood and iron, the blow rumbled deep in the stone and made the gates groan under the strain. Gripho felt the blow deep in his stomach. The force of it unnerved him. He fought to keep down his fear as the Franks rolled the ram back and smashed into the gate again.

More ladders scaled the walls. Heden scurried among them, harassing them with pike and sword. No one had breached the ramparts. Hundreds of arrows fell, overwhelming the wall with dead and wounded. Outside the wall, black acrid smoke rose up off the pitch-covered corpses to darken the walls.

More ladders came, more men. They fought them off. The ram pounded into the gate, its fire darkening the stout wood. Several times, Gripho and his men harried it to a stop, only to have new hands take up the ram to renew its charge. Cheers, on one side of the field or the other, met every attack and repulse. But through the course of the day, the cheers grew weak. Runners brought more arrows and pitch and rocks to the walls. Again and again, they poured death onto their attackers. Late in the day, a horn sounded from behind Carloman's wall, and the attack subsided.

Gripho ordered more rocks thrown at the retreating enemy, but they were of little use. A small cheer rose from the rampart. Gripho was too tired to join in. Up on the far rampart, a lone figure climbed onto the wall and stood fully exposed to the enemy. It was Heden. His body framed against the setting sun, he screamed his battle cry. His mustache and his hair flew back in the wind, and he beat his chest while he raged.

"Thuringia! Thuringia!"

A cry arose from the wall to match his. More voices joined in.

"Thuringia! Thuringia!"

The battle cry spread until pikes and swords and bows were raised above the wall. Swords banged shields, and hundreds of voices shouted into the dusk. Euphoria spread with the cry. Men rejoiced that they had defeated such a mighty foe, even if only for one day. They rejoiced that they were alive.

Gripho found himself laughing. He too climbed the wall and raged at his enemy. The cry cleansed him from the day. They had beaten Carloman.

Later, after they had counted their dead and tended to their wounded, Gripho met Heden in the infirmary. "I told you I didn't need your help," Gripho said, smiling.

"It was a good day, wasn't it?" Heden clapped the boy's shoulder.

"We took the best they had and shoved it down their throats."

Heden laughed. "We did at the wall, anyway."

Perplexed, Gripho waited for the explanation.

"I'm afraid that was just a diversion," the older man explained. "While we were fighting, Carloman brought up the remaining trebuchets. I won't be surprised if tomorrow they begin the bombardment."

Gripho was stunned. He wasn't ready to think about that so soon. "Still, it was a good day, wasn't it?"

"A great day."

Gripho pointed at the older man's side and said, "You took a second wound. You should get someone to look at that."

Heden smiled as he turned to go. "I'm hoping someone will tend to it back in my room."

Boniface stood by the bedside performing the last rites. He anointed the forehead, the lips, the eyes and ears with chrism, each time making the sign of the cross. The body of the once and would-be mayor of Neustria contorted grotesquely in a prolonged spasm of pain. His back arched, nearly lifting him off the bed. The muscles of his face twisted his jaw profoundly, giving him the appearance of an emaciated ghoul.

"Aaaaaannnh," Theudoald gasped, his eyes wild and desperate. "Aaaananaahhn!"

Boniface continued his prayers in Latin, again making the sign of the cross.

A servant appeared at the bishop's elbow, waiting for him to finish. Boniface continued his prayers but raised his eyebrows, inviting the young man to speak.

"Bishop Aidolf of Auxerre," the servant whispered.

Without breaking his cadence or omitting a word, Boniface nodded, and one moment later, the Bishop of Auxerre stood by his side. Without hesitation, Aidolf picked up the Latin prayer and joined in the ceremony with Boniface. As the prayer drew to completion, they made the sign of the cross. "*... per Christum Dominum nostrum. Amen,*" they intoned.

"Unnnnhuh!" Theudoald groaned, spittle dribbling from his mouth. Boniface took his handkerchief and wiped the mouth dry.

"Poison?"

Boniface nodded.

"And you have no idea who could have done it."

"The obvious choice would be Carloman. But he is away at Laon."

"He could have ordered it done. That Johann is enough of a bastard."

"He could have," Boniface agreed. "But Carloman is as devout a man as I have known. Would he forsake the kingdom of heaven so lightly?"

"He's Charles's son."

Boniface shook his head. "When it comes to his faith, he is as much my son as he was Charles's."

"Pippin then."

"More likely than Carloman. But Pippin left before Charles died."

"Was Theudoald able to speak at all?"

"The convulsions are too strong ... it is a violent death."

"Did you question the staff?"

"Of course, but he had many visitors, as you can imagine a potential mayor would have."

"Anything else?"

They paused while Theudoald convulsed, hands lashing out wildly.

"If you would help me hold him down." The two struggled against the man's wild thrashing, and Boniface rolled him to the left, away from them. With some effort, he pulled Theudoald's nightshirt up to expose two sets of parallel scratch marks running down the sides of his back. They were not quite fresh, nor were they healed.

"A woman?"

"One would assume." Boniface rolled the man back onto his back. "The servants said he had spent the evening with the Lady Hélène."

"Hélène? Are you suggesting she poisoned him?"

"It's certainly a possibility. She is close to Carloman's wife, and there were rumors about Charles."

"Carloman is not that subtle," Aidolf said. "Did you question her?"

"Yes. Although distraught, she was very cooperative. She readily admitted to sleeping with him and was appropriately embarrassed, especially about the marks on his back, but she didn't seem to be hiding anything. If she's lying, she's very good at it."

"Still," Aidolf mused, "she has a direct connection to Carloman. Someone should keep an eye on her."

"I've had her followed since yesterday."

"And?"

"Nothing you would not expect from a lady of the court."

Aidolf grunted. "It's not enough to cast doubt on him."

Boniface nodded in agreement.

"Aaannnnth," Theudoald groaned, his eyes bulging out of their sockets. His back arched, again lifting him off the bed. The two bishops moved to restrain him. "Arrrggg," he cried out, beginning to convulse once more. His eyes rolled up into his head, and his teeth gnashed down on his tongue, biting through it. Blood flowed from his mouth, staining the sheets on both sides of his head as it whipped back and forth. Again his back arched, and again he cried out.

His eyes locked on Boniface, begging silently for release. Then something in them shifted. They turned upward, startled, as if he looked upon some other place and time. Suddenly, his tension left him. Groaning with relief, he collapsed back into the folds of his bedding. When his eyes returned to the two bishops, they had a sad but knowing expression. His chest heaved, and in one last great exhale, he expired. In the habit of the newly departed, his bowels released. Its stench filled the room.

The bishops crossed themselves and again bowed their heads to pray.

"Adjutorium nostrum in nominee domini," Boniface began.

Aidolf's response was automatic. *"Qui fecit caelum et terram."*

Pippin and his men couldn't have made any more noise entering the inn. *One day,* thought Bertrada upstairs in her room, *I'll have to teach him about making a proper entrance.* She heard him ask at the desk in a loud voice if she was within. Bounding up the steps and down the hall, he was outside her door. He began to pound on the door and to bellow her name.

"I can hear you!" she called out to him.

It didn't help. The banging and bellowing continued until she crossed the room and opened the door. Pippin stood there, arm raised, ready to pound again. He looked at her the way a hungry man looks at supper.

Bertrada blocked his path, acting as if she didn't know him. "Can I help you, sir?"

Growling, he picked her up and swept into her room, closing the door behind him with his foot. He spun her in the air like a child, and in seconds they were on her bed with blankets, sheets, and clothing flying.

"Pippin!" She giggled. "Give me some time! You haven't even said hello."

"H'lo," he mumbled, his mouth filled with her breast.

"It's so nice to see you again," she continued.

Pippin pulled his head up to survey her body. "You too," he said, grinning. He burrowed his tongue into her belly button.

"And how are you?" She laughed. "Are you well?" Again his response was muffled, this time by the soft flesh just above her pubic hair.

"I beg your pardon?" she said, squirming underneath his tongue. His head moved down the length of her body until Bertrada finally gave in.

When they finished making love, Bertrada asked the question she had been afraid to ask. "How goes the siege?"

Pippin sat up, his eyes no longer playful. "Carloman has lost his way."

Bertrada reached out to him. "It's that bad?"

Pippin nodded. "He won't listen, at least not to me. He's all wrapped up in this religious struggle over Gripho. He thinks he's got to defend the Church. I'm worried that for Carloman, this is only the beginning. He'll rip the wall down to get Sunni and Gripho."

"You can't let that happen," she said.

"I want to talk with Sunni and see if we can stop this before it gets out of control."

"Will Sunni and Gripho agree to leave with you?"

"If I give my word that they have my protection," he said. "But we have to do it before the breach is made."

Bertrada nodded. She had expected as much.

"The men are here," Pippin said, pointing outside.

"I heard." Bertrada laughed. "Let me get dressed. I'll show you the tunnel."

By the time Carloman received word of Theudoald's death, the funeral had already taken place. All reports indicated that the former mayor had died in his sleep from unknown causes. Given the political tension surrounding his death, Boniface had commissioned an investigation and was coming to Laon to meet with him.

When he received word that his godfather was in camp, Carloman ordered a flagon of good wine brought to his tent and awaited his mentor's arrival. Within minutes, Boniface strode through the tent flaps, his figure silhouetted against the light behind him. The wind accompanied him into the tent; the canvas billowed with its force. The bishop's face was still dusty from his ride. Smiling, Carloman rose to greet him, but before he could say a word, Boniface signaled for silence.

"Everyone out!" he commanded.

At a nod from Carloman, Johann cleared the servants and soldiers from the tent. At another nod from Carloman, Johann left as well. Carloman spread his arms, querying his mentor silently.

"Did you do it?" Boniface demanded.

Carloman had no idea what Boniface meant.

"Did you murder Theudoald?"

"Are you daft?"

"Answer me! Did you murder him?"

"I thought he died in his sleep."

"Answer my question!"

"Of course not. I can't believe you would even consider such an accusation."

Boniface looked hard into Carloman's face and visibly relaxed. "I had to ask." He made for the washstand. Pouring water into its bowl, he washed his face and hands. "The bishops insisted on an investigation into his death. They think it was poison."

Part of Carloman was chastened by the news. He too could be a target. On the whole, however, he could not believe his good fortune. Theudoald's death made the issue of succession *so* much simpler. The Church now had no alternatives, and the nobles had no more excuses. Although he never liked the man, one thing left him puzzled. "Who would kill Theudoald?"

"The bishops think you would."

Carloman studied Boniface's face. He didn't like what he saw. "You also thought I could. Didn't you?"

Boniface shook his head. "I didn't believe you would, but you are Charles's son. How well do you know the Lady Hélène?"

It took a moment for the question to sink in. Then a chill ran down Carloman's spine. Hélène? It couldn't be. He could see her smiling provocatively in his mind while they flirted at her party. She had joked that she was Charles's "assassin." *Ridiculous! Still.* But that couldn't be it. Hélène was no assassin.

"She slept with Theudoald the night before he died."

Carloman's stomach tensed. This news shocked him. He had sensed no connection between the two. To the contrary, Hélène only had disdain for Theudoald. Carloman was embarrassed that he felt jealous of the liaison.

"There were scratch marks down his back," Boniface said, watching him.

Carloman racked his brain for answers. How well did he know Hélène? Not well, he admitted. Could she have been telling the truth about his father? Could she have taken his jest seriously? Could she have killed Theudoald? To each of these questions, Carloman had no sure answers. He looked at the man he trusted most in his life, his mentor and confessor. "Would you hear my confession?" Carloman asked.

Startled, Boniface looked at his godson strangely. He pulled up two chairs.

Carloman sat with his head in his hands. "Bless me, Father, for I have sinned ..."

As they approached the northwest corner the city, Pippin instinctively mapped its strengths and vulnerabilities to a siege. From this approach, Laon looked impervious. The walls towered over a steep slope that was only interrupted by a small plateau, perhaps two hundred paces wide. Carloman rightly had used it to house his shield wall, but it would be of little use other than to keep in deserters. The only sortie from this part of the wall was by rope.

At the end of the plateau, the ground fell away again for another hundred feet to the flat farmland surrounding the city. A farmhouse stood at the base of the slope. It looked puny compared to the towering city walls above it.

As they drew close, Pippin could see that the house was in fact much larger than he had perceived. With its back to the slope, the building framed an expansive farm with a barn, three pens for large animals, a stable, and a grainery. It was, he thought, a testament to Bertrada's family wealth. Her father's farm was bigger than many villages throughout the kingdom.

Bertrada led Pippin up to the main house. Although in good repair, it had the eerie silence of abandonment. No chickens squawked, no cows mooed; the animal pens were empty as was the grainery.

"Whatever they couldn't bring into the city," Bertrada said, "must have been scavenged by Carloman. We'll see what is left of the wine cellar." She led him around the back of the house to a set of doors built into the ground. Holding torches aloft, they went underground. At the bottom of the stairs, they found themselves in a long, fortified cavern with hundreds of casks lining the walls on either side. Those closest to the door were missing; some had been forced open with an ax.

"I hope Carloman appreciates your father's hospitality," Pippin said.

Bertrada led him between the casks deep into the cavern. They passed well over a hundred barrels before they reached the far wall. By their direction, Pippin guessed they were well beneath the plateau. This far in, the only disturbance to the dust covering the floor was their footprints.

"Where is it?" Pippin brought his torch closer to the wall, looking for the promised tunnel.

"There," Bertrada said.

He used the torch to disperse a network of cobwebs. "There's nothing here."

"Yes, there is."

Pippin handed her his torch and pushed against the flat stone of the wall. Nothing moved. He used his hands to feel along the left side for an edge. He did the same along the top. There was nothing. On the right side, however, his fingers felt a draft of colder air. He took back his torch and traced the contours of the wall. When he brought it to the right side, the torch fire flared. He threw his shoulder against the stone. It didn't move. He looked at Bertrada, puzzled.

She smiled and handed him her torch. She went to the wine cask to his right. "It's a trick," she said. "The opening is behind the wine. She pushed against the right hand side of the cask, and it shifted away from her, creating an opening in the wall large enough for them to duck through.

Pippin led the way with his torch and found himself in a dirt tunnel that led further into the mountainside. He couldn't see past the light of his torch. Looking back at Bertrada, he saw her nod. Crouching with the torch in front of him, he moved into the darkness. No more than shoulder-high, the tunnel had been dug through the earth and supported by wooden beams and trusses. The air had a musty smell of dead things. After two hundred paces, the slope of the tunnel floor gradually tilted upward. They found themselves before a small wooden door. There were no hinges, no handles, and no latch.

"You said it can only be opened from the inside?"

"We don't need this door to get into the city; we only use it if there is no other way out."

"What can we expect on the other side?"

"A stairway to a storeroom beneath the city. It holds some of my father's treasure. From there, we take a tunnel and another staircase up to the main house. My grandfather built it as an escape route. In the event of a successful siege, our family can flee with at least part of our wealth."

"I'll have Arnot work on it," Pippin said. "I've never known of a door he couldn't open."

"Are you sure you can't get a message into the city to have my father open it?"

Pippin shook his head. "Carloman brought men loyal only to him. This has to be the way."

"Arnot won't be able to get through. We'll have to wait for my father to come out when the wall is breached."

"That will be too late. I need to get them out before that."

Bertrada looked dejected in the torchlight. "I just don't think it can be done."

"We don't have another choice."

Boniface stood over his godson, appalled by the implications of the confession Carloman had made. If Lady Hélène really was Charles's assassin, Carloman could be found guilty despite his intentions. Even if the bishops heard of it, they would weaken Carloman beyond all recognition. They had already pushed him into agreeing to raise the Merovingian. Carloman would lose the support of the Church and, very likely, would fail to put down Gripho's rebellion and any of the pagan rebellions that might follow.

"I know that you intended no harm, but the responsibility may lie at your feet nonetheless." Boniface was sweating. This must not disrupt his life's work. Carloman was the key to a Christian kingdom. Boniface was sure of it. There had to be a better way. Boniface folded his hands and crossed Carloman's Spartan-like tent to the small altar the man had erected. Kneeling before the cross, Boniface prayed for forgiveness and then prayed for guidance.

His mind leapt to the rebellions brewing in the east. Surely the pagan uprisings wouldn't end with Gripho's siege. With every rebellion, calls for tolerance of the pagans would be raised. Some states might even declare themselves pagan. If Carloman failed to put them down, would Pippin? In truth, Boniface didn't know.

Everything hung in the balance. *Damn that woman!* Boniface quickly crossed himself. He would have to handle this carefully. Being bound by the seal of the confessional was helpful since he could not disclose Carloman's confession to the bishops. That, however, was not enough. He would need to divert the investigation away from Carloman altogether. And that would require some effort.

As to Carloman, as long as he was required to atone for his sin, the Lord's work would be done. That much Boniface could do. The question was: how evil a sin is it? It could be interpreted either way. Carloman surely suspected that his sin could be serious. He had, after all, requested the confession.

Boniface considered the potential in this. Carloman's faith was so absolute that a serious breach of that faith would devastate him. Or perhaps, with guidance, push him to be more assertive ... Carloman had been reluctant to take on Gripho. And with Theudoald no longer a threat, Carloman might relent. Any hesitancy would be taken for a sign of weakness, and other rebellions would certainly follow. That could not be allowed.

Yes, atonement could be a powerful tool to keep Carloman on course.

Crossing himself again, Boniface rose, bowed to the figure of Christ on the altar, and turned to face his godson. He walked to Carloman's chair and placed one hand on his godson's shoulder.

"You have spoken in the sanctity of the confessional, my son. That was wise. Your sin will not pass my lips again. On one level, this is a political matter. Let me deal with it as such. I will talk to the bishops. I will resolve their questions. You must never speak of it again."

He turned to face his godson. "As to your sin," Boniface said in his gravest of voices. "Although your conversation was unintentional, it was mired in desire. No, don't protest! You flirted with that woman just as assuredly as I stand here before you today. And you flirted with the thought of murder."

Carloman's face flushed with embarrassment.

"God has an uncanny way of listening to the desires in men's hearts. Your earthly passions have led you astray and to horrible consequences."

Carloman nodded.

"This is no venal sin, Carloman," Boniface cautioned. "This is mortal sin. You have compromised your life with Christ."

Carloman looked as if he had been struck. He knelt before Boniface.

"This cannot be," said Carloman. "I have sinned but not by intent. I raised no hand against Theudoald."

"Although it was not committed by your hand, your heart and your desires administered the poison to your rival just as if you had done it yourself."

"Surely, it is not the same!"

"Murder is the gravest of sins," Boniface said, his voice rising with passion. "Even wishing it taints your soul. In His Sermon on the Mount, Christ said, '*Thou shall not kill, and whosoever shall kill shall be in danger of the judgment.*'" Carloman was visibly shaken. Without sympathy, Boniface continued, "'*But I say unto you that whosoever is angry with his brother without cause shall be in danger of the judgment.*'"

"This will take more than an Act of Contrition to resolve, Carloman. For this, you must atone."

In a gesture that Boniface had taught him at seven years old, Carloman reached down to pick up the hem of Boniface's robe. Bringing it to his lips, Carloman kissed the garment and then prostrated himself on the ground before Boniface. The bishop smiled. He made the sign of the cross over his godson and sighed audibly.

"Your penance will be heavy, my son."

Boniface could barely hear Carloman's response. But when he heard it, he knew his instincts had been correct.

"Blessed be God forever," Carloman said.

"Are you all right, Father?" Drogo asked.

"Yes, son, I'm fine."

"You don't look well," the boy said.

They had gone up the hill with Johann to inspect the damage inflicted by the catapults. Finding the wall still largely intact, Carloman had unleashed a torrent of reproach on the captain of the catapults. Although visibly shaken, the man stood his ground. The wall was holding, he explained, because to a great extent it was backed by solid earth. While some of the city was built above ground, the wall encased the hillside as much as it shielded the city, and its thickness negated much of the catapults' impact.

Carloman ignored the obvious truth of the man's argument and threatened him with a ride on his own catapult if the walls were not soon breached.

It had been two weeks since Boniface had visited. After hearing Carloman's confession, the bishop had insisted that Carloman atone for his sin prior to asking forgiveness. Until then, he said, the gates of heaven were barred. Boniface had returned to Paris, leaving him adrift on a sea of doubt.

While Carloman struggled to accept such a dire consequence for a sin so unintentional, he had to acknowledge the truth in Boniface's words; lusting after a woman in your heart was a sin just as grave as adultery. The scripture held the same true for murder. Had he wished Theudoald's death? His own words haunted him. *Can you take care of that one for me?* He had killed many times in combat and had never questioned the morality of it. That was justice. *But killing by poison?* A small thread of guilt coursed through him, and the more he tried to deny its existence, the stronger it became. He racked his conscience, seeking absolution, but none came.

For three days, he consumed nothing but water and lay prostrate in prayer before the altar. Though hunger savaged his body, he received it gladly to assuage the guilt in his soul. His fast, however, brought no solace. No path to redemption appeared, and the touch of God still escaped his grasp. He was desolate, weak, and confused.

He next threw himself into commanding the siege. No report was of too little consequence for his attention. First he dealt with Father Daniel's followers, "the Faithful," as they now called themselves. Their presence once had bolstered his belief in the righteousness of his war with Gripho. But their numbers continued to grow while Carloman's supplies grew short. He had put them on half rations to protect the food supply. The Faithful protested, demanding that Carloman keep them nourished. They seemed to care little for his explanations of siege warfare.

The Knights in Christ were equally furious with his decision, insisting that the Faithful be cut off entirely from food distribution. But Carloman had no intention of fulfilling their request. He would not abandon those committed to his cause in Christ, especially after the visit from Boniface.

He sent troops as far as Soissons to requisition new provisions.

Discipline was also becoming a problem. Without combat to keep them occupied, the men grew restless. Carloman ordered twice the usual number of daily drills and had his captains regularly inspect the men and their equipment. Exhausted men were less likely to grumble, and Carloman didn't care to hear any more grumbling.

Disease too had struck. Daily, Carloman received reports of those newly dead or too sick to serve. The list grew longer each day. Carloman forced himself to read through the names, absorbing their losses like body blows.

The fate of the siege, it seemed to him, had been reversed. Famine and disease were supposed to ravage those inside the walls, not outside them. Carloman took this as yet another sign of God's displeasure.

The cost of the siege was growing with each day, and thanks to Heden's destruction of the catapults, the wall's demolition could take twice as long as he had planned. Every day, Carloman climbed up the hill to the wall in hopes of seeing some sign of its imminent collapse. He always returned disappointed.

He often met Pippin there. Despite his brother's admonitions, Carloman was reassured by the presence of his younger brother. In some ways, his brother was—as he always had been—at home on campaign. Carloman would find Pippin laughing with the soldiers, poking fun at one man's scar or teasing another about the size of his penis. The men were drawn to him. Pippin was relaxed, confident, and fearless—qualities that the men respected and Carloman envied.

But something had changed. Pippin had surprised him by supporting Trudi in her decision to marry Odilo. More surprising still was Pippin's condemnation of the siege against Gripho. And he was furious over Carloman's agreement with the Church to raise a Merovingian to be king.

"Father would never support that," he had said. "And I won't support it either."

Pippin was no enemy—they shared the same blood and the same faith—but his younger brother was becoming a force to consider.

Carloman's thoughts returned to the concern on Drogo's face. "Yes, son. I'm fine," he had said. But he wasn't. He had abandoned, and been abandoned by, his Shepherd. He was lost. He could no longer see the way or walk in the light. The state of grace eluded him.

Atone. Boniface's words haunted him. He must atone.

Chapter 12

Pursuit

Bradius awoke the day after the beating, wincing with pain. Spying his clothes folded on a chair in the corner, he struggled out of bed, hobbled across the room, and stepped into his pantaloons. He could see but not clearly. One eye was swollen shut, and the other, although partially open, watered relentlessly. Bruises covered most of his body, and his left hand was so swollen it looked like a cow's udder. When he tried to wriggle his fingers, they moved, but pain shot down his arm. Two of his teeth were missing, both on the upper right side of his mouth.

Trudi. He had to find her. A wave of nausea passed over him. He needed to sit down.

Myrna appeared in the doorway. "What are you doing?"

Bradius raised his hand to cut her off. He had trouble forming the word "Don't—" before continuing to dress.

"You're not going anywhere," she said. "Look at you. You can barely stand."

Bradius ignored her.

Myrna's voice softened. "They would have come here anyway, Bradius. They would have found her without me."

He said nothing. She had set them up to be captured. She had betrayed him.

"You and I both know who she is." Myrna shifted to anger. "I don't understand why you were protecting her. What is she to you?"

He continued to dress.

"Have you forgotten what they did to you? Have you forgotten what her family did to Unum?"

"It wasn't her."

"It was her *brother*. How can you let your boy's death go unanswered?"

"Unum is buried. You've no right to dig him up." Bradius picked up his sword belt and fumbled to put it around his waist.

"You're in no condition," Myrna pleaded. "You can't possibly do anything for her."

Bradius glared at her through his swollen eyes. Myrna tried to meet them but again had to look away. He fumbled with his belt. His hands were useless. After a painful minute, Myrna took his hands away. She adjusted the sword and scabbard for him and cinched the belt. She made him sit down on the chair and knelt to pick up his boots. One by one, she put them on and laced them. When she was done, she stood, picked up his cloak, and held it out for him. Tears filled her eyes. With some effort, he stood and shrugged himself into the garment. She picked up his saddlebag and lifted it over his shoulder. He winced. Surveying the room, he assured himself that he had all his belongings.

Myrna's eyes pleaded with him. He returned nothing but anger.

Sighing, she looked down, drew a solidus and several denarii from her pocket, and put them into the pocket of his cloak. She walked to the door, opened it, and stood aside to let him pass.

Without a backward glance, he walked past her. She let him get outside before breaking the silence that had fallen between them.

"Don't you want to know where they went?"

He stopped on the landing, his back to her.

"North, along the Roman road," she offered.

He turned.

"Forgive me." She began to cry.

"Myrna."

"No. You must forgive me, Bradius. I made a mistake. I didn't know. I can't take it back. But I am truly sorry. I didn't understand how important this was. Forgive me," she said. "Please, Bradius."

Bradius reached out to touch her cheek. Myrna leapt into his arms, sobbing.

"I'm sorry. I'm sorry. I'm sorry," she whimpered.

"I am too," he whispered and left.

Trudi found a trail up the mountain and pushed her warhorse throughout the day to gain some distance from the Lombards. It was a grueling pace, but she wanted to reach Wissembourg by nightfall. There, at least, she could have a hot meal and sleep in a bed. The effort, however, was taking its toll. She was lightheaded, exhausted, and her shoulder racked with pain. During the latter part of the day, she cradled her arm, praying that the wound would not reopen.

She rode into Wissembourg with the sun setting behind her. It was a small city with only one main street. She found a house with a sign out front that pictured a bed and knocked on the door to ask for a room. A gentle maiden lady took her in, paid a boy out front to stable Trudi's horse, and poured her a bath. She helped Trudi undress and gasped at her injury. The woman's face grew hard.

"A man did this." It was a statement, not a question.

Trudi nodded.

"You're trying to get away."

Again Trudi nodded.

"You will be safe with me." The older woman doted on her like a child, helping her to bathe and to dress, then taking her downstairs for a meal of hot lamb stew and mead. As soon as it was finished, she insisted that Trudi get to bed. She even brought in an extra blanket and tucked her in. Trudi was so touched by the woman that her eyes welled with emotion at the gesture.

The next morning, Trudi couldn't bear to face the road again. She succumbed to the woman's urging to stay for the noonday meal before heading down the mountain into the Rhine Valley. She told Trudi where to find a ferryman to cross the river and gave her a stout coat to fend off the cold.

The delay, however, was a mistake. Voices drifted on the wind behind her. Pausing to be sure, she heard the familiar clank of armor and knew, somehow, the Lombard soldiers had tracked her east. Damning herself for her carelessness, Trudi picked up her pace.

She thought about using the same tactics Bradius had employed to elude Pippin but quickly rejected the idea. Her only possible path of escape was speed. Any backtracking or subterfuge would allow the soldiers to cut off her only route of escape. She would have to outrun, not elude, her pursuers.

Her best chance was to obtain passage across the Rhine before the Lombards could catch her. She climbed a small hill to look down over the valley and was stunned by the size of the river. It was ten times the size of the rivers she knew.

To the south was the fishing village where the ferry would be. If she could reach it first, they would have to wait for the ferry's return before resuming the chase.

She spurred her warhorse and drove him hard over the rugged terrain. Speed was difficult in many places; the road often didn't allow for more than a walk. In some spots, she had to dismount to guide her horse over the broken landscape. Even where the path was even, it meandered, making it difficult to give her horse its head. She made no effort now to hide her tracks. She couldn't afford the time.

The weather began to warm as the day progressed. Sweat dripped from her forehead into her eyes, making them sting and tear. Trudi rubbed them, using the cloth from her sling. The path began to improve, and she spurred her mount for more speed. She stole a glance behind. Although she saw no riders, she knew they were still behind her.

As the road turned toward the river, no trees remained to protect her from view. She turned back to gauge the distance from her pursuers. Her eyes caught a glint of sunlight off metal far up the road. *They're too close,* she thought. *I won't have enough time to cross the river.* All her instincts screaming, she spurred her horse and sprinted toward the river. She crossed into the open landscape, knowing she would be seen.

She was. Shouts echoed in the distance.

She reached the river and turned south, looking for the ferry across the Rhine. Her horse's breath became labored. His nose was full of froth. *I'm not going to make it.* She passed into the small fishing village and stopped to look back. Soldiers appeared on the road behind her, twenty or more, black against the reddish brown landscape. They turned toward her.

Up ahead, she saw the ferry, a broad, flat raft capable of holding ten horses. Buoyed by empty barrels and long pontoons, it was held against the current by a long rope, anchored on both shores, which passed through the eyeholes of three large posts on the ferry's north end.

She pulled up alongside the ferry and searched for the ferryman. She found him in a small shack with four stout men playing dice. A large, balding man with brown cracked teeth, he stank of fish. The men looked up briefly at her entrance and then returned to their game.

"I need passage," she said.

"Have to wait," he said. "One woman and horse, not much fare."

"I'll pay double," Trudi said.

The ferryman looked up at her curiously and then shook his head. "Nah." He went back to his dice.

"Triple," she said.

Again the ferryman looked up. This time his eyes squinted in her direction. "And a denarius tip for the men."

"Done. But we have to leave now."

The ferrymen scrambled to their feet while Trudi made partial payment on her passage. Making their way outside, the ferrymen began to untie the craft from its mooring while Trudi led her horse onto its deck.

"Hurry!" she called. Looking north to gauge the progress of the Lombards' pursuit, she saw them clearly with dust billowing behind them as they bore down on the village. "Hurry!" Trudi urged, her eyes still on the soldiers.

"Trouble?" the ferryman asked. "I'll need an extra denarius from the looks of those soldiers. I don't want any trouble."

"I'll give you two if we leave now." Trudi glared at the man. He nodded to his men, and the ferry moved out into the river.

It was painstakingly slow. The ferry dragged in the Rhine's current. The men pulled on the rope, straining under its weight. They had gone no more than a third of the way across when the Lombards reached the bank of the river. She could see them clearly, their horses lathered and the men frustrated. Trudi walked to the edge of the deck. She recognized Aistulf among them.

"Ferryman!" the prince of the Lombards called out. "Ferryman, bring her back, and I'll double your fare!"

"Triple!" called the ferryman to Trudi's shock.

"Done." Even from this distance, Trudi could see the smug look on Aistulf's face.

The ferrymen stopped pulling on their rope and began to reposition themselves to haul the ferry back to the western shore.

"Sorry, miss." The ferryman smiled down on her with his brown teeth. "Money is money."

"I'm sorry too," Trudi said, pulling her hand out of her sling. She patted her horse's neck and sighed. "We almost made it, didn't we, boy?"

The ferryman turned away from her to supervise his men. As soon as his back was turned, Trudi pulled her sword from the scabbard on her horse's saddle. Moving it to the left side of her body, she took three steps to reach the western side of the ferry and swung the sword at the taught ferry rope.

"Stop!" the ferryman cried. Several of the men let go of the rope and moved toward her.

The rope held. Trudi swung again. This time, she threw her weight into it. Her shoulder lanced with pain, but the blow was true. The rope snapped, flinging one end west into the river and the other east, slithering through the eyeholes that held the ferry to the rope. It moved with amazing force. Two of the men holding the end closest to her were thrown overboard. The two others were quick enough to wrap the retreating rope around the middle post, straining against the burn as the rope passed through their hands.

Grunting with the effort, they called for help. The ferrymen leapt to the rope, trying to anchoring it to the boat's remaining pivot. The craft swept downstream with the current, arcing steadily toward the eastern shore.

"I'll kill you!" the ferryman shouted, anger contorting his face. He spat in her direction and then turned back to his struggle with the rope.

"A deal made fast is a deal made." Trudi tossed the agreed upon balance on the deck of the ferry. With an effort, she mounted her horse and turned it to face the fast approaching eastern bank of the Rhine. Just before it reached the bank, she spurred the horse forward and leapt to land.

Her horse skittered up the bank, struggling to find footing. Seconds after Trudi's mount found firm ground, the ferry slammed into the bank, splintering its pontoons and shattering its barrel floats. One of the ferrymen threw himself into the water to secure the raft to shore.

Trudi turned her horse east and spurred its flanks. On impulse, she looked back to her pursuers across the river. Spying Aistulf, Trudi waved and smiled. The prince of the Lombards merely shook his head and waved back.

Trudi purchased provisions and headed east toward Canstatt. She figured that without a ferry, Aistulf would lose a day trying to get across the river. She imagined that he would waste more time searching for some news of her passing.

To use that time to her advantage, she asked for alternative routes east, and finding one, struck out before night fell. She walked her horse through streams to hide her tracks and backtracked in an attempt to throw off her pursuit. She didn't think it would buy her much time, but she needed to do something.

It was getting late. The moon had waned in the past few days and could no longer light her path. She needed a safe place to sleep. A footpath off the road to her left led to a small lake nestled among trees. She dismounted and walked her horse along the trail until it reached the water. Still visible from the road, Trudi continued to search for a good place to hide. She led her horse through a dense outcrop of underbrush and around a series of large boulders to reach a secluded stream flowing out of the lake.

After tethering her horse in a spot shaded by several tall oak trees, she knelt next to the stream and drank her fill of the cool water flowing through it. Using one of her sacks as a pillow, she lay down beneath the trees. Her eyes followed the trunks skyward. They reached up into the evening light like hands trying to grasp the firmament. Birds chirped and flitted from branch to branch above her.

She hadn't realized how tired she was. The threat of capture was so intense that it had kept her going long into the day. Now she could barely keep her eyes open. She rested them, listening to the birds overhead and to the water flowing softly into the pool beside her. She didn't even notice falling asleep.

Groaning in her discomfort, she rolled away from her wounded shoulder and got to her knees. The sun had moved back across the sky. She must have slept through the night and half the morning. Pushing herself upright, she chastised herself for losing so much time. She packed her gear, watered her horse, and started to retrace her steps back to the road.

When she had reached the boulders near the lake, the bark of a man's laugh cut through the quiet. Trudi froze in place, straining to concentrate on the sound. She heard several voices, all men. Trying to stay low and out of sight, she made her way to the boulders and hid herself behind the largest of them. She could hear the men clearly now but couldn't see them.

"Why do you care?" a growling voice asked.

"Don't matter to me," a second voice replied. It had a nasal quality to it that, excepting the accent, made Trudi think of Pippin's man Arnot. "I do what they tell me. But it seems crazy spending all this time searching for a girl. We could have been back on the peninsula for all the time we've spent here."

How did they find me so quickly? Trudi's dread returned. Wanting to see her hunters, she searched for a vantage point behind the rocks. She found one, but it required climbing onto one of the boulders to peek through an opening higher up on the rocks. She found a handgrip and using her left arm pulled herself up to a small sliver of an opening between the stones.

They were Lombards. One stood in the clearing, letting the horses drink from the lake. The other was below Trudi's vantage point, squatting in the underbrush.

"Think on it, man," the growling-voiced soldier said. He was older, fat, and jowly. "Our Aistulf marries Charles's daughter, and what does that make their son? He'd be heir to the kingdom, both kingdoms."

"Where do you think she's hid?" The nasally voiced soldier was the one defecating in the underbrush. "She couldn't have gotten too far."

"Won't matter. Our trackers can find anyone. If she's on this road, we'll catch her."

"I'll bet a pint of grog we find her before tomorrow night."

"I'll bet we have her tonight," the first said. "Once Aistulf tracks his prey, he never loses them."

The nasally one came into view, pulling up his breeches. He joined the fat, jowly soldier in the clearing.

"She's crafty, I'll give her that," the nasally voiced soldier said. "That trick with the ferry was pretty good. Good thing there was another ferry an hour south."

Trudi had an odd sensation that she was missing something, something essential. She couldn't put her finger on it. The two men were talking casually by their horses. She was safe, out of sight behind the boulder. Yet her sense of dread grew with every breath. Her eyes searched frantically for what could be wrong.

The horses. There were three, not two.

She scanned the camp for the third rider. He was nowhere to be found. As quietly as she could, she backed down off the boulder.

Just as her foot touched the ground, she heard a sound behind her.

Her heart sank. She tried to turn, but her limbs refused to respond. Before she could see her assailant, an arm grabbed her from behind, and a knife was at her throat.

"Found her!" a delighted voice called from behind her ear. To her, it said, "Settle down now, miss. I expect you'll be coming with me."

They escorted her to the great room of an inn where she was kept under guard for the better part of the day while soldiers went to find Aistulf. For supper, they brought her stew with bread and water. She savored it, thankful for a warm meal. The fire in the hearth was also welcome. She had forgotten what it was like to feel warm.

"So nice to see you again." Tall and elegant, Aistulf strode into the room, smiling at Trudi. He seemed relaxed, confident. He wore beautifully tailored black clothes, black boots, and a gold and white cravat around his neck. *He might be bearable,* thought Trudi, *if he wasn't so goddamn condescending.*

"Do you always assault your fiancées?" she asked.

"That was very unfortunate," Aistulf said. "I have already disciplined the soldier, explaining quite forcefully that no one is ever to touch a hair on your head."

"Why have you been chasing me?"

"You surely know the answer to that question. Have you forgotten our engagement?"

"I have thought of little else for several weeks now. Does it concern you that I don't love you?"

"Not in the least. I never expected to marry for love. That is for people who don't have kingdoms to run. We're marrying for one reason only, our children. Our poor lives are but a link in the chain. It is our children who are important. Your sons will be direct descendants of Charles Martel, every bit as much in line for mayor as is Drogo—or Pippin's son—if Pippin ever has a son. My son will inherit the Roman peninsula. If our son is one and the same?" He let the idea hang there.

"I know the argument," Trudi said. "I come from a long line of mayors."

"Was this merry little chase, then, really necessary?" Aistulf asked. "Do you find me so unattractive?"

Trudi rolled her eyes.

"Ah, well, you don't need to answer. But tell me this: how can you be sure that this man you chase across the continent is really in love with you? Or is he, perhaps, as interested in your progeny as am I? And is he able to protect your children as well as I can? You have considered it, haven't you?"

Aistulf should have taken vows, thought Trudi. The man loved to preach.

"Regardless, the running ends here. I'm surprised you've lasted this long even with your brother Pippin and that renegade, landless knight you found."

Anger soared within her at the jibe.

"Young women, particularly those of marrying age, should not be prancing around through the forests alone. From now on, you will travel with me and under guard. We will be on the Roman peninsula within a fortnight. Once there, if it is lovers you desire, you may have as many as you wish—but not until you have *my* son."

The more he spoke, the more appalled she became. "Is this your idea of a proposal?"

Aistulf laughed. "How delightful! A woman with a sense of humor. I look forward to our journey south. We leave in the morning."

"I can't wait," Trudi said.

Aistulf stood and bowed. "One more thing," he said as he made his way to the door. "I've sent for more appropriate attire than that peasant dress. And please don't wear that silly armor any longer. People on the peninsula would find it … odd."

The only thing Trudi could think to do was stick out her tongue. Aistulf left, laughing.

She had to get away … *had to*. She was escorted upstairs to a bedroom. A guard was placed at her door. *Just like a child,* she thought, *I'm being sent to bed*. She went to her closet and found her two sacks on the floor.

Opening the heavier, she took out her armor. "I'll show you odd," she said.

She put it on and stowed her dress in the other sack. She was surprised to find they had also left her sword in the closet. *They must think I'm playing dress-up.* Her wound still gave her trouble holding the blade in her right hand alone, but she felt more confident just having it with her.

She went to the window. It was already dark outside; the only light on the street emanated from inside the inn. Looking down, she guessed she was fifteen feet off the ground. A small ledge circled the second floor. Without hesitating, she doused the one candle in her room, threw her sack over her shoulder, and climbed out onto the narrow ledge. She moved carefully down the length of the building until she spied one of Aistulf's men watching the road. He moved at a leisurely pace, staring out into the darkness. After a few moments, he turned and walked back along the road beneath her toward the door of the inn where the light was better. She pressed on, passing to the far corner of the house. There were no guards on that side of the building.

She jumped. It was farther than she thought. Her legs buckled under the impact, and her armor clattered against the cobblestone road. With a groan, she got to her feet and backed up against the wall. The guard she had passed came into view, investigating.

"Who's there?"

She didn't move. He stepped cautiously in her direction. "Who's there?" he repeated, peering into the darkness. He took two steps toward her ... and then two more. He was about to turn away when he saw Trudi's sack. Bending down to pick it up, he saw Trudi in the darkness.

"Who—"

Something out of the darkness struck him in the back of the head, and he went down. A beggar stood behind him. He wore a hooded cloak that obscured his face. He motioned for her to follow. Without hesitation, she left the wall, retrieved her sack, and raced behind her disappearing savior. They moved down two streets, him ten steps ahead. He cut through an alley, and then a second, stopping eventually at a stable. Motioning her to wait, the beggar went inside and returned with two horses. They were not of the same caliber as her warhorse, but she didn't have any choice.

"Who are you?"

The beggar pulled off his hood and stared at her. It was dark and his face was large and misshapen. She moved him out to the street and into the moonlight.

"Who are you?" she repeated. But he didn't need to answer. Recognition dawned on her, and she would have hit Bradius in the face if it wasn't already so damaged. "No," she seethed. "Not with you!"

He made hand signals to quiet her down while his eyes searched the alley. "We must go now!"

"Go back to your *pious widow,*" she retorted. "I don't need you." But shouts erupted nearby. The guard had been discovered, and Trudi sobered. Racing to the horse Bradius held, she pulled herself up.

"Follow me," he whispered, mounting the other horse.

Trudi hesitated. Then, for once, she decided to listen.

Pursuit was immediate. Had it not been for Bradius's elusiveness, Trudi knew they would have been captured before a thousand paces. She watched her vassal with amazement as he backtracked, planted false trails, hid their tracks, and used the talents of the hunters against them. Yet when Trudi and Bradius paused to listen, the sounds of their pursuers always drifted to them on the night air.

More than a few times, Bradius and Trudi hid off the trail to let their pursuers pass. Shielded only by the cluster of a few convenient trees, they watched from their saddles as their hunters lumbered by unaware. Bradius, relentless in his art of deception, never missed an opportunity to hide their tracks in an available stream or to follow hard ground to make no tracks at all. Trudi had to admit that he was good.

A range of mountains blocked their path east. Bradius led them north, where the mountains were less imposing. They never camped; they rested. They never ate; they snacked. To avoid detection, neither of them spoke. Bradius used simple hand signals to guide their movements.

After a day's ride, they finally turned east into a vast wood, thankful for the cover it provided.

Tall ancient trees towered over them, with great branches stretching outward only at the very top of the forest. Massive limbs formed a canopy that filtered out much of the light and created a shadowy realm beneath its shield. The undergrowth was sparse, and the forest floor was covered with a thick layer of decaying leaves that muted the sound of their passage. Bradius signaled for her to pick up the pace.

From the moment they entered the deep forest, however, Trudi's breath grew short. She leaned forward in her saddle and strained to see into the shadows. As on her journey from Metz, shapes threatened her from the darkness. The hairs on her arms lifted from her skin. No birds chirped. No animals scurried. No wind rustled. In the permanent twilight of the forest, Trudi became unsure of the passage of time.

Bradius, his damaged face stern and uncompromising, led them steadily eastward. He left no room for questions or discussion, so Trudi had to content herself with trailing behind him as he navigated the woods.

When the ground began to slope steeply upward, Bradius meandered to ease their climb. They rode across the western face of a mountain for an entire day, only to spend the next meandering down its eastern face in similar fashion. Always, they headed east. Always, they made their own trail.

She hardly noticed when it first started to rain. The forest's natural cover sheltered them from the worst of it. But as the downpour grew in intensity, it penetrated the canopy and drenched them both.

The ground became sloppy. Their progress slowed. The air became colder. They tried to ignore the elements and push on, but the weather's continued hostility slowed their pace. Trudi's hands grew cold, and she began to shiver. She withdrew as best she could into her winter cloak and fell into her habit of concentrating on Bradius's back to block out the elements and her exhaustion.

Trudi refused to ask him to seek shelter. Her anger with him had not waned. If anything, it had intensified over the past few days. He had been so terse with her that she would not let herself be weak in his eyes.

He had said almost nothing since they reunited. He never discussed his choices or consulted her opinion. She merely followed him over one mountain after another until the day it stopped raining.

It was midmorning. Despite his habit of forging their own path through the forest, Bradius had taken a small trail that led gradually downward. The forest thinned with their descent. The sky was gray, and the rain had lost its force. The wind too had abated. Like a shutter opening on daybreak, the rain ended, and the sun broke through the cloud cover.

Trudi looked up, stunned. A great valley, broad and flat, swept out before them. She could see for a hundred miles. A small city was nestled into the mountain to their left. *Canstatt,* she thought, surprised they had come so far. Mountains crowded the horizons to their north and south and pinched together at the end of the valley far in the east. Shafts of sunlight lanced down on the farmland before them, creating a colorful display of lush greens and yellows.

Trudi began to laugh. It started as a chuckle but warmed into a full-bodied laugh, rich with irony and affection. Bradius reined in his horse sharply and turned to her.

"We lost them days ago, didn't we?' she accused him.

"What?"

"You heard me. We lost Aistulf days ago, and you've kept up this silence to avoid talking to me. I've been following you blindly for almost a week now, and I suddenly realized that I haven't heard them in days. We lost them, didn't we?"

After a long and embarrassed look, Bradius shrugged.

Trudi shook her head in wonder. "Idiot!" she said, letting him wonder if it was meant for her or for him. She swung out of her saddle and began to take off her armor. Bradius looked at her with shock.

"What are you doing?" he said.

"Taking off my clothes."

A strange look crept across Bradius's face. His horse shied to the left. "Why?"

Trudi had gotten down to her undergarments. "Because I'm soaked through," she said, exasperated. "And I'm sick of staring at your back."

Finding a tree limb that stretched into the sunlight, Trudi pulled her peasant dress out of her sack and spread it across the tree.

"We should get out of the open," said Bradius, searching the landscape.

"You must be joking," Trudi said. "We haven't seen anyone in days. Aistulf isn't anywhere near us, and I need to get dry. If you had any sense, you'd do the same."

Bradius was staring at her strangely. Looking down, she lifted her shirt at the shoulders to fluff the garment out. She found a large boulder facing the sun, climbed up on top, and lay back in the sunshine.

Bradius stayed in his saddle for a long time before he dismounted and took off his armor. He climbed up onto the boulder next to her.

"How did you find me?" she asked without opening her eyes.

"I followed Aistulf. He never bothered to cover his tracks."

She relaxed, letting the warmth of the sun seep into her, enjoying the feel of air on her skin. The relief she felt, however, was tinged with disappointment. "I'm not naïve. I saw the way you were with Myrna at the inn. I know you slept in her room. If that was what you wanted, you could have just told me and let me go on my way. You didn't need to rub my face in it." She hadn't meant to say that. "I can take care of myself."

"Myrna thought she was protecting me."

"Now who do you think is naïve?" she asked and lay back down to face the sun.

Bradius didn't automatically respond. In time, he said, "She is in love with me ... and maybe she didn't like my being with you."

I don't care about Myrna, you ass, Trudi thought. "Why did you come back?" she whispered.

"It's hard to be a vassal when your liege lord is in custody," he said, pushing his jaw to the right until it popped into place. "I met your intended."

Trudi sat up again, a new realization dawning on her. She examined his face. The swelling had gone down, but the yellowish-blue discoloration remained. She touched his cheek. She had been wrong. Her eyes welled at his pain.

"Aistulf did this?"

"He had it done."

Trudi knelt before him and explored his injuries. She gently measured the damage to his eye, following the bruise to his face and neck. She untied his shirt to follow the discoloration to his chest and ribs. She placed her palms against his ribs and pressed firmly inward. He winced, a soft grunt escaping his lips. She took off his shirt to probe his arms.

"You are hurt."

"It's hard to breathe. And my eye won't stop running. My hand is starting to heal. I'll be fine."

Her hands had not left him.

"Your ribs are broken," she said, her voice choking on the words. "Oh, Bradius, I am so sorry. I hadn't realized."

Without thinking, her arms encircled him, and she hugged his head to her chest. She rocked him back and forth like a baby. "I'm so sorry," she said. And then she was kissing his face and his lips and holding him against her.

It took several moments before she realized he hadn't moved. He didn't resist her, but he hadn't returned her embrace. She felt the color bloom in her face as the horror of his rejection took her. She let go of him and tried to stand without considering that they were still on the boulder. She climbed down clumsily and made her way to where her clothes hung on the tree.

"These are dry enough," she ventured, ignoring the fact that they were still quite wet. "I suppose we should get going." How could she have been so stupid? He didn't want her. Not her.

"Trudi," Bradius said from the rock.

"Just let me get my armor back on," she said. "It won't take but a moment."

"Trudi," he insisted.

Holding up her hand, she said, "I understand … I do. It was a mistake … I just thought …" She turned back to her clothes, throwing the dress into her sack, and pulling her armor back on piece by piece. Reluctantly, he followed her, donning his armor and regaining his horse.

"Ready?" she said.

He nodded, and Trudi headed east. She preempted his usual role of taking the lead. She didn't want him to see her cry.

They rode in silence. The broad valley made their passage easy and their progress quick. The weather too blessed them with comfort. The sun rose lazily through puffy, white clouds and offered them the warmth and promise of spring. Without discussing it, they relaxed their pace and turned their faces to the sun. Tension left their shoulders, and the shadow of pursuit left their eyes. It was almost like a casual ride in the country.

Except neither of them spoke.

Trudi had shown Bradius little other than her back since he had refused her embrace on the rock. It was of little help that she knew he was right. He had done what needed to be done. She was who she was, and he was who he was. There was no more of a chance for them than there was for a pig to love a goat. But it did not change the way she felt, and she could not face his rejection.

That night, Bradius built a fire, fixed a small dinner, and then removed himself a short distance to savor his wine. It usually took two or three cups before he would relax. Sometimes more. He tried to strike up a conversation with her, but she would have none of it. She gave him little more than one-word answers to his questions and never offered a thought of her own.

They passed the next days moving steadily through the broad valley. Always, they arose at daybreak, broke their fast, and rode till sundown, stopping only for supplies, lunch, and to relieve themselves. Rarely did they talk. When they did, it was to convey basic information.

"We'll camp here," he'd say, or she would announce, "I have to pee." They spoke about little else.

Their progress through the valley had taken them steadily between the two ranges to where the mountains converged before them, barring their path east. Their only road snaked upward into the foothills and promised a long and arduous journey ahead.

"We'll be in the mountains for a while," he said. "It will be tough going."

"And after that?" she asked.

"We continue east until the Wormitt River. We follow it south to the Danube, then east to Regensburg."

"And after that?" Trudi reined in her horse, forcing him to stop. "What happens after that?"

He shrugged and looked away. "You marry Odilo."

"Is that what you want?"

His eyes focused on the mountains in the distance. "It's what you want."

"You don't know what I want."

Bradius did not respond.

"What happens to you?" Trudi moved her horse close to his. "What happens to you if I marry Odilo?"

"I don't know," he said and looked at the ground. "I don't know."

"Damn you." She shoved him. "Look at me!"

He didn't.

The back of her hand struck his shoulder. It was ineffectual. Her second blow was more forceful. She used the heel of her palm to punch his chest. She began to cry and unleashed a torrent of blows on him. He made no attempt to block them. Instead, he grabbed her elbows to constrict her ability to hit him.

"Stop," he said. "You'll hurt your shoulder."

Trudi pulled away from him, wiping away her tears. Failing to staunch them, she dismounted and started to walk away. Bradius followed. "Please, Trudi," he said, "stop." When he reached her, she turned and stood very close to him, her eyes looking up into his.

"You feel it," she said at last. "You … feel something for me." Her voice was almost a whisper. "I know you do." She took a big breath and plunged on. "Even when I was your prisoner, there was something. Then you saved me from Ansel. You came after me again, even after Aistulf beat you. And when we were out on that rock, and you looked at me—"

He took a long time to respond. "I am your vassal," he said, "and you are to be the mother of kings."

"That is not it," she said. "That much I know."

Bradius's looked at his hands. "I …" He cut himself off with a shake of his head.

She waited for him, but he wouldn't continue.

"What happened on the rock?" she asked.

"I … couldn't," he stammered. "I wanted …"

"Tell me," she whispered. Her hand touched his face, drawing his eyes to hers. He tried to look away, but she grabbed his arm, and again her eyes found his. They bore into him and saw his pain. His eyes welled with tears. He shook his head, unable to speak. "Tell me," she said, laughing softly, "or I'll have to hit you again."

He laughed, but it was a long time before he spoke. "I know what you feel. I feel it too. I have for a long time. But I also see things. Strange things. My nightmares come now even when I am awake. When you kissed me on the rock, I saw blood covering your face and hands."

"Blood?" Trudi asked.

"Unum haunts me. He shadows everything I hold dear. And everything I hold dear turns to ashes."

"I am not my brother," Trudi said. "I'm not."

Bradius turned away. "I know," he said, shaking his head. "But it doesn't matter. Unum mocks me. He mocks my failure to prevent his death. How can he let me embrace the sister of his murderer? How can I embrace the sister of my enemy? Tell me, could you do that? I have sworn to serve you. I have pledged fealty. That much I can do. But when I think to touch you or kiss your lips, I see his blood everywhere."

"Oh, sweet Jesus," Trudi said.

"I don't know, Pippin." Arnot stretched in the open space of the wine cellar, and Pippin had to stifle a laugh. Arnot's entire body was covered with dirt. His eyes squinted when he spoke, and his hair stood out in several directions at once. "It's a tough one. That door is imbedded in a stone. I can't break through it, and I can't dig around it. I've been tunneling on either side of it and hitting solid rock."

"Can you go under it?" Pippin offered.

"I tried. I wouldn't count on us getting through that door soon."

"Do you need more men? I've got several who are in need of a little activity."

"No. I can hardly breathe in the tunnel as it is. More men will suck up all the air that's left. I've got to come out regularly to catch my breath."

"I'll send someone down to help. At least you can take turns."

"What are you going to do if we can't get Sunni and Gripho to come along?'

Pippin was surprised by the question. "Of course they'll come. Any fool can see they're losing."

"Or maybe they're waiting for help."

"If they are, it will have to come from the east," Pippin said. "Hunoald and Waifar won't leave Aquitaine." For over a century, the nobles in Aquitaine had worn out their enemies by locking themselves up in their castle-cities. They'd withhold taxes and send no men or food, knowing that it required four times the number of troops to take a city as it did to defend it. To them, rebellion was a game of attrition. Gripho would get no immediate help from them.

"Then the Alemannians and the Bavarians?"

"More likely." It was one of the reasons Pippin wanted to stop the siege and negotiate a peace with Sunni and Gripho. If the regions west of the Rhine rebelled, Hunoald and Waifar would starve them of resources while the Saxons and the Lombards took advantage of their preoccupation and expanded territory.

"We don't need war. We need peace," Pippin said.

"Huy-yah."

"You had better get back to it," Pippin said, nodding toward the tunnel.

Arnot picked up his pick and shovel.

"Pippin?" Arnot called to him. "What if I can't find a way in?"

"There aren't any other choices, Arnot," Pippin said. "You need to get through that door."

Time had begun to heal their wounds. *At least the physical ones,* Trudi thought. The bruises on Bradius's face had moved from purple to yellow to almost nothing. His hand was less swollen, and he now could use his fingers. They decided to stop at the village they saw at the foot of the mountains to pick up dried meats, an assortment of cheeses, bread, and, of course, wine for Bradius. As always, fearing pursuit, they were discreet. She stowed her armor and wore a dress to blend in. They entered the village separately. They gently probed merchants about soldiers asking questions. They haggled over prices to make sure no one commented on their wealth.

From the moment they arrived in the village, however, Trudi was struck by a heightened sense of activity. Everywhere she went, Trudi heard discussion about something called "the telling." It was as if everything was connected to it. "We will wait for that till the telling," a shopkeeper had said. And a girl lamented to a friend that, "Himmelt won't ask me till the telling."

Afraid to stand out, Trudi refrained from asking what "the telling" was. When it came up, she merely nodded her head as if she understood and discreetly gathered supplies so that she and Bradius could take their leave. She was about finished when she heard a shout from the street. "She speaks! Hurry, she speaks!" Sales stopped mid-transaction, cows were left half-milked, water was left half-pumped from the well, and if it were possible, Trudi thought, women would have stopped mid-birth to answer the call. The villagers flooded into the streets and headed for the north end of town.

She saw Bradius across the street. He nodded toward the eastern road. Trudi shook her head, nodding instead toward "the telling." She had to know what it was. Curiosity had the better of her. It seemed as if Bradius was about to insist, but he shrugged and stepped into the road, following the crowd. Smiling, Trudi stepped into the street behind him.

The sun was warm, the sky a bright blue, and the excitement of the crowd was catching. It took less than five minutes to reach the north end of town. By that time, the crowd had swelled to over a hundred villagers. Green fields rolled gently before them, and as the villagers crested each successive rise, they looked like a human wave flooding the landscape. Far ahead in the distance, Trudi could see smoke from a small fire.

It burned atop a large stone in the middle of a clearing surrounded by a circle of large, broad, flat stones. The villagers did not violate the circle. Instead, they swarmed around its perimeter and maintained a respectful distance. *There was something almost religious about it,* Trudi thought. *Almost like a mass.*

Sitting cross-legged before the fire on the stone was a young woman of twenty years, naked to her waist. Rune lettering tattooed her skin. The symbols snaked up her arms, circled her shoulders, and ran down between and underneath her breasts. Her eyes were closed, and she rocked back and forth before the fire, apparently deeply entranced.

Her hair was long and black and adorned with what looked like dozens of small bones. When her head moved, they clacked in a ghoulish fashion. Her nose and ears were pierced with small silver rings to which tiny bells were attached. These provided a gentle chiming accompaniment to her movements.

"Who is she?" Trudi asked the man next to her.

"A sibyl," he answered. "She sees beyond the illusion of our lives."

With a moan, the sibyl stood and lifted her arms. Her hands opened skyward as if she were begging from some celestial body. Two women moved to her side and, kneeling, produced two small drums. Without any apparent direction, they began to play an odd syncopated beat. The sibyl swayed to its rhythm. In time, women in the crowd mimicked her movements. Several men began to chant.

Trudi squeezed between two people so that she could see. She found herself in the circle closest to the altar. She noticed Bradius had done the same. They were, at most, ten paces from the altar and five from each other. A host of smells accosted her.

Trudi recognized the fumes of several trance-inducing plants Sunni had shown her. Sunni, however, had never used more than one at a time. Trudi was shocked that the woman could move. Even at this distance, every breath Trudi took sent her reeling.

The crowd began to move in a slow, undulating motion to the strange beat of the drums. Trudi moved with them, losing herself to the fumes of the fire, the closeness of the bodies, and the rhythms of the dance. The chanting grew louder and the dancing more pronounced.

Without warning, the drums stopped. The dancing stopped. The sibyl stopped. And she opened her eyes. She was staring directly at Bradius.

"Death," she said into the silence. Her face paled and resonated with loathing. She closed her eyes. No one moved. No one breathed. The sibyl started to sway again but stopped. She moaned and opened her eyes. This time, she looked directly at Trudi.

"Life," she said, then quickly amended, "No." She closed her eyes again and held out an outstretched palm as if to ward off Trudi. "Abomination." The sibyl reeled backward in disgust. She shook her head, bones clacking violently. "No!" She pushed her palm into her forehead, as if squeezing the word from her mind. "Absolution," she said.

The sibyl dropped her arms and stared at Trudi, her eyes suddenly clear and clearly alarmed. "Who are you?" she demanded.

The entire crowd turned to Trudi.

CHAPTER 13

Breach

"Quiet," Gripho whispered, securing one end of a coiled rope to a stone post just inside the rampart. It was night. Bart, Petr, and Gripho stood on the rampart looking out over the wall. Gripho had not wanted to include Heden's sons on his plans. Soldiers would have been better, but the risk that they would warn Heden or Sunni was too great. The boys, he could manage, although he regretted bringing Petr. The boy was too weak. Again, secrecy had driven his decision to include the younger brother. If he hadn't been included with Bart, the boy would have turned to his father. That, Gripho couldn't allow.

Once he was sure that the rope was secure, Gripho tied the other end to a bucket of pitch and then carefully lowered the pail over the side. When the rope slackened, he pointed to Bart. "You first," he said.

Bart chuckled and gave a quick smirk in the direction of his younger brother. He took the rope in his left hand and scurried over the wall. Petr shuffled nervously as his brother disappeared.

"Don't step in the bucket," Gripho whispered into the darkness.

"You next," he told Petr. When the boy hesitated, Gripho said, "Go ahead. I'll be right behind you." Gripho was growing frustrated with

Petr. The boy was such a baby. Eleven years old, but he acted more like six.

Petr had trouble getting over the wall. Bart's weight had pulled the rope taut over the edge of the rampart, making it impossible for Petr to grab hold. When he saw the boy hesitate, Gripho extended his hand to lower him over the edge so that he could grab the rope where it came away from the wall. Gripho watched him disappear into the darkness.

Gripho had chosen the north end of the city for their midnight escapade. Its slope was the steepest of any surrounding the city, and he hoped that it would be the least watched. For days, he had waited until the moon waned. The weather too had cooperated. An overcast sky blocked the light of the stars, and the air was so moist it muffled sound and limited visibility.

With little ceremony, Gripho followed his two companions over the wall and caught the rope blithely as his body slid over the rampart. He moved down the rope hand over hand, using his legs to relieve some of the pressure on his arms.

"Watch out," a voice below him whispered.

Gripho's foot touched something. Petr had stopped his descent.

"Petr," Gripho whispered. "Don't stop. Keep going."

"Can't," the boy whimpered. "I just can't."

"Hand over hand, Petr, just like I told you."

"I can't."

"Petr, I swear I'll skewer you right here if you don't start moving." Gripho let go of the rope with one hand and started to pull his sword from its scabbard. When the hushed scrape broke the silence, Petr renewed his descent with considerable speed. They reached the ground without further incident, and Gripho smiled into the darkness.

"Let's go get that catapult."

The three moved quickly and quietly into the night. Cautiously, they approached the dirt wall Carloman had built around the city. Every thirty paces, torches adorned the barrier. Their flames threw off a reluctant glow that succeeded only in providing light for three or four paces apiece. The boys headed to the darkest part of the wall. Crouching next to it, they grew still, breathing softly to listen for movement. There was none. Bart made a move to climb over the mound, but Gripho held his arm and signaled him to wait.

After a few moments they heard footsteps striking the wooden planking on the other side of the wall. The sound grew as it approached them and then receded as it moved past. When they could no longer hear it, Gripho signaled for Bart and Petr to scramble over the wall. Gripho climbed up after them and handed the pitch bucket over the side. Relieved of his burden, he too dropped to the planks, and the three crouched inside the wall, waiting for the sound of alarm. It didn't come. Silently, they moved down the hillside away from the siege wall, the light, and the soldiers. They followed the outline of the wall east.

The steepness of the slope slowed them. At times they slid their way downhill to circumvent campfires and pickets that barred their path. Their clothes grew wet and heavy with the earth's touch. The boys moved silently and steadily east, fighting the incline to stay in sight of the wall.

Gripho listened as soldiers spoke to each other in the darkness. The men's words were low and muted to match the mood of the night. No tension marked the voices droning through the dark. The men were bored. They were not ready for attack.

It took more than an hour for Gripho to lead Bart and Petr around the eastern end of the city. Above them on the hill, torches surrounding two of the catapults shone in the night. Separated by twenty paces or more, the machines sat on platforms facing the city wall. Gripho led the boys straight for them.

Their journey had taken them farther downhill than he had anticipated. They were well downslope of the nearest catapult. The incline, however, was easier to navigate here on the southern side of the city. Moving slowly upward, Gripho scanned the pickets. There were two, one east and one west of the machines. Three men manned each post, one to patrol the wall, and two to guard the catapults. Gripho nodded to his companions, and they separated. Bart moved uphill and climbed onto the catwalk into the path of the guard patrolling the wall. Before he was seen, Bart acquired a pronounced limp.

The guard halted. Bart took a few more dramatic steps.

"Excuse me, sir." Bart collapsed.

The guard moved to the boy's side and knelt down next to him.

"Where did you come from, boy?"

"My dad brought me up here to look at the wall." Bart looked miserable. "He stopped for a drink at that campfire north of the city. When I tried to get him to come back with me, he let me have it good." Bart rubbed his cheek for emphasis. "I ran off and tried to make my way back down, but I fell and got lost."

"Who is your dad, boy?"

"His name's Wilhelm. He's with the Austrasians."

Without taking his eyes off Bart, the guard called to his colleagues.

As the rest of the eastern picket moved to investigate, Gripho and Petr climbed onto the catapult's platform behind them. Silently, they closed on the backs of the two pickets and, with knives drawn, attacked.

At least Gripho did. He drove his blade deep under the ribs of the man nearest him. The man collapsed, reaching out for the guard kneeling over Bart. The guard turned and attempted to catch his falling comrade. The effort pulled him off balance. Just as Gripho had planned, Bart drew his knife and thrust it up through the stomach of the guard who held him into the man's heart. Blood spewed from the wound and covered both of them. Bart rolled the man to his left and got to his feet. The dying soldier grasped futilely at his belly in shock.

Shit, Gripho thought. Petr hadn't moved. Neither had the third soldier. The man stood frozen in his tracks, watching the life drain from his two comrades. He managed half of a shout and an attempt at his blade before Gripho kicked him in the groin. The guard doubled over, and both Bart and Gripho descended upon him. Their knives came away bloodied and successful.

The damage, however, had been done. Footsteps thundered from the western side of the catapult to answer the alarm.

Goddamn that lump of cowshit! I never should have brought him, Gripho thought. Seizing the bucket of pitch and a nearby torch, he leapt atop the back of the nearest catapult. "Run!" he called to his companions. Gripho poured the pitch onto the machinery and shoved the torch into its workings. He hoped that would do it. Fire licked along the black ooze just as the soldiers reached the catapult. Gripho took one backward glance. Petr still hadn't moved. Bart was nowhere to be seen. As the soldiers gained the platform, Gripho threw himself off the catapult into the darkness of the hill below.

On instinct, Gripho curled into a ball. He did the best he could to protect his head while his body banged down the steep hillside. A sharp rock caught him in the ribs, and his right leg hit a sapling. He didn't think his leg was broken, but the pronounced pain that rippled along his shin and into his knee made him worry. This was not a good time to be lamed. His tumbling body encountered a thicket of large bushes, and he threw out his arms and legs to break his momentum.

The bushes raked through his hands, but the effort was enough to stop him. He came to rest downhill of the thicket, his head facing up toward the city. The catapults still shone in the torchlight high in the distance, but he could see little in the darkness. Gripho squinted to see into the lighted space and swore under his breath. They had put out the fire. He slumped into the grass beneath him. His plan had failed.

Three torches moved down the hillside toward him. He roughly pushed his frustration aside. They would expect him to move parallel to the siege wall to find a way back to the city, so Gripho headed downhill. He ran and fell toward Carloman's camp to put distance between him and his pursuers. He hoped they would limit their search to farther up the hillside.

When he had descended an additional hundred paces, Gripho moved west rather than north and east, the way he had come. He could barely see the torches that lined Carloman's siege wall in the mist, but it was enough to guide his progress across the incline and around the city.

He abandoned any thought of searching for Bart and Petr. They would be far better off making their way back alone. Bart would find a way. But Gripho wasn't so sure about Petr. The boy was useless. When Gripho had turned back to tell them to run, Petr was still rooted to the catwalk like a tree.

Gripho's mud-covered body helped him to blend into the brownish black landscape created by the hill and the night. Twice he was forced farther downhill to avoid patrols looking for him. He passed the Soissons gate and knew that the main road up to the city lay ahead.

When he reached it, he began to despair. It was heavily patrolled along the length of its meandering path. Gripho sat behind a large bush off to the side of the road and tried to devise a plan of attack.

"Halt! You there! Stay where you are," a voice cried out from the darkness. Gripho swore under his breath and looked for a place to run. It was a moment before he realized the soldiers weren't speaking to him.

Less than fifty paces uphill from him, a short figure covered in mud raced across the road past the soldiers and disappeared into the shrubbery on the other side. It was Petr. *He must have tried to follow,* Gripho thought. When the soldiers, including those nearest to Gripho, scrambled after him, Gripho used the distraction to cross the road unseen. He heard Petr cry out as the soldiers found him.

"Gripho! Gripho!" There was a dull thud, and Petr fell silent. *Damn him!* Gripho knew he must abandon the boy. He could not risk being caught. The soldiers scrambled back to the road and began searching the area where Petr had first appeared. Without looking back, Gripho continued to move west.

After an hour, Gripho entered an area thick with trees. The ground had begun to slope upward. He decided he should turn northward and move upslope to circle back to the north side of the city, where he could find the rope. The undergrowth and the trees made this part of his journey difficult, but it was preferable to being out in the open. He climbed up, his leg aching. He found he needed to stop regularly to catch his breath. His ribs hurt. His leg hurt more. He hoped he would make it before dawn.

The night was changing hue when he reached the northwest corner of the city. Gripho turned east, out of the woods, and traversed a steep slope just below a plateau where Carloman had formed his siege wall. It was far more difficult to navigate, and Gripho slid regularly down the face of the hill. He began to worry. He would need to make a move soon. Once the sun began to rise, he would be as visible outside the city as a bug on linen.

The slope gradually began to decline, and he judged he had begun to move east on the north side of the city. He climbed closer to the siege wall. Going back over it would be more difficult since the wall was higher on the downslope side. He needed to find something to help him scale it. He moved parallel to the catwalk trying to find something, anything, to help him over the wall. Near one of the torches, he spied several crates. Gripho waited for the guards to pass before attempting the climb. When the soldier had gone twenty paces, Gripho sprinted for the catwalk.

He did little to hide his movements since he didn't have much time before the guard came back. He picked up one crate and stacked it. It was heavy. He doubted that he could lift a third high enough to stack on the first two, so he climbed on top, hoping that he was tall enough to reach over the wall.

He jumped, but his hand failed to gain purchase on anything that could help him pull his way over the siege wall. A guard shouted, and footsteps thundered toward him. He looked around frantically trying to find something that would aid his flight. Seeing the torch, he pulled it from its holder and threw it into the night. He leapt toward the now-vacant holder, caught it, and pulled with both hands. He swung his right leg over the wall. His calf caught on a jagged rock imbedded in the top of it. Despite the pain, Gripho used it for leverage and hauled himself over. It sank deep into his flesh.

There were more shouts as he pulled himself up and over the wall. Other jagged rocks scraped his chest and stomach, but soon he was dropping the short distance to the ground on the other side. He hurried uphill toward the city wall, praying that the rope would still be there.

Arrows flew. Archers were trying to pick him out in the gray half-light. Shafts sank into the turf near him. He was limping. Blood ran down his calf into his boots. He made twenty paces and then twenty more. He fell. An arrow sank into the earth a hand's length from his face. He got up and kept on until he reached the city wall. There, he paused to catch his breath. He was out of arrow range but far from safe. Soldiers were scrambling over the siege wall to give him chase.

Gripho tried to judge how far he was from where they had descended earlier that night, but he had no point of reference. He had to guess. He moved east along the wall. His leg was stiff, and each step brought a stab of pain. He used the wall for support and struggled against the incline. The soldiers were gaining.

He saw the rope. It was another fifty paces. The soldiers were closer. He wouldn't make it.

Again, arrows were flying, but this time from the city wall. The soldiers pursuing him had become targets. They huddled behind their shields under the hail of shafts. Twice they tried to regroup and charge after Gripho, only to be overwhelmed again. Twenty lay wounded on the field between the walls. The others retreated.

Only one soldier continued the chase.

Gripho was near the rope. He sprang for it awkwardly. Climbing hand over hand, his progress was slow without the use of his right leg. The soldier appeared below him, reached out for the rope, and then he too began to climb.

"Shoot him!" Gripho screamed to those above. "Shoot him!" But the man was below Gripho and effectively shielded from the arrows above. And he was gaining. Gripho didn't want to think about his chances against the man given his bad leg. They were high enough for a fall to be fatal. He threw all his might into the climb.

Shouts and cheers came from both the siege wall and the city as the two raced skyward. Gripho's arms ached, and his leg was on fire. He was two body lengths from the top. He felt the soldier's hands below him just as arms reached over the rampart's edge above him. In a mad scramble, Gripho redoubled his effort, pulling his body upward. The hands above him grabbed him by the shoulders and lifted him up and over the wall.

When his feet touched the catwalk inside the rampart, Gripho seized a sword from a nearby knight and swung the blade at the rope he had just climbed. With any luck, he could sever it before his pursuer could slide back down. His first blow failed.

Incredibly, a hand crested the rampart and tried to grasp the rope where it crossed the wall. The soldier was coming over the wall. Gripho held the blade aloft at eye level, tried to gain sure footing, and waited for the man's head to show. Gripho saw the helmet and began his lunge. A face appeared.

Bart.

Gripho recognized his friend too late to stop his lunge, and the blade jabbed out across the wall, into nothing. The face was gone.

"It's me," Bart called from below the rampart. "It's Bart. I stole the uniform."

Again the face appeared, and hands reached over the wall to bring him up. Once on the rampart, Bart jumped into Gripho's arms, and the two hugged each other in celebration.

"That was too close!" Gripho laughed.

"That was reckless." A stern voice shocked them to silence. Gripho and Bart turned to find Heden standing over them.

"Where's Petr?" he demanded.

Both boys found other places to occupy their eyes.

"Well?"

"The last time I saw him, he was chasing after Gripho," Bart said. "One of the soldiers grabbed him, but Petr slipped away and followed Gripho down the hill."

Heden focused his attention on Gripho.

"He was captured," Gripho said. "He tried to cross the road, and they caught him. He didn't have the sense to wait."

Heden's head rolled away from Gripho as if he had been struck. Pain lanced through his eyes. "Are you sure? Are you sure they caught him?"

Gripho nodded.

"What were you boys thinking?" Heden asked, spittle spraying from his mouth when he spoke. "That mission didn't have a chance to succeed."

"It would have," Gripho growled. "If it wasn't for Petr. That little coward never raised a blade."

Heden's backhand caught the Gripho on the cheek and sent him flying backward. "You'll find I can," Heden said.

Gripho lay at Heden's feet, fury streaking through him. He stood to confront the tall Thuringian. "How dare you strike me?"

Heden had him by the throat. With one hand, he lifted Gripho up and pinned him to the rampart. When he struggled, Heden tightened his grip. Gripho could not breathe. He started to panic.

"*You* led an ill-conceived raid that had little chance of success," Heden railed. "*You* took the service of untrained boys without permission from their liege lord and father. *You* left my son behind. *You* failed."

Gripho felt his eyes bulge as Heden's grip shut off his throat. Desperately, he searched for someone to intervene. No one moved. Looking back into the Thuringian's eyes, Gripho saw the possibility of his own death.

"Father," Bart called.

Heden turned to his son and after a moment dropped Gripho to the catwalk.

"Because of you," he said to Gripho, "I will have to beg Carloman to let my son go." Heden picked up the sword Gripho had used and, with a curse, threw it over the wall and into the night. "I doubt the bastard will acknowledge an offer to parley," he said. "And even if Carloman does agree to talk, I won't have anything to barter with—except you. If you have any sense, boy," Heden growled, "you'll make yourself scarce."

Gripho did.

It's Heden's fault, Gripho thought. It should have been clear to everyone that as mayor, he was in charge. But you couldn't tell that by the way people knuckled their heads to the Thuringian. Everyone acted as if Heden were mayor. Even Sunni deferred to him. He couldn't believe she was sleeping with the man. Gripho rubbed his jaw. And the bastard actually had hit him.

A bone-jolting boulder from one of Carloman's catapults hit the wall and interrupted Gripho's thoughts. The catwalk beneath his feet gave a little beneath him, dropping nearly a hand's width. Gripho reached to the rampart for balance. A plume of dust rose from the base of the wall, and repair crews scrambled to reach the weakened section. Gripho frowned. The southeastern wall was almost ready to fall. Huge cracks of daylight streamed through it. *Laon was a mistake,* he thought. *I can't understand why Mother chose it. We should be closer to our allies in Aquitaine or*

Alemannia or even Bavaria. Gripho grunted and wondered about the possibility of aid from the east. Where was the "pagan revolt?"

Gripho spied Samson far away, shuffling down the street. *Another I could do without,* Gripho thought. *I can make up predictions as well as he can.* Gripho had asked the lore master to repeat his foretelling, but the old man had told him no. The stones "said what they said." They couldn't be redone. Gripho had come close to stabbing the old cow fart. What does it mean to be betrayed by your past?

When Gripho heard the sound, he had trouble recognizing it for what it was. Pitched low and loud, it howled against the evening like a wounded animal and grew in volume until it drew every eye to the wall. There was a crunching noise, a prolonged silence, and then a loud rumble as the wall began to fragment and the stones to sluice outward like water behind a collapsing dam.

"Breeeach!" Gripho's cry was echoed on both sides of the wall. Outside, Carloman's catapult teams scurried to reorient all their trebuchets to the wall's damaged site. Inside, armed men streamed to the gap in the wall to prevent incursions while engineers hauled wooden trusses to bolster the rest of the sagging stones.

Gripho checked over the wall to ensure there was no imminent attack and then descended from the catwalk to direct the reinforcement. His damaged right leg, however, slowed his descent. By the time Gripho reached ground level, Heden was already taking charge. *Damn him!* Gripho had avoided the Thuringian since Petr had been captured. But now there was little choice. Gripho strode directly to Heden.

"I will take over here."

The large Thuringian looked at Gripho and grunted, barely acknowledging him. Heden turned back to the engineers.

Gripho raised his voice. "I said—"

"I heard you," Heden said.

Gripho seethed with anger. "You, there … you, that's right. Put down that planking. Everyone needs to focus on the wall."

The engineer hesitated and looked to Heden. Gripho erupted. "You don't need to look to him! I am mayor. You do as *I* say!"

Work around them ground to a halt. Soldiers, engineers, workmen, and servants turned to watch the two nobles. Heden looked around at their audience, breathed a huge sigh, and put his hand on Gripho's upper arm.

"Get back to work," Heden shouted at those on the wall. "The mayor and I have something to discuss." Before Gripho could protest, Heden nearly lifted him off the ground by his arm and shoved him to a distance out of earshot of the wall.

"You will not cross my path in this." Heden's voice seethed with fury. "Do you have any idea how to defend a breach? Have you ever seen a breach assault?" Gripho glared back with anger but did not respond.

"I have. It's a death march. Hundreds, maybe thousands will be killed assaulting the gap in our walls. It will be the most vicious fighting you will ever see. It will require a Herculean effort to stop them. Many of our best knights will be killed. But Carloman can be stopped. *I* can stop him. *I* know how.

"Or you can continue to play mayor and put yourself between Carloman and the city. They have six thousand soldiers. They will come at you in wave after wave using their numbers to overwhelm your defense. And when they succeed—" Heden's eyes focused on a distant point, seeing the assault with his inner eye. "The men who claw their way through a breach won't just take the city. They will rape it. And don't think they will stop with the women." Heden looked at Gripho. "Boys are just as prized."

Gripho wrested his arm away from Heden and moved to walk away.

"Most nobles in this situation abdicate," Heden said. "They give up rather than unleash such a torrent of violence."

"I won't give up." Gripho spat, turning his back to Heden.

"Stay out of my way, Gripho," Heden said. "Your stupidity has already led to Petr's capture. I think that's enough."

Gripho stalked away only after making the most obscene gesture he could remember. He stormed up the first street he passed and turned at the first corner. He stopped to hear Heden giving orders back at the wall.

"The mayor has agreed to let me handle the defense of the city,"

Heden said in a voice that projected to all those working on the wall. A collective chuckle answered him. "I want the gap reinforced with stone and timber. Inside the gap, I want a narrow gauntlet built using pikes and timber. That will be our first fallback position. We will make an interior wall to surround the gauntlet *tonight* and put a catwalk with defensive positions for the archers. That will be our second line. By tomorrow, I want this area inside the wall to be a killing field." Heden looked up at the rampart walls. "They will mount parallel attacks there," he pointed, "and there. I want pikes, arrows, and soldiers in position by daybreak."

Gripho stood with his back against the wall, raging at his own impotence. He hated that the Thuringian was right about him. But he didn't know what to do. He wasn't going to let Heden humiliate him in front of the men. *A pox on him, but he will pay,* Gripho thought. *He will pay.*

Carloman stood on the catwalk just above the northern gate of his siege-wall. Drogo stood beside him holding his banner. It fluttered lazily in the southern breeze that swept up the hillside. The sun's early morning light glanced off their armor with a glint that could be seen for miles.

Gripho had been foolish to lead that boy into the night. What value could he have been to such a mission? But as a captive, he had great worth. Carloman had yet to determine what price Heden would pay for his son. But it would cost the Thuringian dearly. So far, Carloman had refused all attempts to parley for the boy. If not for Heden, Carloman would have already taken the city, and Gripho would be in chains. Heden would pay. The only question was how.

Carloman surveyed the gap in the wall and watched his trebuchets systematically widen it. The gap in the wall formed a crude *V*, with stones on either side creating a river of rock outside the city. Climbing that river up to the breach would be the challenge. It was a steep climb, the height of three men. It would be grim work. Many would die trying it.

Inside the city, hundreds of people had gathered on the ramparts. They stood two and three deep, peering out over the wall. *They are waiting for me,* Carloman thought. He, in turn, was waiting for the bulk of his six thousand men to ascend the steep, winding road up to the city.

Given the narrowness of the road, the men marched in units of five across and ten deep. Every man in every row stepped in time to a military drum, their knees rising and falling as they ascended the mount. On every fourth step, their fists slapped their chest plates in unison. On every twelfth, they shouted "Huh-yah!" The sound of it echoed off the hillside and rolled over the flat landscape behind them.

Their progress had been steady since daybreak. Over a thousand men were in position behind the siege gate awaiting his orders. A second thousand were well on their way, and already there was little room left on the hill behind the siege wall. Carloman would have to attack soon, if for no other reason than that they were running out of space.

"Father?"

"No, Drogo," Carloman said. "You cannot lead the attack on the breach." He smiled. Drogo's company was the only comfort he had found since his visit with Boniface.

"It is the battle's greatest honor."

"Only because so few survive it."

"You did."

"I was much older than you."

"Will we be part of the attack?"

"At the right time, son."

"When will that be?"

"The battle will tell us."

Three of Carloman's Knights in Christ rode up to the gate. They dismounted and fell to one knee before Carloman. As a father would a child, Carloman made the sign of the cross with his thumb on the forehead of each. They rose to their feet.

"Drogo, these are the knights who will lead the assault on the breach. May I present to you Rhinehart, Jolin, and Friedrich of Austrasia." The men bowed deeply, and Drogo returned the gesture.

"I bid you strength and valor to overcome our enemies," Drogo said.

"For the glory of God!" Rhinehart raised his sword in salute.

"Huh-yah," echoed his companions.

Carloman reached into his pocket and handed Drogo three small, red, triangular pennants. Each had Carloman's cross and fleur-de-lis. He nodded for Drogo to give them to the knights.

"Take these tokens with you into battle," Carloman said. "May they bring awe from your enemies and honor from our men. They are symbols of the highest bravery; you will be honored to the end of your days." The knights fastened the pennants to their chain mail just above the left breast. Carloman made the sign of the cross. "In the name of the Father, the Son, and the Holy Ghost."

"Amen," the three said. They rose, bowed to Carloman and Drogo, and took their places at the gate. Behind them, more than a thousand knights were arrayed. Some carried ladders. Many carried pikes. Most carried swords and shields. They jostled restlessly, crowded behind the gate.

Carloman faced them, his armor shining in the sunlight. He raised his sword high above his head. A shout rose from those nearest the gate and was picked up by the men behind them. Soon, score upon score lent their voices until the whole army had joined in the visceral roar. They banged their shields and slammed their breastplates. A rhythmic beat began to emerge from the cacophony. This sound overtook the shouting. Others joined in until the entire army seethed with the rhythm.

At a signal from Carloman, Father Daniel, dressed in white, strode out onto the catwalk beside Carloman and Drogo. Silence took the ranks. The priest lifted his right hand, and the ranks closest to the wall dropped to one knee. Behind them, each successive unit knelt, creating a wave of obeisance before the Church's representative.

"In the name of the Father, the Son, and the Holy Ghost," the priest intoned.

"Amen," echoed the ranks.

The priest paused, waiting for attention. When he spoke, his voice resonated with a deep and clear timbre that projected far over the ranks of men.

"Holy knights ... God's soldiers ... Army of the Church! Today, *you* are the hand of God on earth. *You* carry His sword, His pike, and His lance. *You* bring righteous retribution to those who have desecrated His holy church.

"Because you have faith, and because your purpose is just, when you pass through these gates, you will be absolved of all sin. Should you fall today bringing justice to the pagan, you will sit at the Lord's right hand. You will have a place at His table.

"But many of you will not fall. Many of you will survive the fury the pagans will unleash. Many of you will cross the breach and overcome the wall to bring God's justice.

"I beg you, do not hesitate. Do not hold back your hand. Do not spare the pagan from your wrath. Let none who stand before you rise again to offend His name. Let none who harbor them live to sin again. In the name of the Father, the Son, and the Holy Ghost." He made the sign of the cross with large sweeps of his right hand.

"Amen," chorused the troops.

Carloman raised his sword high in the air.

"Austrasia!" he shouted.

"Austrasia!" they returned.

As the gate opened, horns blared, and Rhinehart, Jolin, and Friedrich of Austrasia ran onto the battlefield, leading a thousand soldiers toward the breach.

Dressed in a blue robe, Sunni stood next to Heden high on the wall so both armies could see her. She would not cower in her room while brave men fought and died for her son. In truth, she dreaded this moment. She had hoped to avoid its unnecessary bloodshed, but Carloman had forced her hand. She would not turn away from Gripho's destiny.

Despite the early hour, the sun beat down on her like a blunt instrument, assaulting her before the day's battle even started. Making matters worse, the dust from Carloman's assembling army billowed through the morning air, making it difficult to see and breathe.

She stiffened as a thousand voices roared from the other side of the shield wall. A horn blared, the gate swung open, and a torrent of men swarmed onto the battlefield, racing toward them in an incoherent rage. Sunni blanched at the sheer menace of it. Instinctively, her hand found Heden's arm.

They streamed toward the wall, stumbling into and over the trenches and barricades Heden had placed in their path. The city's archers had little trouble finding their target. Sheets of arrows flew from the wall, striking with a staccato sound that thrummed along the phalanx of soldiers. Scores fell under the barrage.

The attackers advanced until the next flight of arrows was launched. At a barked command, the soldiers slowed and crouched under their shields until the arrows hit and then resumed their mad dash when the sound had passed. They advanced and retrenched, advanced and retrenched, in a ragged dance with the arrows across the battlefield. To Sunni, they seemed to rise and fall like a morning tide.

As Carloman's army drew close, three concerted assaults began to take shape. The main body struck for the breach while two flanking attacks moved to scale the wall with ladders to the east and west of it. The city's defenders rained rock and stone down upon them. The rock-throwers wreaked havoc, slicing through the ranks of men in ghastly swaths of destruction.

Heden's men were particularly successful in keeping the ladders from the city walls, but less so in stopping the attack at the breach. At the forefront, one man led the army into the gap of the wall. He shifted his shield onto his back to free his hands and scaled the boulders before it like a goat. A rock knocked him off balance, and he fell. Then he was up again, pulling himself forward. A dozen men behind him scrambled up to keep pace, shouting, "Austrasia! Austrasia!"

Burning pitch fell on them, and their screams filled the air. The charge, however, had brought its own momentum. Soldiers scrambled over their fallen comrades and advanced through the wall into the city.

Sunni turned her attention inside the rampart. Heden had set up a shield wall inside the breach, trapping their attackers at the wall. With no time to form a wall of their own, Carloman's men were being cut down like wheat before a scythe.

With a guttural roar, a handful of men charged. One knocked aside a pike, swept his sword upward, and in a continuous motion leapt high above the shield in front of him. His sword slashed down, splitting the defender's head from the back of his skull.

Falling forward, he rolled over the dead defender and stood up behind the shield wall. Without hesitation, he began to hamstring the line's shield holders.

"To me! To me!" He pushed forward, his sword killing in fluid circular blows as he moved from foe to foe. The line was breaking. A handful of men appeared at his side, and he led them deeper inside the wall. The way now open, Carloman's men poured deeper into the city.

A dozen paces in, they saw the trap. Heden had erected a gauntlet inside the breach, with newly erected ramparts above it. His archers had Carloman's men at close range.

They raised their shields to fend off the arrows, but it was too much. They fell in droves, slaughtered before the battle was an hour old.

Heden pushed thoughts of Petr roughly aside. He couldn't afford to be distracted.

"More arrows! More arrows!" he shouted above the din. As the attack pressed up into the breach, the city's archers could not sustain their barrage at those newly entering the battlefield. The focus of the battle moved closer and closer to the city, and more of Carloman's men crossed the battlefield untouched.

It bode ill that Carloman refused to parley over the boy. What could be gained by keeping his son captive? He was a child! Heden thought of Petr, bound and alone, crying into the darkness. He wanted to howl in frustration.

"Shields left! Shields left!"

The shield walls had held against the initial rush, but the bulk of Carloman's attack was still to come. As the sun climbed higher in the sky, the sheer weight of Carloman's army bore down on the city's defenders. Ladders scaled the city walls, and pockets of invaders grew on the ramparts. The main body pushed its way through the breach, forcing Heden's men to retreat to his first fallback position.

Carloman's men streamed into the gauntlet of pikes and wood trusses that Heden had built and met a new wave of death. They surged at the wall, their voices rallying in wave after wave of battle cries and screams. Hundreds came, and hundreds died under the barrage of arrows, rocks, and burning pitch that Heden and his men poured down into the gauntlet. The slaughter was merciless, the onslaught relentless. Death followed death that followed death.

Heden's hands itched for action. Now, at last, it had come. He ordered a surge to beat back the Franks on the ramparts and left to join the reserves. He found Gripho with them at the gate, holding his horse at the ready. Heden signaled for the gate to open and led over one hundred cavalryman into the field. They waded into the Franks, their blades descending in rhythmic butchery. Their sortie cut through the main body of Carloman's attack, leaving those in the breach cut off from support and fighting on two fronts.

Gripho led a separate mission to strip the wall of ladders. Heden waited until the walls were denuded before ordering the cavalry back to the gate. The maneuver cost him twenty men but bought precious time for the wall's defenders to regroup. Once inside, Heden sprinted back to the ramparts to survey his defenses. Carloman was sending more men than Heden had expected. The fighting was more intense, and the losses were higher. His men were being strained to their limits. Heden repositioned some of his reserves along the rampart to fill in the gaps on the wall and ordered new supplies of arrows and rock to be carried up to the catwalk.

By Heden's count, Carloman must have already lost almost a thousand men, a heavy toll for any army. But Carloman had plenty more in reserve. Heden heard a shout from the rampart and looked out over the wall. Fresh troops had entered the field. Carloman was starting over. He hadn't even bothered to change his battle plan.

Heden shuddered at Carloman's detachment. No cost seemed too dear for the man. He tried not to think of Petr, but new fears and fury bloomed inside him.

"Here they come!" he shouted. Ladders rushed to the east and west walls as the main phalanx drove again toward the breach. Heden grabbed a pike and headed toward the Frankish ladders. His rage had found another outlet.

From across the field, Carloman surveyed the approach to the breach. The river of rock had become a river of corpses. The dead lay in waves across the field, grotesquely disfigured by the burning pitch or descending rocks. Some were still alive, pierced with arrows and screaming in pain for help or the chance to end their torment. The ground was thick with blood. Carloman shook his head and dabbed the trickling mucus from his nose. He had lost nearly a third of his army.

He received reports of a gauntlet set inside the walls of the breach. If Heden had one fallback position, he was likely to have a second. The Thuringian was clever. He had been prepared. The cavalry sortie had bought the city time and cost Carloman hundreds of men. But the tactic would only work once. Carloman had sent for his own cavalry units to be brought up the hill. If Heden tried it again, Carloman would isolate the Thuringian on the battlefield and take him hostage.

The sun was setting over the western horizon. In the morning, Carloman would direct greater numbers of men to the ladders. He had to overwhelm those manning the city's ramparts. At the very least, he had to distract them. Otherwise, getting through the breach would be too costly. Too many men were dying.

"In the morning, Father?"

"No, Drogo. I told you I would let you know." For the first time since he had left Paris, Carloman wondered whether he had enough men to take the city.

Heden heard the horns. Carloman's army withdrew from the field. His men cheered, but he had trouble sharing it. Petr was still a captive.

Looking down into the breach from the forward rampart, he was appalled by the slaughter they had committed that day.

His wound had reopened. Exhausted, Heden leaned against the wall for support, waiting for the reports to be brought to him. The scaffolding of the gauntlet had been burned. Casualties were high, supplies low. *They would not survive another day like this,* he thought. Carloman had too many men.

Heden called for his head engineer. It was dark by the time the small, wiry man made his way up to the rampart. Torches lit his way. Heden could see that the man too had been wounded; the engineer's bandaged left arm hung useless by his side.

The engineer nodded in greeting, exhaustion plain on his face.

"We held," Heden said.

"Today."

"Can you fix the gauntlet?"

The engineer shook his head. "I'm surprised this rampart still holds. Their catapults did a lot of damage."

"What if we collapsed what's left of the rampart into the breach?" Heden asked.

The man looked from the rampart down into the breach and back to the wall. He descended one flight of stairs to the level below and returned several minutes later. A smile took the corner of his mouth. "Might be able to do that," he said.

"By daybreak?"

"Won't do any good by noon."

Heden put every available hand at the man's disposal. Within the hour, he had the interior wall lit and scores pulling on ropes lashed to the rampart. Others levered the portions of the wall with planks. In the end, they had to use their own rock-throwers to weaken the forward rampart. "It's all about leverage," the engineer said.

Two hours before dawn, a number of stone blocks came loose roughly halfway up the wall.

"Pull!" shouted the engineer from the top of the opposite rampart, and the ropes snapped taut. The entire forward section collapsed into the breach, burying the bodies of those who had fallen that day. A cheer rose from the men, and the engineer did a little dance from his perch on the rampart.

Heden ordered the men to throw everything they could find into what was left of the breach: planks, wheels, carts, beds, pews from the church, even the altar.

"It will give you some time," the engineer said when Heden joined him, "maybe a week, no more."

Once it was clear that the repaired breach would hold, Carloman silenced his trebuchets. Under a flag of truce, he led scores of men back onto the field, not with weapons and shields, but with wagons and litters to carry away the broken and mutilated bodies they had left behind from the previous day's battle.

He had risked much, seeking to overwhelm the Thuringian, and instead had taken horrendous losses. A sliver of doubt pierced his thoughts. What if he failed? The thought surprised him. Never before had he felt such doubt on a battlefield. But then, of course, Charles had been in command.

Carloman's eye caught a piece of red cloth wedged into the armor of a corpse. Dismounting, he knelt beside the body. It was Friedrich. An arrow pierced his neck. Carloman closed the man's eyes, said a short prayer, and tucked the pennant behind his chest plate. Regaining his horse, he circled the battlefield to acknowledge those who had died at his command. The trip was long, his corpses many.

Regaining his tent, Carloman closed the flap behind him. He took off his armor and placed the red pennant beside his makeshift altar. Despite the early hour, exhaustion swept over him, and he sat down. He had trouble catching his breath, almost as if he had just been in battle, and struggled to regain his composure. He found himself staring at the red pennant and wondered at its ability to hold him transfixed.

"I am not my father." The words came unbidden to his lips. Yet he heard the truth in them. All his life, he had been so assured, *so righteous* in his faith and his family's destiny. Now he was not. And in his hour of greatest need, everything that made him secure in purpose had come untethered: Charles, Pippin. Trudi, Boniface, the Church, his faith. He never felt more alone. He was not his father. His father would know what to do.

Atone. Boniface's voice echoed in his mind, and Carloman bowed his head in acknowledgment. Faith was the key to his salvation. He must find a way to restore his path to the light. Until then, he was lost.

Hands trembling, Carloman knelt before the makeshift altar and began to pray. His voice sounded strained, even to his own ears. "*Confitéor tibi in cíthara, Deus, Deus meus: quare tristis es, ánima mea, et quare contúrbas me?*"

He bent his mind to the meaning of the words and tried to capture the cadence of the prayer. "*Confiteor Deo omnipoténti—*" The words had always swept him up in their power and their beauty. He used his voice to punctuate each phrase.

"*—Beatæ Mariæ semper Vírgini, beato Michaeli archangelo, beato Joanni Baptístæ, sanctis apostolis Petro et Paulo et omnibus sanctis: quia peccavi nimis cogitatione, verbo et opera …*"

As his passion rose from within him, he tried to ignore the trickle of fear that accompanied it. His skin flushed with expectation. His right hand closed around the holy icon he wore around his neck, and he clutched it to his chest. The swell of emotion surged through him. He extended his left hand before him, humbly offering his soul to God.

"*Mea culpa, mea culpa, mea maxima culpa.*" With his right hand still holding the relic, Carloman bowed and struck his breast three times. He waited for the fervor to take him.

It never came.

Choking back his desperation, Carloman whispered, "Please, Lord. Restore me to the path of righteousness; show me the way."

He bent to the right of his prie-dieu, his hand reaching for the instrument of his devotion. He felt the soft leather handle of the flagellum, and he shuddered at the menace of its tongues. Again, he began to pray.

"*Deus, tu conversus vivificabis nos. Et plebs tua lætabitur in te.*" This time, as the cadence of the prayer moved him and the passion of the words surged within him, he held out the flagellum and lashed it over his left shoulder to punctuate the prayer.

"Ostende nobis, Domine, misericordiam tuam. Et salutare tuum da nobis."

The tongues snapped against his skin, ripping the scabs off welts not yet healed and raising new ones beside them.

"Domine, exaudi orationem meam. Et clamor meus ad te veniat."

His body stiffened, and Carloman drew the force of pain into the throes of his passion. *"Oramus te, Domine, per merita sanctorum ..."* He struck again, this time over his right shoulder. "... *tuorum, quorum reliquiæ hic sunt, et omnium sanctorum ...*"

With each blow, he thrust the sacred words through his clenched teeth until his body convulsed. "... *ut indulgere digneris omnia peccata mea.*"

Again he stretched out his hand. *"Mea culpa, mea culpa, mea maxima culpa."* But the touch of the Savior again was withheld. It took him a long time to withdraw his hand. When he did, Carloman nodded in obeisance. "Thy will be done," he said, tears welling in his eyes.

Johann ducked his head into the tent, his eyes taking in the flagellum and the blood on Carloman's back. "Father Daniel requests an audience."

Although exhausted, Carloman nodded. "I'll need a minute." He dried himself with a towel, pulled a chemise over his head, and sat down to wait for the priest.

From the moment the man entered the tent, Carloman sensed that something was different about him. Gone was the dirty cassock that Carloman had come to associate with the priest. The garment had been washed and allowed to dry in the sun. He had bathed and run a brush through his long, white hair and beard. The priest stood erect and dignified, waiting for Carloman's permission to enter. That too was different. Father Daniel had the unnerving habit of strolling into Carloman's tent unannounced. He waved the holy man toward a chair.

The priest didn't move. His eyes had a strange cast to them as if he gazed at some remote place rather than at the confines of Carloman's tent. His pupils were almost nonexistent against the pronounced blue of his eyes. The effect was unnerving. It was, Carloman suspected, the look of fervor.

"I have had a vision," Father Daniel said. "I have been sent by Michael the Archangel to bring you strength and purpose. The time has come to strike a blow against the pagans."

It was too much. Carloman stood and turned his back on the priest. "Tell me, Father, what more would you have me do? Two thousand men died yesterday trying to storm the city. And we failed! Now before we can attack again, they *somehow* have resealed the breach. Another attack would be foolhardy, and I can't just *pray* my men inside the wall. I've got to let the trebuchets do their work. Now if you will excuse me—"

"There are blood stains on the back of your chemise, Carloman." Father Daniel's words were soft, almost a whisper. "You seek strength through the flagellum?"

Surprised by his tone, Carloman turned back to face the priest. "I have sinned," he said.

And with that acknowledgment, the anguish and despair overwhelmed him. It was as if the abyss of hell yawned wide before him. His eyes welled with tears, and he knelt before the priest, the words tumbling from him, raw with trepidation. "I have fallen from His path and am unworthy to receive His grace. I have fasted. I have prayed. I have mortified my flesh. Yet His touch eludes me. And I am lost without it."

Father Daniel bent to take him by the shoulders. "Rise, Carloman. You need not kneel before such a humble priest. You carry the Lord's burden. It is I who should kneel before you."

Carloman shook his head. "You don't understand."

"You flay yourself just as the Romans flayed Christ. And like our Savior, you suffer from the same doubt He suffered on the cross. Your Father has not forsaken you, Carloman. But neither will He let this cup pass."

Carloman clung to the priest's words, trying to grasp their meaning.

"I had a vision," the priest repeated. "I've been sent by the Archangel

Michael to give you strength and purpose. God's hand is withheld because your task is yet unfinished. You will not feel His touch again until your duty is complete."

A test, Carloman thought, hope stirring within him. *I am being tested.*

"You among men have been chosen by God to redress the desecration of His church. You are His sword." The priest paused. "It is true that the pagans have won the day. Now you must show them the price of standing against the legions of Christ."

"I don't know what else I can do."

"You have the son of the pagan general."

Carloman nodded.

"You must show them the wrath of God's hand."

Carloman shuddered. The boy was younger than Drogo.

"He is no innocent!" the priest thundered. "He desecrated God's mass, riding into church on horseback. He took to the field of battle, nearly destroying your catapults. He openly worships the pagan faith. He is an affront to all who are holy.

"While your men and the Faithful starve and die of disease outside these walls, the pagans remain inside, comfortable and content in their sin and safe from your prosecution. It is not enough to defeat them Carloman; the pagans must be made an example for all those who would think to desecrate His holy ground."

He offers me penance, thought Carloman, blanching at its weight. "I must pray for guidance," he told the priest.

"Don't pray too long. The day of our salvation is upon us. Only in victory will you return to grace and sit in the palm of our Lord's hand."

CHAPTER 14

Choices

Those nearest Trudi backed away and formed a semicircle around her. On the open side, the sibyl stood confronting her. No one spoke. Still affected by the smoke, Trudi was swaying slightly. She didn't know what was expected from her. Bradius started to say something but was silenced with a wave of the sibyl's hand. Trudi started to speak and then closed her mouth as well. She could think of nothing to say.

The sibyl approached Trudi. She walked with the seductive grace of women endowed with great beauty or great wealth. Calmly, she lifted Trudi's hand to examine it, exploring her palm, her knuckles, and her nails. Next she felt Trudi's forearm and bicep. She took Trudi by the chin and looked deep into her eyes. The sibyl's eyes widened in surprise. Releasing her, the sibyl walked around Trudi slowly. Trudi felt like a mare being evaluated for sale. She stood very still and tried to maintain as much dignity as possible.

"You are a contradiction," the sibyl said in a voice all could hear. "You are a woman but have a soldier's strength and hands. You dress like a peasant, yet your eyes are noble. You are church-born, yet are *conscious.*"

The sibyl moved toward Bradius, her hips undulating as she walked. The crowd's eyes never left her. Her eyes never left Trudi. "And there is something about this man," she said, running her fingers seductively along Bradius's arm. "Your fates are intertwined. Like lovers. Or siblings. It is yet unclear to me. There is love and death in him, violent death. And the blood of it," she said, nodding to Trudi, "taints you as well."

The sibyl returned to Trudi and crossed her arms. Trudi had the sense that the sibyl was debating something. When she spoke, she spread her arms and raised her voice to embrace the crowd.

"All life exists on one of three worlds: Asgard, the home of the gods, Midgard, the home of humanity, and Utgard, the home of the dead. Our life force is connected to the other worlds through the tree of life, but powerful wards protect us from them. If these wards are damaged or broken," she glanced at Bradius, "the result is madness.

"*Your* life force," the sibyl looked at Trudi, "is a whirlwind. Its power is strong, so strong that it disrupts the lives of those around you. You are the center. The wind of your choices steers their choices. And all of your choices are of consequence. You will choose life, you will choose death, or you will choose absolution."

The sibyl shuddered and closed her eyes. "But you do not belong here," she said. "Your path lies elsewhere." She looked at Bradius. "You both must leave. The blood of your past stains these fields as well as your heart."

Some of the villagers shifted their weight from one foot to another. It was nothing overt, a change in posture, no more. But it caught Trudi's eye. The villagers were no longer spectators. They were tense and hostile, waiting for some signal.

"You will come with me," the sibyl said. "The stain needs to be cleansed and—" The sibyl looked as if she was about to say something more but shook her head. Looking to one of the villagers, she said, "Bind their hands. Find their horses. I must take them to the tree."

A murmur of assent rippled through the villagers.

Trudi tensed. She could not stand the thought of being bound again. She searched for a route to escape. But Bradius stood near her, offering the villagers his wrists to bind. At a nod from him, she mimicked his gesture and proffered her wrists.

With a clatter of bones and a tinkle of bells, the sibyl threw back her head and strode sinuously through the crowd toward the town. The villagers gave way before her, bowing as if she were royalty. She never looked back. Behind her, they fell into two broad phalanxes, one beside Trudi, the other beside Bradius. They marched back to town over the fields, across the roads, and down the streets into the village where Trudi and Bradius were promptly put on their horses. The two women who had played the drums in the field also found horses for themselves and the sibyl and joined the party. The sibyl, who had by this time covered her nakedness with a shawl, led them east out of the village. Several miles later, they reached the foot of the mountains.

Only then did the villagers leave them.

The five rode most of the day in silence, following a narrow path up that forced them into single file. The sibyl led. Trudi and Bradius followed. The two women brought up the rear. They came to a small clearing, and the sibyl drew reins. She gave a signal to the women, who dismounted and untied Trudi's and Bradius's hands.

"You are free to go," the sibyl said. "But I would suggest you avoid taking the road back. If you return to that village before I pass this way again, you will most certainly be killed. People here take their harvest very seriously. And blood is a bad omen. I took you captive in part to gain your freedom."

Trudi shuddered. She wasn't sure if it was from dread or relief.

"We weren't in any danger until you started talking about our blood staining the fields," she said. "If you were worried about saving us from the villagers, why did you say anything at all?"

"I see what others cannot. The villagers come to me to understand their lives. 'Will the harvest be plentiful?' they ask. 'Will my baby be healthy? Is this love true?' I could see none of these things today. My visions were only of death and the whirlwind. I am bound to the truth I see. And the truth must be spoken. They came to hear about their lives. Instead, they heard about yours.

"Everything I said today was true. To cleanse the stain, I must take you to the tree. But that is a path only you can choose. I will not take you unwillingly to the tree. I cannot help you unless you ask to be helped."

Trudi hesitated.

"If you do not come," the sibyl said, pointing to Bradius, "he will die."

Trudi looked to Bradius. His face was red. He clearly believed the sibyl. Trudi took no more than a moment to decide.

She took them far into the mountains. They scaled several, suffering steep climbs and dramatic descents. Although there were no markings on the path, the sibyl led them confidently through fork after fork, frequently stopping to collect grass and dirt into a small cloth rag that she bound tightly with twine. Singing softly over the newly formed sack, she hid it in the limbs of a tree at the crossroads.

"What is she doing?" Trudi whispered to Bradius.

"Protecting our path," he said. "She thinks we are being followed. She leaves a spell to make our pursuers choose the wrong path."

"Does it work?"

Bradius shrugged.

Along the way, the sibyl stopped to pick mushrooms and to harvest wild plants. Sometimes she took leaves, other times the roots. Some plants she kept on her person, others she kept in sacks tied to her horse. Often, she would take the two women with her into the woods, instructing them on how to find the right plants and the best way to preserve them.

At night, the sibyl allowed a small fire but forbade Bradius his ritual with wine. She asked them to eat nothing but bread and water and made them each a necklace consisting of thin pieces of twine held together by a series of complicated knots. These she made by firelight, mumbling incantations over her work as each knot was finished.

"This wards off the shadows of Utgard," she told Bradius, tying the thick cord around his neck. "It will not prevent their passage because the path is well trodden. But it should help you to sleep."

To Trudi, she gave a thinner necklace with many more knots. In several places, human hair and flowers were woven into its design. She also had attached to it a bone that had been removed from her hair. "This," she said, tying the necklace around Trudi's neck, "honors the three eternal sisters. They are the Fates. Einbet gathers the fibers of our existence, Barbet spins them into the thread of our lives, and Wilbet weaves the pattern of our passage. Together, they shape our past, our present, and our future. Each of them reaches out for you. The pull of their hands creates the whirlwind of your life. This necklace offers homage to all three in hopes that their touch will be kind."

Their path turned south. Behind them lay a series of steep mountains with rounded peaks. A narrow valley snaked its way around them, giving Trudi the dizzying impression that they traveled at a great height above the ground. A lone peak stood before them. Beyond that, a great expanse of land stretched as far as the eye could see. A river cut a path through it from north to south. *The Wormitt,* Trudi thought.

"There is our destination," the sibyl said, pointing to the last mountain. "There stands the tree."

As they descended, Trudi's heart began to pound in her chest. *I'm not ready,* she thought. Sunni's ministrations had been rudimentary. They had only focused on her passage into womanhood and the power that implied. She wasn't ready for this. Dire warnings from Boniface surfaced in her mind, rituals of witches riding animals in the night sky and demons who mated with humans.

When they reached the valley, the sibyl blindfolded Trudi and Bradius.

"Once, the path to the tree was known to all, so that all could come to worship. Today, we must guard the location of the trees. The robe wearers burn them."

Trudi suffered the discomfort of the blindfold, but it only increased her anxiety. The horses meandered up the mountain path, stopping and turning at the sibyl's direction. Trudi lost all sense of direction and time. The pounding of her heart grew more pronounced.

"We have arrived," the sibyl pronounced in a whisper. They dismounted, and Trudi waited while the sibyl's assistants removed her blindfold. She found herself in a broad clearing surrounded by trees. On closer inspection, the trees formed a perfect circle, thirty paces across. Ten paces from the perimeter, a single tree stood tall and straight in the evening light. It was an ash tree, gray, graceful, ancient, and majestic.

Trudi could see how these people believed that it linked the three worlds of existence. It was beautiful. She started to approach the tree, but Bradius grabbed her arm.

"No one is to touch the tree outside a religious rite," he said.

She turned to look at him and found his face a mixture of awe and trepidation. "Are you afraid?" she asked.

He nodded.

"What will she do?"

"For each, the experience is unique."

"We won't be together?"

"I don't know," he said.

The two women had taken their horses and supplies into the woods. When they returned, they brought the makings of a small fire, which they built and lit in a shallow pit before the tree. They next brought several of the sibyl's pouches as well as bread and several jars of what looked like honey or jam. They set these in places on either side of the fire. The day was fading. Already darkness filtered through the light, eroding its sharpness and stealing its clarity.

"You must disrobe," the sibyl said. When Trudi hesitated, Bradius's eyes pleaded with her. She untied her peasant dress and let it fall.

The two women took their clothing into the woods. The sibyl went with them and returned with a small bowl filled with a blackish, tar-like substance. With a reed-like stick, she stirred it, approached Bradius, and began to draw a symbol just above his right breast. It was a vertical line with two slanting lines falling off it to the right.

"This is Ansuz, the rune of Yggdrasil, the ash," she intoned. "All who come before the tree must wear its mark." Above his left breast, she drew a second symbol. It also had a vertical line. At its center, however, two equal lines formed an angle that peaked to the right. "This is Thurisaz," she said, "the rune of the giants. It is a mark of strength and resistance." She drew a third symbol, this time on his abdomen. It was a vertical line with two downward slashing lines. One came from the left, touching the bottom of the vertical line. The other started from the top and slashed downward to the right. "This is Eihwaz, the rune of the bleeding yew—mark of death and regeneration."

When the sibyl turned to her, Trudi recoiled. A sharp look from the sibyl stilled her. Embarrassed, Trudi leaned forward, allowing sibyl to repeat her ritual. Save for the ash, none of her symbols were the same as those the sibyl made for Bradius. The second mark looked like an arrow pointing skyward. The sibyl called it "Teiwaz, the god-rune symbolizing victory through sacrifice." The third rune, placed on her abdomen, had two vertical parallel lines connected at the top by an angle that dropped sharply between them. The sibyl called this rune "Ehwaz, the rune of the horse." She said it was the mark of "an unbreakable bond."

The sibyl continued her work, painting smaller runes on their faces and hands while the soft grayish light of the sky held back the darkness. Little by little, that light too disappeared. By the time the sibyl had finished, the forest trees were an impenetrable darkness. The ephemeral red-and-gold lambency of the firelight danced off their bodies and defined the limits of their world. And at its limit stood the ash. Tall and godlike, it rose before them out of the mysteries of the earth and disappeared high above them into the unknown.

The sibyl asked them to sit facing the fire and the tree. She disrobed and sat down on the other side of the fire. Her two assistants sat behind her near the bread and the jars they had brought out earlier. They too were naked, and although older, sparingly marked with runes. The sibyl's runes looked menacing in the firelight.

"You each have a journey." She took a pouch and emptied its contents into the fire. A powerful scent lifted off the blaze and struck Trudi like a blow. She could barely inhale it. "You also must eat this," the sibyl said. Her two assistants proffered bread with the tar-like substance smeared onto it. The sibyl whispered incantations into the fire. With a reassuring nod from Bradius, Trudi took a bite of the bread. It smelled of mushrooms and tasted like bark. She made a face and turned to Bradius.

Suddenly, she was outside her body—above it—watching herself make a face and turn to Bradius. Panicked, Trudi looked to the sibyl. The woman was staring directly at her, not at her body, but at her. The sibyl smiled, and the world tilted to one side. Trudi was back in her body.

"Look into the fire," said the sibyl. As the fire drew her gaze, it grew larger and larger until Trudi lost herself in its dance of consumption.

It was a crisp fall day. The sky was a sparkling blue with soft, billowy clouds gently hovering above the trees. The leaves of the wood had turned yellow and red with a tinge of gold streaking through them. *They are perfect,* thought Bradius. *Just perfect.*

Unum was beside him. As usual, they spoke little, contenting themselves with each other's presence on such a beautiful day. The landscape rolled by them, almost as if they stood in place, and the path passed quietly beneath their walking feet. Bradius turned his face skyward and felt the warmth surround him. The muscles in his back and neck relaxed, and for the first time in ages, he smiled.

"What did my mother look like?" Unum asked.

A pang touched Bradius's heart. His hand reached out to stroke Unum's hair. It was a familiar subject, but for some reason, Bradius could not remember.

Someone stood in the road just ahead. Bradius tried to turn Unum around, but the path kept rolling by them, drawing them nearer to the man in the path.

It was Carloman. His sword twirled casually in his hands, its blade glinting in the sunlight.

Finding a sword in his own hands, Bradius attacked. Their blades arched toward each other. The two spun, collided, separated, and spun again. Blade caught blade, time and again. Bradius had never fought so well. His attack was a furious combination of feints and kicks that forced Carloman to retreat down the path. Then it was Carloman who attacked, and it was Bradius's turn to fend off blow after blow as he retreated from his nemesis.

"Tell me where she is," Aistulf said, his blade breaking skin.

Confused, Bradius stepped away from his attacker.

"Tell him." Myrna stood naked beside him. "Tell him where to find Trudi."

Bradius shook his head, knowing that if he did, he would die anyway. Aistulf grabbed Myrna by the hair and put his sword at her throat.

Bradius began to tremble. He mustn't tell. He couldn't.

Unum stepped between them. Carloman again swung his blade. Bradius countered. Unum's head fell from his body. Bradius couldn't tell whose blade had done it.

As he tried to put Unum's head back onto his body, Bradius heard the whisper of a blade and saw Myrna's body fall.

"All roads lead here," Carloman said.

Bradius looked up in time to see Carloman's sword pierce his chest.

Trudi was eight. Her father had just come home from campaign, and she wore her bright blue dress and flowers in her hair. She danced with her father, her feet on his feet and her hands lost in his. She was singing, and Charles was laughing. When the song ended, he whisked her up in the air with his hands and twirled her around for all to see.

"And who among you," Charles called to the nobles, "will marry my little girl?"

She was twelve. They were riding. Charles had stayed home from the hunt to be with her. He raced his huge warhorse against her brown mare. He had given her an enormous head start. As he passed her at a dead run, he scooped her off her saddle and plunked her down behind him. He hadn't slowed his horse a step. She hugged his back, immersing herself in the smell of him. He let the horse have its head, and they rode with the wind whipping through her hair.

"Austrasia!" she shouted. Charles laughed and shouted with her.

"Austrasia! Austrasia!"

She was naked. Aistulf had taken off her armor and then her leathers. He had her backed against the wall in her room at the inn. He bent to kiss her, his mouth enveloping hers. She strained against him but felt her body respond nonetheless. She felt the heat churn within her and pressed herself against him.

"It is only about the children," he whispered.

She was naked. She was submerged in a small lake looking up through the water. Ansel was above her, masturbating. His face contorted in anguish as his stroking became more frantic. She tried to cry out, but water filled her mouth. She stretched out her hand to stop it, only to feel the semen strike it as Ansel cried out.

She was naked. She lay back against the boulder, basking in the afternoon sun. Bradius was above her, taking off his clothes. He smiled at her lovingly as his eyes devoured her body. His hands explored her skin, tracing ancient runes over her body.

When she looked down, the runes were made of blood.

Trudi moved her hand to her mouth and wiped away drool. She was weak with exhaustion and covered with the grittiness of dried sweat. She opened her eyes and found Bradius lying next to her on a blanket near the fire. They were both still naked. He was unconscious, his skin deathly pale and splotched.

The sibyl sat opposite them on her own blanket. The fire had been stoked; it blazed brightly before them, providing warmth against the night's chill. Clearly, she had been waiting for them to awaken. She handed Trudi a cup of water to drink.

Instead, Trudi moved to Bradius, propped up his head, and poured a trickle into his mouth. He coughed and spewed a mixture of blood and spittle over her. His eyes flickered. Recognizing her, he allowed her to pour more water into his mouth. This time, he kept it down. Trudi cradled his head in her lap.

"What have you done? He looks like death."

The sibyl nodded. "He has died many times tonight."

"Has he been healed?"

"His trials remain unfinished."

"He won't survive another one," Trudi said.

"His demons besiege him. And you have yet to make a choice."

"What does this have to do with me?"

"You are the center," the sibyl said. "And your choices are of consequence."

"Do you mean that I will decide whether he lives or dies?"

The sibyl nodded. "Your choices will."

"And if I choose wrong?"

"There are no wrong choices."

Bradius struggled to sit up. "Are you all right?" he asked, coughing more blood. She nodded and wiped his face with her hand. He looked haggard and weak.

As before, the fire defined the circle of their existence and cast its flickering light onto the ash. Shadows danced along its trunk, creating the impression of images carved into the wood. *Except those aren't just shadows,* Trudi thought. The tree had changed. She looked curiously to the sibyl.

"The sacred symbols of the ash," the sibyl said. "Only in the dark of night may we remove the tree's exterior. I must restore it before daybreak."

Trudi peered through the darkness. Carved into the core of the ash's trunk stood a large cylindrical pole. Carved into it was the likeness of a woman. Her hands were joined together in front of her abdomen, her palms facing outward. It looked startlingly like the phallus from Trudi's fertility ritual.

"It's a phallus," Trudi said.

"It is the symbol of our oldest gods' joining," the sibyl said. "The woman symbolizes Freyja, the mother, the pole, Freyr. This tree celebrates that which we hold most holy, the creation of life."

"You said our lives were tainted with death," Bradius said.

"So they are," the sibyl said.

"We're not finished yet, are we?" he murmured. It did not sound like a question.

The sibyl shook her head and lifted her hand. The two young women appeared on either side of Trudi and Bradius. They carried a brackish liquid and more bread. This time a whitish substance was spread onto it.

Without hesitation, Bradius took a drink of the liquid and bit into the bread. Reluctantly, Trudi did as well.

"Choose well," the sibyl said, looking into Trudi's eyes.

Trudi took Bradius by the hand, and the world fell away.

Trudi was playing with her son. They were sitting cross-legged on the floor of the inn. The top she had spun veered wildly off course and then circled crazily back to where they sat. The little boy laughed, and Trudi could not help but smile at his innocent joy. He tried to grab the top and accidentally knocked it over. It rolled out of control across the floor. Trudi got to her feet to retrieve it.

"It won't work, you know," a voice said from behind her. It was Aistulf. He strode into the room as if it belonged to him. He was dressed exquisitely in black and gold. "You can't hide from who you are. Your life is full of consequences." Something about the word "consequences" made Trudi flinch. She spun the top again for the boy. "Your son is the direct descendant of Charles Martel. He will very likely be an heir to the throne. You cannot hide him any more than you can hide yourself."

"I don't want him to be part of your world."

"It is not mine. It is just the world."

"He does not need to be king."

"It is not about what he needs." Aistulf sighed. "It is about who he is. As long as he is alive, he will be a contender for the throne. He won't be left alone. He may not be left alive."

"I can hide him. Others have done it." Trudi spun the top again for her son. It flew across the floor, hopping wildly until it found its balance. The boy scurried on chubby legs to follow it, delighting in its alluring movement.

"Maybe you could," said Charles. She was no longer at the inn. She was at home in her room at Quierzy. Her father was squatting down beside her, watching her son chase the top.

"But one day someone will lure him away. He will learn of his birthright. And he will dream of becoming king. Oh, what a dream for a boy to have!" Charles's eyes were far away and gleamed with an inner light. But when they returned to Trudi, they hardened to stone. "And then he will align himself with whoever will have him, and he will fail." Charles shook his head. "Why else do kings marry their children into powerful families? It is to protect their progeny. An alliance is temporary, a birthright forever."

Her son squealed. The top was losing its force and beginning to teeter.

"What of love?" Trudi demanded. "What of happiness?"

"It is time to grow up, Trudi."

"Is there no room for love?" she insisted, her eyes brimming with tears.

"It is just a very poor strategy," Charles said, combing the boy's hair with his fingers. "And what, pray tell, is my grandson's name?" he asked.

"Unum," she said, smiling. "His name is Unum."

Bradius was lost. Worse, he was alone. The woods were dark. It was night. He searched through the underbrush, the plants scratching his hands.

"Unum!" he shouted. "Uuunummmm!"

There was no response. He followed the path for a hundred paces, calling out his son's name. He backtracked and searched in the opposite direction, again to no avail. "Unum!" he screamed, his voice cracking under the strain. He listened, but there was no response. "Unum," he called again, weaker this time. "Unum," he whispered.

He realized that he had been here before. He had seen these landmarks. He knew that tree and the rock next to it. He knew this wood. He began to run. There had been no path, but he remembered the way. Past the birch trees. Past the lake. And the ash. Through the clearing. Beyond the oaks. He found it. It was as he had left it. He could have found it by its smell.

The ground was still soft and broken. Weeds and grass had begun to take hold, but for the most part, the massive grave remained untouched. Gagging from its putrid air, he made for the headstone and fell to his knees. Sinking his hands into the soft black dirt, he began to dig. At first his hands were cautious, brushing away the earth with care. His urgency, however, overwhelmed him, and he tore through the earthen tomb, his hands raking through the decay.

He found his son, his decomposing head next to what was left of his body. Gently, Bradius took off his coat and used it as a shroud to carry the boy. He retreated past the oaks and through the clearing. A dark figure stood in his way. It was Carloman. He was swinging an ax in a lazy figure eight. He looked at Bradius expectantly.

Bradius ignored him. He walked past him to the other side of the clearing and into the woods. He didn't care that Carloman followed. He came to the ash. A fire burned before it. On a blanket nearby, a woman slept. She was naked. He laid his shrouded burden on top of the fire and watched the flames lick the contours of its newfound fuel. Carloman stood beside him in silence, watching the orange flames rise up to consume what was left of his son.

"Now for the tree," Carloman said. He turned to the ash and raised his ax. Bradius found himself on his knees. He couldn't move. He couldn't watch. He wept for the tree, knowing he could not save it.

A hand touched Carloman's shoulder. It was the woman on the blanket. Carloman turned, clearly surprised to find her there. "No," Trudi said to her brother. Looking back over her shoulder at Bradius, she said, "I choose you."

Daylight found its way around the corners of Trudi's eyelids. At first, it was just a brushstroke of red against the blackness behind her dreams. Then the red deepened and yellowed, pushing away the dark. She tried to resist. She clung to the darkness. She felt rested and warm. She wanted no part of the light. But it would not be denied.

She awoke to find Bradius next to her. They were wrapped in a blanket together near the dwindling fire, the length of him entwined in her arms and legs. She checked to make sure he still lived and was relieved by the regular rise and fall of his chest.

No sign of the pagan priestess or her assistants remained. The ash tree had been restored to its original form, its exterior as seamless and as graceful as it had been when Trudi first saw it. Their horses grazed nearby, and their clothes had been returned, folded on a rock by the fire. A thin, morning dew had formed on the outside of the blanket, and Trudi shivered at the chill of the air against her skin. She ducked back under the covers to the warmth of Bradius's body.

They had survived the night. Surprisingly, she felt fine. In fact, she felt refreshed. She tried to remember her visions from the ritual, but she retained only glimpses. Two stood out in her mind. One involved her father and a little boy. The other had to do with Carloman and an ax. That one she remembered.

Bradius groaned and shifted his body toward her. His face burrowed into her shoulder. When his eyes opened, he smiled at her dreamily. She almost laughed out loud when he suddenly realized how close they were. He didn't pull away, however. She felt his body relax in her arms.

"Where is the sibyl?" he asked, peering out from beneath the blanket.

"They've all gone," she said. "I think the rite is over."

His eyes took on a faraway look.

"Are you all right?" she asked, her hand touching his chest. "Was it difficult?"

He nodded.

"Do you think she healed you?"

"I don't know," he said. "I don't think it works that way. I think she finds a way for you to heal yourself." He stretched his arms outside the blanket and yawned. "Are you all right?"

"I feel wonderful." She brushed the hair out of his eyes. A stray thought took her, and she laughed despite his seriousness.

"What?" he asked.

"No, it's nothing," she said, trying hard to restrain her smile.

"You laughed."

"It's just those runes on your face look a whole lot sillier by daylight."

He shifted his weight, rolling her onto her back. "You think yours look any better?" They both laughed. Then he kissed her. She wasn't surprised by it. It was what she had hoped he would do. His lips touched hers lightly and then again, but harder. His tongue darted inside her mouth, and she met it with hers, playfully engaging it. He stopped to gauge her reaction, and she smiled a great wide smile to show him the happiness she felt.

It wasn't the only thing she felt. She wanted him inside her. She tried to spread her legs, but they were pinned by the blankets. He rolled on top of her, hoping that would help, but it only trapped her beneath him.

She laughed. "You're going to have to loosen the blankets," she said.

"Only a little," he replied. "I like being wrapped up with you like this." He struggled with the blanket, shifting their weight, first one way and then another. She arched her pelvis upward to let him pull the cloth free, and he slid into her.

It startled both of them. They laughed and relaxed in each other's arms. She liked the hardness of him filling her. She pivoted to better feel the length of him, and he started to pull back.

"No, no," she said softly. "Stay there a moment longer." Her eyes closed, and she concentrated on the fullness she felt. A smile again took her face, and she opened her eyes. "Now." She giggled.

In time, the blankets loosened, and Bradius straightened his arms to lift his upper body off her. She held his waist, urging him faster and opened her legs wide. When he tired, she rolled him over and sat astride him, rocking her hips forward and back so that she always had him fully inside her. The muscles in her abdomen clenched, and she ground herself down onto him. With each thrust, the tension and heat within her built until it was overwhelming. Deep within her, a dam broke, releasing spasm after spasm until the tension was gone.

Bradius pulled her to him, arched his back, and whispered, "Oh," as if he were surprised. His body convulsed, and then he sank back into the blanket with her on top of him. They lay together for a long time. Neither spoke. At last she sat up, holding him hostage with her legs. She leaned forward and kissed him on the lips.

"She does good work," Trudi said, smiling. He looked confused. "The sibyl!"

Bradius grinned. His brows knit together as he had remembered something. "Did you ever make your choice?" he asked.

She looked into his eyes and said, "Yes."

Trudi and Bradius washed themselves in the Wormitt River, delighting in its cool, fresh water. They splashed around like children and wound up making love in its shallows before they were finished. Back on shore, they donned fresh clothes and decided to head south on the well-traveled path that bordered the river. They made their way leisurely, relaxing in the surprising warmth of the early spring day and taking pleasure in each other's company. Less than half of the morning had passed before they left the road to make love again. Trudi seduced him again after dinner.

As day followed on day, they began to travel less and make love more. They made their way south, stopping as often as they could in nearby villages and towns to enjoy the local wines and to explore each other's bodies. Sometimes it was a look that triggered their passion, at others, just a touch. Bradius would laugh and carry Trudi into the bushes, or she would tackle him behind a tree to pull off his clothes. Trudi was amazed at Bradius's ability to find clever places in which to conceal their lovemaking.

Neither asked where they were heading. Neither wanted to know. In the weeks that followed, the journey became their destination, their lovemaking a way of marking time. Trudi refused him nothing. In fact, he rarely had to ask. She had never been so happy. And he was a changed man.

Although he had insisted on showing her his method for savoring wine, he drank only sparingly. He slept irregularly at first and then well and through the night. Nightmares rarely haunted him, and never during the day. The dark circles under his eyes began to fade. And more often than not, he smiled. Trudi was amazed at how such a simple thing as sleep could change a man's face.

She asked him questions about paganism and was moved by his passion for his beliefs. He told her the ancient stories of the founding of the three worlds and of the gods' discovery of the runes. He showed her how to draw each of them and helped her to memorize their meanings. As they traveled, he pointed out runes made naturally by the branches of trees or by stones alongside the road. Trudi saw them in the handiwork of the villagers they met. She realized suddenly that she had always seen them on intricately carved canes or woven into the fabric of clothes. She just hadn't recognized them for what they were.

Wherever they stopped, they were welcomed. The villagers recognized new love when they saw it and warmed to the couple instantly. Although the people they met were kind, their accents were harsh. In some places, their accents were so guttural that Trudi could barely understand what they said.

Trudi put flowers in her hair and wore her dress instead of her armor. This she did more for convenience than anything else. She wanted little to stand in her way when the desire took them. She had even stopped wearing undergarments.

She sang to Bradius as they traveled and told him stories of her past. When she spoke of her father, Bradius would retell the tale from the perspective of those Charles had conquered. When Bradius boasted of his military exploits, Trudi would describe the fear and suffering he had caused. Together they slowly bridged the gaps between their lives, resolving their shared history through conversation. But it was the lovemaking that bound them together. Again and again, they each lost themselves in the passion of the other and forged a bond that held them both tightly.

When they arrived at the outskirts of Donauwörth, instinct led Trudi to avoid the city. A marketplace at the confluence of the Wormitt and the Danube, Donauwörth was home to travelers from all parts of the continent. Trudi feared discovery. They circled widely to the west around the city and stayed in a small town on the north side of the Danube. They found a small inn and took a modest room.

The innkeeper, a thin, balding man with a curved back and hunched shoulders, was quick to settle them in but slow to excuse himself. He chattered continuously. He commented on the weather, offered suggestions for shopping in the town's small market, and confirmed Trudi's worst fears. Foreign soldiers, the old man explained, were in Donauwörth and offering good money for information on a woman wearing armor. They had been in the city several days. He suggested that this was no cause for alarm since the soldiers never came this far west. When the innkeeper left their room, Bradius took Trudi in his arms. She wept against his chest.

"I chose you," she said when she had composed herself. "We'll go wherever you want. We can go back into the mountains or we can go north. I don't care where it is, just so long as it is away from Aistulf and Carloman and all the rest of them. I just want to be with you."

They were, however, trapped by geography. With the Wormitt to the east and the Danube to the south, they could go no farther as long as Aistulf blocked their way. Without access to the bridge in Donauwörth, their choices were few.

"We'll leave in the morning," Bradius said. "We can head back north to put some distance between us and Aistulf. We'll find a way across the Wormitt somewhere along the way. But tonight we stay here. I like the look of this bed."

Trudi laughed at his obvious leer. She pushed him playfully, and he fell back on the bed. "I'll be right back," she said, turning. She walked to the door, closed it, and turned the key in its lock.

Bradius emerged from the inn whistling. It was an old song his mother had taught him. He no longer remembered the words, something about young lovers and springtime. He was in search of wine and cheese and bread to sustain them on the trip north, but he tarried at the stalls in the marketplace to purchase a bracelet for Trudi.

The vendor directed him to the east end of town where he found a merchant named Tobias, who sold local wines. The two engaged in a spirited conversation about the vintages he possessed and about the best the two had ever tasted. Tobias was from Provence and had traveled the world but had settled near Donauwörth for the love of a woman. He disparaged his cellar as "unworthy," but it was more than adequate for Bradius's needs. Recognizing Bradius as a true lover of wine, Tobias opened several flagons, and they tasted each, commenting on the distinctive flavors and colors. Bradius purchased eight of them and told Tobias he would be back. He strolled back into town with his knapsack on his back and his face tilted toward the sun.

He heard the horsemen before he saw them. He looked for places to hide, but there was not enough time. The horsemen thundered into the town, disrupting those afoot and forcing the merchants to scramble to protect their wares. To hide, Bradius had to content himself with turning away from them and assisting a pottery vendor in shielding his stock.

They were Lombards. They thundered past, ignoring those they inconvenienced, and left the merchants enveloped in the dust of their departure. Curses and obscene gestures followed them out of the marketplace.

Bradius began to sweat. He had no way to warn Trudi. The Lombard knights would reach the inn on horseback long before he could get there on foot. And they would, of course, check the inn. They would find her. He began to panic. He could not lose her, not now. His heart pounded in his ears, and his breath became short. *Do something!* His mind screamed at him. *Do something!* He started to run, his feet following the hoof prints the riders had left. In his heart, he knew it would be too late. They would take her. She would be gone. He would have nothing.

His chest began to pound from the exertion. He slowed his pace to avoid exhaustion and discarded his knapsack to rid himself of its weight. He grew lightheaded, and his legs throbbed. *I mustn't panic,* he thought. He steeled himself into the calm he used in battle and forced himself to breathe. He began to plot strategies for tracking Trudi's captors and executing her rescue. His pace slowed to an even, determined stride that he could sustain all the way back to the inn.

He never noticed his tears.

The soldiers were already at the inn. He was too late.

Their warhorses were tethered outside, and two soldiers stood guard at the door. Bradius had slowed to a walk before reaching the inn to avoid attention. He walked past the building, cursing himself for his carelessness. Of course they would go to the inn. He had to find the innkeeper. He had to have news of Trudi. His heart pounded despite the fact that he was no longer running.

Two streets past the inn, he turned left. Two streets more, he turned again. He walked another three before turning again and heading toward the rear entrance of the inn. Unfortunately, it too was guarded. He waited for over an hour, hoping to see one of the servants. He saw only soldiers.

Frustrated, he returned to the front of the inn and found an inconspicuous place across the street from which to watch. He didn't know what else to do.

Near dusk, he saw the innkeeper leave the inn. The old man looked frantic. Despite his age, he moved quickly, heading east down the main street of the town. As discreetly as he could, Bradius followed, setting a walking pace that was faster than the old man's. It took Bradius four streets to catch him. The innkeeper was muttering to himself and spitting as he walked. When Bradius stopped him, it took the man a moment or two to recognize Bradius. When he did, the old innkeeper flew into a rage.

"You!" he shouted, hitting Bradius ineffectually in the chest with his fist. "They nearly killed me. It's you they've been looking for! And you knew it all along," he said. "I even told you about the soldiers! Why didn't you leave? Have you any idea what you have done?"

"What about Trudi?" Bradius asked. "What about the girl?"

"They found the armor! That's all they needed to know she was here."

"What about the girl?" Bradius was shouting.

"I haven't seen her. She was out when they arrived. They sent word to Donauwörth."

Hope bloomed inside Bradius. "Where is she?"

The innkeeper shook his head. "I don't know." He shook his head again. "I don't know. I thought she was with you."

Bradius was so intent on news of Trudi that he didn't hear the horses until they were almost upon them. When he did look up, Bradius knew that it was too late to run.

There were three of them. And the lead rider was Aistulf. He drew reins before Bradius and the innkeeper. He signaled his men to stop. He placed both his hands on the pommel of his saddle and looked down at Bradius.

"Bradius, isn't it?" he said.

Bradius nodded.

"How unfortunate it is to find you here." Aistulf signaled to his men. They dismounted and took Bradius by the arms. In the meantime, Aistulf turned his attention to the innkeeper.

"And you, sir?"

"An innkeeper, your grace," the little man said, bowing repeatedly.

"The inn at which this man stayed?"

"Yes, your grace."

"I have only one question for you, good sir. Did he and the girl share a bed?"

"Yes, your grace. They did." The man leered up at the prince. "Tight as two squirrels, they were, and as loud."

"More unfortunate, still," Aistulf said. He dismounted and drew his sword.

Bradius struggled against the two men holding him. They shoved him back against a wall. Aistulf lifted his sword so that its point was inches before Bradius's face.

"I thought," Aistulf said, "that I made myself clear, when last we met, that Charles's daughter was no longer your concern. And now I find you here, again in her company. Do you make a habit of sleeping with other men's fiancés?" The sword flicked, and a line of red split Bradius's cheek. "Where is she?" he asked. Bradius said nothing. The sword flicked again. A second red line appeared on the other cheek. "Where is she?" Aistulf insisted.

Bradius said nothing.

"You must realize that I cannot let you live."

"At least let me die with a sword in my hands," Bradius said.

Aistulf frowned again, considered the request, and then took a step backward and bowed mockingly. "Give him your sword," Aistulf said to one of the men holding Bradius. Although surprised, the Lombard soldier did as he was told. Aistulf, Bradius noted, was not a man to give an order twice.

Bradius moved into the street and took his stance. He held the sword before him, the blade right to left across his body. Aistulf strolled casually in front of Bradius and took his position. He didn't bother to raise his blade. Instead, he left its point resting idly on the ground. Aistulf bowed to Bradius, waited for him to nod in return, and attacked.

Bradius had never fought a man so quick with a blade. He fell back immediately and parried. Twice they engaged. Twice Bradius retreated. On the next assault, Aistulf's blade caught Bradius on the shoulder. Aistulf backed up a step to let Bradius recover and then attacked again. Bradius continued to retreat before the onslaught, desperately looking for some advantage. He found none.

Aistulf attacked, paused, and then attacked again. It didn't take long for Bradius to realize that Aistulf was mocking him. The prince was trying to drive home the point that he was by far the better swordsman. Aistulf stalked him relentlessly, skillfully, and never left Bradius an opening.

Once, after their blades caught above Bradius's head, Bradius tried to kick the Lombard in the groin. Aistulf deftly blocked the blow with his thigh. Bradius tried to take advantage of his imbalance by charging Aistulf in an attempt to knock him to the ground. The Lombard casually sidestepped Bradius and sent him reeling with a kick to the side of his knee.

Bradius recovered and, with an effort, resumed his stance. Sweat was streaming down his face and into his eyes. His chest was heaving. Aistulf, by comparison, had yet to break a sweat and was breathing easily. Hopelessness began to creep up Bradius's spine. He couldn't beat Aistulf, even if he were lucky.

Aistulf smiled, as if he had fought a hundred men who had been forced to come to the same conclusion. Anger seethed inside Bradius. As Aistulf parried his next blow, Bradius slammed his forehead into the Lombard's face. Aistulf stepped back stunned. Bradius launched a furious attack and poured his rage into every blow. Now it was Aistulf's turn to retreat. The fury of each blow forced the Lombard prince to stagger. Bradius pursued, seizing every opportunity to attack.

Bradius spun left, kicking at Aistulf's knee. Aistulf spun as well and caught Bradius in the chest. Bradius backed away, his lungs heaving for air, and again took his stance. Aistulf wiped the blood away from his face.

This time, when Bradius attacked, Aistulf caught every blow. It was the same for the next attack. Bradius realized that Aistulf was exhausting his rage intentionally. The prince parried methodically, purposefully. And when Bradius's anger began to fade, he would have little left to fight with except fear.

His arms began to tire. He had trouble returning to his stance and holding his sword high. A crowd had formed around them in the street, and Aistulf began to play to them, smiling after each of Bradius's attacks, deflecting every blow, and strutting like a cock before he attacked. In the end, Bradius could do little more than keep his blade between himself and Aistulf.

A change came over Aistulf's eyes. It wasn't anger or hate. Bradius wasn't sure, but he thought it looked like boredom.

With a flourish, Aistulf spun to his left, forcing Bradius to turn with him, and after three quick blows, sent Bradius's sword flying from his hands. Aistulf lunged forward and pierced Bradius through the chest. Bradius stared down at the blade, almost relieved that the battle was over. He sank to his knees. With another flourish, Aistulf withdrew his sword, spun, and struck again. This time, the blow was aimed at Bradius's head.

The blow missed. Bradius had collapsed to the ground as the blade fell. He lay on his side, blood spreading in a pool beside him. He could no longer move. The pain in his chest was immense. It felt as if the sword was still in him. He looked up at Aistulf. The Lombard stood above him, the point of his blade at his throat.

"You're very good," Bradius said to the prince, blood bubbling from his mouth.

Aistulf smiled and saluted him with his sword.

This is what it is to die, he thought. *How useless my life has been.* He thought of Trudi and was ashamed he could no longer help her. Then, like a vision, a familiar face appeared in the crowd. A man long dead. No. It was just the wine merchant he had visited. But he had the face of a man once loyal to him. Once, long ago. Darkness closed in on Bradius, and he could not tell if the man was real or a ghost. "Take care of her," Bradius said before his eyes rolled back into his head.

"Oh, I will." Aistulf wiped his blade on Bradius's coat. "Throw him in the river," Aistulf said to his men. "And find the girl."

CHAPTER 15

Betrayal and Sacrifice

Sunni would have given anything to see Carloman's face when he awoke to find the gap in the wall repaired. It didn't take him long, however, to renew his barrage. She wondered how much time Heden's gambit would buy. Almost a week had passed, and the pounding had been relentless.

Until that morning. She found the silence threatening. She and Heden climbed the rampart to investigate. Gripho, Bart, and Samson followed.

Four workmen were erecting a structure outside Carloman's shield wall. In full view of the city, they sunk a large cylindrical post deep into the ground. A perpendicular wooden beam was affixed to it, supported by two shorter boards for strength. They attached a pulley from one side of the beam with a thick rope threaded through it. A hangman's loop dangled from one end. They had requested a parley with Carloman. This was his response.

"It's for Petr," Heden said. His voice sounded ancient.

"Bastard!" Sunni seethed. "How can he be so harsh? Petr is just a boy."

"He was old enough to attempt destroying the catapult," Heden said.

"It was little more than a prank," Sunni argued, throwing a glance at Gripho.

"Only because they didn't succeed," Heden said.

"Why wouldn't Carloman parley?" Gripho asked.

"He wants to make a point," Heden said.

"And what point is that?"

"That the time for talking is over."

One of the workmen inserted an arm through the hangman's loop, and two of his coworkers pulled on the other end of the rope. Sunni shuddered as they drew him aloft. She looked to Heden. He stood apart from them, stoic, regal. She was humbled by his strength and devastated by what it must cost him.

Satisfied that the gallows were sound, the workmen lowered their comrade to the ground and signaled to the siege wall. Within moments, horns blared, the gate opened, and Carloman rode out, flanked by two knights. Each carried a banner. One was Carloman's red banner with the lion of St. Mark. The other was the banner of the Knights in Christ, a simple red field with a white cross. Together, they rode to the gallows. The knights took positions on opposite sides of the gallows while Carloman planted his horse directly before it, placing himself between the noose and his audience inside the city. He looked up at them expectantly.

Gripho began to pace, limping as he went. Bart stood at the wall, staring at the scene below. Samson moved downwind of them and began marking his face with a black paste.

A priest dressed in white came through the gate on foot. With him was a dark-haired boy. A full head shorter than the priest, he looked like he was there as an afterthought.

"That's Petr," Heden said, his voice hollow. "I can tell by his walk."

"Oh, Carloman," Sunni whispered. "Don't do this."

As Petr came into view, Sunni could see he had been bathed. His hair was combed, and he wore new clothes. His face was deathly white. His hands were bound in front of him. He had been crying.

When the boy saw Heden on the rampart, he collapsed to the ground.

"Father!" he cried. "Father!"

Carloman never looked at the boy.

"Father!"

The priest lifted Petr by the arm and dragged him to the gallows. Petr struggled against the priest, futilely turning to look back at the rampart. "Please, Father!"

Sunni was aghast. How had it come to this? Her lover stood beside her on the rampart, his hands gripping stone shards, impotent to respond to his son's cries. His face was hard, but his eyes were filled with pain. He twitched every time Petr called for him. Sunni's breath caught in her throat. She choked back a sob.

The priest signaled for one of the workmen to lower the rope. As the stout cord descended from the cross beam, the priest pulled it over the boy's head.

"Father! Father!" Petr screamed.

Heden's face crumpled. His head fell back, and a howl filled with pain and impotent fury erupted from him. "Petr!"

Hearing him, the boy tried to struggle against the priest, but the rope held him. "I'm sorry! I'm sorry!" he wailed pitifully. "I didn't mean it. Father!"

"Oh, my son," Heden whispered.

Samson, his face marked with paint, faced the sun, spread his arms wide, and lifted his staff high in his right hand. *"I call Ansuz, the Ash,"* he incanted, *"the World Tree and Tree of Life."*

"The ash which binds us," Sunni answered softly.

"Father!" Petr shrieked as the priest tightened the noose and stepped back. At his signal, the two workmen pulled as one until the rope found resistance.

Heden stood tall and still on the rampart as tears coursed down his cheeks. Seeing him, Petr stopped his struggle. He too stood up straight, and although he wept, he mirrored his father's dignity. Their eyes locked, and they spoke no more words. With a mighty heave, the workmen hauled Petr off the ground by his neck. The boy's small body twisted.

His legs flailed. He tried to grasp the rope with his bound hands. When he failed at this, he stretched his arms toward his father. The workman tied their end of the rope to the main post. Petr's face turned red and then blue.

"Yggdrasil, you who link all the worlds of creation," Samson said.

"You are the source of human kind," Sunni answered.

Carloman raised his hand, and the two workmen took hold of the rope above where it had been tied and pulled the struggling boy high off the ground.

"Take your divine breath from this boy."

"Take him to Utgart, the land of the dead."

Carloman's hand fell. The workmen let go of the rope and Petr's body fell. The cord snapped taut, breaking the boy's neck. He hung limply at the end of the rope as it swung in small circles above the ground.

"He has known little joy and much sorrow."

"Let his soul find peace and his body renew the earth."

Heden's body jumped involuntarily when Petr's neck snapped. Sunni reached out her hand to sooth him, but instead her touch pierced what was left of his composure. The huge man she had come to rely on for strength wept openly in long racking sobs that shook his body. He hurled wordless howls of rage over the rampart until his body was exhausted. Bending under the weight of his sorrow, Heden fell to one knee, still holding the wall with his two hands. Bart ran to him, and Heden folded his only living son into the hugeness of his arms. He rocked the boy there, shaking his head back and forth, his mouth forming words but without sound.

In a rage, he was up again, his arm on Bart's shoulder, "Carloman," he screamed. "Carloman!"

Carloman sat calmly on his horse, staring up at Heden's grief. For just a moment, Sunni thought she saw a flicker of doubt touch her stepson's face. But Carloman turned away, leading his knights back through the siege-wall gates, their red-and-white banners held high in the air. The priest and the workmen followed.

"Bastard," Sunni whispered and then wept. She wept for the death of Charles's family. She wept for the suffering she had caused Heden. She wept for the sweet boy who swung at the end of the rope below them, knowing he had been too gentle for such a violent fate.

Samson took a small pouch from his coat and poured its contents into the palm of his hand. Holding it aloft, he let a fine dust drift into the wind.

The catapults started anew.

All told, filling the breach had given them ten days. They had used the time well. Wounds were dressed, dead were buried, and defenses reinforced. But Petr's death had taken a horrible toll. A moment after he died, the city's will diminished. The stones slamming against the outer walls had become a death knell.

The catapults had reopened the breach at dusk. Carloman was expected to renew his attack that morning.

Heden was up. Sunni was not. She lay coiled around her pillow, the blankets tucked up under her chin. Heden had just returned from the latrine and was sitting at the end of the bed. Sunni could see only the outline of him. His elbows were on his knees, and his head was in his hands. He had not moved in a long time.

"Can you beat him?" Sunni asked.

The room was still dark, but an early light had begun to seep into the room through the small spaces around the door and windows.

"Can you beat Carloman?"

When he responded, his voice sounded ancient and hollow. "Yes," he said.

"How?"

"The only way to win a siege is by making the price of victory too high."

"He had six thousand men. How many will he sacrifice?"

"It takes four times as many men to take a castle as it does to defend one. Carloman already has lost a third of his men. Every day we survive is a victory. Every day improves our odds. With the losses he has incurred, he is already wondering if this siege has been worthy of its cost. The only thing we don't know is what price is too high for Carloman to pay."

Something in Heden's voice unnerved Sunni. She stretched her hand across the mattress to touch his back. He didn't move. She unwound herself from her pillow and moved languidly to him, encircling him with her arms. She spread her chest across his back and buried her face in the crook of his neck.

"What do you mean?"

"Many more will die today." Heden stared off into the darkness, and an odd silence fell between them. He had spoken little since Petr's execution. Sunni had tried in small ways to comfort him, reassuring Heden more with her touch than her words. But there was no time for her following Petr's death. Her lover had immersed himself in the preparations for the coming battle.

He had spent every day at the wall pushing the men to prepare for the attack. He ran his captains through detailed strategies to cover every contingency. He ordered more reinforcements and stocks brought to the wall. The men moved quickly and assuredly to do his bidding, but they were unnerved by his presence. The luster in Heden's voice was gone. The humor that had buoyed the men through every day of the siege had disappeared. His eyes were hollow.

He was very far away even when he lay next to her in bed. She broke their silence. And when she did, her voice was trembling. "You must promise me something," she said. Heden didn't respond. Sunni started again, hesitated, and then said firmly, "You must promise me something."

"What is it that you want?"

"Promise me that you won't kill Drogo."

For the first time that morning, Heden turned to face her. "Will he be on the field of battle? Will he carry a sword? Will he attack defenders of the city?"

Sunni grabbed his shoulders and looked deep into his eyes, trying to find the gentle man she knew to be somewhere inside the cold warrior before her. "Don't seek him out, Heden. Don't order him killed. Don't become the murderer of children. Carloman is a monster. Don't let him make you one." Her eyes pleaded but brooked no compromise.

"Soldiers die. Drogo is not immune," Heden said.

"Not by your hand. He's not to die at your hand."

"Why do you think he killed Petr?" Heden stood. "What military value did he hold? Carloman murdered my son to make the price of victory too high. Drogo is his only heir. He is worth a thousand men to him. Two thousand! It may be the only price Carloman won't be willing to pay."

"I'm not willing to pay it either."

Heden stared at her with hollow eyes. "I cannot make you such a promise, Sunni. And you have no right to ask it of me. Not after Petr."

"He is my grandson."

"Not by blood."

"Nonetheless, he is mine."

Heden turned from her. "There is a chance that we may prevail, but it is a small one. Many will die."

"What would you have me do?" Sunni asked.

"I came here for you, not for Gripho. Tell your son to abdicate."

"Gripho will never agree to renounce his rights to succession."

Heden sighed and shook his head. "And there is no help coming?"

"The note Odilo sent by carrier pigeon said he was raising armies to fight Carloman in the east. He's not coming."

After a long time, Heden nodded. "Each day we survive, Carloman will have to decide whether another day is worth the price. So must you. It is a game of attrition. Our soldiers and his. I will give you another day. Consider it a betrothal gift."

Sunni tried to smile but could not. Her eyes brimmed with tears. They heard one of the men shout outside the villa.

"You had best help me get ready," he said. "It's well past dawn. I can hear the men taking their positions."

Sunni rose from the bed and opened a cabinet from which she drew fresh bandages to rebind his wounds. She took off Heden's undergarments and unwound the stained bandages that lay beneath. She probed each of his wounds gently, looking for decay, and spread a fresh poultice on each before rebinding them.

"Tightly," he said as she wrapped the wound at his side. She complied, ensuring that nothing she bound would give way during battle. Completing this, she helped him with his chemise, his pantaloons, his chain mail, his belt, and his chest plate.

When he reached for his sword and scabbard, however, something about it alarmed her. Her face grew hot, and her breath grew short. Her heart hammered in her chest. Panic snaked down her spine.

"Wait," she said, stopping him, her hand flat against his chest. He looked at her with hardened eyes. Her gaze held him to her. "Heden," she said, her voice catching. "My love—"

He put his fingers to her lips, but she shook her head, insistent. "I have been so selfish. I am ... so humbled by your love." Tears fell from her eyes, and her voice became a whisper. "To have come to me after so many years, and to have it cost so much—" She shook her head, desperate to gain control over her emotions. "I love you so."

She saw in him a flicker of emotion, but it was no more than that. A shout from a thousand voices came from outside the city, and instinctively Heden moved toward the door. Sunni threw herself at him, hugging him to her chest.

"Come back to me," she said.

Heden hesitated and then left without a word.

Heden looked up at the sky. The sun was high, and the ramparts were flooded with Franks. So was the breach. Heden had made several attempts to retake the wall, only to be frustrated by the Franks' sheer numbers. If he didn't do something soon, the day would be lost. He would need to give his soldiers more time.

His eyes searched for a solution. It would have to be quick. He raced down the scaffolding to the ground where he found Gripho leading what was left of the reserves to reinforce the shield wall in the breach.

"Come with me," Heden said.

Gripho's eyes gleamed back at him.

"We're going to make another sortie with the cavalry," Heden said.

"It won't work," Gripho said. "Didn't you see Carloman bring up his cavalry?"

"There is a way," Heden said. "We'll do it in stages. I'll lead the first sortie to cut off their attack on the breach and to pull down the ladders. Carloman will send his cavalry in to cut off my retreat—"

"You want me to lead a second sortie to cut off his cavalry," Gripho said appreciatively. "It'll be a pincer movement between us."

Heden smiled. "You'll make a good commander someday."

They assembled the cavalry, and Heden split them into two groups. There weren't as many as he had hoped, but it would have to do. At his signal, horns blared, and the gate began to open. Heden led his Thuringians into the field.

Although the cost of the battle had been high—much higher than it should have been—Carloman knew this attack would succeed. The tide of the battle had turned. Once the ramparts had been taken, it was only a matter of time before his soldiers would overwhelm those defending the breach.

The Thuringian had been a noteworthy opponent. He had prepared the city well and had executed a flawless strategy. It was the sheer size of Carloman's force that had won the day. Many would have been unwilling to take such losses. But Carloman knew this day would be remembered long throughout the kingdom. Few would doubt his willingness to win again.

He heard a horn and turned his head to the wall. The gate was opening. It was a cavalry charge. *Heden is not that stupid,* thought Carloman. *He must be desperate.* Carloman turned to Drogo while signaling to the cavalry. "It's time, Drogo."

"Time?"

"I told you the battle would tell us when it's time to join the fight. The time is now. Get your horse."

Father and son descended from the siege wall to mount their warhorses and take their places at the front of the cavalry line. With horns blaring, they entered the field.

Heden went for the ladders first. As long as they stood, there was little chance to stop the attack on the breach. The cavalry chopped its way through to the ladders and then pulled them down with grappling hooks. Cheers rose from the ramparts, where renewed counterattacks began to take shape.

Heden wanted to be far enough away from the wall to tempt Carloman into cutting off their retreat. That meant clearing out the walls first and attacking the main body second. As soon as the ladders were down, he signaled to his men to regroup and turned on Carloman's main force.

They cut a bloody swath across the back of Carloman's attack on the breach. The foot soldiers were no match against his cavalry. With the battle lust in them, Carloman's soldiers could think of little more than reaching the breach. They didn't expect to defend their rear. Heden waded into them, creating havoc at the back of their line.

The cavalry blades fell again and again, forcing Carloman's army to turn and fight. In the ensuing confusion, a counterattack at the breach pushed the Franks back out through the gauntlet and out onto the river of rock.

With one eye on Carloman's advancing cavalry, Heden kept his line of men together and savagely slaughtered dozens of foot soldiers. Heden looked up. Carloman was leading the cavalry. Drogo was with him. It took everything in Heden not to react to the advancing cavalry. *Take the bait,* he willed. *Take the bait!*

Carloman's cavalry thundered toward the gate and swept past it to cut off Heden's retreat. Heden was euphoric. *Now we will see what price is too high!* He waved the signal cloth he and Gripho had agreed upon and turned his cavalry to face Carloman with swords already well stained by Frankish blood.

In the distance, behind Carloman, Heden could see Gripho and his cavalry assembled outside the closed gate. But they did not move. Gripho sat in his saddle with his hand up, holding his men in abeyance. With a sinking heart, Heden knew that there would be no second cavalry sortie.

With two of his most trusted servants, the Compte de Laon made his way through the tunnels underneath the city to his storeroom. They moved away the large boxes that covered the secured doorway and drew back the huge iron latches that protected the door from the inside. Once free, the door swung inward, and the three descended the stairs to the treasure room.

Booty from battles over a century past lay next to buckets filled with solidi and denarii. Gold and silver chalices, plates, knives, and candlesticks lay in chests beside stacks of armor and a row of shields and swords.

The compte and his servants focused on the buckets of gold and silver coins. They moved these down a flight of stairs to a landing with a small door. Made of hard wood and iron and imbedded in stone, it was secured by a lock that held the latch in place. The compte produced a key, freed the latch, and struggled with his two servants to open the door. It swung inward with a high-pitched groan.

A head covered with soot poked through the door from its other side. The compte let out a shout.

"*Thank* you," said the smiling face, turning up to them. "You have no idea how grateful I am that you opened this door." He scrambled through the aperture. The compte's servants helped him up and then pinned him against the wall.

"My good Compte de Laon," the man said, the smile never leaving his face. "My Lord Pippin sends his regards and bids you join him and your daughter for a spot of ale, just outside the city."

"Do you jest?" the compte said.

"Have you any idea how long I've been stuck in that tunnel?" the man asked. "I could use a spot of ale myself."

With a nod to his servants, the compte and his men followed Arnot back through the tunnel, taking as much of the treasure as they could carry.

Heden had split the cavalry by nationality, taking the Thuringians into the field with him and leaving the Neustrians to Gripho. *A fatal error,* thought Gripho, a smile creeping onto his face. He stood in the gate with soldiers loyal to his mother, holding up his arm casually to keep them in place. Horses pranced around him anxiously. The men looked to him, confused.

"Hold," Gripho said, keeping his voice confident. "Not yet."

Heden's strategy had worked. Carloman had taken the bait and swept past the city gate to cut Heden off, leaving himself exposed to a counterattack from the rear. The gates had opened on Heden's signal just as the two had planned, only Gripho had not charged. He fully intended to take the field, but only after Carloman had exhausted his men dispensing with the arrogant Thuringian. Once Heden was dead, Gripho would attack his half brother's exposed rear and push Carloman into a forced retreat. The day would end with the city intact, Carloman forced from the field, and the Franks' army reduced to half strength. Gripho would offer to parley in the morning to negotiate a settlement. The siege would end with his right to succession intact.

"Milord!" Jean-Claude, one of Gripho's captains, pushed into the line next to him. "Milord, the Thuringian is vulnerable! We must enter the field."

"I said, hold," Gripho growled.

"We can save them," Jean-Claude said. "We must attack."

Gripho saw the rest of his men nodding in assent. They knew the moment was at hand. He reached for his knife.

"I give the commands here."

"But, milord, they will be slaughtered."

Gripho's arm slashed in an arc across his body. His knife sank easily into the soft throat of his captain, the only unarmored spot within reach. Gripho enjoyed seeing the surprise on Jean-Claude's face as the man realized his death was so near. He attempted a lunge at Gripho but merely fell off his horse. Jean-Claude lay on the ground face down, drowning in his own blood.

"Anyone else wish to challenge my command?" Gripho asked. The men shifted in their saddles, but none spoke.

Gripho's eyes returned to the battlefield searching for Heden. Gripho found him charging the center of Carloman's line. Clearly, Heden had realized his jeopardy and was attempting to get to Carloman before the strength of his opponent's larger cavalry took its toll. A desperate strategy to be sure, but it could never work. By the time he reached Carloman, Heden would be exhausted. Carloman would best him without effort.

Unless ... a second thought crept into Gripho's mind. It was far more sinister and had perhaps a better chance of success.

Maybe he's going after Drogo.

Heden used battle flags to signal his men for a third time, hoping they recognized his latest order. He pushed his mount forward, accelerating the speed of the charge to catch Carloman's troops before they could effectively form a line.

He waded into the Franks, his Thuringians behind him. They approached in a ragged formation, hoping to engage Carloman's knights in hand-to-hand combat.

Heden used his shield to absorb the first blows, awaiting an opening to drive home the point of his blade. He caught his first opponent just below the armpit. His second fell after Heden severed the man's arm.

Carloman, however, proved to be no fool. He formed the bulk of his cavalry into a line and charged the Thuringian position in formation. As they closed, Heden wheeled his horse and waved his sword frantically.

"Retreat! Retreat!" he shouted. The Thuringians needed no further prompting. They disengaged and charged after Heden. A cheer went up among the Franks as they watched their enemies flee before them.

A nervous thrill surged through Drogo as the cavalry clashed with the Thuringians. He was in the front line, near the Thuringian point of attack. Everything moved so quickly. Shields clashed, swords fell, blood and viscera filled the air. He was appalled and transfixed by the sight. Unsure of what to do, he mirrored the knights to his left, who checked their mounts.

"Hold!" one of them called. "Form a line."

Drogo took his position, pike forward, and waited for the order.

"Charge!"

They closed on the ragged line, and Drogo felt the shock of his pike hitting the shield of an enemy soldier. The force knocked the spear from his hand. He pulled his mount back to draw his sword. In a blur, the Thuringian was on him, and Drogo barely fended off the first blow with his shield. Pain shot up his arm. Looking up into the face of his attacker, Drogo saw the wild eyes of a madman. Fear lanced through him. How could he defeat such fury? The man swung his sword again, and again Drogo blocked it. He tried to thrust his sword, but he was too hesitant, too slow. His enemy brushed it aside and began to rain blow after blow onto Drogo's shield. Drogo cringed behind it, afraid to leave the man an opening.

"Retreat! Retreat!" a voice called, and the man before him turned to flee the field.

Even Drogo knew what it implied. *Victory,* his mind sang. Elation surged through him. Many of the Knights in Christ surged to the kill. Heels sank deep into the flanks of their horses as the battle lust took them. A blood-curdling cry sprang from Drogo's throat, and he spurred forward with the Franks, brandishing his sword in anticipation. *They* would be the killers, not the prey.

Drogo heard his father shout for order but knew it would be hopeless. The Siren's song of slaughter had taken his knights. The first of the

Franks chased down the stragglers, butchering them before they could turn. The rest raced forward in hungry expectation. Several knights passed Drogo on faster horses, and he whipped his mount to gain speed. They closed on the backs of the Thuringians, who rode desperately away from them. *Victory,* thought Drogo. *Victory!*

The Thuringians turned.

Those farthest from the Franks were the first to wheel in the face of the oncoming charge. As each of the Thuringians reached the new line, they too wheeled in turn. Within moments, the Franks faced an organized cavalry line. With their forward ranks so spread, they would have little chance to form one of their own. *It happened so fast,* thought Drogo. *It could only have been planned.* As a maneuver, the tactic was a thing of beauty.

He wished, however, that he wasn't in the forward ranks.

Heden ordered the charge. His Thuringians advanced with a wall of pikes that slammed into the ragged forward Frankish line. His men swept through a third of Carloman's cavalry like a wave, leaving few alive behind them. Only small pockets of Frankish knights in the first line survived, having recognized their peril and formed themselves into squares. The ploy was a defensive one that would only work if the rest of Carloman's cavalry could advance far enough and fast enough to save them.

Drogo was in one of the squares, off on Heden's left flank. They used their pikes to fend off enemy horses and their swords to fight close in. Several of Heden's knights peeled off the line to attack. Heden pushed forward with the main body of his line.

Carloman had regrouped what was left of his cavalry into three stout lines and ordered a charge of his own. The two cavalries converged. Horses slammed into horses, and shields clashed with shields. Pikes skewered horses and knights alike. The Thuringians fought ferociously, but Carloman's greater numbers still worked against them. Heden looked again to the city gate, in desperate hope that Gripho would come. The Neustrians still did not move.

Heden knew that if he didn't do something soon, the battle would be lost. He signaled to the ragged line of knights near him, and together they wheeled away from the main body to find Drogo's square.

As a commander, Carloman watched the battle unfold dispassionately. He noted Gripho's Neustrians at the gate and wondered at their refusal to help the Thuringians. Tactically, it made no sense as it put the bulk of the defender's army at risk. Despite this, Heden had proved resourceful, using a feigned retreat to seduce Carloman's forward line into giving chase. The result had been predictable. Discipline on the battlefield was essential. You lose your discipline, you lose your life.

Carloman also was pleased that most of his cavalry had not lost their self-control. They still blocked Heden's way back to the city and still had the greater numbers. It was only a matter of time before they won the day.

As a father, however, Carloman's heart quailed at the sight of his son being duped into a reckless charge. He had sent Johann after the boy. The blond knight had been smart enough to realize their jeopardy and to corral a number of knights into a defensive square. That would buy some time for the main force to advance. Carloman worried, however, that it wouldn't be enough.

He threw his warhorse into the fray, intent on challenging the Thuringian himself. He chopped his way through to the right flank, taking his second line with him, hoping for an opening that would take him to Heden. He was surprised to see Heden wheel and take a number of men with him. It took little thought to divine where he was heading. Carloman spurred his horse in pursuit.

"To me!" he screamed. "To me!" He didn't wait to see if anyone heard.

Gripho frowned. Heden was good. He took comfort in the fact that Carloman had greater numbers. He didn't see how the Thuringian could win.

"Milord, please!" a call was shouted from back in the ranks.

"Silence!" Gripho commanded.

"They're being slaughtered!"

"Hold your positions!" Gripho shouted.

He heard movement behind him. Someone was trying to break ranks. Gripho turned to intercept, but too late. A lone horseman sprinted toward the battle.

"I said, hold!" Gripho barked.

On his right, a second horseman broke ranks, and then a third. Gripho turned to face the men and drew his sword.

Two knights on his cavalry's left flank bolted for the battle. Those behind them bolted as well. Soon, the whole flank streamed out of the gate toward the Frankish rear. The right flank was next. Then even the soldiers nearest him wheeled left and right to circumvent his horse. The Neustrians had joined the battle. Gripho was left standing in the gate alone.

He had only one course of action left. He spurred his horse and joined the fray.

Although Johann's square was behind the Thuringian cavalry line, Carloman's position on the right flank put him physically closer to Drogo than Heden. His only disadvantage was that he would have to fight his way there, and Heden would not. The surprise of his charge, however, had caught much of the Thuringian cavalry off guard. There still was a chance that he could reach Drogo first.

Carloman knew that his mad dash to save his son was a military blunder. It introduced an element of risk where none was necessary to win the battle. The howling in his heart, however, made it imperative that Carloman charge. He *had* to save his son. He slashed his way through

Heden's left flank, cutting a path to Drogo's position. His eyes never lost sight of the Thuringian's progress toward the square. *It will be close,* he thought, trying to push back his panic.

Then, out of the corner of his eye, he saw Heden draw reins. Something had taken the man's attention. He was looking toward the city. With a short punch of his shield, Carloman stunned the man fighting him and dispatched him with a thrust of his sword. Carloman turned to see what Heden had seen.

The Franks were under attack from the rear. Sweat leapt from Carloman's face as he realized that his charge to save Drogo had effectively split his cavalry in two. A line of knights had followed him around the flank while his main force had turned to face the threat from the rear. Heden could see it. And he was redirecting half his force to the flank—to cut Carloman off from the rest of his own cavalry.

Carloman said a short prayer and spurred his horse forward to Drogo's position. With Heden's force redirected, he met little resistance reaching the boy. The two joined forces. Carloman nodded quickly to Johann. Johann saluted.

"Father!" Drogo said, clearly glad to see him.

"Form a line!" Carloman shouted, searching the battlefield for an advantage.

Carloman smiled at his son reassuringly. "Learn anything?" he asked.

"I won't do that again," the boy replied.

Carloman returned his attention to the Thuringians. Heden had succeeded in breaking the cavalry into two parts and was forming a line to advance on their position.

On this part of the battlefield, Carloman realized, the Franks were outnumbered.

"Stay with Johann!" he called to Drogo and spurred to rally his left flank.

The sounds of battle had always struck Heden as uniquely macabre.

Most people could recognize myriad sounds from their daily lives: water from a brook spilling into a pool, fire crackling through a wet log, a horse's hooves clopping against hard earth. No one had to see these things to know what they were.

Soldiers knew sounds of a whole different kind: arrows puncturing lungs, swords cleaving arms, pikes penetrating horseflesh. These were catalogued alongside the death rattle of a man's lungs, the scream of a soldier being mortally wounded, and the whimper of a man seeing death come for him. Heden knew those sounds all too well. He had heard them throughout his life. He heard them now. The opposing cavalry lines came together with a sickening crunch. The crux of the battle had begun.

The Franks fought well. They were disciplined and methodical. They didn't panic over being isolated on the battlefield. They simply bent to the task of fighting a larger force. Heden wondered how much longer he would have. Gripho's Neustrians had attacked the Franks' rear guard in a ragged formation and hadn't the numbers to succeed. All Heden could hope for was a sustained fight that kept the bulk of the Frankish force occupied while he went for Drogo. The stark truth settled on him like a shroud; there was no other choice. It was either Carloman or the boy. He made for the boy's position.

Heden's cavalry line had disintegrated, and the battle had become a melee. Heden charged the Frankish knight before him and surprised the man by slashing the neck of his horse before they engaged. The steed collapsed, throwing its rider forward and off balance. Heden slammed the man with his shield and knocked him to the ground.

Heden thrust his sword into the face of a second knight who leaned backward to avoid the blade. Heden lifted his wrist to shift the weight of the blade. He sliced upward with it and brought its edge down on the man's exposed thigh. The Frank screamed and pulled forward, just as Heden thrust again, catching him in the stomach. The blade caught there, temporarily leaving Heden exposed.

He warded off a blow from his right by throwing his shield over his right arm to protect his shoulder. A second blow fell, followed by a third. He yanked frantically at his blade until it came free. Then he turned to face his attacker. His horse sensed his newfound liberty and surged into the attack. Heden held his shield high above his head and thrust his sword beneath it, disguising the blow and catching his assailant's armpit before the man could react.

Heden had always excelled in melee, in part because he was a good horseman. He could feel his horse tense for the next attack and knew by the way it shifted where his enemy would be. It was not unusual for Heden to thrust his sword in one direction and extract it to counter a blow from another.

Two Frankish knights assailed him at once. He retreated, backing his warhorse up to gain space, and then spurring it forward and to the left. This had the effect of positioning both of his attackers to his right, one behind the other. The ploy, however, cost him dearly. The closest knight cut Heden's right leg deeply when he passed. Heden punched the Frank with the pommel of his sword and shoved him off his horse. Gritting his teeth to fight through the pain, Heden pressed forward.

Pippin allowed time for a hasty reunion between the compte and his daughter back at the inn. He had hoped that the meeting would lift Bertrada's spirits. She had been cool to Pippin since Carloman had hung the Thuringian boy. She seemed to hold it against him somehow, as if he had been the one holding the rope.

The compte too seemed to blame Pippin for Carloman's siege. He railed for half an hour over the lives lost and the damage done in his city. When Pippin explained his strategy for stopping it, the compte dismissed his plan out of hand.

"That won't stop Carloman. Perhaps you might have convinced him before the siege, but not now. Too many lives have been lost. Your plan, however, might save my city. All Carloman wants is Gripho's head on a pike. If you walk out with him, Carloman might end the siege and leave Laon to bind its wounds. For that, alone, I'd take you inside the wall."

Bertrada saw them off. Pippin watched as his lover kissed her father on both cheeks and then hugged him to her breast.

"Be careful," she scolded the man. "I'm not sure how you got into this mess, but I'd consider it a favor if you got yourself out of it."

Her father smiled at her warmly and winked.

She kissed Pippin on the cheek.

"I'm doing the right thing," he blurted. She ignored him and shifted her attention to Childebrand and Gunther. They too received little in the way of warmth. She offered each her hand and then curtsied. They had just been dismissed.

Once outside, Pippin and his men mounted their horses and rode east toward the farmhouse with the wine cellar and their tunnel into the city. The Compte de Laon moved alongside Pippin, and the two rode in silence for some distance.

"You've got some work to do, young man," he said.

"Oh, I think Sunni will see the wisdom in this," Pippin said.

"I meant Bertrada, you oaf."

Pippin's face reddened. He looked away.

"You'd have to be blind not to see it," the compte continued. "And I know her well enough to know that she won't get over it with time."

"But it's nonsense! I had nothing to do with it." Pippin said it more loudly than he had anticipated.

"So I understand. But your family has a history, a rather violent one. I was there to see a good deal of it myself. My family," he waved toward the walled city of Laon to their east, "benefited from it.

"But to Bertrada, that history is nothing more than a few ancient stories she's heard embellished over the years at fireside. Petr's execution," the compte shook his head sadly, "made all those stories real for her. She is not sure she wants to be part of a family like that."

"Ruling is not always a gentle art," Pippin said, quoting his father.

"Nor does it require murdering children," the compte said. "For some time, my daughter has been enjoying the company of a pleasant, young, and very wealthy nobleman named Pippin. Now she has to confront the reality that he is part of a family legacy. And that legacy has often been violent and cruel, and it dates back generations."

"My family has also brought peace and order," Pippin said. "We have protected the kingdom from invasion after invasion. We have fought back the Vikings, the Goths, the Saxons, and the Saracen. We have made the roads safe for travel and used the king's edict to establish a rule of law. If we did not rule, who would?"

The compte held up his hand. "You don't have to defend your family to me. You have to defend it to her. And because I like you, I'll give you a piece of advice. Don't talk to her about the Vikings and the Goths and the benefits of your family's rule, as important as those things are. Speak to her about what kind of ruler *you* are."

"I'm not sure I know yet."

"Yes you do. Or I wouldn't be taking you back through this tunnel."

Pippin wished he shared the man's confidence.

The day was waning rapidly when they arrived at the farmhouse. They quickly stabled their horses and moved to the wine cellar. The compte led them past the hundreds of wine casks and through the trick door, down the long, narrow tunnel, through the small door, up the staircase to his treasure room.

Childebrand whistled at the size of the compte's treasure trove. Pippin hurried them through the room and up the stairs to the tunnel and then to the villa.

The compte led them through his villa into his personal quarters. They encountered few servants, and Pippin doubted that they had been recognized.

Childebrand whistled again, this time at the villa's sumptuous décor. The compte chuckled in response and thanked him for the compliment. The view from his rooms faced the north, away from the battle, but the compte closed the curtains anyway, fearing someone would discover their presence. Before he left, he made a point of shaking Pippin's hand. "Good luck, son."

In a rush of feeling, Pippin embraced the man, and then the compte was gone.

From her balcony, Sunni watched with alarm as Heden took the field on his second sortie. It wasn't until she saw the ragged Neustrian charge that she understood her lover's strategy. Even then, she recognized it for what it was—desperate.

Heden and Carloman had moved their cavalries across the battlefield like giant chess pieces throughout the afternoon. Carloman played a patient game of strength, Heden, an endless game of feints and traps, always hoping to tempt his opponent into a mistake that might even the odds. Sunni's heart leapt when Carloman split his cavalry to protect Drogo's square. She cheered when Heden moved to take advantage.

Heden fought with passion, his horse moving with grace and purpose while his blade arced and thrust in a flurry of blows. He dispatched knight after knight. Sunni gave a short cry when Heden lost his shield. But he quickly replaced it with his short sword and continued the fight unabated.

His killing spree now had a purpose, Sunni realized. Heden cut a path directly to Drogo. Tears streamed down her face. She understood Heden's need. The battle was desperate and nearly lost. Yet the horror of the past few weeks overwhelmed her. The cost was already too high, far higher than she ever imagined. And she was responsible. Her stubborn refusal to jettison her son's rights had brought her and Heden to this place.

She could see Drogo clearly from her balcony. Johann was with him. The blond knight wheeled his horse furiously to fend off attackers. Sunni understood Heden's point that Drogo was on the battlefield to kill and so could be killed in turn, but in her heart, Drogo was the young boy she had seen in parley, the one with the innocent wave and the embarrassed smile.

Sunni turned her eyes to Heden. Even from her balcony, his fury was evident. His hair and mustache flew around him in a whirlwind as he howled in incoherent rage. His blades seemed part of him, descending and plunging with precision and skill. He cut through knight after knight in successive fury, dodging and pivoting on his warhorse. Soon, there were only two Franks left between Heden and Drogo. Both attacked Heden at once. One of them was Johann.

Across the battlefield, the Neustrian line collapsed, and Sunni grasped at the wall. *I could lose them both,* she thought. Despite the fading daylight, Sunni found her son. He was attempting to organize a retreat to the gate. Several knights had clustered near him. They battled fiercely, working their way to the wall. Her relief, however, was short-lived. His retreat had left Heden and his men alone. The bulk of the Frankish cavalry turned back to the Thuringians. Heden's cavalry was caught between two Frankish lines. There was no way back.

Sunni's knees were trembling. Carloman was again racing to reach Drogo. She watched as the two men closed on his position, leaving a wake of dead in their paths.

With his short sword, Heden deflected a two-handed, overhand blow from the first knight. It glanced off Heden's blade and cut into his shoulder. Heden screamed with rage at the wound and hurled a sweeping blow with his long sword. The blade caught his foe just below the ear. Gore splattered them both. His horse wheeled protectively, turning Heden to face his attacker. It was Johann. Swords rang as Johann pressed his advantage. The horses wheeled again. Johann struck a blow, just above the waist. Heden hunched over in his saddle, his sword pointing out awkwardly before him. Johann charged again. Heden didn't move. Just as Johann's mount reached him, Heden pulled his horse to the side and lunged, impaling the blond knight on his broadsword. It ran Johann through. Heden had to struggle to push Johann off his blade.

Drogo was alone. Heden spurred to close the distance between them. Drogo hesitated. Heden's speed accelerated.

Sunni doubted Carloman would reach Drogo in time. Heden was nearly on the boy, and Carloman was a good fifteen horse-lengths away.

At last, Drogo spurred to face the threat, but his attack lacked momentum.

"No!" Sunni screamed from the wall. "Please, Heden, no."

Drogo swung his blade in a high overhand arc. Surprisingly, Heden did not strike. Instead, he crossed his two swords and caught Drogo's blade between them. With the pommel of his long sword, Heden slammed a backhanded blow to the side of Drogo's head, knocking the boy off his horse. Drogo lay on the ground vulnerable. He looked up at Heden, waiting for the deathblow.

Heden ignored him and turned to wait for Carloman, blood streaming from his shoulder and his side. His hair and mustache were drenched with the gore and sweat of the battle, and his armor was dented and scored. He tried to sit straight, but the wound to his side forced him to hunch over it.

Sunni wept at his nobility.

Carloman closed on him with all the power his warhorse could bring, attempting to use his shield as a battering ram.

With startling speed and grace, Heden moved. His warhorse pranced aside, and Carloman hurtled past. The two turned to face each other again. This time Carloman was more wary. The two horses danced to gain advantage. Their masters exchanged blows and retreated only to close again. Their swords rang together repeatedly into the growing darkness.

Heden grunted with every blow. Even from her distance, Sunni could see that he was favoring his side. One of Carloman's blows fell, and Sunni did not hear the clang of a sword blocking it. Carloman backed his horse away from Heden, waiting.

The Thuringian leaned forward in his saddle. He straightened with significant effort, raised his sword again, and closed on Carloman. Carloman blocked his blow and struck. Again, Sunni heard no clang of sword meeting sword. And again, Carloman backed away.

Heden was now hunched far over his horse, his head close to the steed's neck. Slowly, he pulled himself upright. It took much longer this time to raise his sword. Carloman's horse pranced slightly to the side as its master held the animal in check. Sunni held her breath, wondering what was causing Carloman to wait.

With military precision, Carloman raised his sword aloft, its point skyward, and touched the blade's pommel to his forehead, saluting the Thuringian.

Heden spurred his horse. They closed. Carloman thrust his sword past Heden's short bade and drove it into the Thuringian's chest. The momentum of the two horses's charge sent the blade through Heden's body to the hilt, bringing the two men face-to-face.

Sunni howled into the growing darkness. She shook violently as she watched Carloman catch Heden's slumping body and hold him upright in his saddle. Carloman drew the Thuringian to him in an intimate embrace and whispered into his ear. Sunni's knees gave way as Carloman eased her lover's body to the ground.

CHAPTER 16

Endings

Trudi had collapsed when Bradius fell beneath Aistulf's sword. She didn't care if they found her anymore. She didn't care about anything. She was numb. A man tried to help her up. She shook her head, waving him away.

"I am a friend of Bradius," he whispered. Trudi looked up through her tears, astonished. "I saw you fall. I knew it had to be you. You must leave, lass—now!"

Trudi shook her head. It was too much.

"By the Sisters, woman. Get to your feet! You must leave this place!" He pulled her up by the armpits and walked her toward the nearest side street. When they had turned the corner, he handed her a knapsack. "Take this to the docks and give it to a man named Heinrich. Use the name 'Tobias' and tell him you need a place to hide. I will come and get you after I recover his body."

Trudi turned back to look at the square. Aistulf had wiped his sword on Bradius's shirt. "Go!" Tobias whispered, pushing her down the street. "Find Heinrich."

She stumbled away, trying to contain her grief. It couldn't be. It just couldn't be that Bradius was gone. Yet, in her heart, she knew he was.

And each time the thought surfaced, she stopped and wept for him. She wanted to pray but didn't know the pagan words to say.

Without knowing how, she made it to the river and found the docks. There was a boathouse there run by a disheveled, bearded man in a filthy greatcoat. She asked for Heinrich.

"Who wants him?"

Trudi searched for the name. "Tobias."

"What does that old badger want now?"

"I need your help."

Heinrich looked her up and down. "You look like it, lass. Come inside." He took her into the boathouse and had her sit by the stove. "Here." He gave her a cup of wine. "Not the like stuff Tobias drinks, but it will help."

"He said to give you this." She held out the knapsack.

Heinrich took the pack, looked inside, and made a low whistle. "This is some of his best." He frowned. "You must be in trouble, girl."

Trudi nodded, still numb. "They're coming for me. I need to hide."

Heinrich stood, went to the front of the boathouse, peered outside, and hurried back to the stove. "By the Gods, they're coming. And Tobias with them! You didn't say there were soldiers!!"

"Please," she said.

Heinrich frowned and then pointed to a boat. "Get in. I'll cover you with a blanket. Don't make a sound until I say so."

She heard Heinrich walk away. In a moment, he was back and motioning for her to get out of the boat.

"That old codger is going to get us all killed." He tossed ropes and several anchors into the boat and began to untie it from the dock. "Lass, you need to stand just inside the opening over there by the dock." He pointed to the front of the boathouse and then quickly outlined Tobias's plan.

From her position near the dock, she could not see Tobias, but she could hear him talking with one of the soldiers. She had a full view of Heinrich as he rowed the boat out of the boathouse and up to the dock. Heavy and cumbersome, the craft sat deep in the water.

"Why don't we just throw him in the river?" the soldier said.

"With this current, he'll just wash up on the next dock. We'll need to take him out where it's deep with ropes and anchors to weigh down the body. I hired some help to heave him over the side. Had to pay extra for that. Not everyone will touch the dead."

The soldier grunted. "Just be quick about it."

In a minute, Tobias and Heinrich were laying Bradius in the bottom of the boat. Trudi nearly wept at the blood that covered him.

Heinrich started to climb on board and sat at the stern of the craft, his back toward shore.

"Just a minute." The solider stepped forward to search the blankets in the boat. Trudi withdrew into the shadows. All the man found were anchors and ropes.

"Satisfied?" Tobias asked.

The soldier grunted.

Tobias put out his hand. "My payment, good sir."

"Not till the job is done."

Tobias shook his head and walked past the soldier off the dock.

"Hold on," the soldier said, following.

Heinrich came back to the boathouse and took off his coat. "Here." He held it out for her. "Put the hood up."

"I'm no fool," Tobias said. "Payment in advance."

"One denarius now, and the second when you return."

Trudi donned the coat and peered out of the boathouse. Tobias again made as if he were leaving. The soldier's back was to the dock. Trudi slipped out and climbed into the boat.

"Done," Tobias said. "I'll take the one now."

The soldier fished into his pocket for the denarius. Tobias made a great deal of fuss over biting into the coin and holding it up to the light to ensure it was real silver. Eventually, he nodded and turned to the boat. Trudi turned her back to the shore. Tobias boarded and pushed off the dock. The heavy craft teetered, and the two boaters moved to redistribute their weight. Tobias knelt next to the body, and they paddled out into the river. When the current took them, they struggled against it to move the boat to midstream. The craft complied reluctantly, listing heavily toward one side.

"Is he breathing?" Trudi whispered from her seat at the stern.

"Keep paddling," Tobias said. "And keep your face to the far shore. We don't want that soldier to realize that Heinrich has suddenly become a woman."

"Is he alive?"

"Just keep paddling."

When they reached midstream, Tobias placed the anchors in the blanket and fashioned ropes around it to make it look as if a corpse lay within. Then, with a signal to Trudi, the two threw it overboard. The weight of the stones dragged it under the current. Tobias stood in the bow of the boat and waved back to the soldier far upstream. The man waved back.

"Now let's look like we're trying to get this monster to shore," Tobias said. "The current will take us out of sight. Then we can see if our friend here is still alive."

"Who are you?" Trudi asked. "And why are you helping me?"

"I'm paying a debt to an old friend," Tobias said. "One that's long past due."

Ignoring protests coming from Tobias, Trudi threw herself into the bottom of the boat and placed her face next to her lover's, her ear close to his mouth.

"He still breathes," she said. "He's alive."

Tobias scrambled to the stern of the boat to steer as Trudi ripped open Bradius's chemise to expose the wound. A small cry escaped her lips. The wound gaped high on the left side of his chest, its edges puckering like a mouth trying to close. She searched frantically for something to use as a bandage. Finding nothing, Trudi stripped to her undergarments and ripped her dress into strips. She dipped several into the river and scrubbed away the blood near his wound. She rolled others into a compress that she pushed into the crude orifice. As best she could, she wrapped them into place and then turned him on his side to dress the exit wound on his back.

"He's blue," she said. She laid Heinrich's cloak on the bottom of the boat, rolled Bradius onto it, and then worked it around him until it wrapped his body. "We've got to get him to shore," she said.

Tobias shook his head. "There are soldiers everywhere. We've got to get east."

"He'll die," she said.

Tobias nodded. "He might, but he'll die for certain if we land near here."

Tears sprang to Trudi's eyes. She didn't think he could make it. She leaned close to Bradius's ear. "Stay with me, my love," she pleaded. "Please, stay with me." She lay alongside his body and pulled him into her arms. His body was limp and difficult to move. She pulled his face to her chest, wrapping her arms over his shoulders.

"Please, Bradius," she whispered. "Our life together has just begun. We have so much to do. Stay with me." Turning to Tobias, she demanded, "How much longer?"

He looked out at the shore and shrugged. "The Danube has a fast current, but this boat is heavy. It sits low in the water. We are just now passing Donauwörth. We need to be a good distance east before we could even think of landing."

"As soon as you can," she said and turned back to Bradius.

He still had a bluish cast to his skin. Trudi began to rub his arms, willing life into them. She begged him to hold on and described the life they would lead together. She counted the children they would raise and the flagons of wine they would drink.

He gave no response. Trudi looked again to Tobias. Again, Tobias shook his head. "Not yet."

At long last, she felt the boat heave to one side as Tobias used the oar as a makeshift rudder. The bow turned to starboard, and the heavy craft began its slow journey to shore.

"I'll need your help now, miss," Tobias said, paddling furiously. Trudi moved to the port side and picked up the second paddle. With a final look down at Bradius, she bent to pull the paddle through the water.

Tobias had chosen the far shore, the southern shore, where few trees lined the banks. Most of it was farmland, flat and unrelenting. Trudi understood Tobias's reluctance for landing. They could be seen for miles. Slowly, ever so slowly, they moved toward the shore.

When they reached it, Tobias leapt from the craft into the water with a long rope. One end was tied around his waist, the other attached to the bow. His feet struggled to find footing in the strong current. At last, they found traction, and Tobias hauled against the rope, pulling the bow of the boat around to face him.

He worked his way to shore, pulling the boat in as he went. At the riverbank, Trudi helped by standing in the stern and forcing the bow skyward. Tobias grabbed it and slid the boat onto shore. Together they carried Bradius to a spot under a tree.

Tobias produced a flint, and after rounding up fallen twigs and branches, he soon had a fire to warm their patient. Trudi went in search of a willow tree. She found one, peeled off a healthy piece of its bark, and headed back to camp.

Once there, she used a rock to grind the bark into a black and white powder. She stirred the powder into a cup of water and, propping Bradius's head in her lap, poured it into his mouth. At first it dribbled out the sides, but when she replaced it, he coughed and swallowed. She repeated the process until he had drunk half a cup.

Tobias examined Bradius's wound and sighed. "We'll have to sear the flesh." He drew his knife from the scabbard at his belt, wrapped the handle in spare cloth left from Trudi's dress, and held it near the base of the fire to heat the blade.

Trudi nodded, knowing the shock could kill Bradius. "We have to try." She unwound the sodden bandages, amazed at the amount of blood. She rolled Bradius onto his side so that both wounds were accessible. Again she held his head in her lap. Tobias approached with the knife outstretched and touched the blade to the wound in Bradius's chest. The flesh smoked and blackened. An acrid smell bit at Trudi's nostrils.

Bradius groaned but did not waken. Tobias pushed the blade in deeper. This time Bradius bucked against the probe. Tobias moved to the exit wound. Again Bradius's body heaved against the touch. Again a groan escaped his lips. Tobias continued probing all open parts of the wound. When he had finished, they rewrapped Bradius's bandages and laid him back against the ground.

Trudi stood, walked away from her lover, and vomited. Angry at her weakness, she wiped her mouth and turned back to Tobias. She vomited again. This time, the liquid hurled from her in a great fountain, emptying everything in her stomach.

"I'm sorry," she said, embarrassed.

"I'm surprised you held on so long," Tobias said. "A loved one's flesh is like one's own."

They sat on either side of Bradius as day fell into night.

"Tell me how you know him," Trudi said.

"It was a long time ago. Back then, I carried a different name. I was a lieutenant in the army that Bradius raised to fight Charles Martel, may the darkness take his soul.

"I joined along with all the other young men of my village, Jen, Carl, and Janus. We were all so proud to serve! He was a great man, your Bradius. He had such faith.

"We reveled in his early triumphs and swaggered through villages, proud to be Bradius's men. But in the last battle, our unit was left to face Charles when Bradius split the army to save the sacred tree. Without him, we were no match for such soldiers. Charles's cavalry butchered us. Every one of my friends fell before their swords."

"How did you survive?"

Tobias stared into the fire as if he had not heard her. Trudi waited.

"It happened so fast." Emotion choked his voice. "They were on us, and in a moment everyone was dead. I fell to the ground and pulled Carl's body over me until the fighting passed." Tears welled in Tobias's eyes. "I never lifted my blade in their defense."

Trudi reached across Bradius to touch his hand. He wept at her touch. It took a moment for him to gain his composure.

"I fled the battlefield in the dark of night, crawling over the corpses of my friends. I was too ashamed to go home, so I came east over the mountains and changed my name. A year in Donauwörth, I met a young widow, converted to Christianity, and started a new life as a wine merchant.

"Today I saw Bradius in my shop. I nearly shouted his name just for the joy of hearing it aloud. He didn't recognize me. And as we chatted about wine, it struck me that perhaps he didn't want to. Perhaps he was trying to leave the past behind. I contented myself with deeply discounting the best wine I own.

"When it was returned a while later, I became alarmed. A fellow merchant had found the knapsack by the side of the road and thought it might have been stolen. It could only mean one thing. Bradius was in trouble. I stared at the eight flagons nestled in the knapsack and wrestled with the ghosts of my life. I thought this was perhaps a chance to redeem myself. I closed the shop and went to find him.

"I was too late. I arrived just in time to see that bastard put a sword through him.

"But he saw me." Tobias's voice cracked, and he struggled to hold his tears. "He *knew* me. And he gave me one last command." He looked at Trudi. "He said to take care of you."

"You had a different fate than your friends," she said. "I am glad you are here to help me." When Trudi explained who she was, however, Tobias's face turned a ghostly white.

"What have I gotten myself into?" he said, burying his face in his hands. Trudi smiled and again reached across Bradius to take his hand. They talked for hours. She didn't remember falling asleep but found herself dreaming of sibyls and sex and trees and soldiers.

"Trudi," a soft voice called to her. She awoke. It was Bradius.

"Oh, my love," Trudi whispered as she scrambled to Bradius's side. She lay next to him, folding her body to his as they had every night.

"I never thought I'd see you again." He smiled at her.

"I'm here. You're going to be fine."

Bradius tried to laugh but coughed instead. A bubble of blood escaped his lips.

"I am so sorry," Trudi said, her voice breaking with emotion. "I'm so sorry." Tears fell from her eyes.

"My fault," Bradius said, his voice barely audible.

"No, my love. It was me. I made the choice. I made the choice. She said to choose well, and I didn't. I didn't. I should have known they wouldn't let me leave. If I had chosen Aistulf or Odilo, they would have left you alone. I chose you." Her voice broke. It took her a moment to continue. "I chose love. And look what they've done."

"You chose well," he croaked. "I ... was dead without you." Bradius closed his eyes and coughed. A liquid sound. Blood trickled from his mouth, ran down his cheek, and pooled near his ear.

"Stay with me," Trudi said. "Don't leave me now. We'll go to Regensburg. Odilo will protect us. It's just down the river. We have a boat. We're almost there."

"Shhhh," Bradius said.

"We'll have children." She started to cry. "We'll renounce their claim. We'll live in the mountains."

"I love you," Bradius said.

"We'll grow grapes and make wine." Her face crumpled. "We'll have each other." She held his face in her hands. "Stay with me, my love," she whispered. "Please, stay with me."

But he was gone.

Night had fallen. The battle had ended. Horns had blown, and Carloman's forces had retreated behind their shield wall. The thin curve of the moon cast an eerie light over the battlefield. Sunni stood on her balcony looking out over the devastation left by the defense of the breach. Despite the rout of Heden's cavalry, they had survived another day. The Frankish army had lost close to a thousand men, and yet the city still lived. Gripho was in the courtyard below celebrating with complete ignorance of the loss Heden represented. Sunni had heard rumors of Gripho's betrayal. He had said the sortie was folly and had refused to waste his men.

Heden's body was left on the battlefield where it had fallen. Sunni stared into the darkness. She could no longer see it. A chill wind lifted up off the killing ground and made her shiver. Goose bumps pricked her flesh.

"The night spirits, milady," Samson whispered behind her. "We must leave."

"I see them," Sunni said. "They call to me."

"Do not listen."

"They howl my name."

"Come away."

"They beg for their mothers."

"They steal your soul."

"So many died this day—"

"Milady, please."

"It is me they blame."

"Not all."

"No," she said at last, "not all." They stood silently for a long time. When she spoke again, her voice was barely audible. "I can't hear his voice," she said, her words catching.

"He's not here. He's found his place in Utgard."

"We had so little time."

"He is part of the pattern the Sisters weave."

Sunni spun on Samson in anger. "The *Sisters,*" she sneered, "widowed me twice. The *Sisters* have left me bereft." Her voice fell to a whisper that lost none of its fierceness. "I am alone."

"Yet the pattern does not end here," Samson said.

Sunni grunted and turned back to her vigil.

Gripho came to her rooms before dawn. Sunni refused to see him. He stood outside her door boasting that today's battle would be a victory. *The fool!* She had, at last, seen him for what he was. She had heard how he betrayed Heden on the battlefield and no longer doubted that he was responsible for burning the church. Samson's words echoed in her mind. "Your past will betray you." Gripho was doomed by his own hand. *Oh, Heden!* Her heart wailed. *How I failed you!*

The Compte de Laon also had requested a meeting. She wondered at Samson's nod. "The pattern does not end here," he had said. With a coldness of heart she had never felt before, Sunni rose and checked her reflection in the mirror. Her hair was disheveled. Her eyes were bloodshot. Dust from the battlefield outlined the tracks of the tears she had shed. She made the compte wait. She took her time changing her gown, washing her face, and combing her hair. She would not greet the future powerless.

When Samson opened the door, Sunni sat on her chair as on a throne. She lifted her chin so that her stare would look haughty and cold. She extended her hand regally to the compte as he entered. He accepted it as such, kneeling before her and kissing her ring. Her composure faltered, however, when she saw who accompanied him into her chambers. Pippin, Childebrand, and Gunther stood waiting to be recognized.

Sunni couldn't breathe. It wasn't possible.

"Friend or foe?" Her voice was but a whisper.

"Ah, Sunni. I came as soon as I could." Pippin opened his arms, a sad, loving smile on his face. "I am sorry it took so long." Emotion caught on his last words.

Sunni went to him and folded herself in his embrace. She was surprised at the great sob that escaped her lips. But as the strength of him enveloped her, Sunni allowed herself to weep openly in his arms. Gunther, Childebrand, and the Compte de Laon could do little but look away.

When she had composed herself and listened to Pippin's proposal, she could not help but show her disappointment.

"It won't work," she said.

"It will."

"He's not going to let you walk out of here with Gripho alive."

"But if I give you my oath of protection, he'll have no choice," Pippin countered. "He knows I'll fight to preserve it."

"He's got three thousand soldiers on that field."

"He won't fight me."

"He will, Pippin. He's different."

"He will honor my oath."

"He honors nothing."

Pippin stood and crossed the room, clearly thrown by her intransigence.

"The world has changed," she said. "You must change with it."

"No," Pippin replied, with a vehemence she had never seen in him. "I will not change. If I don't do this, I am complicit in it. Carloman has his reasons for doing this. I don't agree with them, but he believes he is in the right. Three thousand soldiers can't make this right. If I don't do this, there will be no consequence of this betrayal.

"I am the consequence," he said, pounding his chest with his fist. "My oath is the consequence. If he insists on taking Gripho, he breaks my oath. If I stand before him, he either comes to his senses and compromises or faces a lifetime of war with me."

Pippin's eyes had grown cold. Sunni shuddered, knowing that this was why men followed him. She thought of how much of Charles lived in his son.

"We will go with you," she said. "But know that the man you meet in parley is not the brother you have known."

"Who is he then?"

Sunni matched the coldness of Pippin's stare. "A monster," she said.

After Pippin had gone, Sunni sent for Gripho. When he arrived, she handed him a cage with pigeons fluttering inside. A large red ribbon hung from its handle.

"What are these?" he asked.

She gave him a look that suggested the question was stupid.

"I mean, what are they for?"

"They're to signal our allies of Carloman's victory."

"He hasn't won."

"Yes, he has."

"We repulsed the best he had yesterday!" Gripho shouted. "We will do it again today."

"Heden bested them yesterday. *You,*" she said, "sacrificed him out of vengeance. Without Heden, we're finished." Sunni picked up the pigeon cage and walked outside onto her balcony. Gripho followed. "Ask the simplest soldier you can find," Sunni said. "He'll tell you. They all know. You killed our only hope. You've abdicated without even realizing it. Carloman still has three thousand knights. We barely have enough men to stand in the breach. We're done."

"I can do this, Mother. I can. There are enough Neustrians left who are loyal. The Thuringians will follow Bart. If we stop Carloman again today, we can negotiate. We came so close yesterday. Give me one more day."

"No." Sunni opened the cage and reached her hand in to secure one of the birds.

"No!" Gripho shouted, backhanding the cage and sending it to the floor. The violence of the act startled Sunni, but she stared at her son, refusing to be intimidated.

"Will you sacrifice me next?" she asked. "Will you leave me to die as you left Heden? Will you burn me in effigy as you burned the priest? '*Your past will betray you,*'" she quoted to him. "I know now what that means. You did this to yourself. You brought about the end to your own succession. You've lost your place in history. Your power ends here."

"No, Mother, you can't do this. It is my destiny."

Sunni picked up the cage. She opened its door and found another bird. "This is your destiny," she said, letting it go. It hurtled down off the wall and climbed straight up the rampart into the sky. Within moments, it was a speck against the dawn.

"Please," Gripho said. He was desperate.

"You have one chance left," Sunni said as she released another bird.

"Anything," he replied.

"Pippin is offering his oath of protection against Carloman. He believes Carloman will honor it."

"No, he won't."

"I see no other choice." Another bird flew into the morning sky. "We either walk out with Pippin, or Carloman takes us by force. I doubt either of us will survive if we choose Carloman. We have a chance with Pippin."

"I don't need Pippin," Gripho said as he paced up and down the balcony.

Sunni released the last of the birds.

Rain swept over the battlefield. It was not a cleansing rain that washed over the streets and fields. It was a sodden rain. The dead on the battlefield sank into the muck, becoming indistinguishable from the brackish earth.

After such a battle, it was commonplace for opposing commanders to offer a truce to clear the battlefield of the dead. Carloman had no intention of letting that happen. He had lost half his army pressing the breach and would not allow the city's soldiers to repair its wall again. He had to finish the siege today. A delay would drive up the number of men it would take to overcome the breach defenses. And Carloman was already unsure that he had enough to do the job.

He stood inside the shield wall on his makeshift rampart. His men formed into ranks before the gate. Soldiers were always less willing on the second day of a breach attack. Three new men knelt before him so he could thumb the cross on their foreheads. Again the priest came forward to speak as he had spoken the day before. Father Daniel gave his blessing and offered absolution to those who were about to make war.

He again raised his sword high above his head to draw their cheers. Although they came, they were muted and lacked luster. *Their hearts are not in it,* Carloman thought distantly. *Nor is mine.*

His attitude perplexed him. The defeat of Heden was honorably done. It paved the way for him to take the city. Surely, Gripho could not mount a comparable defense. But the memory of Heden turning from Drogo to face him haunted Carloman. Heden could have easily killed Drogo.

Carloman feared the symmetry between life and death. Even the Bible spoke of it. *An eye for an eye, a tooth for a tooth. You reap what you sow.* Heden could have repaid the debt of his son. He could have extracted a heavy toll for taking the city.

But he didn't. There was no honor in killing such a man. If anything, Carloman felt shame.

Looking up, he saw his army standing before him. The priest stared at him quizzically. Carloman realized that they expected him to speak. He had, after all, drawn their attention by raising his sword. Turning away from them to regain his composure, his eyes fell on the battlefield. Thousands of mutilated corpses lay before him on the muddy field. His face flushed in anger. He was furious for being so weak.

"We must not fail," he said, almost to himself. Resolve swept through him with a rush of blood. "We will not fail!" he shouted so that all could hear. "The death of our comrades yesterday has paved the way for our victory today." Several shouts rose from the ranks, but Carloman waved them away.

"Their deaths were given freely to avenge the desecration of our mother Church. Their deaths were given freely to declare sanctuary for the holy men and women who practice our faith. Their deaths were given freely to ensure that this land of ours remains a haven for those of the true faith!

"I accept their deaths in God's name. And I promise you as I promised them, we will not fail!" Murmurs of agreement bubbled from the ranks.

"Yesterday, I killed the commander of the pagan army." Cheers answered him. "I accept his death in God's name." Carloman paused, his doubts returning. "He was an honorable man. And I take no pleasure in killing honorable men." His voice fell. "I took no pleasure in killing his son." The blood of innocents. Carloman could feel the quiet expectation of his men. Ruthlessly, he pushed aside his reservations and thrust his sword into the planking at his feet. "But they were not innocents!"

Shouts of agreement answered him. "They entered the fray as men of free will and took arms against the house of God. I take their life forfeit!" Cheers erupted before him. "I claim their deaths for the Church!" He shook his fist, and the cheers rolled before him into a roar. "Standing before me, they stood against the will of God.

"His will be done." Carloman ripped the sword from the planking and raised it above his head. As the men screamed their battle cries, Carloman pointed his sword and signaled for the gates to open.

Rain was a bad omen. The day would be troublesome. Sunni was already drenched to the skin and miserable. She hated rain.

Pippin began arranging his men into formation. Sunni rode on his right with Gripho beside her. Childebrand flanked him on the left and carried his green banner. In the rain, it looked black. Gunther too carried a flag, the flag of truce. It too was sodden. The rest of Pippin's twenty men rode behind them. *We look so small,* Sunni thought.

Samson also stood with them, though slightly apart from the group, his staff in hand. He had insisted on accompanying her. The lore master had been right to warn her of the night spirits. The ghosts would not let her go. Sunni felt their presence outside the gate and heard them calling to her as if they were still alive. She could not clear her head. She felt trapped between the worlds of the living and dead.

Despite all her misgivings, Sunni nodded to the guards on the wall, and the gate opened before them. Pippin led. They moved out over the tortured battlefield, navigating between the bodies and barricades.

The ghosts of the battlefield besieged her. They swarmed around her, their faces frozen in the grimace of death. They called to her, beseeched her, and Sunni did not shrink from them. She would not cower. Silently, she acknowledged them all, recognizing the debt she owed them. In time, they retreated to a respectful distance and allowed her to focus on the living.

They were midway across the battlefield when a great, roaring shout, the voice of thousands, rose from behind the shield wall. Pippin raised his hand, and his small band halted to await Carloman's army. The shield-wall gate pushed open.

Sunni was unprepared for the charge of Carloman's army. A thousand men surged onto the battlefield, their shields raised high above them. Their voices screamed, and their legs pounded across the earth. Their numbers devoured the battlefield with a fury that shook Sunni to her core. *How do men stand against such force?* She quailed before the sight, every instinct screaming for her to run. Yet Pippin sat on his warhorse unaffected. She clung to his courage like a lifeline. She held herself straight in her saddle, sitting regally next to him despite her certainty that they would be overrun.

Just as the first of Carloman's soldiers reached them, trumpets sounded from the battlements, and Carloman's army confusedly came to a halt before them. The men stared up at their party dumbly until recognition set in. Word passed through the ranks that Pippin rode with Sunni and Gripho.

Everyone waited. All eyes remained on Pippin. He continued to sit comfortably in his saddle, his eyes focused on the gate of the shield wall. No one moved. Silence took the battlefield.

Carloman came. He guided his warhorse through his troops. Men gave way before him, and as he passed, they closed ranks behind him. He pulled within ten paces of their party and halted. Sunni noted that the priest she had seen at Petr's hanging rode with Carloman. His face was grim and red with anger.

"Brother," Carloman said.

"Carloman," Pippin said, his voice familial. "May I present the Lady Sunni, wife of Charles, son of Pippin of Herstal, and our half brother, Gripho?"

Carloman's horse shied slightly, and he corrected it. He nodded to each in turn. "Sunni. Gripho." His body was tense and rigid.

"May we parley?" Pippin said.

Again Carloman nodded. Both parties dismounted and approached each other. They formed a rough circle. Sunni stayed next to Pippin.

"What in hell is this?" Carloman said.

"A parley," Pippin said. "Didn't I just say that?"

"This is no game, Pippin."

"No, Carloman, it is not." Pippin's eyes seemed lit by a fire of their own. "I'm ending this."

"There is only one end to this, and it has nothing to do with you."

"It has everything to do with me."

"Their rights to succession are forfeit," Carloman said. "I am taking them into custody."

"You will not touch them. I have extended my oath of protection. We are going to leave this place now and will negotiate a settlement to this crisis later."

"They are going with me, Pippin."

"Not until I am dead."

Silence held the two brothers as they stared into each other's eyes, each testing the will of the other. Sunni held her breath, knowing neither would give way.

"Look around you, Pippin," Carloman said, breaking the silence. "I have three thousand men here to support my cause. Who supports yours?"

"Who will support yours if you violate my oath? The country is already on the verge of civil war. Would you pit yourself against me too?"

"I will not let you take them, Pippin."

"You have no choice, Carloman."

"This is ridiculous!" The priest in white stormed into the circle, his face wild with anger. He pointed to Sunni and Gripho. "Seize them!" the priest commanded. He pointed at Gripho. "The devil incarnate walks before us, and we parley? We should strike him dead where he stands!"

Gripho shoved the priest down into the mud and drew his sword. The sound of blades being drawn from scabbards echoed across the plain.

Carloman's sword was at Gripho's throat.

"This is a parley, Carloman." Anger seethed through Pippin. "I don't know what this priest's role is here, but everyone will step away." Without looking over his shoulder, Pippin called to Gripho. "Put away your sword."

Gripho withdrew his sword and then spat on the blade at his throat. "A pox take you!" he shouted at Carloman.

Carloman withdrew his blade and slammed the pommel of his sword into the side of Gripho's head. Gripho went down into the mud next to the priest. Carloman's blade returned to Gripho's Adam's apple.

"Carloman!" Pippin shouted.

"No, Pippin," Carloman said. "It ends here."

Betrayal. Samson's voice echoed in Sunni's mind.

With a quickness that startled Sunni, Pippin's weapon leapt into his hand.

They buried Bradius under a tree. They could not find an ash, so Trudi instead chose the willow where she had harvested Bradius's medicine. It was an ancient tree; its limbs drooped down over his grave in a great cascade of yellow and brown. An ash would have been better.

Despite his conversion to Christianity, Tobias had spoken ritual words from a pagan burial ceremony. He could not remember much but did the best he could. At the end, he drew dust from the ground and allowed the wind to carry it away. It was supposed to be Bradius's soul passing into the next world, but it was Trudi's that wafted into the wind.

She didn't know how she could go on. She was not sure it mattered. Bradius's loss took away her will to eat, to breathe, to wake, to bathe. Sleep was the only thing she craved. Tobias was worried. Trudi could tell by the way he fussed over her. She tried to reassure him that she would be fine but could not find the strength to say the words. She was exhausted. She lay curled up in the bow of the boat as they made their way downstream toward Regensburg, Tobias sat in the stern, steering with his paddle.

She knew her appearance was hideous. Bradius's blood was crusted on her underclothes and clumped in her hair. They hadn't had time to wash. More importantly, she no longer cared.

It was the crying that unnerved Tobias. In all truth, it worried her as well. She could not stop. Tears leaked from her eyes in a never-ending stream that she could not control. At first she had tried to wipe them away, but had given up when they would not stop. She was sure that they drained something from her, something vital, something that kept her alive. She was so tired. The incessant motion of the boat made her head feel like it was splitting apart. Worse, it nauseated her. She had already vomited several times into the water.

Sensing her discomfort, Tobias had turned the boat to shore. He leapt into the shallows and fought the river's current to beach the craft. He tied it to a small tree. Trudi didn't move. Tobias returned to lift her, mumbling something about getting her "cleaned up." He struggled against the current. When he found his footing, he lowered her into the water and attempted to wash the blood off her. He apologized for needing to touch her body. Trudi made no effort to help.

Tobias lowered her head into the water and released one hand in an attempt at washing her hair. The shift in his grasp made him lose his hold on her. He shouted as her body moved downriver with the current. Tobias stepped to retrieve her and stumbled. While he tried to regain his footing, Trudi's head slipped below the water. His hands scrambled after her. They failed to catch hold.

She welcomed the silence. Air bubbled from her nose and mouth. She let it go. It was then that she discovered there was a choice to make. She could breathe in the cool water and slip from this world, or she could pull herself out of the shallows. The last of the bubbles left her. They floated upward, entrancing her as they wobbled toward the light.

She stood. The waters of the Danube swirled around her waist as her feet found traction.

Shocked into silence, Tobias stood before her in the shallows, dripping wet. Trudi pulled her wet hair over her shoulder and twisted the water from it.

Tobias smiled. "If I had known that drowning you would bring you back to your senses," he said, "I would have done it yesterday."

"I'm sorry, Tobias," she said. "I'll be all right. I wasn't sure I wanted to live."

"Not to worry, girl. You're not the first I've known to be with child."

"What?"

"My wife cried for a month. She—"

"I'm not with child!"

"Well, I'm no midwife, but all that crying and puking usually means a baby's coming."

Trudi couldn't speak. She stood in the swift current, her hands exploring her belly. She focused her senses and tried to feel evidence of life inside her womb. She looked at Tobias questioningly, and he nodded with some assurance.

All she felt was nausea.

Every sword on the battlefield was suddenly in hand. Pippin's blade was pointed at Carloman. Carloman's pointed at Gripho, and a Knight in Christ had his blade at Pippin's throat. Gunther and Childebrand formed their retinue into a circle around the parley facing out while Carloman's army surrounded the circle facing in.

"I gave them my oath," Pippin said to Carloman through clenched teeth.

"I gave my oath to God," Carloman said.

"You have no right to do this."

"It is God's will."

They stood frozen in place, their swords poised in an extended chain of death. The rain fell. No one dared breathe. Of those on the battlefield, Sunni alone could see into the eyes of both Pippin and Carloman. And what she saw there appalled her.

Death's shadow touched them both. Neither would back down. She watched as Carloman's head turned slowly back to Gripho, his eyes certain and cold. She saw the muscles in his back tense and his sword arm roll slightly to the right. His face stretched and grimaced in anger.

Pippin's face mirrored his brother's. His sword arm rolled as he prepared to thrust. A low growl escaped Gunther's throat. *We all will die,* Sunni realized. The shadow touched them all.

Sacrifice, Samson's voice cried inside her head. *Sacrifice!*

"Stop!" Sunni commanded, pushing herself between them. "Stop!"

Everyone froze. Sunni fought to clear her head.

"Sunni?" Pippin called to her. "Sunni!"

"I abdicate," she said. "We abdicate."

"No!" Pippin shouted.

"I release you, Pippin, son of Charles, from your oath. I freely abdicate my role as regent and abdicate Gripho's role as mayor."

No one moved.

"Put down your swords," she said.

Still, no one moved.

"Pippin," she said, "it is the only choice worth making. Someone has to sacrifice or death will reign today. It is a price too high."

Pippin's eyes were unfocused; his sword still pointed at Carloman's throat. "He violated my oath." His voice was unrelenting.

"Not if I abdicate. Put down your sword." The shadow still touched him.

"Pippin." She had to reach him. His arm tensed. "Pippin!" He looked ready to die.

"I guarantee their safety," Carloman said. "No harm will come to them."

"Pippin!" Sunni's voice was urgent. "This is the only way." She saw his eyes squint.

"Swear it, Carloman!" Pippin said. "Swear it by God."

Carloman hesitated.

"Swear it!"

With a sigh, Carloman said, "I swear by God that no harm will come to them. I guarantee their safety before His eyes."

"Gripho?" Pippin called out to his half brother. The boy hesitated. He still lay on the ground, looking up at the blade held to his throat. Then he looked to his mother. Sunni nodded.

"I abdicate," he said.

Pippin yelled so that all could hear. "If either of them dies suddenly in the night, Carloman, I will come for you." To the priest, Pippin whispered, "And for you, charlatan, I will come for you too."

He withdrew his sword. Sunni nearly wept with relief.

At a nod from Carloman, two of the Knights in Christ stepped forward to escort Sunni and Gripho to their horses. They led them wordlessly to Carloman's retinue. Carloman regained his horse and turned to face his brother. Pippin had not moved.

"You should not have meddled," Carloman said. "You never understood what was at stake."

Pippin looked away. It broke Sunni's heart. *He's been shamed,* she thought. *I have brought him to this.* But when Pippin's eyes rose to meet his brother's, they were defiant. "I understand, brother. More than you know. You think this is about religion. You think this is about God and faith. It is not." His voice rose with anger. "It's about the power. Despite all your upbringing, despite all your training, despite all your armies, you aren't prepared to hold it. You have given it away to everyone else. You've agreed to raise a Merovingian as king. You make war at the Church's bidding. You raise arms against your own family." Pippin shook his head. "You abdicate without knowing it."

"Huh-yah," Sunni whispered.

Carloman stared at Pippin, unmoved.

"You will never see me again without an army at my back," Pippin said.

Carloman was almost to the shield-wall gate with Sunni and Gripho before his army realized that they had won. A single shout penetrated the silence, was picked up by others, and three thousand voices cheered wildly in victory. Carloman's soldiers danced in the mud, embracing each other in celebration.

The sound swept over Sunni, bringing with it the full weight of her decision. Her face reddened, and her eyes misted, but she rode with her back straight and her head held high. Gripho rode beside her, his head down. He was already cursing her.

Trudi had no clothes. All she had left were undergarments, and they were covered with blood. She couldn't travel like that, nor could she show up in Regensburg unclothed. They made a small camp. Tobias built another fire. Then Trudi dispatched him to a village to buy supplies and a dress.

She took some solace in the fact that they were less than half a day's boat ride from Regensburg. She didn't think, however, that she could get back into the boat. The thought of being afloat brought waves of nausea to her. They would have to walk.

Tobias's departure gave her some much-needed privacy in which to bathe. She needed a more thorough cleansing than Tobias's cursory scrubbing in the river. The bath, by itself, seemed to reinvigorate her. She used sand to wash her skin and her undergarments. What was left of these, she pounded on a rock. She found a secluded spot in the trees in which to hang her things.

She lay down to bask in the heat of the afternoon sun. As she relaxed, she began to consider the possibility that she was with child. She found the idea warmed her as much as the sun. It was as if Bradius had left behind a gift for her.

If Bradius was the father. Trudi counted the weeks. It had been more than three months since the boar hunt. It wasn't likely that the child was Odilo's. She frowned. She didn't need Sunni to map out the politics. *It will have to be his now,* she thought.

"Trudi!" Tobias's voice called from the camp. Trudi laughed under her breath. He was making quite a commotion to allow her time to dress.

"I'll be right there, Tobias!" Trudi scampered into her undergarments, thankful that they had, for the most part, dried in the sun. She rushed back into camp, drawing her fingers through her hair to try to untangle it. "I can't wait to see what you got—"

Tobias lay on the ground inert. Trudi stared at him dumbly, trying to figure out what he was doing. She looked up and around him.

Ansel. He stood ten paces from her to the right of Tobias, his sword in hand. A ragged scar angled across his face where his left eye had been. The skin there was lumpy and puckered loosely where it covered the socket. It was his right eye, however, that frightened her. It had a crazed look, veering wildly over her body. He reeked of malevolence.

"I knew you would come," he said, smiling. "I just had to wait. The only question was on which side of the river."

Trudi's eyes went back to Tobias. He didn't move. Ansel's eyes followed hers.

"I wouldn't make that mistake twice." He smiled. "It's just you and me now."

"I can't go with you," Trudi said. "Please, Ansel. I'm almost there." Trudi began to circle to her right around the camp.

"I made a sacred vow to bring you back," Ansel said.

"Did your sacred vow include feeling my breasts?" Trudi spat. He reddened. "Did it include touching yourself?" His eye grew frantic.

"Silence, witch!" he shouted.

Trudi ran for the boat. Ansel crossed the camp to intercept her. He was slow but was able to land a glancing blow to her shoulder with his left arm. It knocked her into the air. She had forgotten how strong he was.

He moved between her and the boat, cutting off her escape. Trudi circled to her left to keep him off guard. He moved to his right. Again he lunged for her. She spun left and kicked him in the side of the head. He went down. She raced for the boat. She reached it but could not untie it before Ansel was on her. She had to run again.

She sprinted alongside the river. She saw a horse. Ansel's. She dashed, searched his saddle, and found the scabbard for his short sword. She pulled the blade from its sheath and turned back to Ansel, the horse between them. She would not run again.

Ansel slapped the horse to send it away and stopped when he saw the blade. Trudi twirled the short sword, testing its heft and balance. She circled to her right, this time toward his blind eye. This forced Ansel to shift his body to the left and his sword arm forward. Trudi feinted left, then right, looking for an opening.

Ansel stalked her, trying to narrow her room to maneuver. She left him a false opening. He saw it and refused to attack. He waited for her, clearly knowing she could only win if she led him into making a mistake. She had only one choice. She attacked. Her blade arced to his right, again forcing him to turn. She spun left, behind him, attacking down on the backs of his legs. Her blade caught the back of his thigh, slicing through the meat of it. But she didn't feel bone. He turned to face her. He favored the leg greatly but was still standing.

She attacked again. This time he was ready. Her blade met his. She spun. Their blades met again. She reversed. Again blade struck blade. Ansel attempted an overhand blow. She raised her blade in time to stop it, but its force was too strong. She collapsed into him. She pushed off only to find him staring stupidly at her nakedness.

She feinted, spun right, kicked at his cut leg, and swung at his head. He ducked. The force of her failed blow turned her so that her back was to him. Something hard hit her in the back of the head.

He was above her. She tried to move her legs, but they were pinned beneath his. He ripped from her what was left of undergarments and then fumbled with his pantaloons. She beat on him with her fists, punching him in the chest. He pinned her arms above her head and held them in one of his massive hands. She could smell the stench of his breath and the sweat pouring off him. His right hand returned to the cord that held up his pantaloons. He pulled at it until it gave way. His erection loomed above her, large and serpentine. He stroked it with his free hand, watching her.

"No, Ansel!" She squirmed beneath him. "You can't do this." He reached down between her legs. A grunt escaped his lips. He looked at her oddly and then grunted again. This time more forcefully. His face looked confused as if he wasn't sure what to do next. His eye looked down at her breast. He grunted again.

He pushed off her, rising to his knees, and turned. Tobias was behind him, stabbing him with a knife. Ansel caught the hand that held it. Tobias was ashen and afraid. Ansel stood, still holding the merchant by the arm. His right hand closed on Tobias's throat, and Ansel lifted him off the ground. Ansel began to squeeze.

Trudi scrambled to her feet, looking for anything that might do harm. She grabbed a fallen branch and swung it hard against the thigh that she wounded. The branch broke against Ansel's leg on impact. He collapsed to one knee. She saw the short blade just paces from her. Seizing it in both hands, she wheeled back to Ansel. He still held Tobias by the neck, his arm extended. She stabbed upward into Ansel's armpit.

Blood gushed from the wound, flowing down her blade. Ansel dropped Tobias and struggled to turn toward her. Blood cascaded from his armpit, covering his vast nakedness. He looked surprised to find her upright.

"Whore," he said, his lone eye rolling back into his head.

Trudi kicked him in the chest, and Ansel fell backward. She stood above him, screaming in incoherent rage. Ansel's erection still lifted above him grotesquely. Trudi hacked down with her right hand, and her blade sliced off his manhood at its base. She reversed her grip and drove its point down into the middle of Ansel's chest.

The blade bucked on his backbone. Trudi stepped over Ansel's chest, her legs on either side of him, and threw her weight behind the sword until she forced it through him and into the ground. Ansel gasped at the thrust and grabbed her legs, his huge hands circling her thighs. She leaned on the blade until he died. Letting go of her sword, she stepped out of his hands and away from the blade. Her weapon stood by itself, rising out of Ansel's corpse.

Tobias lay facedown on the ground where Ansel had dropped him. He wasn't moving, and blood covered his scalp. Trudi's lungs heaved from exertion, and she bent to put her hands on her knees. Looking down, she was startled by her nakedness and the blood that covered her.

"God help me," she said and knelt to see about Tobias.

By the time Carloman's army reached Soissons, news of his victory had preceded him. Crowds formed alongside the road, cheering as his army passed. Churches held special masses to celebrate his triumph, and the city officials gave long speeches to honor his name. By the time Carloman reached Paris, his march had become a parade.

Virgins dressed in white twirled long red-and-white streamers in the air. Priests followed behind them carrying crucifixes on long poles. They led hordes of parishioners carrying makeshift banners sporting the cross and Carloman's lion of St. Mark. Crowds lined the road on both sides and cheered each passing contingent. At the sight of Carloman, they erupted into shouts of acclaim. Children scurried to march alongside the infantrymen. Local pipers and drummers joined in with the military musicians and took up their marching songs. Mothers lifted their babies to see the conquering hero.

By the time they reached St. Denis, the parade had become a carnival. Boniface allowed himself a broad smile. He stood before the Church with Bishops Wido of St. Wandrille and Aidolf of Auxerre as Carloman's army approached.

"You're right, Boniface," Aidolf said. "We should leave the matter of Theudoald's death to you. After this," he waved at the festivity unfolding before them, "any further protest would fall on deaf ears."

"He will always be a champion of the church," Boniface said. "His faith is unquestioning."

"Yes, but what about the brother?" Wido said.

"He stood with the pagan," Aidolf said. "What will we do about him?"

"For the moment, nothing," Boniface said, frowning. "War erupts around us in every part of the kingdom. Aquitaine has seceded. Bavaria is in revolt. The Saxons are taking advantage in the east, and the Alemannians are burning churches. My sources tell me that Pippin is raising an army to fight Hunoald and Waifar. As long as he is putting down rebellions, Pippin serves our purpose."

"Does he?" Aidolf asked.

"Does he support raising the Merovingian?" Wido asked.

Boniface shook his head.

"Is he still allied with Carloman?"

Boniface shrugged.

"Will he side with the pagans?"

"No. No. He is Christian," Boniface said, a little too quickly. He knew that Wido and Aidolf held their suspicions. He looked away into the distance. He would not confirm them.

"I fear, my good bishop," Aidolf said, patting Boniface's shoulder, "that we have yet much to do."

"What about the sister?" Wido asked. "The pope is concerned about the Lombards."

"She is missing," Boniface said. "I fear she is dead."

All three bishops crossed themselves.

"I was surprised," Aidolf said, "that Carloman left that witch of a stepmother and her son alive. As long as they breathe, they are a threat to him."

"That surprised me too," Wido said.

"They abdicated," Boniface said. "It would have been murder."

"Yes," Aidolf said. "You are quite right, of course ... forgive me."

"Yes, yes, of course," Wido said. "What was I thinking?"

A long silence ensued.

"And where is your godson keeping them?" Aidolf asked.

"Sunnichild was taken to the nunnery at Chelles," Boniface said with some satisfaction. "She has shaved her head and taken holy vows. The boy is being held at Neufchateau in the Ardennes under house arrest. They will cause no more trouble."

"To be sure," Aidolf said. The two bishops exchanged glances. "No trouble at all."

Sunni dismissed the novice with a kiss to her cheek. The girl curtsied and then scurried from the garden, leaving her alone with Samson, who toiled quietly by a tree near the wall that kept the nuns from the world outside. She approached him, touching lightly the herbs that grew under his care. Instinctively, she bent to pick a leaf from a rare herb at the edge of the row and tucked it into the pouch at the front of her habit.

Samson looked up as she approached and smiled.

"Beautiful girl," Samson said.

"Yes, she is. And generous to an old woman tired of the life outside."

"Not so old, not so tired," Samson said.

"It is a sin for her to be locked up in here."

"You must pray for her." Samson smiled.

"No you don't, my ancient one," Sunni chided him, smiling. "Don't mock my choices. I have taken the vows of my own free will. My life is now inside these walls."

Samson nodded. "Your thread is still strong."

"Stop. You know I have forsaken the lore," she said. "I've lost so much. There is nothing left out there that matters. Here, I am comfortable. I want for little. And there is little here I can lose. I will be content here for the rest of my days."

"The Sisters weave the pattern," Samson said.

"I no longer care what they say," Sunni said. "Besides, in here, you would have a difficult time holding a rite of foretelling." She kissed him on the forehead and made her way back across the garden to the convent halls.

Samson waited until she had gone and then ambled toward the ash tree in the corner of the garden. He uncovered a small square stone that had been placed among its roots. From his pocket, he produced a small clump of weeds that had been moistened and hardened into a ball. From this, he cut a plug and placed it inside his cheek. With his knife, he cut into the palm of his left hand and let a trickle of his blood fall onto the stone. He closed his eyes, and his body began to weave in circles.

It was late in the day. The sun descended gracefully over the blue water west of Regensburg. A horn sounded inside the city gates, signaling a changing of the guard. New soldiers stepped into place on the wall, saluting smartly in the twilight.

It was a stout wall. Built by the Romans in the first century after Christ, it surrounded the city and was protected by four large towers, one at each of its corners. The Romans had built the fort to protect their army of the Germanic territories. For four centuries, it had served its purpose well. Recognizing that a landed aristocracy could manage their assets better, the Romans eventually abandoned the massive fort. They turned the administration of their territories over to a land-rich aristocracy that had, over time, evolved in the territories. The Agilolfings moved into the fort and made it their family's center of power. From there they ruled Bavaria.

Entrances, each with two arches, faced the four winds. The main archway faced north less than one hundred paces from the banks of the Danube. Guards on the western wall saw the lone soldier first. They shouted down for instructions. It was near dark, and entrance to the city was forbidden at night. The soldier would not make it in time. He traveled on foot, leading a horse, laden down with a large burden.

As the soldier drew closer, the guards' ability to see dimmed with the fading daylight. It was not until he had stepped into the light of the gate's torches that they saw that the soldier was, in fact, a young woman. She wore men's clothes that were clearly too large for her and sported a long sword across her back and a short blade at her side. Her face and clothes were covered with blood and dirt. A body lay across her warhorse, tied clumsily to the saddle. It was not clear that the man was dead or alive. Exhaustion haunted the woman's face. The guards barred her way.

"The gates are closed," one said. "You can enter in the morning."

"I am here to see the duc."

The guard hesitated. "State your name and business." The question seemed to tap a resource deep inside the girl. Her back straightened. Her head lifted. Her eyes cleared and took on a diamond-like sparkle that had not been present only moments before.

"I am Hiltrude," she said in a clear voice that carried in the night air, "daughter of Charles the Hammer, son of Pippin of Herstal. I'm here to marry Duc Odilo of Bavaria."

One of the guards laughed at the absurdity of her claim until he saw the look of death cooling her eyes. He ran for instructions.

Author's Note

Although this story is drawn from history and is set in a very real time and place with many real characters and real events, it is fiction ... pure and simple. Please don't take offense if I have treated a beloved personage harshly or seek to "set the record straight" if I've made a character come to life in a way that you find inaccurate or offensive. I make no claims to know the personalities of those who lived over twelve hundred years ago.

History for this period is sketchy at best. Most of what is recorded was written long after the fact and usually by those who prevailed in the conflicts of the day. As a result, their biased perspectives defined what was "true."[1] Most historians readily recognize this fundamental flaw and work hard to piece together the record from what limited sources exist into a common thread of what happened and what did not. And even then, they don't always agree.

For those who are interested in knowing which pieces of the story come from that common thread of facts versus my fiction, I offer the following:

---

1 Paul Fouracre, *The Age of Charles Martel* (Harlow, Essex: Pearson Education Limited, 2000), 6: "Modern scholarship has picked away at this picture of unqualified Carolingian success by taking on board the fact that the sources reveal only one point of view, and that late-eighth century and early ninth century writers were, in the main, working under the patronage of the Carolingian family itself."

General Plot Outline

For much of Frankish history, the power behind the Merovingian kings was ensconced in the office of the "Mayor of the Palace." Mayors were men who commanded the military and ran the government over one or more of three primary states in the Frankish Kingdom (Neustria, Austrasia, and Burgundy), much akin to the way the Shogun in Japanese history ruled in the name of a "divine" emperor. Other states within Francia operated somewhat more independently as "duchies." These included Alemannia, Bavaria, Thuringia, Hesse, and Aquitaine, all related through agreements and fealty to the offices of mayor, although some were allies to a greater or lesser degree. Often passed from father to son, the office of the mayor created powerful families that ruled large territories over many generations. By the beginning of the eighth century, the power of the mayors had coalesced into two regions, Austrasia and Neustria, and increased so substantially that the Merovingian kings of this time are often referred to as "puppet" or "shadow" kings.[2]

Much of this consolidation of power was due to the military and diplomatic machinations of Pippin II of Herstal. After seizing power and the title of mayor through force of arms in Austrasia in 675, Pippin and his family spent much of the next twelve years battling for control over neighboring Neustria. Following a rash of assassinations and a decisive battle at Tetry in 687, Pippin II succeeded and ultimately took the title of mayor in Neustria as well. By the time of his death in 714, Pippin's influence dwarfed the power of dukes in the other states of the Frankish territories.

Pippin and his wife, Plectrude (from a powerful Austrasian family), had two sons named Drogo and Grimoald who stood to inherit the bulk of this power. Drogo died in 708, leaving Grimoald as the only legitimate heir. Shortly before his death in 714, Pippin named Grimoald mayor of Neustria. Unfortunately, Grimoald was murdered in the chapel of his patron saint, Saint Lambert, shortly after Pippin's death.

---

2 Ian Wood, *The Merovingian Kingdoms 450–751* (Harlow, Essex: Pearson Education Limited, 1994), 287.

Grimoald's assassination set off a cascade of events: Plectrude sought to retain control over both states by naming Grimoald's six-year-old son, Theudoald, mayor of Neustria and another grandson, Arnulf, mayor of Austrasia. She imprisoned Charles, the twenty-six-year-old bastard son of her late husband, to prevent him from asserting a claim. The Neustrians revolted, displaced Theudoald, and tried to establish their own mayor. Charles escaped, battled Plectrude and her allies, seized his father's treasure and, using it to buy support, named himself mayor. Ultimately, this displaced both his nephews as mayor and pulled much of Francia into a civil war. One by one, Charles fought the states within the Frankish kingdom to assert his claim as mayor and reconquered what today constitutes Western Europe.[3]

Historically, Charles is most famous for the battle of Poitiers in 732. There, he stopped an invasion of the Saracen (Muslim) army under Abd ar-Rachman, then governor of Spain. The Saracen advance threatened Tours, which was where many of the kingdom's holy relics were kept. Charles's army stepped in to arrest the Saracen progress north. The battle ended in the death of Abd ar-Rachman and the rout of the Saracen army. It was for this battle that Charles was named "Charles Martel" or "Charles the Hammer." For over a thousand years, historians credited him with saving Christianity in Europe.[4]

Charles reigned as mayor of the palace for twenty-seven years. His power grew so great that in the last years of his reign, he openly ignored the rights of succession of the Merovingian kings. When Theuderic IV died in 737, Charles refused to elevate another Merovingian to the throne and led the kingdom himself, without a king, for four more years until his death.

Charles Martel had four children. His eldest three, Carloman, Pippin, and Hiltrude, were born of his first wife, Chlotrude. Charles had a third son, Gripho, from a second marriage to a Bavarian princess from the powerful Agilolfing family. Her name was Sunnichild.

After putting down a rebellion by Maurontus in Septemia and

---

3 Ibid., 270–275.

4 Fouracre, *The Age of Charles Martel*, 2.

Provence, Charles Martel died at home in his villa in Quierzy on September 22, 741. No cause is listed for his death. Just before he died, he named all of his sons mayor and divided the kingdom equally among them.

History shows that upon Charles's death, his two eldest sons warred against the younger Gripho and his mother, laying siege to them at the city of Laon where they had taken up residence. Sunnichild and Gripho were captured and imprisoned. Gripho was sent to Neufchateau, and Sunnichild to the nunnery at Chelles. Questions have arisen among historians as to whether the two older brothers were actually united in this endeavor. Later events clearly indicate that the two may have disagreed on the treatment of Gripho as well on the question of raising another Merovingian to the throne. There is no question, however, that the two brothers divided Gripho's territories between them.[5]

The succession following Charles's death was immediately renounced by Hunoald, Duke of Aquitaine, and his son, Waifar.[6] A challenge to the succession was also raised at the time by Theudoald, the above-mentioned grandson of Pippin of Herstal and Plectrude. I have suggested that he may have been aided in this by Bishop Wido of St. Wandrille. Given Theudoald's lineage, his claim would have had considerable merit. His challenge for the office failed, however, due to his untimely death. One text indicates that Theudoald may have been killed but did not specify by whom or why.[7] The poor man died so suddenly that year, however, one must wonder at the turn of events.

A scandal during that time involving Charles's daughter, Hiltrude, plagued the family well into the ninth century. Much to the consternation of her two older brothers and their court, Hiltrude fled to Regensburg following Charles's death to marry Duke Odilo of Bavaria, the uncle of Sunnichild. Hiltrude met Odilo during a prolonged visit he had made

5 Ian Wood, *The Merovingian Kingdoms*, 289–290.

6 Bernard S. Bachrach, *Early Carolingian Warfare, Prelude to Empire* (Philadelphia: University of Pennsylvania Press, 2001), 37.

7 *Annales Laureshamenses* 741, ed. Georg Pertz, MGH SS, 2, p. 24, quoted in Roger Collins, *Charlemagne* (Toronto: University of Toronto Press, 1998), 31.

to Charles's court. Further complicating matters, Odilo was suspected of fomenting rebellion among the states of the Frankish empire and leading the kingdom into civil war.[8]

Religion

None of the texts I have read refer to the civil war that followed Charles's death in religious terms. The Church had long had a strong hold on the ruling aristocracy of the Franks. The Merovingians had been Christian since Clovis was baptized by Bishop Remigius of Reims in 496 (after a military victory against the Alemans). Most of the regions of Francia are believed to have been Christian by the mid-700s. Recognized exceptions to this are few. In Spain, the Saracen ruled, and paganism prevailed in the Frisian and the Saxon territories.

That being said, there is evidence, cited below, that Christianity's hold over Europe was not so comprehensive in the mid-eighth century, particularly in the eastern regions. And given the role that religion has played and continues to play in violently dividing peoples, I felt comfortable in sowing the seeds of rebellion in a clash of faiths. For the skeptics, I offer the following:

St. Boniface was a missionary who spent most of his life in the eastern Germanic countries converting the pagans to Christianity ... particularly in Frisia, Hesse, and Bavaria. The bishopric at Regensburg, which Boniface founded, was not established until 739, two years before our story begins. If Europe were already Christian, this life's work would not have been so worthy of Boniface's attention, let alone the papal recognition he received for it.

Another indication of Christianity's tentative hold on Bavaria is the lack of Christian symbols buried along with its dead. Prior to 800 (nearly sixty years after our story), few in the Regensburg region were buried with crosses or other symbols of Christianity. In fact, most corpses were buried with treasured artifacts and enough wealth to sustain them through the afterlife. Christians need no such help in the kingdom of

8 Fouracre, *The Age of Charles Martel*, 167–168.

heaven. According to a leading archeologist of the region, this practice stopped abruptly and almost entirely after AD 800. This indicates that Christianity's reach into the countryside was still new to the region and that Christianity wasn't dominant among the populace until years later, during Charlemagne's time.[9]

There is also ample evidence that the Church was very concerned over the continuing practice of pagan rituals throughout the kingdom. As late as 830, Halitgar, bishop of Cambrai, produced a handbook for confessors. It was an example of the questions a confessor should ask a penitent about specific beliefs and practices.[10] The Church issued specific warnings about pagan practices (it was upon these that I drew many of the rituals I describe in the novel). These infractions involved penances so light that one must assume that the practices were still widespread at the time.

Two other facts pushed me into the direction of having religion be a critical factor for the rebellion following Charles's death. When the story begins, Trudi presses Sunni about Charles's intervention in Bavaria and recounts a tale of how Sunni's uncles married the same woman and practiced pagan rituals to heal their dying hexed son. This story is documented history.[11] Clearly, if the nobles of Bavaria were practicing Christians, they were still only "practicing" and were not above resorting to paganism when they felt the circumstances warranted it.

Much of the ritual and source of the pagan religion I describe originates in the Nordic and Germanic countries. The use of runes and the mythology surrounding them, I pulled from a short book on runes by Nigel Pennick.[12] As mentioned above, I also drew upon the Church's

9 Interview with Dr. Andreas Boors, MA Archeologist, Historisches Museum der Stadt Regensburg, May 2005.

10 Alan Charles Kors and Edward Peters, eds., *Witchcraft in Europe 400–1700* (Philadelphia: University of Pennsylvania Press, 2001), 55–57; John T. McNeill and Helena M. Gamer, *Medieval Handbooks of Pennance* (New York: 1990), 305–306.

11 Fouracre, *Age of Charles Martel*, 108–109.

12 Nigel Pennick, *Complete Illustrated Guide to Runes* (London: HarperCollins, 2002).

condemnation of pagan practices, which matched the practices Bishop Haltigar describes. Finally, I drew from an older religion that likely preceded the Norse Gods to Eastern Europe, namely Hinduism and particularly Tantrism. For the Tantric rituals, I drew on several sources, but primarily on a book by André Van Lysebeth on Tantrism.[13] Since older religious practices and rites are often "adopted" by newer religions, as is evident in the adoption of Greek mythology into that practiced by the Romans and also Christianity's adoption of rites and symbols from many cultures, I felt comfortable merging some aspects of the older Tantric faith with the "newer" Nordic religion.

Characters

Sunnichild: Also called Swanahilde in the history texts, Sunnichild first appears in history following Charles's intervention into Bavaria to solve civil unrest in the territories. As mentioned earlier, Trudi recounts this story early in the book, alluding to the fact that Charles Martel returned with Sunnichild as both his hostage and bride. Coming from the powerful Agilolfing family, Sunnichild would have been considered an advantageous political marriage for Charles.

There is a great deal of evidence, however, that over time, Sunni won Charles's love and confidence as well. She was empowered by Charles to run his government while he was out on campaign. I chose to portray this influence in a scene between Sunni and a fictitious "Brother David" where Sunni first divines Charles's impending death upon the discovery of a donation of the chateau at Clichy to the monastery at St. Denis. Much as is described in the novel, Sunni did impose taxes on the merchants at the Fair of St. Denis in Paris (much to the consternation of the merchants) and did sign off on the charter for the donation of the chateau at Clichy in exchange for Charles's burial at St. Denis.[14]

More importantly, Sunni's influence over Charles can be seen in

---

13 Andre Van Lysebeth, *Tantra, Cult of the Feminine* (Boston: Weiser Books, 1995).

14 Fouracre, *The Age of Charles Martel*, 163–166.

Charles's provision for Gripho with prized land for a "middle kingdom" when it came time for him to split the kingdom amongst his sons. Given his young age at the time, this created great consternation among Frankish nobles and likely would not have happened if her influence was not great.

Nothing in the history texts describes Sunnichild as pagan. Given her Bavarian background, however, and the practices of her uncles (see above), I felt I had adequate license to describe her as such.

Boniface: It is also clear that Boniface (née Wynfreed) now St. Boniface, held great sway over Charles and at least Carloman. A legate of the pope, Boniface personally ministered to Charles's family, was godfather to Charles's sons, and a close advisor to the family. A passionate missionary who spent much of his early life converting the pagans, Boniface was named by the pope a "bishop at large." Boniface held enormous influence over the other bishops of the region and was partly responsible for gathering the synods to address Charles's taking of Church lands.

Hiltrude: There is no evidence that Charles intended for Hiltrude to marry Aistulf. At the time, however, she was certainly past marrying age. And since her sudden marriage to Odilo was deemed such a scandal (well into the ninth century), I surmised that other plans must have been in place. Aistulf would certainly have been a likely candidate.

Carloman: As Charles's eldest son, Carloman was actively involved with his father's rise to power and was considered a formidable military force as mayor. Tutored by St. Boniface, Carloman was also greatly influenced by religion throughout his life. In the novel, I credited Carloman with founding the "Knights in Christ." No such organization existed at the time. Given the later rise of several formal religious orders among the knights (The Templars, etc.), I felt at liberty to define the "Knights in Christ" as an early prototype under Carloman's care.

Pippin: As Charles's second son, Pippin (also referred to by historians as Pepin), would have been on campaign with his father from early adolescence (he was twenty-seven at the time of Charles's death). Unlike Carloman, however, Pippin left Charles's court to be educated and live with the Lombards on the Roman peninsula (in what today is Italy). Pippin was, in fact, "an adopted son" of King Liutbrand and would have been a contemporary of Prince Aistulf. Pippin's sojourn to the Roman peninsula would have likely diminished Boniface's role in his upbringing. Therefore, I've portrayed Pippin as the less religious of the two older brothers.

Pippin did have a relationship with Bertrada, daughter of the Compte de Laon, early in his adulthood. Some historians suspect that relationship was critical in ending the siege of Laon.

Odilo: Duke Odilo of Bavaria came to power following Charles's intervention in the "civil unrest" there. He was likely to have had blood ties, as well, in Alemannia. Although some historians have questioned his leadership role in bringing Francia into civil war following Charles's death, many still describe his role as the ringleader.

Gripho: Like his mother, Sunnichild, there is no evidence that Gripho (or Grifo) was pagan. Having cast his mother and her uncle (Duke Odilo) in such a light, it was only logical for me to continue the tradition where Gripho was concerned.

Given the reaction to Charles's decision to grant Gripho a "middle kingdom," it is likely that Gripho was not beloved by his stepbrothers from Charles's first marriage. As to the spoiled nature I have given him, it seems to fit the behavior he demonstrates later in life.

Theudoald: As described above, Theudoald was named mayor at age six by his grandmother upon the untimely death of his father (Grimoald) by assassination. Theudoald survived to challenge Charles's sons over the title mayor, only to die suddenly of unknown causes. Although clearly, Theudoald had support among many nobles for his claim, all of those described in *Anvil* are fictitious.

Bishops: Bishops during this time period were men of great power. In addition to their religious duties, bishops exerted tremendous influence through the monasteries within their domain. Great tracts of land donated over time to monasteries by nobles seeking to buy a place in heaven led to great religious wealth and military power. Many bishops held standing armies and were on occasion known to command the armies themselves.

So great was this wealth that Charles Martel often confiscated men and lands from the Church to reward his followers. Legend has it that this "theft" damned Charles to a place in hell. It is said that his corpse was even dragged there by a dragon.[15] It was this pillaging that the Church sought to redress through the synods following Charles's death.

Two of the bishops described in *Anvil* correspond to bishops of the time. Wido of St. Wandrille and Aidolf (or Aidulf) of Auxerre were both considered powerful men. As to Wido's height and Aidolf's sexual orientation, those were figments of my imagination. The sexual misbehavior of priests, however, was addressed strongly in the Church synods of the day, particularly by St. Boniface.

Duke Heden: Charles certainly felt the Franks were entitled to sovereignty over Thuringia as he left the region to Carloman in 741. Little, however, is known about Thuringia during this time period because there were no organized churches in the region.[16] There is evidence that the

15 Ibid., 2: "This view developed in the ninth century and found expression in a vision in which the great warrior's tomb in the monastery of St. Denis was opened and found to be empty. What could be seen, however, were scorch marks which indicated that Charles had been dragged off to hell by a dragon. The reason for his grisly fate was that he had plundered the lands of the church."

16 Ibid., 110.

political situation there was unstable due to persistent Saxon incursions from the north, but most of the history of the dukes in Thuringia in the later seventh and eighth century is almost impossible to reconstruct.[17] There is reference to a Duke Heden early in Charles Martel's reign who donated lands in Hammelburg for the foundation of a monastery. Heden's religious credentials, however, come into question in Willibald's *Life of Boniface*, which states that Christians of Thuringia were oppressed by Heden and were subjected to pagan rule until he was driven out.[18] History does not reference Duke Heden after 717.

Given the lack of solid information as to Duke Heden's death and the recognized fragmented political situation in Thuringia, I chose to keep Heden alive, although marginalized, in *Anvil*. There is no evidence that he ever had a liaison with Sunnichild and none whatsoever that he aided her at Laon. It is likely, however, that Sunnichild had help from someone to withstand the siege of Laon by Carloman. As Gripho was only fourteen and still an adolescent, a noble or contingent of nobles must have been on hand to assist her cause. I merely chose one for the job. No known children are attributed to Duke Heden.

Fictional characters: Bradius and his friend Tobias are fictional characters. Both were created out of the need for champions to aid Trudi, much as Duke Heden was resurrected to defend the interests of Sunnichild. It is unlikely that Trudi undertook her flight to Bavaria with anyone's blessing, so she must have had help in getting halfway across the continent to Regensburg.

As for Bradius, it is true that Pippin was not present at Charles's death because he had to put down an uprising in Burgundy with his Uncle Childebrand. Connecting Bradius to this uprising as well as to paganism and to Maurontus (in Provence) was my idea.

Obviously, Carloman could not have witnessed the killing of Bradius's son, Unum, or taken the life of Heden's son, Petr, as neither existed.

Two other figments of my imaginations made their way into being

17 Ibid., 112.

18 Ibid., 113.

minor characters of note: Father Daniel, the priest in white, personifies the fanatical element of Christianity at that time while Lady Hélène brings to life the art of assassination in kingly politic. Neither character has any direct reference in history, although, as I have noted above, assassination was certainly very much a tool of statecraft at the time.

Other personages: Where I could, I used the real names of the dukes and warlords of the time. Hunoald and Waifar of Aquitaine existed and were a constant thorn in the side of the Carolingians. King Liutbrand and Aistulf ruled the Lombards on the Roman peninsula and did indeed threaten Pope Gregory. Aistulf was also a renowned swordsman who won prizes at the Spoleto tournaments, much as is described in *Anvil*.

Ateni of Provence and Radbod of Frisia were names of lords from those respective regions, but their rule did not coincide exactly with this timeframe. Unfortunately, they were as close as I could find. I did not lose too much sleep over this as it was common during this era for names to be passed along from father to son (as was true with Charles, Carloman, and Pippin).

There is also no record of the name of Carloman's wife, so I supplied one. The fact of this, I find odd. As the wife of the mayor and the mother of Drogo, she should have been important enough for her name to be recorded.

Places

Little construction exists today that existed in the eighth century. Charles's palace at Quierzy along the river Oise is gone. Quierzy still exists. It is a very small farming community with little remaining historical reference (although I did find a civic building there named the "Salle de Charlemagne").

Reims too still exists, as does the arch at its entrance and the labyrinth of tunnels beneath its city. Much of the world's champagne continues to be cooled in these underground tunnels. Reims, as was noted above, was home to the baptism of Clovis. It continues to hold the elements of his baptism in the "Palais du Tau" museum next to the Cathedral of Reims.

(One can also find there a talisman that Charlemagne is often pictured with, which he wore to his grave.)

The walled city of Laon still stands atop a ridge northeast of Soissons. Although the city has grown and protects far newer buildings than were present in the mid-eighth century, it is still possible to stand on the southern wall and imagine Carloman's army approaching across the vast plain below the city. Dozens of tunnels beneath the city have recently been excavated. Many were created to protect the wealth of its residents.

The basilica of St. Denis was built in 451 above a Gallo-Roman cemetery. The monastic community there was founded in the seventh century. The church that stands there today was built after the turn of the millennium and post-dates the story in *Anvil*. The tombs that housed the remains of French kings, sadly, were sacked during the French Revolution. St. Germain des Prés, the church Carloman visits in the novel during his stay at Isle de la Cité, still stands and was frequented by the Carolingians, although the portion of the church that existed during that time is closed to the public. There is no evidence that Carloman was married or received his first communion at St. Germain des Prés.

Donauwörth and Regensburg still stand along the southern banks of the Danube. Little is left of the Roman fort I described that was built in Regensburg during the first century after Christ. Part of one tower and one half of a double-arched entryway still exist, as does a portion of the southeastern wall. I was greatly helped in visualizing this by a schematic drawing of what the fort should have looked like, provided by Dr. Boors, chief archeologist of the Regensburg museum. Dr. Boors gave me a guided tour of the museum and what was left of the fort walls. He was also kind enough to show me those artifacts from the region attributed to the eighth century. The value of this tour was extremely helpful in that it resolved several open questions in my mind. These included the use of Roman coin during this time period (Dr. Boors showed me a treasure trove of solidi and denarii), the existence of spurs, and more importantly, the Christian artifacts (or rather the lack thereof) among grave sites in the region.

As can be deduced from the footnotes, I have relied heavily on Paul

Fouracre's account of the period, which is detailed in *The Age of Charles Martel*, published by Pearson Education Limited in 2000. Much of the summary I've recounted above, I pulled from his text, specifically the pages that dealt with Church influence and the death of Charles Martel (160–176). It is one of the clearest texts on this period that I have read and magically appeared on the bookstore shelf just in time for the research phase of *Anvil*. For that, I am eternally grateful. I did not always take his lead, however, and have tried to cite some of the other choices I made throughout this note.

I also drew heavily on the writings of Ian Wood's *The Merovingian Kingdoms 450–751* and Bernard Bachrach's *Early Carolingian Warfare, Prelude to Empire*, the latter of which was extremely helpful in characterizing battle armor and tactics of the time.

Other important texts upon which I relied include: *Carolingian Chronicles, the Royal Frankish Annals and Nithard's Histories*, translated by Scholz and Rogers (Ann Arbor: The University of Michigan Press, 1992); *Two Lives of Charlemagne* by Einhard and Notker the Stammerer, (New York: Penguin Classics, 1979); *Frankish Institutions Under Charlemagne* by Francois Louis Ganshof (New York: Norton Library, 1970); *Sieges of the Middle Ages* by Philip Warner (Barnsley, S. Yorkshire: Pen & Sword Military Classics, 2004); *Witchcraft in Europe 400–1700*, edited by Alan Charles Kors and Edward Peters (Philadelphia: University of Pennsylvania Press, 2001); *Charlemagne* by Matthias Becher (New Haven: Yale University Press, 2003); *Charlemagne* by Roger Collins (Toronto: University of Toronto Press, 1998); *Charlemagne, Father of a Continent* by Alessandro Barbero and translated by Allan Cameron (Berkeley and Los Angeles: University of California Press, 2004); *Complete Illustrated Guide to Runes* by Nigel Pennick (London: HarperCollins, 2002); and *Tantra, Cult of the Feminine*, Andre Van Lysebeth (Boston: Weiser Books, 1995).

CPSIA information can be obtained at www.ICGtesting.com
Printed in the USA
LVOW13*0932090314

376607LV00005B/26/P